INTO HELL

THE ROAD TO HELL SERIES, BOOK 4

BRENDA K DAVIES

GILMOUR-COX PUBLISHING

ALSO FROM THE AUTHOR

Books written under the pen name

Brenda K. Davies

<u>The Vampire Awakenings Series</u>

Awakened (Book 1)

Destined (Book 2)

Untamed (Book 3)

Enraptured (Book 4)

Undone (Book 5)

Fractured (Book 6)

Ravaged (Book 7)

Consumed (Book 8)

Unforeseen (Book 9)

Forsaken (Book 10)

Coming 2019/2020

<u>The Alliance Series</u>

Eternally Bound (Book 1)

Bound by Vengeance (Book 2)

Bound by Darkness (Book 3)

Bound by Passion (Book 4)

Coming August 2019

<u>The Road to Hell Series</u>

Good Intentions (Book 1)

Carved (Book 2)

The Road (Book 3)

Into Hell (Book 4)

Hell on Earth Series

Hell on Earth (Book 1)

Into the Abyss (Book 2)

Kiss of Death (Book 3)

Coming Fall 2019

Historical Romance

A Stolen Heart

Books written under the pen name

Erica Stevens

The Coven Series

Nightmares (Book 1)

The Maze (Book 2)

Dream Walker (Book 3)

The Captive Series

Captured (Book 1)

Renegade (Book 2)

Refugee (Book 3)

Salvation (Book 4)

Redemption (Book 5)

Broken (The Captive Series Prequel)

Vengeance (Book 6)

Unbound (Book 7)

The Kindred Series

Kindred (Book 1)

Ashes (Book 2)

Kindled (Book 3)

Inferno (Book 4)

Phoenix Rising (Book 5)

The Fire & Ice Series

Frost Burn (Book 1)

Arctic Fire (Book 2)

Scorched Ice (Book 3)

The Ravening Series

The Ravening (Book 1)

Taken Over (Book 2)

Reclamation (Book 3)

The Survivor Chronicles

The Upheaval (Book 1)

The Divide (Book 2)

The Forsaken (Book 3)

The Risen (Book 4)

To Jamie.

Thank you so much for all your help and for my sanity!

GLOSSARY OF TERMS

- **Adhene demon** <Ad-heen> - Mischievous elf-like demon.
- **Akalia Vine** <Ah-kal-ya> - Purple black flowers, orange berries. Draws in victims & drains their blood slowly. Red leaves. Sharp, needle-like suckers under leaves.
- **Barta demons** <Bartə> - Locked behind the 55th seal. Animal of Hell. Now part of Lucifer's guard.
- **Calamut Trees** <Cal-ah-mut> - Live in the Forest of Prurience.
- **Canagh demon** <Kan-agh> - Male Incubus, Female Succubus. Power thrives on sex but feed on souls on a less regular basis than the other demons. Their kiss enslaves another.
- **Carrou Vines** <Kar-oo>- Thick black vines. 6-inch-long thorns. Grow around Canagh demon nests.
- **Craetons** <Cray-tons> - Lucifer's followers.
- **Drakón** <Drak-un> - 101st seal. Skeletal, fire breathing dragons.
- **Erinyes** (furies) <Ih-rin-ee-eez> - demons of vengeance and justice. 78th Seal.

- **Fires of Creation** - Where the varcolac is born.
- **Forest of Prurience** <Proo r-ee-uh nce> - Where the tree nymphs reside. Was also the original home of the canaghs and wood nymphs.
- **The Gates -** Varcolac demon has always been the ruler of the guardians of the gates that were used to travel to earth before Lucifer entered Hell.
- **Gargoyle -** Claws contain a paralyzing agent they use on their prey. When victim is paralyzed, they peel away their skin one strip at a time and eat it.
- **Ghosts -** Souls can balk against entering Heaven, they have no choice when it comes to Hell.
- **Gobalinus** (goblins) <Gab-ah-leen-us> **-** Lower level demons, feed on flesh as well as souls. 79th seal.
- **Hellhounds -** The first pair of Hellhounds also born of the Fires of Creation, with the first varcolac who rose. They share a kindred spirit and are controlled by the varcolac.
- **Jinn** - 90th seal. Can grant wishes.
- **Lanavour demon** <Lan-oh-vor> **-**The 3rd seal. Can speak telepathically and know people's inner most secrets and fears.
- **Leporcháin <**Lepor-cane> - Leprechaun looking creatures. Half on Kobal's side, the other half are on Lucifer's. Only ten in existence.
- **Madagan** <Mad-a-ghan>- A beast from Hell. Resembles a boar with a giant tusk in the center of forehead. Mottled red and black skin, plumes of smoke from a blowhole in top of head. Extended, round skulls, cloven hooves.
- **Manticore** - 46th seal. Body of a red lion, human/demon head.
- **Ogre** - 33rd seal.
- **Ouroboros** - 82nd seal. Massive, green serpent.
- **Palitons** <Pal-ah-tons> - Kobal's followers.

- **Púca** <Poo-ka> - 80th seal. Shape changers which can take on animal or human form. Could also be the source of vampires as they drain their victim's blood.
- **Revenirs** <Rev-eh-ners> - Mummy-like skeletons. Debilitating cry. Suck life from victims with "kiss."
- **The River Asharún** - River in Hell.
- **Rokh** - 81st seal. Large birds of prey.
- **Skelleins <Skel-eens> -** Guardians of the Gates.
- **Tahanusi** <Ta-ha-nusee> - Sea creatures that reside in the Asharún river.
- **Tree Nymphs** - Live in the Forest of Prurience. Men and women. Striking and very free sexually. Smaller than wood nymphs and live in the trees.
- **The Wall** - Blocks off all of Washington, Oregon, California, Arizona, New Mexico, Texas, Louisiana, Mississippi, Alabama, Georgia, Florida, South Carolina, North Carolina, Virginia, Maryland, Delaware, New Jersey, Connecticut, Rhode Island, Massachusetts, Vermont, New Hampshire, and Maine. Blocks parts of Nevada, New York, Pennsylvania, and Arkansas. Similar wall blocks off parts of Europe.
- **Wood Nymphs** - Resided in the forest before they were locked behind the 77th seal for drinking the blood of demons while they were having sex with them. May be the source of vampirism in human mythology.
- **Wraith -** A twisted and malevolent spirit that the demons feed from. On earth they only come out at night.
- **Varcolac demon** <Var-ko-lack>- Born from the fires of Hell. Only one can exist at a time. When that one dies another rises from the Fires of Creation. Fastest and most brutal of all the demons. They are the only kind that can create and open natural gateways within Hell as well as close them. They control the hellhounds.

Demon Words

Achó <Ach-oh> - Attack.
Ainka <Ayn-ka> - Easy.
Crahán - Looney
Gallha - Go.
Harga <Har-gah> - Here.
Helka <Hell-ka> - Hell king.
Mah Kush-la ˈMɑ: <kush-la> - My Heart.
Mjéod <Myod> - Mead or a demon drink.
Partka <Part-kah> - Stay.
Rhála — King
Rejant —Queen
Senché — Silence.

Glossary Of Symbols

Humans took some of them and turned them into what became known as the Elder Futhark, also known as runes.

Eiaz <E-az> - (Tilted Z) - Speed, heightened senses, and protection.
Risaz <Ree-saz> - (Straight line with a triangle attached to the middle) - Force of destruction.
Sowa <Sow-ah> - (Backwards E with sword piercing the center) - Blade of fire.
Zenak <Zen-ach> - (Three wavy lines) - Eternal fire and life.
Ziwa <Zee-wah> - (Two V's with a line connecting the top, like fangs) - Guardian of the hellhounds. Mark is considered gift of strength, endurance, and virility. Considered a blessing and a curse as well as marks bearer as having a piece of the hellhound's soul within them.

CHAPTER ONE

Kobal

"What is this?" River inquired.

Her amethyst eyes widened as she gazed at the river of red Hell water winding before us. Jagged black rocks stuck up from the middle of it, forcing the water to flow around them and creating strong currents. Those currents were capable of smashing to pieces anything caught within them. A few feet away from us, calmer water lapped against the rocky shoreline of the pathway we traversed. The color faded from River's face, her head tilted back, and she blinked at the sharp rocks jutting from the ceiling.

"The River Asharún," I replied. This place had never bothered me before, but seeing the dread in her eyes and knowing her reaction to wraiths, I didn't intend for her to be here any longer than necessary.

"Are we here to travel on the river?" First Sergeant Sue Hawkson asked from beside her as he ran a hand through his short, dark brown hair. He stood with his broad shoulders thrust back, and his blue eyes filled with determination as he gazed at the Asharún.

"The Asharún is the quickest and safest route," Corson replied.

"We will not be traveling on the Asharún," I said and clasped River's elbow. "There are other ways to my chambers. Come."

Her eyes swung toward me. "Why aren't we going to travel it?"

I pulled her a step closer and cupped her cheek tenderly in my hand as I studied her. She tried to hide it, but I knew being in Hell tired her. As Lucifer's only living descendent, and with her angelic and demonic abilities, she had been able to make it this far into Hell. However, sweat beaded her forehead and stuck her dress to her body. Her flushed skin warmed my hand, and her exhaustion beat against me, yet she refused to let me carry her as we made our way to my private chambers—chambers where I had once slept and lived when I resided in Hell, but I hadn't been to them in years. I had no doubt they would still be secure, as few others had known where they were located. Those who had known of them wouldn't have dared to enter them while I was away.

We'd done nothing but walk since leaving the chamber housing the Fires of Creation behind hours, if not days, ago. I had no way of knowing how much time had passed. Before I'd left Hell, it wouldn't have bothered me. There was no concept of time in Hell, no sun to mark the passing hours, but now that I'd lived on Earth, I wondered about the time of day.

There were only the constant fires in Hell, and I found myself missing the sun. That was something I never would have believed possible months ago. Then River had walked into my life, changed my perspective on things, and become my home. Before, I had always planned to return to Hell to reign, but now I would take my throne from Lucifer and leave this place behind to live on Earth with her.

I brushed back a strand of River's raven-colored hair from her cheek. Her eyes closed as she turned into the palm of my hand, her full lips brushing over my skin. The scar at the corner of her right eyebrow was more visible against her flushed skin, as were the freckles on her slender nose. Her sweeping black lashes fell to shadow her eyes as her inherent scent of earth, fresh spring rain, and flowers assailed me.

My gaze latched onto my marks on her neck. The evidence of my four fangs piercing her skin was unmistakable to everyone standing with us and all those we encountered. Even if she didn't bear my marks right now, every demon would know she was my Chosen. I had claimed her, and I was never going to let her go.

I would keep her protected from the countless things looking to tear us apart and her weaknesses. Unfortunately, that included the Asharún river. Reluctantly releasing her, I lowered my hand to my side again.

"Why aren't we going to travel it?" she asked again.

"Because, Mah Kush-la, the Asharún is a place for the damned spirits who enter Hell. Some of the souls we feed on become so weakened that they are ensnared by the currents of the water."

Her full mouth parted on a breath of realization. Goose bumps broke out on her tanned arms before she ran her hands over them to ease the chill. "Wraiths," she murmured.

"Yes. Countless numbers of them are trapped in the water." And wraiths weakened her, something we couldn't afford to let happen now.

"So is this like the River Styx?" Hawk asked.

"Human mythology twisted the Asharún some. It's not the boundary between Hell and Earth, but basically yes, the humans who glimpsed the Asharún river through veils separating Hell and Earth called it the River Styx," Magnus replied.

Hawk frowned at the water. "Why did they call it Styx if it's Asharún?"

"In the human's Greek mythology there are five rivers separating Hell from the living. They were wrong about there being five of them. There is only the Asharún. However, the Greeks did name one of the five rivers the Acheron, the river of woe," Magnus said. "But to many humans, Styx became the most popular and well known of the rivers. Probably because it was easier for them to pronounce, and we all know humans don't like to tax their tiny brains."

Though River wasn't entirely human, and Hawk no longer was, they both scowled at Magnus. His eyes shone with amusement when he smiled back at them.

River glowered at him for a minute more before focusing on me. "Okay, so it's the river of woe—"

"And of anger, forgetfulness, hatred, and hostility, amongst *numerous* other things," Magnus interjected.

"Enough," I growled at him, and his mouth clamped shut.

"But it's the safest and fastest way for us to reach your chambers?" River asked me.

I lifted my head to glare at Corson for mentioning it in the first place. Corson's citrine eyes warily held mine as he stepped away from me. Magnus and Bale inspected the ceiling while the skelleins all studied the blades of their swords and the hellhounds padded away to explore the water.

Corson had nowhere else to look as I pinned him to the spot with my stare. In the dim light playing over this part of the river, Corson's hair appeared midnight blue. His pointed ears stood out from the curls falling over them. Thankfully, since we'd entered Hell again, he no longer had the earrings of the human women he'd slept with dangling from his ears.

At six foot four, Corson's lithe build and usually easygoing demeanor often caused others to underestimate him, but as an adhene demon, he was one of the deadliest creatures I'd ever encountered. He was also one of my most loyal followers and closest advisors.

"The Asharún is full of wraiths," I said to River. "I'd prefer not expose you to them any more than necessary. We will stay on land."

She glanced back at the swirling water as a wraith broke the surface. A hand rose into the air, its fingers opening and closing as it sought to grasp something. The shifting currents of water spun the wraith around before sucking it under once more. Trapped by the flowing waters, some of the wraiths took on their human form again, while others remained the twisted spirits they became after demons fed on them for long periods of time.

When River started rubbing her arms again, I knew she recalled how cold the wraiths made her feel. I knew she was remembering discovering that her father, a man she'd never known when he'd been alive, had been sent to Hell when he died. In his wraith form, her father had used his abilities to help Lucifer bring down the seals one at a time.

"I'd prefer not to be around the wraiths, but if it's going to be quicker and safer to travel the Asharún, then we should," she stated. "Are we supposed to swim it?"

"No." The tips of my claws dug into my palms as I glanced from her to the water and back again. "We don't swim. The ferrymen are called to take travelers on their journey."

"Call them then."

"River, the Asharún is not a good place to be."

"Kobal, we are *literally* standing in Hell. I don't think anywhere is a good place to be."

"No, it's not," I grated through my teeth. "Can you handle being that close to so many wraiths?"

"Yes." She rested her hand on my arm. Her fingers ran over the symbols marking my flesh as she spoke. "If you're with me, I can handle it. Your presence helps to shelter me from their cold, and these are weakened wraiths; they won't affect me as badly as the others did, or my… father."

Her nose wrinkled at the last word, and her mouth pinched together as if she'd eaten something unpleasant.

"You can't know that they won't affect you as much," I told her.

"Maybe not, but I *do* know that avoiding the best route because of me is dumb. Besides, it's hot as Hell in here; I could use a little cooldown, and the wraiths do provide that for me." Her mouth quirked in a teasing smile, but no amusement shone in her somber eyes. "I'll be fine. How long will we have to be on the Asharún?"

"It will probably feel like a few hours of human time, at least."

No one else would have seen it, but I didn't miss the twitching muscle close to her eye. She said she would be okay, that she would handle it, but I felt her uncertainty.

"A few hours is nothing in the grand scheme of things," she murmured and turned away from me. "Call for the ferrymen, send up a smoke signal, knock down a rock from above, or whatever it is you have to do to get their attention. We're going boating."

I glanced over at Corson who stared at River with a pained look. When his gaze lifted to mine, I didn't see fear there this time, but more guilt and a reluctance to do as she'd instructed. "Call them," I commanded.

Corson bowed his head and stepped closer to the Asharún. Water ran over the tips of his boots, turning it from a blood red hue to a pinkish one when he knelt beside the river.

"You can change your mind," I said to River. "No one here will blame you for that." I didn't bother to look at the others; they would have no choice in the matter.

Her hair waved about her shoulders when she shook her head no. "No matter what it takes, I want this over with. The sooner Lucifer is dead, the better we'll all be. If this will get us to your chambers and eventually to Morax, Verin, and the rest of your followers faster, then we are going to do it."

At River's words, Corson rested his fingers in the water. Closing his eyes, he drew energy from the wraiths caught up in the Asharún's currents. As weak as they were, it was easy for him to feed on numerous wraiths at once.

River winced and stepped back when a wail reverberated through the air. The forlorn cry of the wraiths echoed off the rocks until the sound became an inescapable cacophony that vibrated the ground.

"It will stop soon," I promised her. Releasing her elbow, I wrapped my arm around her waist and drew her against me. I cradled her head to my chest as thousands of wraiths broke the surface of the water.

CHAPTER TWO

River

I began to regret my decision to make this boat crossing when the wraiths bobbed up in the water. Their dipping and rising motions reminded me of buoys bouncing on top of the ocean water. Except these buoys weren't colorful lobster pot or channel markers. No, these buoys were the blackened souls of the damned, and there were so *many* of them.

They churned the water like piranhas in a feeding frenzy. Their frantic movements caused the current to shift and change as their hands clawed at the air. They seemed to be trying, and failing, to grasp something that would pull them free of the tumultuous waters. I couldn't help but pity them as their desperation beat against me.

My shoulders drooped as the muggy air in the cavern, easily the size of football field, made me feel like a wilted plant. The stagnant pond aroma of the Asharún clogged my nostrils as the current flowed from an archway on my right. I couldn't see beyond the archway, and when I turned my head, I couldn't see past the twist in the rocks to my left, but the water coursed that way.

I yearned to clap my hands over my ears and shut out the awful, wailing of the wraiths, but I refused to show any weakness in front of them. Kobal embraced me against him and bent his lips to nuzzle the top of my hair. His innate, fiery scent filled my nose.

My fingers curled into the rigid muscles of his back, drawing him closer. In his arms, I could almost shut out the hideousness of this bleak cavern, screaming souls, and jagged rocks that I swore were really a demented Hell creature waiting to devour us.

We were deep into Hell, and after the things I'd seen in this place, the rocks coming alive and eating us wasn't far-fetched to me. If someone were to fall on one of those rocks, or if one of them suddenly broke free from above and plummeted down, they would cut through a person or demon as easily as a knife sliced through warm butter.

I shuddered and pressed closer to Kobal. The solid beat of his heart lulled my eyes into closing as I took comfort in the strength he emitted —a strength that flooded my body with life and caused the tips of my fingers to emit midnight blue sparks. His hand slid through my hair until his fingers cupped the back of my skull, and his lips moved down to caress my cheek.

Despite the screaming, churning wraiths, I couldn't stop my body's intense reaction to his. Love for him swelled within me. When Kobal's lips brushed against mine, the electric jolt of contact went all the way down to my toes.

Pulling back, he gazed down at me from his entirely obsidian eyes. There were no whites to his eyes, not until they shifted into the amber color they became when he was enraged, highly emotional, or aroused. A foot taller than my five-nine height, I had to tip my head back to take in his square jaw, pointed chin, aquiline nose, and high, broad cheekbones.

I didn't have to see the four fangs that emerged, two upper and two lower, when he was ready to fight to know he was lethal. It radiated from the carved muscles of his body and the power flowing through him. Those fangs had pierced me more times than I could count as he'd taken me and marked me repeatedly. I didn't have fangs, but my bite marks on his neck were still visible against the bronzed hue of his skin.

Reaching up, I brushed back a strand of deep brown hair from his forehead. The only hair on his body was on his head, eyebrows, and lashes. I trailed my fingers over his cheeks to run them across his full lips. For a second, gold color flashed through his eyes, but he tamped it down.

He'd lost his shirt during his recent battle with Lucifer, leaving him bare to my perusal of the etched muscles of his abdomen, chest, and arms. I couldn't stop myself from running a finger down the center of his chiseled abs as my gaze traveled to his tapered waist and the pants hanging low on his body. We were all in some serious need of clean clothes, but I couldn't help admiring the way his blood-splattered, torn pants hugged the thick muscles of his thighs.

I forced my attention away from the obvious bulge in those pants to the markings on his chest and arms. On his left arm, flames started at the tips of his fingers and ran up the back of his hand. They wrapped around his wrist and rose to encompass two hellhounds on his thick bicep. From there, the flames traveled up to the base of his neck and licked over his flesh before dipping down to encircle his left pec. I knew, from the many times I'd explored his bare body, that his markings created the same circular pattern on his back.

On his right side, flames also started at the tips of his fingers before wrapping around his wrist and arm. There were no wolves there as those markings were made up entirely of intricate symbols within the flames. The symbols were a part of his ancient, demon language and had been on him when he rose from the Fires of Creation exactly as he was now.

The Fires of Creation had made him different than the other varcolac demons who had risen before him. None of the other varcolac demons had been marked with the symbols he possessed. Symbols like Ziwa, which made him more volatile but also stronger. Having Ziwa on him was considered a gift of strength, endurance, and virility. It was also considered a curse as it marked its bearer with a piece of the hellhound's soul.

Kobal was also the only varcolac to ever house two hellhounds within him. All of those who had come before him had controlled the hellhounds, but none had been born with the creatures inside them. My gaze fell to the two hellhounds on his arm again, Phenex and Crux, a mated pair. When Kobal chose, he could set them free to rain down destruction, and they did so with glee.

The varcolac demon was meant to have been the rightful ruler of Hell, but Lucifer's arrival here, six thousand years ago, changed that. Kobal had spent his entire fifteen hundred sixty-two years of existence trying to reclaim a throne stripped from his ancestors millennia before he'd been created.

"Here comes one of the ferrymen," Corson said.

My attention turned away from Kobal and back to the Asharún. Corson removed his fingers from the water and rose. The echoing wail of the wraiths ceased abruptly, and they all disappeared beneath the surface. The abruptness of their departure robbed me of my breath.

From around the corner of the archway, a boat drifted into view. Ripples flowed away from the boat as the figure standing at the far end used his staff to steer the vessel through the water. The boat resembled the pictures I'd once seen of the gondolas in Venice. On the bow of the boat, the narrow nose of it rose at least five feet before curving over. Something had been nailed to the bow, but I couldn't quite make it out.

"What about the hounds, Kobal?" Magnus inquired.

My attention turned to Magnimus, or Magnus, as he preferred to be called. The last demon of illusions had saved my life more than a few times. He'd made me better at drawing on my ability to harvest life from things, instead of using my fire when I was panicked, but there were still times when I couldn't tell if I liked him or wanted to choke the arrogant demon.

With his ice-blond hair, silver eyes, and perfectly chiseled features, I would have thought Magnus better suited for an angel in Heaven rather than a demon. The only thing making him look at all demonic were the two, six-inch-long black horns curving against the side of his head. His hair covered most of those horns, but the tips and outlines of them were still visible.

"Send out the call for another ferryman," Kobal commanded.

"How many of them are there?" Hawk asked.

"Three," Lix replied.

Lix was one of the five skelleins left who had come with us on our journey and who had also survived the battle with Lucifer at the seals. Some of the other skelleins had split off before the battle to go with Morax and Verin to try to keep Lucifer distracted. The rest remained on Earth with Shax, Erin, and Vargas, but the skeletal-looking creatures had sustained a lot of losses at the seals.

Because he was a little taller than the other skelleins, I could differentiate Lix from them. Though they all looked nearly identical, I'd also started to pick out subtle differences in the other skelleins. That one's skull had a small flat spot in the back, and the one beside it had longer fingers, but unlike Lix, the others had never introduced themselves to me.

All the skelleins were shorter than five feet, and most of them were only about four and a half feet tall. The first time I'd met the skeletal, drink-loving, riddle-asking creatures, they'd unsettled me, but the better I got to know them, the more I liked them.

On Earth, the skelleins wore something to differentiate their sexes and personalities. In Hell, they had no adornments and tried to blend together once more. I hoped that when we made it out of here I'd get to see them in their costumes again and Corson wearing his earrings.

This black pit of despair had stripped all of them of their more jovial sides and turned them into unrelenting, savage demons once more. I welcomed their savagery if it helped to keep us all alive, but I wanted to see the skelleins swigging beer and dressing eclectically again.

Corson knelt at the shoreline again and dipped his fingers into the water. I wanted to stick my fingers in to learn if the water was hot or cold, as thick as the blood it resembled or as flowing as the waters on Earth. I didn't go anywhere near it though. With that many wraiths in it, I had no idea what effect touching that water would have on me. I bet it wouldn't be a heartwarming, let's all lock arms and sing experience.

The wraiths started to wail as they rose out of the water again.

"And all three of the ferrymen are as ugly as sin," Lix stated.

"They can't be any uglier than some of the other hideous creatures we've seen in here," Hawk said.

Lix planted the tip of his sword on the rocky ground and leaned on it as he spoke with Hawk. "Oh, young former human, you've only seen the tip of the proverbial iceberg when it comes to the ugliness of this place."

Hawk glowered at Lix when he called him a former human, but it was true. If it hadn't been for Lilitu's canagh blood mixing with Hawk's after she sliced him open, Hawk would be dead. Instead, her blood had altered his genetic makeup, turning him into a canagh demon and making it possible for him to venture this far into Hell with us. It also meant he now fed on sexual energy and wraiths, like the other canagh demons did. Hawk wasn't exactly thrilled about his newly turned, demon status, but he agreed it was far better than death.

"That's reassuring," Hawk said to Lix.

"There's nothing reassuring about Hell," Lix replied.

The boat came close enough for me to see what looked like a bull skull staked to the bow. However, this skull was more protracted than a bull's and its red, two-foot-long horns curved up until the tips of them touched in the middle. I didn't know what kind of creature that skull belonged to, and I never wanted to encounter its live counterpart.

Kobal stepped away from me as another boat emerged from the shadowed tunnel and glided toward us. The hellhounds prowled the shoreline before moving to either side of me and Kobal.

Some of the massive hounds brushed by me as they walked. They rubbed their heads against my sides and nudged me until I rubbed their sleek, black coats. They resembled wolves but they were larger than lions and could rip my head off with the swipe of a paw, but I knew the beautiful animals would never hurt me.

Corson rose and stepped away from the water once more. With his connection to the water broken, the wraiths slid back beneath the surface. A grating noise sounded as the first boat slid in between two man-sized rocks to settle on the shore before us.

I glanced at Hawk when he inched back. He may be a demon now too, but this was all as new to him as it was to me. He looked about as thrilled as I felt to climb onto that craft with the robed ferryman.

Entrenched in shadows, and with the hood of its black cloak pulled over its head, it was impossible to make out many details about the ferryman standing at the stern. However, if the skelleins considered it ugly, I was content not to see its face.

"Mah rhála," the shrouded figure greeted in a voice that brought to mind dusty crypts housing mummies. I wouldn't be surprised to learn this thing hadn't spoken in hundreds of years.

"English, Carion," Kobal commanded.

"My king," the dry voice grated out. Its head twisted an inch to the side; I couldn't see its eyes, but I sensed its attention had shifted to me. "My queen," it murmured.

Shivers ran over my flesh when I caught a glimpse of two burning red orbs in the area where the ferryman's eyes would be.

"Shit," Hawk said in a voice so low I didn't think any of the others heard him.

The other boat slid onto the shore with a grating sound. The rocks lining the water's edge looked like they could pierce through flesh, but they didn't do any damage to the boats. *At least they're solidly built*, I thought. Always a bonus when about to take a ride on the river of woe.

Another shrouded figure stood at the stern of the second boat, and an identical skull hung from the front of it. My fingers instinctively fluttered up to touch my shell necklace before I recalled that I'd lost it during my battle with the lanavours. My hand fell to my side as the second figure stepped forward.

"Mah rhála, mah rejant," it said in a voice as dry as the first one.

My king. My queen, I realized.

"Speak English, Charant," Kobal replied and the creature bowed its head.

Turning back to me, Kobal extended his hand and I took it. He walked me over to the first boat. I inspected the skull on the front as Kobal lifted me over the side and set me in the boat.

CHAPTER THREE

River

I couldn't tell how Carion steered the boat. If the thick wooden staff he dipped into the water propelled us forward, or if he dug it into the bottom of the river and guided us that way. However he did it, the boat glided seamlessly through the currents. He showed no signs of strain as he effortlessly pulled the pole from the water. Gnarled and with twisting coils of thicker wood going around it, the staff could crack someone's head open with one blow.

Carion drew the staff out of the river and swung it over to the other side of the boat. I resisted touching the red drops that fell from the pole to glisten against the wooden bottom. I had a feeling the wraiths permeated every ounce of this water, even what fell outside of it.

Magnus and I sat on the single bench seat stretching across the middle of the boat. The others all stood with their legs braced against the current and their eyes searching the bleak passageways we traversed. I kept waiting for something to leap out at us or the rocks to come to life, but the only sound and movement came from the wraiths, the ferrymen, and the boats.

My muscles ached as I held myself rigidly and searched for any hint of danger, but at least the wraiths weren't having an overwhelming impact on me. Goose bumps danced over my cooler flesh, but I didn't feel as if my bones would shatter, and I could breathe without a problem.

Occasionally, a wraith would break the surface of the water near us. Hands would grapple at the air, or a warped face would emerge before the soul was dragged under again. Sometimes, the peaceful lapping of the water flowing against the hull would be broken by the thump of a wraith hitting the side, but they mostly left us alone.

My hands locked around my seat when a wraith bumped the boat. The smooth, polished wood of the boat was chestnut in color. Grains ran through it and there was an occasional, darker knot in the panels. There wasn't enough life flowing through the wood for me to draw from it, but it was there.

"What are the boats made from?" I asked.

"Calamut trees," Kobal answered.

I looked up at where he stood before me. "The calamut trees allowed themselves to be cut down?"

I couldn't picture those colossal trees—with their sweeping limbs and ability to create walls with their branches—allowing anyone near them with an ax. I'd watched those branches pierce an ogre straight through before dragging him away. I preferred not to think about what they would do to someone who tried to chop one of them down.

"That would never happen," Magnus said.

"The wood was harvested after the calamut died," Kobal said. "It doesn't happen very often, but occasionally one of them does die or is killed."

"I see," I replied and ran my hand over the seat before rising.

Bracing my legs apart, I easily maintained my balance on the shifting vessel. A feeling of rightness stole through me at being surrounded by water again. I hadn't spent much time on boats back home, but I'd spent enough time near the ocean to know its ebbs and flows well. The Asharún may not be the beautiful, rolling blue sea I loved so much, but the sway of its currents called to me.

The boat glided around a corner, and the jagged walls closed in on us. Kobal bent his head to avoid being stabbed by the rocks. The scent of brimstone and fire grew heavier on the air.

A wraith rose out of the water only a few feet away. Its human-looking hands clawed at the air before its elongated jaw and sightless eyes broke the surface. Seeing the human qualities on the deformed figure was more disturbing to me than witnessing them when they were entirely the twisted monstrosities they became.

I tried not to recall the image of my father as a wraith, but watching the spirit being pulled under the water again brought forth the memory of my father being sucked into the Fires of Creation and destroyed.

To keep myself centered in the here and now, I focused on the boat behind us. The hellhounds all sat within it, their amber eyes bright in the gloom.

Something bumped against the side of the boat with more force than the wraiths had exhibited so far. The bow went slightly off course before Carion corrected it.

"What was that?" I whispered.

"Probably a tahanusi," Bale replied and pushed a strand of fiery red hair over her shoulder. Her skin held a red hue to it and her eyes were a penetrating lime-green color. Bale was one of Kobal's second-in-command; the other one was Corson. She was one of the most stunning women I'd ever seen with her lethal curves and flawless features, but she was just as ruthless as Kobal and Corson.

"What is a tahanusi?" Hawk asked.

"A sea monster," Magnus replied as casually as if he'd revealed they were starfish.

"A what now?" Hawk reached for one of his guns, but he no longer wore his weapon belt. Our human weapons had been lost during the battle with Lucifer.

Magnus's mouth quirked in amusement when Hawk glanced

between him, the Asharún, and back again. The realization we shared this water with something more than the wraiths made the hair on my arms rise. I scrutinized the water, trying to pierce through its murky depths to see what lay beneath, but the river refused to yield its secrets.

"The tahanusis won't bother us," Kobal said and rested a hand on my shoulder.

"But they're sea monsters?" I asked, unable to tear my eyes away from the water.

"They're Hell creatures who also feed on wraiths," Kobal replied. "They rarely bother the boats."

"You throwing that word *rarely* out there isn't as reassuring as you think it is," Hawk said.

Something else hit the side of the boat, causing it to veer off course again. I bit back a gasp as I strained to see the creature beneath us. Not being able to see them made knowing they were there so much worse.

"They occasionally bump against the boats by accident, that's all," Bale said.

From fifteen feet away, a rounded back broke the surface of the water. It rose higher as it slid through the water like a serpent. The water streaming over the creature caused its scales to glisten like black diamonds before it finally vanished again.

Then, a tail lashed out of the water and flicked out behind the creature. I couldn't stop my stomach from turning when I realized the tip of the tail resembled a rattlesnake's. With a shake, the creature threw off drops of water, and its tail created a high-pitched rattle that reverberated like a gunshot over the walls of our close confines.

Beside me, Kobal stiffened. Magnus slowly rose to his feet. I glanced between the two of them as the gray tail slid beneath the surface of the water. Only a small ripple indicated where it had been. Carion planted his staff in the water and the boat halted. The vessel behind us stopped a few feet away. The foot-long talons in the back of Corson's hands extended. The hounds all rose to their feet as a hush descended.

In the distance, another rattle echoed through the cavern, drawing my attention to the winding tunnel we'd already traversed. The curves in the rocks made it impossible to see more than twenty feet ahead or behind us. Kobal and the others all turned to face the direction we had come from.

Another rattle sounded from somewhere ahead of us. The strength of it vibrated off the walls and created ripples across the surface of the water. As the boat swayed, Kobal's hand tightened on my shoulder and he drew me closer to him. His black fingernails lengthened into three-inch claws that could eviscerate someone.

My heart pounded out a drumbeat against my ribs. "Kobal—"

I didn't get a chance to finish my question before he spun toward me. He wrapped his arms around me seconds before something launched itself out of the water. Kobal jerked against me, and we were both shoved roughly forward. The boat listed precariously to the side, nearly tipping over. Leaning back, Kobal planted his foot on the other side of the boat and pushed it down before we were all dumped into the water.

"Are you okay?" I demanded of him. I tried to twist in his arms to see what was going on when the coppery scent of blood filled my nostrils. *His blood.*

Fury at anything injuring him caused fire to dance across my fingertips, and Kobal's flames emerged to circle his wrists. The boat rocked as the weight within it shifted, but I still couldn't see around Kobal as he kept his body enfolded protectively over mine.

"Corson!" Kobal barked.

"It went down before we could get it," Corson replied.

"Get us to shore, Carion, now!" Kobal commanded.

"Are you okay?" I demanded again.

"I'm fine, Mah Kush-la, do not worry. What was it?" he asked the others.

"Lower-level demon," Bale replied.

"In the Asharún?" Magnus asked, his tone disbelieving.

"They know the World Walker is here," Lix said.

Another loud rattle sounded from somewhere beyond the cavern. Kobal lifted me up and spun me around as a demon came out of the water behind us. More fire flared around Kobal and lashed out of his back in a protective wave. The demon screamed, and Kobal's low growl resonated in my ear. Moving to the side, I twisted away from him enough to see the scorched demon falling into the water as another creature loomed out of it.

"Kobal!" I shouted at the same time he turned and launched a punch.

The creature's nose flattened and its cheek caved in from the force of the blow. Blood oozed from its mouth before it spit out its teeth. I recognized it as a lower-level demon because of its animalistic features seconds before Kobal clutched its head and snapped it to the side.

The demon's body went limp, but its eyes still rolled in its head. Kobal continued to twist its head to the side until he wrenched it from the demon's shoulders. Yellow blood spilled forth to mix with the red water.

Something crashed against the side of the boat, spinning it sideways in the water. I staggered back, my arms pinwheeling to steady my balance. Righting myself, I placed my foot against the wood behind me to brace myself as a splash sounded.

Something hit the boat with enough force that the wood shuddered and beads of water formed around the edges of the boards. I edged my boots away as the red water slid toward them.

Corson plunged his talons straight through the neck of another demon while Lix and the other skelleins eagerly hacked at them with their swords. Kobal lashed out at another one when it erupted from the water. Fire danced over my fingers as I searched for another threat and positioned myself so that my back was against Kobal's. Kneeling at the side of the boat, Magnus and Hawk waved their arms as they shouted something I couldn't understand.

It took me a second to spot Bale swimming through the water toward us. I realized she'd created the splash I'd heard. Magnus and Hawk grabbed her arms when she made it to the boat and hauled her over the side. Water dripped from Bale as she sat for a second before leaping to her feet with a murderous gleam in her eyes.

"Destroy them all," Carion hissed.

My eyes widened when I realized his hood had fallen back to reveal his features. Lix had been completely right, the ferryman was ugly and not in the disconcerting, 'I'm not used to seeing something that looks like this' kind of way, but in a flat out, 'I'm going to have nightmares about him for the rest of my life' kind of way.

His gray skin flaked off and fell around him as he lifted the staff and slid it back into the water with far more speed than he had before. There were no lips to his mouth, only a clear view of his yellow, pointed teeth. The white cheekbones beneath his eye sockets were visible. Two glowing red lights burned out of his head from where his eyes should have been. However, none of that was as bad as all the things wiggling beneath his crusty skin like worms burrowing through the earth.

I finally succeeded in tearing my gaze away from him, but his face was forever seared into my memory.

Another demon burst from the water and came over the side of the boat at Bale, Magnus, and Hawk. Against my back, Kobal's body moved fluidly while he worked to fight off more demons with the skelleins. On the boat behind us, the hounds howled, but their vessel remained unaffected by the demons swarming us.

Lifting my hand, I released a blast of fire into the face of a hyena-looking demon. The demon yelped and fell into the water as more of them emerged. Some fell back beneath the surface, but others caught the boat and held on as they tried to pull themselves inside.

Drawing on the vast power Kobal emanated, I fought my growing dread as the boat rocked precariously and the shouts and grunts of fighting filled the air. Fear brought out the fire in me, but right now I needed my ability to wield life. It was a far more lethal weapon against these creatures.

Deep blue sparks danced across my fingertips. I worked on growing the energy as a splintering sound rent the air and the boat shuddered to a stop. Expecting the boat to break in half, I glanced nervously around, but I couldn't see any damage to it. The boat following ours came to a stop and from somewhere behind us another rattle sounded.

"What—" I never got to finish the question as the wood beneath my feet suddenly gave way and I plummeted into the water.

CHAPTER FOUR

Kobal

I leapt forward to grab River, but she was already gone. A snarl tore from me as my hands clenched empty air. Water surged through the gaping hole the demon had torn into the boat. They'd dared to touch her, dared to take her from *me*, and they'd taken her into the *Asharún* with the wraiths and the tahanusis.

"Kobal!" Bale shouted as I turned and dove over the side of the boat.

The warm water of the Asharún enveloped me when I plunged beneath its surface. Kicking hard, I dove deeper as I searched for any sign of River, but I couldn't see my hands before me.

The demons wouldn't kill her—Lucifer wanted her alive—but they would take her to him. And what he would do to her…

No. It would *not* happen. I'd get her back before they managed to take her from here. On my right, a spark burst through the darkness before going out. I swam toward the light. River had created that spark, but the water would extinguish her flames, and the wraiths would make it difficult, if not impossible, for her to draw on her ability to wield life.

A tahanusi, angered that others had entered its water, brushed against my chest. Its scales scouring my flesh drew blood. I was their king, but they tolerated only the wraiths in the water with them. It was the reason I'd believed traveling the Asharún would be safer.

I had underestimated Lucifer's control over these lower-level demons, if he'd somehow convinced them to brave the wrath of the tahanusis to capture River. The demons must have been hiding and waiting to see if we would come this way and slipped into the water when they heard the approach of the boats.

Another thick-skinned body abraded my flesh, and a rattle sounded through the water. If the tahanusis planned to attack me, they would have by now, but king or not, they wanted me out of their water and they were letting me know it.

I wildly searched for any sign of River in the murky water of the damned. The demons would have brought her back to the surface by now to keep her from drowning. But then, lower-level demons weren't known for their intelligence, and they wouldn't require oxygen as often as she did. They may not realize she would need to breathe already.

With a fierce kick, I propelled myself back to the surface. Bursting free of the water, I inhaled deeply and treaded water as I spun in search of her. Our boat no longer skimmed across the surface, but hung heavy in the water as Carion steered it sluggishly toward the shore. Now that River wasn't within it, the demons had ceased their attack on it.

From deep within the cavern, another rattle reverberated off the walls, but this time it was followed by a low wail that the tahanusis released as one. There would be no more warnings. The tahanusis would strike to kill now.

The hounds all whimpered and moved toward the end of their boat. "Partka," I commanded them to stay. The tahanusis would cut them down without hesitation, and they could do nothing to help in the water.

"There, Kobal!" Corson shouted and pointed fifty feet away from me, toward the other side of the cavern.

Hawk made a move to jump into the water, but Magnus and Bale both jerked him back as River broke free of the water. She gasped for air before turning and swimming toward the boat. I swam as fast as I could to get to her. She only made it ten feet before something jerked on her body, pulling her under again.

Diving beneath once more, I swam for where I'd last seen her. A burst of orange came from twenty feet ahead of me, but River's flames were extinguished by the water.

River

I kicked at the demon holding my ankle, but his grip didn't ease. My hands clawed at the water in a vain attempt to stop my downward momentum. I had no idea how deep this river was, but it seemed endless as the dark, cold depths of the Asharún became all I knew. My entire life, I'd been drawn to water; now I was certain it would be the death of me as my lungs burned for air.

It took everything I had not to open my mouth and inhale greedily. Panic growing, fire burst from my fingers only to be extinguished immediately by the water surrounding me. I tried to draw on the flow of life around me. Even if this was a place for the dead, the tahanusis still lived and thrived in this environment. Instead of life, all I felt was the chill permeating further into my bones until ice encased the marrow of them.

The wraiths. Their presence may not have affected me much when I was on the boat, but being in the water with them was an entirely different story.

I kicked against the hold on my ankle again, but the weakness seeping into my limbs and my lack of oxygen made it increasingly difficult to fight off the demon. I'd always been a strong swimmer and able to hold my breath longer than most, but I was being pushed to my limits right now.

No! I will not die like this!

The adrenaline fueling me caused another burst of fire to erupt. I almost screamed when the flame briefly illuminated the round, eel-like mouth full of piranha teeth coming straight at me. The soulless green eyes of a tahanusi filled my vision before darkness descended around me once more.

My arms flailed in the water as I tried to swim backward to avoid the course I'd seen the sea monster taking. I kept waiting for that mouth to lock on me and gulp me into its body. I'd slide down that tube-like throat as smoothly as a raw oyster. I felt on the verge of hysteria when I realized it was oddly fitting that being consumed by a water creature would be my demise considering all the fish I'd eaten in my life.

I jerked when a scaly body slid down the front of me, scraping the flesh of my collarbone as the tahanusi dove deeper into the water. I had no idea why it hadn't eaten me, what game it was playing. Perhaps they were like boa constrictors and it intended to squeeze the life out of me before making a snack of me. My already frantic heartbeat went into overdrive at the idea of the tahanusi preparing to wrap itself around me.

Stars danced before my eyes as lack of oxygen started to affect my brain. The ridged edges of the tahanusi's rattle brushed against my face. After the roughness of its solid body, the softness of the rattle threw me completely.

Unable to stop it anymore, my lips instinctively parted for breath as the demon's grip on my ankle released. Water rushed into my throat and poured into my lungs as I tried to close my mouth, but once I'd inhaled, I couldn't stop. My body convulsed as water expanded my lungs. I struggled to get my wits together enough to swim. I thought my feet kicked toward the surface, but then I realized they were barely moving at all and I was sinking deeper.

Something solid slid between my legs. Before I had time to process what it was, it propelled me upward. Water flowed so fast around me that it stung my cheeks. My hands encircled my throat when another gulping breath of the Asharún filled my lungs. The stars vanished, blackness filled my vision, and I slumped weakly against the creature.

I knew I broke free of the Asharún only because I felt the rush of air against my cheeks, but I still couldn't see anything. Water spewed from lips as I coughed it out of my brutalized lungs.

Whatever was between my legs slid away. I fell back beneath the surface before I could stop myself. More liquid filled my mouth and nose. Something else slipped beneath me and feeling as if I were seated in a swing, I was lifted again.

Breaking free once more, water sprayed from my lips and ran down my chin when a round of coughing racked my body. Every one of my bones hurt, all my muscles and organs felt bruised, but I was alive.

My hands fell onto the scaly body of one of the tahanusis, my dress kept me protected from its rough skin as it slid beneath me. It held me above for a second more before slipping away. This time, I managed to weakly tread water instead of plummeting beneath.

All around me, the wraiths broke free of the surface. One of their hands fell through my shoulder, causing my teeth to chatter. I expected the Asharún to start icing over around me, but the current remained flowing steadily onward, taking me with it.

I tried to figure out where I was in the river, but I couldn't see beyond the twisted souls encroaching on me. My kicking slowed as the wraiths steadily weakened me. More of the wraith's hands fell through me. More twisted faces whirled before my eyes.

If I didn't get away from them, I would go under again, and this time there would be no coming back. I tried to draw on my fire or the flow of life, but both eluded me in this world of water and death.

CHAPTER FIVE

River

Through the sea of black, I saw two lower-level demons slicing across the water toward me. I jerked when an arm locked around my waist and my back was pulled against a solid chest. Even before Kobal spoke, I knew it was him.

"Easy," he murmured, his lips brushing over my ear. "I've got you, Mah Kush-la."

His familiar endearment for me, meaning *my heart*, briefly warmed me. My feeling of being safe didn't last long as the two demons reached us and a third burst out of the water in front of us. Kobal curved himself protectively around me. The thuds of fists hitting his flesh sounded. He grunted, but made no other noise.

"K… Ko… bal?" I managed to chatter out.

He didn't respond as he released me with one of his hands and swung out behind him. Craning my head, I watched as he sliced his claws across the neck of one demon before driving his fist through the chest of another and tearing out its heart. The third sliced its claws down Kobal's side.

I cried out and lunged for the demon. I may not be able to do much with the wraiths and the water all around me, but I'd choke that thing to death for hurting him. Kobal's powerful legs kept us both afloat as he seized the demon's arm and snapped it back. Lunging forward, he sank his fangs in the demon's throat, reared back and spit the demon's flesh out.

Resting his hand on the Asharún, Kobal released a wall of fire from his fingertips. It raced over the water in a fiery blaze that illuminated the cavern. The demons screamed and fell back as the fire whipped around us to create a half-circle of protection. The popping sizzle of their flesh and the burnt stench of it filled the air.

Keeping his arm locked around my waist, Kobal's powerful body cut through the water while fire continued to stream from his hand. I lost sight of the demons and the wraiths vanished when Kobal approached. I spotted the others standing on the shore with the hounds, waiting for us. The rattling of the tahanusis ceased, but the arched back of one slid out of the water a few feet away.

"They saved me," I said when Kobal's body further eased the chill in me.

"They may not like us in their water, but you are their queen," he replied.

"I knew the demons accepted me as their queen, but these creatures too?"

"Any who are loyal to me will be loyal to you, without question," Kobal said.

"Where are the rest of the demons who attacked us?"

"If the tahanusis didn't feast on them, then they've fled like the cowards they are."

The idea of being feasted on by a tahanusi made me gulp.

When we made it to the shoreline, Kobal carried me onto it. Despite the heat of Hell, and him, I continued to shiver in his arms. His hands ran over my body, rubbing my back and arms to defrost my limbs.

I craned my body to see over his shoulder and gasped at the flayed open skin of his back. He shifted to hold me so I couldn't see it again. "You're wounded!" I cried.

"I'm fine," he said gruffly.

"Kobal—"

"It will heal soon," he said and set me gently on my feet. Water dripped from his hair and down his face as he clasped my chin. His golden eyes surveyed me from head to toe before he circled around me. He kept his back from my view as he moved.

"I'm a little wetter than before, but no harm done," I said when he stepped in front of me again.

"Hmm," he grunted in response.

His fingers skimmed the flesh where the tahanusi had abraded my collarbone. With the way I'd been healing since I'd started coming into my powers and claimed Kobal as my Chosen, the marks wouldn't be noticeable soon. "I'm fine," I assured him.

He stopped before me. A muscle twitched in his cheek as a vein throbbed to life in his forehead. "Aside from the lungful of water."

"Yeah, that sucked," I admitted and shoved a strand of wet hair out of my eye. "Let me see your back."

"It will heal."

"I know that, but I want to see it. Maybe a bandage would help it heal faster."

"Not likely."

Still, he turned to allow me to inspect his raw and torn flesh. I didn't dare touch it. He may be acting like it didn't hurt, but it must. I rested my fingers on his sides before bending to kiss an undamaged area of his back. He'd sustained this damage to protect me.

He turned and lifted me into his arms. "You are mine to protect, always," he said, as if he'd read my mind. He carried me the remaining ten feet to where everyone else stood.

Carion had pulled his hood back into place. His eyes blazed as he surveyed the damage the demons had wrought on his boat. "Lucifer and his followers must pay for this," he hissed to Kobal.

"They will," Kobal promised as he set me down.

"Are you okay?" Hawk demanded of me.

"Fine," I said as I ran my hands over my arms.

Pulling his hands away from me, fire erupted from Kobal's fingers and ran up to his wrists. He made sure the flames didn't touch me as he ran them along my body. His flames wouldn't burn me, but they would burn the dress off me, and neither one of us wanted me traipsing around Hell naked.

Two of the hellhounds rose and came closer to me. They pressed against my sides, their warm fur helping to further ease the rattling of my bones. I rested my hands on the hounds' heads as my gaze ran over the black rocks surrounding us.

"Can we get out of here?" I asked.

"We can," Bale replied. "Are we still heading to your chambers, Kobal?"

"We are," he said.

Kobal extinguished his flames as he stepped back. Glancing down at the dress the tree nymphs had given me, I realized I was almost completely dry.

"Lucifer doesn't know where my chambers are located," Kobal continued. "He is trying to block us every way he can to get at River. The demons who attacked us got lucky when they stumbled across us here."

Lifting a piece of my hair, he ran it through his fingers. "But Lucifer will never have you," he vowed.

I smiled at him, but I had a bad feeling about all of this. My premonitions were never directly about me. However, my instincts screamed at me to get out of Hell as soon as possible.

Kobal

Taking River's hand, I helped to steady her as she climbed over the jagged rocks lining the shore of the Asharún. Numerous abrasions from the rocks marred her skin. Her wounds healed quickly, but the fact she sustained them at all set my teeth on edge. The fine blue veins in her eyelids were now visible and her cheeks had hollowed out, as she labored to fight off the effects of the wraiths. Before she fell into the water, she'd been handling their presence well, but not anymore.

When I got the chance to destroy Lucifer, I would make him pay for everything she'd endured because of him.

Another wraith broke out of the water and wailed before slipping away again. In response, River's hand trembled in my grasp, but her eyes were defiant when they met mine. It was as if she knew I was considering carrying her so she didn't have to walk anymore.

When she stepped down beside me, I pulled her closer as I stopped to survey the cavern and scent the air for any new threat. The only odors I detected were the faint hint of brimstone, the Asharún, and River's crisp scent that managed to break through the aromas of Hell. If there were more demons waiting to set a trap, they would slip into the water again to avoid my detection of them. After what had happened to their cohorts, I doubted any of them were willing to attempt coming at us through the Asharún again though.

I could stretch my hand up and run my fingers over the lethal tips of the rocks above, but a hundred feet ahead the cavern expanded once more. From past travels, I knew it opened into an area with a pathway winding toward the higher levels of Hell. That path would lead us away from the Asharún and the wraiths, but Lucifer could establish another ambush there—one River was far from prepared to handle right now.

"We're going to change course and go through the oracle," I stated.

"The oracle?" Hawk asked.

"It's a lake of fire where Earth can be looked on by those who reside in Hell. It's the central focus of all the heat in Hell," I explained. "Before I left here, there had never been an angel spotted near the oracle."

"But they could frequent it often now," Hawk said.

"They could," Corson replied, "but it is unlikely. It's a place to look upon Earth, and in case you've forgotten, the fallen angels *really* dislike your former species."

"They really dislike all species other than theirs," Magnus said. "And let's face it, they don't like their own kind much either. They wouldn't be here otherwise."

"True," Corson agreed.

"We'll go through the oracle and on to my chambers. We'll rest there before joining with Morax and the others," I said.

"Have you spoken with Morax recently?" Bale inquired.

"Yes," I replied crisply. It didn't matter that Morax was five-hundred-twenty-years old and had followed me since he'd been old enough to fight, didn't matter I knew he would do everything he could to defeat Lucifer, I hated letting him into my head. Most times, I kept my mind shut down to any type of telecommunication, but it was necessary to stay in contact with Morax now. "They are battling Lucifer's troops. They've sustained losses, but they're holding their own. They haven't gained much ground against him."

"Are you thinking about bringing down more of the demons still on Earth to join us?" Bale asked.

River stiffened beside me, and I knew her thoughts had turned to her brothers. If there were less demons guarding the gateway and the wall, there was a better chance something could happen to her siblings.

"No," I said. "The seals may not be falling anymore, but far too many creatures escaped them before we stopped their collapse. We can't leave the humans guarding the gateway above unprotected. We also need the demons at the wall to remain there. They won't be able to stop everything from getting past them, but they'll stop a lot of it."

"The humans outside the wall will learn of our existence if the wall is breached," Corson said.

"You mean *when* the wall is breached," I replied. "There will be no stopping that from happening."

"No matter how many walls are built, there is no stopping the truth. It always comes out," Magnus said.

Bale scowled at him. "That's insightful, coming from one of the most manipulative beings I've ever met."

Magnus spread his elegant hands before him. "I manipulate what others see. I get them to do my bidding, or punish souls with their worst nightmares. A manipulation of the mind is one thing, but I will always give you the truth if asked for it. I can create images, I can make myself something I'm not, and I can make others something they are not, but eventually those images fade and the truth comes out.

"I brought my carnival to life and made it a *real* thing hewn over centuries of magic, practice, and work. It is no longer make believe; it is reality. However, even *I* cannot make a lie a truth, Bale. Though I thank you for believing me powerful enough to do so."

Bale's eyes became slits as she stared at Magnus. Over the centuries that they'd fought by my side, there had always been an animosity between them. Bale was a ruthless fighter; she went at everything head-on. Magnus was more strategic with a wait and see approach to combat. They were complete opposites who would battle each other until the day one of them died.

When Magnus retreated from the war with Lucifer three hundred years ago, he'd never revealed that he was doing so because he wanted to become better at weaving his illusions. Magnus's reasons for retreating were sound, he'd proven himself loyal since, and put River's life and safety ahead of his own, but Bale remained uncertain of him.

"Play nice, children, or I'll take your toys away," Corson said, drawing lethal looks from Magnus and Bale.

"Enough," I said. They all stopped speaking and looked to me. "The humans will learn at least some of what has happened. There is no stopping that. We can only continue with what we are doing here, and traveling through the oracle is the best way to go."

I slid my arm around River's waist as I turned away from them. Her hand settled on my stomach as we continued along the shoreline and past the pathway leading out of here. Wraiths and tahanusis continued to occasionally break the surface of the Asharún, but the tahanusis' rattle did not sound again.

"Your back is a lot better," she said as she craned her head to look at it.

I had always been a fast healer, but the strength of my Chosen bond with her caused me to heal at a much faster rate than I had before. "It is."

"Will I be able to see my brothers through the oracle?" River asked.

I wanted to tell her yes, to give her that bit of hope in this place of despair, but I couldn't. "It doesn't work that way. The oracle only reveals what it decides to reveal."

"Did you ever look into it and *want* to see something?"

"No," I admitted.

"Then maybe there is a chance it will show me my brothers."

I brushed a strand of hair over her shoulder. She smiled at me and took my hand to flatten it against her face. Healthy color crept across her cheeks as she drew on my life force. My gaze fell to her mouth when a sigh parted her full lips, and her black lashes swept down to shadow her eyes.

For a minute, I was lost to her, but then my attention returned to the cavern when it started to widen out. The angels had never been seen at the oracle before, but that didn't mean demons couldn't be waiting ahead.

CHAPTER SIX

River

Kobal led us away from the Asharún and through a side tunnel. The tip of some of the black and red rocks scraped my skin while I walked through it. Before me, Kobal turned sideways to avoid the rocks before being able to walk straight again. More of those deadly rocks hovered above our heads, waiting to break free and slice someone in half.

The further we moved away from the Asharún, the less I felt the effects of the wraiths. Midnight blue sparks raced across my fingertips when I ran them over the rocks and drew on the pulse of life in them. The ache in my brutalized lungs eased with every breath I took, yet I was beginning to lag.

I thought I'd been hot in Hell before, but it was nothing compared to now. Sweat ran down my forehead and back, adhering my dress to me. I pulled at my soggy collar, trying to get some air against my skin; it didn't help. I wiped the sweat away from my eyes, but no sooner had I done so than more of it stuck my lashes together.

For the first time, I understood what a lobster felt like when it was first thrown into the pot, and I vowed to never eat the crustacean again.

When Kobal glanced back at me, I forced a smile. I didn't need a mirror to know I looked like week-old dog crap, but I refused to let him carry me through here. I'd let him carry me across that cavern filled with the dead monsters who escaped the seals. I wouldn't let him do it again. I had to stand on my own in this place; it would eat me alive otherwise.

I might take a wraith right now though. They may drain my abilities and weaken me, but I would almost welcome their wintry presence to ease my increasing discomfort in this suffocating heat.

I glanced over at Hawk, but he wasn't sweating anywhere near as bad as me. *Because he's a demon now too*, I reminded myself.

Still, sometimes I forgot that this man, who had once been more human than me, was now more demon than me. Hawk could be changed into a demon and have their immortality. If other humans survived the change, they could also have the demon's immortality too. I would never be able to have it without risking my connection to all living things, and Kobal refused to take that risk with me.

I understood why; the last thing I wanted was to become like Lucifer and the other fallen angels, but I would give almost anything to have an eternity with Kobal. I couldn't deny that I still harbored a teeny hope that we would discover it was possible to turn me into a demon without severing my connection to all life.

My gaze landed on Kobal's broad back. I watched his muscles and his markings bunch and flow with every step he took. He was the strongest and most powerful being I knew, yet not even he would be able to stop my eventual death.

Whether my demise be tomorrow or a thousand years from now—some of my ancestors, such as Noah, had managed to live far longer than they should have—I would still die. My ancestors' lengthy lives most likely came from their ability to draw on the flow of life, even if they hadn't known they were doing it at the time.

Kobal stepped out of the side passageway. He turned to extend his hand to me. Taking it, I climbed out from between the walls and into a massive cavern. The heat slapped me in the face with enough force to suck the breath out of me. I wheezed to get air into my shocked lungs as sweat poured down me, soaking me as thoroughly as my dip in the Asharún. I didn't bother to pull my dress away from me again; it cleaved to my body, but extra movement was not an option. Moving would only create more heat and more sweat.

"River—"

"Fine!" I wheezed before Kobal decided to either take me back or carry me through here. "I'm fine. Keep going."

My legs wobbled when I stepped forward, but I steadied them beneath me as a muscle twitched in Kobal's cheek.

Walking caused more sweat to pour down me. My lips cracked and my mouth felt like I'd made sand my new favorite snack, but I didn't ask for the water some of the skelleins carried for me. I'd drink it all if I got my hands on it, and I wanted out of this place more than I craved a drink.

Our footsteps echoed off the walls surrounding us. We couldn't hide that we were coming from anything ahead, but we'd be able to see anything coming at us from over two hundred feet away. Tilting my head back, I blinked at the smooth, rounded ceiling a hundred feet above me. The glow of a distant fire bounced off the black rocks, turning some of them gray. The glow and those gray rocks were the only color in this drab area.

Hell shadows danced over the walls, keeping rhythm with the flickering flames. The shadows moved in a sinuous, almost memorizing dance. They unnerved me with their ability to leap and jump in ways no normal shadow could, but they were fascinating to watch.

When my knees nearly gave out on me, I staggered forward a step before righting myself. "Let me carry you," Kobal grated from between his teeth.

My attempt to swallow was thwarted by my severe lack of saliva. "No."

"It's not a sign of weakness to require help. You are not from here. You'll exhaust yourself by being stubborn."

"Maybe, but this is something I have to do," I croaked.

Kobal growled in frustration and made a move to grab me. For a second, I thought he was going to completely disregard my wishes, but his hands fell back to his sides. His black eyes shifted to amber when they met mine, and I knew what it had taken for him not to do as he wanted.

At one time, he would have ignored my words and tossed me over his shoulder. I had no doubt he would carry me out of here if he believed I was in danger, but for now he'd listened to me.

I almost threw myself into his arms to hug him close. Instead, I smiled at him. He stared at me for a minute before reluctantly turning away.

As we walked across the cavern, I finally spotted the source of the heat and the glow playing over the walls. Fifty feet away, fire rolled onto a rock ledge before receding again. The ebb and flow of it reminded me of the sea. The crackle of the flames almost sounded like the crashing of waves on the sand. Unlike the sea, white plumes of spray didn't shoot up from it when it reached the shore, instead yellow and orange sparks floated through the air before vanishing into the shade above.

"An ocean in Hell," I whispered. "Is that the oracle?"

"It is," Kobal confirmed.

I missed the ocean. Missed the salt of it on my lips, the soothing flow of its waves against the shore, and the cries of the birds soaring above. This crashing fire had none of the teeming life the sea did, but it still drew me toward it.

Stopping at the edge of the waves, I gazed out over the oracle. The fires rolled on for a good hundred yards before slipping beneath the wall across from me. "Where does it come from?" I asked.

"The oracle is an extension of the Fires of Creation," Kobal said from beside me. "This chamber doesn't possess the same amount of power as the chamber housing the Fires, but there is enough here that the human world can be looked upon. Because the fire here isn't as strong, we can get closer to the oracle."

I remembered gazing down into the Fires of Creation that had forged Kobal and thinking how angry and hot the flames looked. Now that heat blasted against me, but nothing would deter me from getting closer to it.

My heart beat faster with every step I took toward the fiery sea. I yearned to peer into the oracle and see my brothers. I *had* to know Gage and Bailey were alive. I'd sacrifice everything for them and would do anything to ensure they had a future.

The trembling in my legs grew, but it wasn't only from exhaustion anymore. No, I feared looking into those fires and discovering my brothers' broken bodies. A lump wedged in my throat. Every step became harder to make, but I continued until I stood at the edge of what could only be called a shore.

I kept my feet away from the rolling inferno as I gazed over the crests. "Will it work for me?" I asked Kobal when he stepped beside me.

"I don't know."

"Do you see anything?" No matter how I tried, I couldn't keep the hope from my voice. I *needed* someone to see something beyond this place.

"The wall," he replied and rested his hand on my shoulder. "Mac is guarding it. The wall still stands."

My shoulders sagged beneath his grip. "Hawk?" I asked when he came forward to stand on my other side.

"I see the ocean, but not this one," he said softly.

"Is it the ocean from home?"

Hawk had lived in the town next to the one I grew up in, but we hadn't met until we were both at the wall.

"Yes, and there are boats on it, people fishing."

My hands fisted as I tried to will something into view. No matter how much I tried, all I saw was fire and the sparks floating through the air. "Do I have to look somewhere special?"

"No," Kobal replied, his hand tightening on my shoulder when I swayed on my feet. "We should go."

"Wait." All I wanted was a glimpse of Bailey and Gage, just one *tiny* glimpse. "A few more minutes."

I sensed the other demons and skelleins closing in behind me. The hounds' claws clicked against the rocky ground as they patrolled the cavern. I didn't look at any of them.

"You must drink," Kobal said and handed me a canteen.

My fingers curled around it, and I lifted it to my mouth. Hot water trickled past my lips. I greedily gulped it down before reluctantly pulling it away. Kobal took it from me and handed it to Lix as I focused on the oracle again. Before me, the waves of fire parted like a curtain pulling back from a window.

My heart plummeted when I saw what the oracle revealed.

CHAPTER SEVEN

River

The Last Stop bar the skelleins built around the gateway into Hell had been on fire the last time I saw it. If there had been any remains of the bar, they'd been cleared away to reveal the charred earth the fire had ravaged. The skelleins who stayed above to help guard the gateway hadn't bothered to rebuild anything.

The scene slid further away to create a panoramic view of the area and the demons and humans camped there. Their numbers were far smaller than I recalled. It didn't take me long to discover why as the oracle revealed the mounds of overturned dirt marking the numerous graves at the edge of the woods.

At the edge of the clearing stood a young girl with her wheat blonde hair falling in ringlets around her shoulders. Her kelly green eyes surveyed the clearing with sadness. Unlike the ghosts everyone could see due to the opening of the gateway, I was the only one who had ever seen the child, Angela. I didn't know what she was, or why she appeared to me, but my instincts said she wasn't a bad thing.

Suddenly Angela's head lifted and her eyes latched onto mine. I didn't have a chance to blink before the scene shifted and I found myself standing before her. Angela's mouth curved into a smile as she gazed at me.

Angela's rosebud mouth opened, but if she spoke, I didn't hear her. She'd never spoken to me before. She'd tried to stop me from doing things with gestures, but never words. Lifting her hand, her fingers attempted to caress my arm. I felt nothing against my skin.

"Are you able to see what I see?" I asked Kobal.

"Not normally, but you might be able to pull me into your vision."

I grasped his hand on my shoulder and pulled it down to envelope it within both of mine. I focused on his large hand until the cavern and the scene in the oracle faded away. All I saw now was Angela, and all I felt was the formidable flow of Kobal's life washing over me.

A pathway opened between us and I pulled Kobal into my vision. The three of us stood together in a world of misty, gray fog. The oracle didn't fuel this anymore, I did.

"Can you see her?" I whispered.

Angela's eyes shifted to where Kobal stood. Her face hardened in a way I'd never seen a child's face harden before. Kobal snarled and stepped toward Angela.

"Kobal!" I tried to pull him back as defiance radiated from Angela, but he refused to budge.

Angela turned toward me. Her hand stretched out as desperation blazed from her eyes, and I sensed her need to communicate something to me. I stretched my hand toward her, but Kobal seized my wrist and jerked it down. He pushed me back and planted himself in front of me.

"No!" I cried when the fog faded away to reveal the rolling tide of the oracle once more. "Why did you do that?" I demanded, poking him in his shoulder blade. "She was trying to tell me something!"

Kobal's head swiveled toward me. His golden eyes blazed and the corded muscles in his biceps bulged as the veins in his arms stood out. I'd seen him enraged more than a few times, but this was something more than rage. If I hadn't known he would never hurt me, I would have bolted from him and straight out of this cavern. Instead, I held my ground while all the others backed steadily away.

"Is that who you've been seeing?" he demanded. "Is she why you took the angel figurine and refused to part with it? Is that the child, Angela?"

I released his hand. "Yes."

"*Fuck*!" The bellowed word bounced endlessly off the cavern walls.

"Kobal—" He lifted me and carried me away from the oracle. "What are you doing?" I demanded. "She's not bad!"

"She's not good," he growled.

"You can't know that!"

He set me on my feet so abruptly that I staggered back before catching my balance.

"*I* can know it." I opened my mouth to protest his words, but he continued speaking. "She is an angel, River, or at least the angels are using her to get to you."

"Holy shit!" Corson blurted and edged further away when Kobal glowered at him.

My mouth closed before falling open and closing again. Questions tumbled so rapidly through my mind that I couldn't grasp one to ask it. I opened my mouth again, but all that came out was, "Huh?"

"The dead child, Angela, is an angel or a tool the angels are using to manipulate you," Kobal said.

"She can't possibly be an angel!" I protested.

"You are correct, dear niece. She is not an angel," a voice purred from the shadows on the far side of the cavern. "However, my long lost, and not at all missed, brothers and sisters *are* trying to communicate with you. They just don't know how."

I didn't have time to process the words before Kobal pushed me behind him. The sound he emitted caused the hair on my body to rise, and I knew that whoever stood in those shadows would not make it out of here alive.

Kobal

I focused on the area where the voice had come from, but whoever stood there remained concealed by the darkness. Scenting the air, I detected a new aroma, but it was so faint that the hounds hadn't caught it. Whoever it was hadn't been there long and must have slipped in while I was immersed in River's vision.

I recognized the odor the intruder emitted as one of the fallen angels. It brought to mind water, but whereas River made me think of fresh rain, this was more like a lake with the minerally tang of brimstone mixed into it. Hell had corrupted the angel's natural scent.

I bared my fangs at a shifting in the shadows and gestured for the hounds to come forward.

"I have not come here to fight, Kobal," the voice murmured. "I would not have revealed my presence to you if I meant to attack. I would have simply struck while the two of you were focused on the oracle."

"Then why not show yourself?" I demanded.

A raven swept out of the darkness to land fifty feet away. Its talons ticked against the ground, rainbow colors reflected off its feathers when it folded its wings against its sides and settled away from the oracle. The bird stood nearly three feet tall and weighed at least a hundred pounds.

"I've shown myself," the raven murmured and River gasped. "As you can see, I could have remained hidden from you. Could have followed you wherever it was you are going and reported to Satan… I mean Lucifer. Even if you scented me, you would not have been looking for *me*."

"What the fuck is with the talking bird?" Hawk blurted.

"It's not a bird," Bale said and drew her sword from the holder on her back.

"I am not here to fight any of you," the raven stated.

River stepped out from behind me. I held my arm in front of her as my body tensed in preparation to attack. If that bird so much as ruffled a feather the wrong way, I'd pluck it bare before shoving its beak up its ass.

I searched the shadows for more enemies. Within me, Phenex and Crux stirred in preparation of a battle, but I kept them locked away when I sensed nothing else out there. That didn't mean the fallen angels couldn't be somewhere nearby, waiting for their chance to launch an attack against us. They could have sent the raven as a distraction.

Hatred coiled within me when my gaze returned to the raven. I despised the angels in Heaven as much as the ones in Hell. I didn't know what any of the angels sought from River, but I knew none of them would care if she lived or died if it got them what they wanted from her.

Every instinct in me screamed to go for the raven, to attack and kill, but I wouldn't leave River's side until I knew what was going on here. If I moved away from her, an angel might come from somewhere else and try to take her. When she was stronger, she could fight them off and cause a lot of damage, but she was too weak for that now.

"Lix, take the skelleins to the other end of the cavern. Get behind the raven and keep an eye out," I commanded.

"My brothers and sisters are not here, and they do not know I am," the raven said.

"That's either extremely good or bad for you. If you're setting us up, I will take the time to make your death especially excruciating," I vowed.

"I have no doubt," the raven replied.

River's brow furrowed as she stared at the bird. "Caim?" she inquired.

River identified more with her angelic side than her human or demon side. Because of that, she'd known the fallen angel Azote's name too when he attacked her, yet she hadn't recognized what Angela was. I suspected that was because Angela wasn't truly an angel, but something the angels were using to communicate with River.

The raven's head tilted to the side; its ebony eyes shimmered with colors while he studied her. "Yes," the raven replied.

"How did you find us?" I demanded.

"I've been flying over much of Hell in search of you. It occurred to me you would know the angels never come here and that this would be a good place for you to travel through. I have not come here on Lucifer's behalf, but because I have some things I must discuss with you."

CHAPTER EIGHT

Kobal

"Show your true self then," I commanded. "If what you say is true, then there will be no deceptions between us."

The raven chuckled and ruffled its feathers. Within those feathers, streaks of rainbow color came to life in the glow of the fire. "Yet you stand with the demon of illusions."

"There are no illusions here," Magnus said and spread his hands before him. "You would see them if there were."

With a ripple of movement and a shifting of the air, the raven vanished from view. In its place stood the fallen angel I knew as Caim. I hadn't known about his ability to shapeshift though. I didn't trust him, but I understood it had been a small olive branch on his part to reveal this to us.

Spreading his six-foot wings out at his sides, Caim displayed more of the differences between him and most of his fallen brethren. After shearing their wings off on Earth, most of the fallen angels had regrown bat-like wings with thick veins running through them. Caim's wings were covered in black feathers. Those feathers glistened with the same rainbow colors the raven possessed. A nearly foot-long silver spike came out of the tip of each wing, and another protruded from the bottom of them.

He settled his wings against his back, tucking them away until all that could be seen of them were the two silver spikes over his shoulders.

"Caim," River said again.

The angel's eyes shifted to her. Like the rest of the fallen angels, his eyes were now black instead of the violet of the angels, but different colors reflected in his eyes. "Yes, my niece," he murmured. "That is my name."

River's eyes narrowed. "Lucifer is not my father; you are *not* my uncle."

"Yet you recognized me in raven-form and you spoke my name before you were told it. I would wager you also knew Azote's name when you encountered him."

I recognized the stubborn gleam in River's eyes as she lifted her chin. "That doesn't make you my uncle, or Lucifer my father," she replied.

"My fellow brothers and sisters are trying to communicate with you from Heaven," Caim said instead of arguing with River over her lineage.

"Why?" I demanded. "What is Angela exactly?"

"Humans call them Guardian Angels; angels call them guides. Because of the laws laid down many years ago, angels will not travel to Earth anymore. Over the years, they have developed guides to get humans to do their bidding. Guides are rarely used as it requires a lot of power. However, because River cannot openly communicate with the angels like some of her ancestors could, they had to find another way to reach out to her. They are using this Angela's spirit, her soul, to connect with you," Caim explained.

"She's only a child," River whispered.

"She's dead; her age doesn't matter," Caim replied bluntly. "They most likely chose a child because she would be less intimidating to you."

"Why am I the only one who can see her?" River asked.

"Because you are the one they want to see her."

"What are they trying to guide River into doing?" I inquired.

"Alas, I do not know the answer to that," Caim replied. "But they are trying to show her something."

"And we're supposed to believe anything you say?" Hawk asked. "You're about as evil as it gets."

Caim folded his arms over his chest. "You are no longer human, yet your mind is still so small. Humans are the ones who deemed angels everything good. They held the angels in such high-regard while they made demons things of evil and disgust. Humans feared the demons because they looked different, yet they worshipped the angels for their perceived perfection in looks.

"When some of those angels fell, humans deemed the fallen more evil than demons. So much eviler that in a great deal of human lore, the humans imagined one of their disgraced angels as the ruler of Hell. They gave Lucifer horns, a tail, turned him red, called him Satan and other ridiculous names, but most of all they made him the ruler of all things evil and *baaad*." Caim waved his hands around his face as he drew out the word bad.

Dropping his hands back to his sides, he continued speaking. "Yet he is not the true ruler of Hell, something you now know. Humans esteemed to be like the angels who remain above, but you missed one vital thing about all three of our species."

"And what is that?" River inquired.

"We are *all* flawed. Perfection can never be attained. Yet you humans kill yourselves trying to become something you can never be; perfect. Angels were created by the being you hold above all else, but even that being is flawed. It has to be flawed; it was created with a world that has imperfections.

"Unlike the being, none of us were created in the very beginning, but we all came into existence in one way or another. Humans and demons evolved in unimaginably hostile conditions. The being forged the angels in the image of man. We are simply more powerful forms of *humans,* and humans are about as imperfect as it gets. It's pure stupidity to believe anything can be perfect, or that it can be entirely good or bad," Caim retorted.

"Pure stupidity does describe a human perfectly," Magnus said and ignored the irritated look River gave him.

Caim's wings fluttered forward. He settled his spikes onto the rocky ground. I stepped forward to launch at him as the hackles on the hellhounds rose and they emitted a low rumble.

Caim held his hands up in a pacifying gesture. "If I had come here to fight, we would be fighting, Kobal."

"Where are the other fallen angels?" I demanded.

"With Lucifer, fighting against your followers," Caim replied. "They believe me to be out doing reconnaissance."

The hounds spread further out around us, creeping forward with their heads low and their eyes locked on Caim. The skelleins watched us from the other side.

"What do you want to discuss?" I asked.

"I was thrown from Heaven with Lucifer. I sheared off my wings with him on Earth and I followed him into Hell, but I cannot follow him in what he is doing now. If Lucifer succeeds in ending the human race, or somehow regains entry into Heaven to continue his war there, it will be the destruction of *everything* and I have no wish to die. I have come here to offer my help to you."

CHAPTER NINE

River

Many things in my life had astounded me, but when Caim announced this, I was pretty sure someone could have pushed me over with a finger. His eyes held mine, the varied colors within them coalescing together. His jet-black hair stuck to his forehead from the sweat running down his flushed face. The black clothes that had transformed from raven to angel form with him stuck to his skin. I realized that, like me, the heat of the oracle affected him more than the demons. That was the reason the angels hadn't been seen near it before.

"Interesting," Magnus murmured.

"Or a lie," Kobal replied and stepped toward Caim.

I grasped his arm, halting him before he could go any closer. The hounds released another low rumble and bared their fangs. "Wait," I said.

"We can't trust him," Corson said.

"The angels are nothing more than flying rats!" Lix declared from across the way.

"*I* am part flying rat," I reminded Lix.

Lix ducked his head and hunched his shoulders. "We like you," he muttered before pulling the top off his flask and taking a swig.

I turned my attention back to Caim, whose gaze remained on me. "How did Lucifer open the gate from Earth into Hell?"

"I don't know," he replied.

"Lie," Bale hissed.

Caim didn't look at Bale as he replied. "It's not a lie. My brother is the only one who knows what he did to open the gateway. He would never tell us. There is power in the mystery, and Lucifer won't give up an ounce of power."

"Can I close it?" I asked.

"I don't know. I do know my brother wants you for himself, badly. It leads me to believe you are capable of many things."

"Why are you willing to help us? Aren't all the fallen angels not evil, but ah… looking to rule or enslave humans and demons?"

Caim lifted his wings from the ground and closed them behind him once more. "Not all of us, or at least not *me*. What Lucifer plans is madness. He refuses to see that he could destroy everything if he continues on this path."

"So this is a save-your-own-ass type of situation?" Hawk asked.

Caim snorted. "Is there any other kind?"

"Yes, there is," I said. "There is protecting the ones you love and there is a greater good."

"I have never been like the rest of my fallen brethren, but that is a woe-filled tale best kept for another day," Caim said. "However, your tender heart will not survive my brother. Perhaps you should let some of your humanity go and face the truth; you must be vicious to live through this."

"I faced that truth a long time ago," I retorted. "But I will not give up what makes me *me*. I will defend and protect my loved ones no matter what it takes. I will *not* become like you."

"The sad thing is, you remind me of myself before the fall. So idealistic, so certain you can make it all better, so determined to do so, but nothing can ever be *all* better again. The fall taught me that."

"Is the fall what severed the angels' bond to life?" I asked, desperate to know the answer and to keep it from happening to me.

"Ah, child, that was a mixture of steps taken that never should have been taken. Once taken they could never be reversed," Caim replied with a flick of his fingers.

"What steps?" I demanded.

The casual way Caim assessed me reminded me of a bird. I had no idea how he had shifted into a raven, but it was clear the bird was a part of him, even in his angel-form. "You fear it happening to you," he murmured.

Kobal took another step toward him. My hand tightened on his arm. There was no way I was going to keep him held back if he decided to go for Caim, but I had so many questions, and I *needed* answers. I doubted all of what Caim revealed would be the truth, but if even a fraction of it was, then I had to hear it.

"Kobal, don't," I pleaded.

Flames flickered to life around his fingers and rose to his wrists as he froze before me. The hounds stayed low to the ground as they crept closer to Caim. I took an unsteady step forward, not realizing how weak I was until my legs nearly gave out. I locked my knees into place and defiantly held Caim's gaze.

"I think it could happen to me," I admitted to Caim.

"You do not wish to be like your father Lucifer."

"He's not my father," I grated. "I've had the misfortune of meeting my father in this place, and he's dead now."

"A soul cannot be destroyed," Caim stated.

"His was," Kobal replied, and out of the corner of my eye, I noticed Bale edging closer to the ocean of fire and trying to come up along the side of Caim.

Caim glanced nonchalantly at Bale before focusing on Kobal again. "That's a first. My brother must be pissed you took his toy away."

"My father's soul wasn't a toy!" I retorted.

Caim shifted so that he stood half in and half out of the shadows. "Your father is Lucifer, my brother. His blood runs strong in you. It has forged you and your line. It will forge your children's line too. If you live to have children."

The sound Kobal made caused Caim to slip further into the dark and the skelleins to raise their swords. "Wait!" I gasped, knowing Caim was preparing to leave. "I deserve answers!"

Caim's face reemerged. I blinked as the shadows surrounding him created the effect of a disembodied head. Then, he rippled his wings, and I realized it wasn't the shadows creating the effect. His body had transformed into a raven, while his head remained a man's.

"The fall started the break in the connection," Caim said. "The shearing of our wings made it so only the slightest of threads remained between us and life. I can still recall my desperation to hold onto that thread with everything in me."

A look of yearning spread across his face, and his head bowed for a minute. "Some of my fellow fallen made choices that severed the last of their thread while we were still on Earth. Others lost it when we followed Lucifer from the human realm into this one."

He lifted his head and those multi-hued ebony eyes met mine. "I felt the snapping of the connection when the gate closed behind us. It was a loss so profound that only madness could follow, and follow it did, for all of us."

"And are you no longer mad?" I asked.

"Sometimes even the lost soul of a monster can rise from the madness to see the truth."

"What is the truth?" Kobal inquired.

"That to continue this path and do nothing to stop it would make me something far worse than a monster. If Lucifer succeeds, he will annihilate all the realms and all those who reside in them. I may be one of the fallen, but I will not be a part of that. I love my brothers and sisters, but I cannot allow them to continue this destruction."

Everything in me screamed that none of the fallen angels could be trusted, that he was most likely here for Lucifer and to manipulate us, but the desperation in Caim's gaze pulled at me. I found myself believing him.

"So you want to know if the severing of the bond can happen to you. It can," Caim continued. "One wrong step can weaken it, and with each weakening, it becomes easier and easier to take those wrong steps until one day it's gone, and all you're left with is…"

"Emptiness," I said at the same time he did.

A small smile curved the edges of Caim's full mouth. He didn't possess the ethereal beauty of Lucifer, but his near perfect features and raven wings were striking.

"Why are your wings different than the others?" I asked.

"I sliced the wings from my body to try to survive on the human realm. However, I could never sever my bond to the raven within me. All angels were created with small differences to give us something unique when not much is unique in Heaven. I am one of the few who possessed a significant difference from my siblings. That difference is my ability to embrace the raven's spirit and form. It's a bond that survived all the things I've done. The raven has made it so I can see past the insanity the loss of my connection to life created. Perhaps it is that bond which also allows me to retain a piece of the benevolence that once ruled me. There are always endless questions, but there are never answers for all of them."

My fingers dug into Kobal's skin as Caim slid further into the shadows again. "If I choose to join Kobal, if I died and became a demon, would it sever my bond to life?" I blurted before he could leave.

This time Caim didn't remerge from the dark as he uttered his reply. "Yes."

My heart sank. I wanted to scream denials at him, but I knew he was right. Kobal had known it for a while now. A crushing sensation squeezed my heart as my last bit of hope for an eternity with Kobal burst like a bubble.

"You cannot embrace your demon side without experiencing the madness," Caim continued. I heard a flutter of wings, and then a shadow rose to swoop across the ceiling of the cavern. "Know that you have someone working with you from the inside now."

The raven dipped to the side before vanishing out of the cavern over the heads of the skelleins. Stunned silence followed his disappearance.

"He could be lying about the experiencing madness thing," Corson finally said, and I knew he was only trying to give Kobal and me some hope.

"He's not." I tore my attention away from where Caim had been and to Kobal. His eyes eased from their amber color to their pure, obsidian depths. "He may be lying about turning against Lucifer, and he probably is, but he's not lying about the severing of the bond." I placed my hand against my chest, over my heart. "I *feel* the truth of his words."

Kobal wrapped his hand around my neck and pulled me against his chest. Tears burned my eyes, but I refused to shed them. I clung to him, my fingers digging into the solid flesh of his back.

He bent his head and rested his lips against my ear. "We have to get out of here. He could be bringing Lucifer back."

I reluctantly released him and leaned against his side as he led me away from the oracle.

CHAPTER TEN

River

"If the angels are trying to communicate with me, it explains what happened when we were in Magnus's cavern," I said sometime later when I felt strong enough to talk now that we were away from the oracle.

Kobal's body stiffened against mine as he led me around a turn in the rock tunnel. I still had no recollection of the strange dream, or whatever it was that had caused me to leap to my feet and say "*The angels*," before collapsing.

"Why do you say that?" he asked.

"I've kept my ability to share another's dreams shut down since I shared that one with Lucifer." I didn't even dare to use it to reach out to my brothers for fear I would somehow draw Lucifer in too. "The angels may have been trying to get me to open it again, or maybe they were trying to communicate with me in a different way that caused my reaction."

"Maybe."

"How did you know Angela had something to do with the angels when you saw her?" I asked.

"Because of her scent. The angels in here, and you, have the scent of rain or water about them. Your scent is crisp whereas the fallen angels' has been tainted, but I detected water on her. Whatever abilities they use for the guides, they can't disguise their scent."

"I see." I tilted my head back to look at him. "You don't want me communicating with them?"

"I don't trust any angel, fallen or not."

I didn't bother to remind him I was part angel and identified more with my angel side. We were both aware of that; it was what would keep me mortal after all.

"They could be trying to help," I said.

"They could," Hawk agreed from behind us.

"Or they could be looking to eliminate Lucifer's line, permanently," Magnus said. I frowned as I glanced at him over my shoulder. He stared pointedly back at me. "Even after what Caim said, are you still trying to convince yourself the angels above are all that is good and right in the world?"

"No," I said. "I know they're not, but we already have enough enemies; we could use some allies, and there is a chance they could be trying to help us."

"I don't think the angels want to kill River," Hawk said.

"Still relying on that misplaced human faith in the angels?" Magnus inquired.

"Still resorting to that douchey demon attitude?" Hawk retorted. "And no, I'm not. I simply don't think they want to kill her."

"Why not?" Corson asked.

"Because if they felt it would solve everything, they would have attempted to kill her by now, but they haven't."

"And they have tried to protect me," I said. "Angela tried to stop me from going into the canagh nest before Vargas and I entered it."

"See," Hawk said and gave Magnus a gloating look. "The angels would have let her stroll on in there without any warning if they wanted her dead."

"There's no way to know what the angels are trying to do. I still don't trust them," Magnus said. "We should have killed Caim."

"We weren't going to reach him before he flew away," Bale argued.

"The fallen have always underestimated the intelligence of the demons and believed themselves above us. Let them think we believe Caim will help us," Kobal said.

"You think he was lying about helping us?" I asked.

"Don't you?"

"Maybe, about some things. In others, I think he told the truth, or at least parts of it. He knows we don't trust him. If he's playing us, he'll report that distrust to Lucifer. If he's not toying with us, I think we'll find out what was true and what wasn't soon enough."

"That we will," Kobal replied and pulled me to a stop before a large slab of gray rock.

His arm slid away from me when he stepped forward and bent down. Something made a clicking sound as he felt over the bottom of the rock before rising to run his hands over the top of it.

Another click filled the cavern before Kobal placed his hand in the center of the slab. The slanted Z symbol I recognized as Eiaz materialized beneath his palm on the rock. During one of the times I'd explored the numerous symbols on Kobal's body, I remembered coming across Eiaz. He'd explained the symbol represented speed, heightened senses, and protection.

Bending again, the corded muscles across Kobal's back bulged as he gripped the bottom of the easily five-hundred-pound rock and lifted it out of the way. My fingers itched to trace every inch of his chiseled body while I watched him work.

I bit my bottom lip and glanced away when he set the rock aside. Turning back, he held his hand out to me. A small smile played at the corners of his mouth as his skin slid into contact with mine. With his heightened sense of smell, I knew he'd sensed the direction my mind had taken.

I scowled at him, which only caused his smile to grow while he led me past the rock. My eyes widened on the austere space we entered. “What is this?” I asked.

“My chambers,” Kobal said. Releasing me, he waited for everyone else, and the hounds, to enter the cavern before lifting the slab and settling it back into place.

I’d suspected that we’d finally arrived at our destination when he’d used his marks to unlock the rock, but I hadn’t expected his chambers to be like *this*.

When we’d been living by the wall on Earth, Kobal’s main tent had been simply decorated with its table, sideboard, lanterns, goblets, and drinks. Books had often been on the table, waiting for him or me to pick up. His separate room had held a large bed, nightstand, mirror, armoire, and other assorted things he’d taken from houses in the nearby town. The possessions hadn’t originally been his, but he’d picked them out and made them his.

There was nothing but rocks here and a fire pit against the far wall. Even with the glow of the flames bouncing off the walls, this place was stark and lonely.

Magnus had decorated his private space in Hell. Corson was different here than he’d been on Earth, but I believed there would still be signs of his personality in his chambers, and that Bale would have something of her own if we ever saw where she lived here.

It was clear how much their time on Earth had changed Corson and the skelleins. Not so clear with Bale, but I had a feeling, if I had known her when she’d lived only in Hell, I would see changes in her now too. I doubted any of the demons saw how different they were on Earth compared to Hell. If they did, they would never admit it.

Kobal had decided that when this was done with Lucifer, he would stay on Earth with me, but I wondered if he realized how much my world had become a part of him too. Living on our plane had changed him more than I’d realized before we ever even met. The Kobal I first encountered had possessed the warmth of an ice cube; the demon who had lived here was the entire iceberg.

"How spartan," Hawk murmured as his gaze ran over the gray rock walls and empty floor.

"No one will be able to get passed Eiaz to enter here," Kobal said.

His footsteps rang off the black stone floor as he strode across the room. He walked behind a section of wall that blended in so seamlessly with the rocks, I hadn't realized something lay beyond. Kobal reemerged with black and red furs tossed over his arm.

"There is water behind there for all of you to clean up with. River and I will be going into my sleeping chambers. You are to remain here. We will rest before leaving to join Morax and the others," Kobal stated.

He handed the furs to Corson and turned to me. I didn't have a chance to blink before he lifted me and carried me across the echoing chamber. Rounding the corner of a different set of rocks, he strode down a small hall. When none of the light from the main area pierced this hallway, I strained to see through the darkness while Kobal continued unerringly forward.

My fingers dug into his shoulders as I thought of him sleeping in this place every night. I settled my head on his shoulder, holding him closer as I inwardly wept for the lonely demon who had resided here. The only one of his kind, the one with the weight of Hell, war, and the lives of his followers on his shoulders. He was still the only one of his kind, still had the weight of war on his shoulders, but now he knew he was not alone.

He had not known that here.

He stopped before another rock and set me on my feet before it. Placing his hands on either side of my head, he kept me pinned before him. My breath came faster as his chest brushed against mine while he worked to move the rock aside. My toes curled, and my gaze drifted over his broad chest as he pushed the rock out of the way.

I didn't turn to look at the room beyond as he lifted me and carried me across the threshold. Lowering me again, he turned to close the rock behind us. I gazed at the small room and the pile of furs tossed into the corner. Nearby was a small pool of water with a lava rock set out beside it. The fire in a pit cast shadows over the walls, but unlike the fire in the main room, I couldn't see the flames within this pit.

"How long did you live here?" I asked.

"From my birth until I went to Earth," he replied.

For over fifteen hundred years he'd slept here, yet there was *nothing* here. "Where are all of your things?"

"There's a small room over there with some of my clothes in it." He waved at an area across the way, and I saw that, like the larger chamber, the rocks hid what lay beyond.

"What about personal items? Magnus had goblets and furs and a whole carnival to keep him entertained."

"I have nothing else here."

I swallowed the lump in my throat. "Why not?"

Cupping my face in his hand, he drew my eyes to him. "Because I sought nothing but my throne while I was here. These rooms were never my home. My home was where my throne is."

"And now?"

"Now my home is with you," he said simply, yet the words robbed me of my breath. "Come."

He clasped my hand and led me across the chamber to the pool of water that was about three feet deep and five feet wide. My skin prickled with excitement over being able to scrub the sweat, stench, and dirt off me.

I untied my boots and yanked them off while Kobal worked to remove his. I went to tug the dress off before recalling the intricate buttons going up the back of it. Mewling in frustration, I nearly burned the material off me.

"Easy," Kobal murmured as he stepped behind me.

Gathering my hair, he draped it over my shoulder before bending to kiss my nape. His warm breath on my flesh caused my pulse to skyrocket as his fingers worked to slide the buttons free. I was caught between throwing myself into his arms or leaping into the water and scrubbing myself for the next hour.

He ran a single knuckle up my spine in a massaging manner before replacing the knuckle with his thumbs. I moaned as his hands rubbed my cramped muscles. His fingers brushed the undersides of my breasts before he slid them away to push the sleeves of the dress down my shoulders.

My nipples tightened in anticipation of his touch as the dress dipped down and air rushed over my flushed skin. My breasts ached to feel his hands kneading them until I could barely stand.

“Exquisite,” he murmured in my ear.

He stepped so close that the heat of his chest branded my back. Bending over me, his body nearly enveloped mine as his mouth pressed against the marks he’d left on my shoulder. His hands pushed the dress down until the sleeves fell completely away and the top of it hung about my hips.

My body jerked and my head fell back to his shoulder when his hands settled on my stomach. They slid down, pushing the dress lower and forming a V beneath my belly button. I waited for him to slip his hands under the dress and between my thighs. Instead, his hands moved leisurely up my stomach. They brushed my breasts in a teasing manner that had my body begging for more. I couldn’t stop myself from arching toward his hands.

He chuckled before nipping at my ear. “Did you miss me inside you?”

“Yes,” I breathed.

His hands fell away, and with a tug, he pulled the dress over my hips and down my legs.

“You are mine,” he stated, and I could feel the ardor of his gaze on my back.

“And you are mine,” I reminded him as I turned my head to look at him over my shoulder.

“I’ve only ever been yours, Mah Kush-la,” he said and pulled off his pants.

The thick length of his swollen shaft stood proudly out from his body when he tossed his pants aside. The bead of precum already forming on the head of it caused me to lick my lips. I clearly recalled the taste of him, of fire and male, on my tongue.

When he stepped against me again, the heavy weight of his erection against my back caused liquid warmth to pool between my legs. My head tipped back as he lowered his mouth to kiss my forehead, nose, and briefly my lips.

His arms swept around my waist, and he carried me to the pool where he descended into the red water. A blissful sigh escaped me when the warmth of the water encompassed my cramped muscles.

CHAPTER ELEVEN

River

Kobal set me down before turning to grab the lava rock sitting at the side of the pool. "When was the last time you were in these chambers?" I asked.

"Before the humans tore open the gateway."

Ever so carefully, Kobal ran the lava rock over my back. I would have scrubbed a layer of skin off in my impatience to get clean, but he wouldn't leave a mark on my flesh. He set the rock down and dipped his cupped hands into the water. Lifting them, he poured water over my hair and down my back. I closed my eyes as it ran over me in red rivulets while his fingers tenderly massaged my scalp and washed my hair.

When he was done, he reclaimed the lava rock and brought it back to my skin. I gasped when his hand dipped below the water and cupped my ass while his other hand worked to wash my thighs. The hand on my ass squeezed my flesh before sliding between my thighs. I pushed back against him, seeking more of his touch.

Slowly, he slid his fingers back and forth across my aching center, spreading the wetness he had created. He kissed my shoulder as he dipped the tip of one finger inside me before pulling it out to run it over my clit in small circles. I pushed more demandingly against his hand as coiling tension began to build within me. He had only to touch me and my body became his to do whatever he asked of it.

"Always so wet for me," he murmured.

His fangs grazed my shoulder. Reaching behind me, I wrapped my hand around the rigid length of him. I gave one long stroke before running my thumb over his head and the thick vein running up the side of his shaft. His obvious desire for me fueled my arousal to higher heights.

"Always so hard for me," I replied.

His hips thrust into my palm before he grasped my hand and drew it away. I mewled my discontent when he brought my hand to my stomach. "Not yet," he said.

Keeping my hand in his, he slid it over my breasts. My heart hammered in my chest when he used my thumb and forefinger to pinch my nipple before rolling it over. I couldn't see his eyes, but I felt his rapt gaze on our hands as his breath came faster against my shoulder. He released my hand, and when I went to let it drop again, he reclaimed it and placed it against my breast.

"Keep touching yourself," he commanded gruffly. "I want to watch you."

This time, when he released my hand, I kept it on my breast. Helpless to resist anything he asked of me, I melted against his chest as I ran my thumb over my nipple. I delighted in the sound of pleasure he released when I pinched my nipple before shifting my hand to my other breast.

He cupped his hand and dipped it into the water before lifting it to my neck. My eyes became heavy-lidded when he let the water trickle down my back. With his lips and tongue, he followed the water to the small of my back, leaving a trail of heat over my flesh.

Rising again, the supple skin and chiseled muscle of his chest slid over my back. His breath warmed my shoulder as he stood over me to watch me caressing myself once more. He wrapped his arm around my waist to pull me flat against him. My back bowed when his palms ran down my belly again and he slid a hand between my legs.

I groaned when he slid only the tip of his finger into me again. Lifting my free arm, I draped it around his neck when he ran his fangs over my shoulder while he continued teasing me.

"Mark me," I whispered, needing his bite almost as badly as him.

He thrust his finger into me at the same time his fangs clamped onto my shoulder. Stretching me further, he slipped another finger into me. A familiar tightening started between my thighs and spread into my belly.

Kobal

The muscles of River's sheath clenched my fingers when she came in a heated rush. Her hand grasped her breast harder as she moaned, and her head fell against my shoulder. Her irresistible, fresh rain scent intensified as her hips continued to follow the demanding rhythm of my fingers within her.

I bit deeper and her fingers dug into my nape as she came again. Legs weak, she slumped against me. I kept my arm locked around her waist while I carried her from the water. My fingers eased their stroking, but I kept them deep within her until my cock could replace them.

Her enticing pants as she tried to catch her breath had my dick demanding release. I lowered her onto the furs and reluctantly removed my fingers from her. The whimper of disappointment she uttered almost caused me to grip her hips and drive myself into her from behind.

I restrained myself as I placed my hand on her back and lowered her to the furs. This time, I would see her face when I made her body come apart. With gentle guidance, I rolled her over until she lay sprawled before me. Her wet hair created a cloud of black silk around her shoulders and flushed face. Her violet eyes shone in the light of the fire at the back of the room.

I ran my knuckles over her cheeks, memorizing every detail of her, *my* Chosen. I wanted to possess her in every possible way, but I wanted to savor her more. If she touched me though, if she stroked me and guided me into her, I would lose control. Reaching over her head, I grabbed another fur and pulled it toward me. I ripped it into pieces before focusing on River again.

"Do you trust me?" I inquired.

The haze of passion slid away from her eyes as she frowned at me. "With everything I am."

I took one of her wrists and slid a piece of fur around it. She continued to frown at me as I took the other end of the fur and bound her free wrist. When I leaned over her again, I slid the looped piece of fur around a rock. She stiffened but didn't fight the bond.

"I'll release you if you ask me to," I promised. "And you can burn the ties away at any time."

She didn't protest or try to break free as a small smile curved her enticing lips. Unable to resist, I bent my head to hers in a claiming kiss. Her mouth parted, her tongue eagerly entwining with mine. The head of my dick pushed against her inviting entrance, but I pulled back before I could enter her. I was determined to relish her for as long as possible.

Breaking the kiss, I dropped my head to the hollow of her throat and ran my tongue over her damp skin, savoring the taste of her salty flesh as I moved lower over her body. I lowered my head to one of her breasts and drew her nipple into my mouth, sucking on it until it stood proudly into the air. Releasing it, I turned my attention to her other breast. When her nipple rose against my tongue, I sank my fangs into her breast, marking her further as mine.

"Kobal!" she cried.

Her body arched off the ground, and her head twisted to the side as she pulled on her bonds. She mewled in frustration, but she didn't fight against her restraints and she didn't burn them away. As the scent of her arousal filled my nose, every instinct I had told me to satisfy her. She was my Chosen, she needed release from *me*, yet I still managed to restrain myself from burying my cock into her inviting body and satisfying us both.

If her hands had been free, if she'd been able to touch me, I never could have held back. Releasing my bite on her breast, I moved lower to run my tongue across her ribcage and flat stomach before tasting her belly button. Her legs fell further open as I maneuvered myself between her thighs.

Sliding my hands under her ass, I lifted her hips to expose her sex to my mouth. The tantalizing sight of her wet curls caused my dick to jump in anticipation as I blew on her clit. River's head thrashed and her ass tightened in my hands. When I blew on her again, her eyes slid closed and her head fell back.

My gaze latched onto her tantalizing nipples and the clear evidence of my bite on her golden skin as I bent my head to taste her. A bead of semen formed on the head of my cock while I delved my tongue into her hot recesses. The feel of the semen on my skin and the fullness of it building within me were things I'd never experienced before claiming River. Now, I couldn't remember a time before her and the sensation of the growing pressure within me. I didn't want to remember it either.

Her hands grasped the furs, and her body moved greedily against my tongue until she was riding it like she did my dick. Throwing her head back, she cried out, and I lapped up her sweet release. Lowering her to the ground, I leveled myself over her. Her muscles were still contracting from her orgasm when I thrust into her.

My body demanded its own release, but I remained unmoving within her, feeling the lingering contractions of her sheath gripping me. She searched my face as I memorized every one of the different flecks of purple within her amazing eyes. The love shining in her gaze was something I'd never considered having in my life before her. Now that I had it, I would never let it go.

Leaning over her, I gripped the furs above her wrists and burned them away. Her arms fell to the ground before her hands lifted to cup my cheeks with her palms. "My heart," she whispered.

"My everything," I told her as I slid out of her before surging forward once more.

She wrapped her arms around my neck; her mouth turned into my shoulder, and she bit down hard enough to break my skin. I growled as she marked me. Her legs encircled my waist, and sparks of life flickered across her fingers as she lost complete control.

From past experience, I knew she could use her ability to harness life to fling me across the room. Now it warmed my skin as power flowed between us and she met my increasing demands of her body.

When she released her bite, my hand entangled in her hair and I pulled her head back to expose her throat to me. I sank my fangs into her, marking her again. Her nails raking my back as her muscles clenched around my shaft nearly caused me to spill my semen within her.

I pulled out of her just as I began to come. The hot rush of my release lashed across her belly and chest as I kept my cock trapped against her stomach. I wanted River to bear my children, but that couldn't happen until Lucifer was dead. I'd spilled myself in her twice now; during our first time, and when I'd been out of my mind with lust in the Forest of Prurience. There was a possibility she carried my child now, but if she didn't, I couldn't increase the chances of her becoming pregnant.

I inhaled a ragged breath as I kept myself from collapsing onto her. Kissing her neck, I reluctantly rolled to the side and embraced her in my arms. With ease, I rose and returned to the pool. She cuddled against me, smiling while she nuzzled my chin with her lips. I carried her into the water and settled her on my lap.

"We're going to survive this. No matter what happens, we're going to get through it," she said.

"We are," I said as I ran my hands over her silken flesh and lifted the lava bar to cleanse her.

When I was done, I carried her from the pool once more. Her exhaustion beat against me as I returned to the fire. She was asleep before I settled her onto the furs again. Lying beside her, I gathered her close to me, but I couldn't sleep. My mind spun with everything Caim had revealed.

The angels were trying to communicate with River, trying to guide her, but what were they trying to guide her into doing? To them, she was only a pawn, a means to the end of the mistake they'd made when they cast Lucifer from Heaven to live on Earth.

When Lucifer figured out a way to enter Hell, he'd become the demons' problem, and now he was once again the humans' problem, even if he wasn't on Earth yet. River might be able to stop him from taking over Earth, or she may be the key to him somehow returning to Heaven and the angels would do whatever was necessary to ensure Lucifer never saw Heaven again.

Before I'd met her, the progeny had only been a pawn to me too, a thing that could possibly be used to close the gateway or to help defeat Lucifer. When River had been brought to the wall, *everything* about the progeny had come to matter to me.

I know what I'd been willing to do with the progeny before meeting her, so I also knew what the angels would be willing to do with her. Her survival would not matter to them if she did what they needed her to do.

Running my fingers through her hair, I breathed in her angelic scent as I cradled her against my chest when she murmured something in her sleep. No matter what it took, I would destroy Lucifer and every angel in existence to keep her safe.

CHAPTER TWELVE

River

"There are so many of them," I murmured as I gazed at the sea of demons gathered below us. The chamber Kobal's followers stood in was the size of an auditorium, but there were so many that they spilled out the archways branching off from this central room.

There had to be at least a thousand of them within the chamber. I had no idea how many stood beyond it, but laughter, cheers, and moans of ecstasy drifted throughout and continued down those side tunnels. A girlish giggle trailed behind a tree nymph as she weaved her way through the crowd. An easily eight-foot demon with yellow skin and hair the color of a clear, summer sky followed her.

Beside me, Lix puffed out his chest before taking a swig of mjéod from his flask. "Ah, tree nymphs," he sighed as he recapped it.

The remaining skelleins chattered as they raised their flasks and clicked them together in the center of the group.

"There will be time for nymphs later," Kobal said. "We have business to attend to first."

Lix's skeletal face fell before he took another drink. "Of course."

I returned my attention to the demons below. They all looked so different from one another, yet there were similarities between some of them. Those similarities marked them as either the same kind of demon, or they were at least part of the same type of demon. Some of them could be siblings.

All the demons bore some resemblance to humans, even the red and green ones with horns and tails, or the blue one in the corner, and the woman who had four arms. Some were short, others were so tall they had to stoop to avoid hitting the ten-foot-high arches of the side tunnels.

I'd seen my fair share of demons at the wall and while camped by the gateway, but nothing had prepared me for the variety of the ones here, or the number of them. On the far side of the room, I spotted Morax and Verin speaking with a group of demons. Verin stood with her hand on Morax's chest and her ear resting over his heart. Morax leaned casually against the wall while he ran a strand of her hair through his fingers.

"These are your followers," I murmured.

"They are yours too," Kobal said and took my hand in his.

On the walk here, I hadn't stopped to think about what would happen when we met up with Kobal's followers. I hadn't allowed myself to consider what they would think of me.

The demons I'd encountered so far had been accepting of me. Bale and Corson were my friends; Lix was my drunken philosopher who made me think about who and what I was. I liked Magnus far more than when I'd first met him. Morax and Verin had never been unkind to me. Hawk had resolutely remained my friend throughout all the crazy twists and turns thrown at us these past months.

I had no idea what to expect from the demons below, no idea what they would think of me and my relation to Lucifer. These demons had remained in Hell to fight the battle here. They hadn't dealt with people, and they more than likely hated humans for opening a gateway into their world. Mankind had thrown their world into a tailspin as much as Lucifer, and I was a reminder of humans *and* Lucifer.

Kobal's Chosen or not, their queen or not, they may hate me for it.

"It will be fine, Mah Kush-la," Kobal said.

My eyes darted to him, and I realized I'd been squeezing his hand. I forced myself to relax my grip on him. "Are some of the ones below still a part of your illusion, Magnus?" I asked. Before we'd left Magnus's corner of Hell to journey to the seals, he'd created the illusion of numerous demon fighters to face Lucifer.

Magnus's silver eyes were unwavering on mine. "No, they are all your followers, mah rejant."

It was the first time he'd ever called me that, and it only served to reinforce what I already knew; this was a monumental thing. I would never again get a chance to make a good first impression. I took a deep breath and blew it out as I struggled not to fidget with my dress.

"It will be fine," Kobal said again, and over his shoulder Corson and Bale nodded briskly.

"Yes, fine, just fine," I murmured. Facing a cavern full of demons who might hate me made me want to vomit, but I would do it.

Kobal had told me that going through his chamber was the only way to reach this place by using the convoluted route we'd traveled to get here. Unless someone knew where Kobal's residence was, could somehow get inside it, maneuver the twists and turns, no one else could come the way we had, so no one was keeping an eye on where we entered the cavern. Because of that, the demons didn't know we were here yet.

As if reading my thoughts, Morax tipped his head back. The glow of the small fire pits within the cave played over him. The different hues of green in his skin gave it a scaly, almost reptilian appearance, but from prior experience of touching him during my training, I knew his skin was as smooth as silk.

Two, six-inch-long black horns curved out from the top of his bald head. They bent toward each other until they nearly touched in the middle. At six foot two, his tail was the same length as his height and a foot thick in diameter. It thumped against the ground when his orange snake eyes latched onto me and Kobal. Both sets of his eyelids blinked at the same time.

His smile revealed all his razor-sharp teeth as he rested his hand on Verin's shoulder and pointed to us. Verin lifted her head from his chest and broke into a grin that lit her face. Her eyes were the same sun color as her hair, and she had a body that could make men and women fall at her feet. As Morax's Chosen though, any would-be pursuers steered clear of her. Both Morax and Verin could stop someone in their tracks; Morax for his intimidating appearance, and Verin for her striking beauty.

Noticing that Morax and Verin had been distracted by something, the demons gathered closest to them turned to look at us too. In the space between one heartbeat and the next, those demons went down on one knee. They draped an arm over their knees as they bowed their heads.

My breath caught in my throat when Morax and Verin joined them. I resisted the urge to hide behind Kobal as more demons noticed the ones kneeling, and the direction they were facing, before they looked toward me and Kobal. Once they saw us, they also knelt.

I'd spent my entire life trying to blend in, to go unnoticed in order to keep my strange abilities hidden. Now, I was on full display, the center of attention, and many of those below probably knew at least some of what I could do. I still wore the ruined dress, yet I felt exposed in a way I'd never been before.

I *hated* it, but awe filled me as the demons went down like dominoes around the cavern. This deference was for Kobal. He was their king, the one who had guided them this far. I couldn't deny my apprehension, but I also couldn't contain my immense pride in the man standing beside me.

The din of conversation and laughter within the cavern died away as more and more demons turned and knelt. It spread outward to the tunnels until the hedonistic moans stopped. I was certain the staccato beat of my heart could be heard over the hush that fell over the cavern.

"Come," Kobal said.

He kept my hand in his, choosing to ignore my increasingly sweaty palm as he led me down the rocky path to the chamber below. I didn't look back at the others, or the hounds, I knew they followed us as the clicking of the hounds' claws sounded against the rocks.

I'd been so concerned with Lucifer throughout all of this that I hadn't stopped to think much about this "queen of Hell" thing. The vast depth of the responsibility slapped me in the face.

Deep breaths.

I inhaled raggedly and threw back my shoulders when we arrived at the bottom of the pathway. I could be a heart-attack-waiting-to-happen mess on the inside, but on the outside I had to act as if I belonged here.

The demons edged back to create a pathway for us as Kobal strode through the crowd with his shoulders back and his eyes focused on Verin and Morax. No one could deny he was the rightful king of Hell. I found his confidence contagious and didn't have to fake it quite as much when I tore my attention from him and back to those gathered around us.

Kobal stopped before Morax and Verin. "Rise," he commanded.

They both rose in one fluid motion. Kobal released my hand to clasp Morax's before taking hold of Verin's and squeezing it within both of his. He let her go and reclaimed my hand. "We have a lot to discuss," Kobal said.

"We do," Morax agreed. "The seals?"

"We have stopped them from falling."

I knew Morax possessed the ability to telecommunicate and had been keeping in touch with Kobal, but apparently it had been brief conversations as Morax breathed a sigh of relief at this news. "Good."

Kobal guided me around to face the rest of the demons. Bale, Corson, and the others had knelt behind us. The hounds sat near the foot of the path with the skelleins kneeling before them.

"You may all rise," Kobal commanded and the demons rose in one united movement.

"Mah rhála," the word whispered through the crowd as they lifted their heads to look at Kobal. Then, their eyes shifted to me. They examined my face, my eyes, and finally Kobal's bites, clearly marking me as his Chosen.

"Mah rejant," they murmured and the greeting spread through the cavern.

I gave a brief bow of my head in greeting while wishing I'd learned some more demon words before coming here.

"It is good to see so many of you again," Kobal pitched his voice to carry throughout the cavern. "And it is time you met your queen, my Chosen, River Dawson."

An excited murmur raced through the crowd. I resisted pulling at the collar of my dress as I met their curious gazes.

"You will protect her life above my own," Kobal continued. I glanced at him, not exactly thrilled by that statement, but Kobal remained focused on the crowd. "We are the closest we have ever been to defeating Lucifer. Our time has come," Kobal continued. "He will be stopped, and we will reclaim Hell."

The crowd shifted, many of them stomped their feet, and a strange, almost guttural cheer went through them. It took me a minute to realize they weren't cheering but saying, *Helka,* over and over again. Simultaneously, each of them lifted a fist into the air and released a shout before their hands fell back to their sides and they became silent once more.

I glanced at Hawk. He looked like someone had tossed him into the ocean and he didn't know how to swim. I felt the same exact way.

"Is there somewhere we can speak privately?" Kobal asked Morax.

"Yes. Follow me," Morax replied.

CHAPTER THIRTEEN

River

The demons split apart as Morax led us through the crowd. Verin sauntered beside him, her hips swaying with each step. Curious eyes burned into me as I walked past the demons, but no one spoke to me again. All of them bowed their heads to Kobal once more, and he paused to speak with some of them before continuing. A few of the ones he spoke with fell into line behind us, while one of them turned and disappeared into the crowd.

I didn't take an easy breath until we stepped out of the chamber and into a side tunnel barely large enough to fit the two of us walking next to each other. A glance behind me revealed Hawk, Lix, Bale, Corson, and Magnus also following us. The hounds created a wall at the back of the pack.

Morax stopped before a boulder blocking the end of the tunnel and stepped to the side. His tail coiled around the edge of the rock. The muscles in his tail flexed when he lifted the rock and set it aside to reveal the room beyond.

I peered in at the gray walls and floor of the room. Each of the four corners had a small Hell fire burning within a pit. The warmth of the room brushed against my skin and caused sweat to bead on my brow, but it was nowhere near as unpleasant as the heat from the Oracle.

Kobal led me inside and the others filtered in to spread out around us. A large, stone slab in the center of the room was set up like a table. It had half a dozen pink quartz rocks surrounding it. The rocks were at least two feet high with a flat top perfect for sitting. Six black goblets sat on the table, and more were displayed on the shelves lining the back wall. To my right, a narrow hall led away from the room, but no one moved toward it.

"What is this place?" I asked.

"Hell has many hidden chambers where demons reside. There is no way to uncover all of them. What one demon knows, another doesn't, and so on," Kobal replied. "This is one of those chambers."

"Our world is always changing and evolving, even when it is staying the same," Magnus murmured. "But Hell is a place for those who have perished and death always bring about change, does it not?"

"It does," I agreed though his words gave me that whole feeling of falling through the rabbit hole again. Magnus had a way of making things confusing, at least to me and Hawk. All the demons understood what he said perfectly fine; he made my head ache. "What does Helka mean?" I asked Kobal.

"Hell king," he answered.

"Oh."

Behind me, the boulder creaked as Morax shifted it back into place and the entrance was covered once more. I glanced over my shoulder at the demons I didn't know. They must be some of Kobal's more trusted allies who had remained in Hell after the gateway opened.

"How many fighters have been lost since you left us?" Kobal inquired.

"About a hundred," Verin replied. "We've taken out at least twice as many of Lucifer's followers."

"But then the lower-levels have always been stupid and weaker and therefore easier to kill. He's keeping his upper-level demons restrained right now and only sending his weaker fighters after us," Morax said. "We engaged with them yesterday, but it was a half-hearted attempt on Lucifer's part."

"Any idea why?" Kobal inquired.

"He's plotting something. What it is, we don't know," a demon with three-eyes answered.

Stepping forward, the demon extended one of his hands to me. Every one of his different colored eyes dared me to take the hand that was easily the size of my head. The eye in the center of his forehead was a striking aqua blue, while the left one was orange and the right green. Easily eight feet tall, he was solidly built and handsome with his broad cheeks and wide jaw.

"I am Calah," he said.

I took hold of his hand the best I could, considering I couldn't wrap my fingers all the way around it. "River," I replied.

He bowed his head before releasing my hand and turning to Kobal. "It is good to see you again, my king. It has been too long."

"It has, my friend." Kobal took Calah's hand and squeezed it. Though Calah was taller and broader than Kobal, the amount of power Kobal exuded made him seem larger than Calah.

The other demons who had entered the room came forward to introduce themselves to me and to reconnect with Kobal before stepping back.

"We must figure out what Lucifer is plotting," Kobal said when the last demon retreated from him.

"We moved everyone here when we realized he was trying to bait us," Morax said.

"How was he baiting you?" Kobal inquired.

"He was keeping us busy by engaging us on one side, but with only a small number of lower-level demons. We destroyed them without much effort, but we know he has more troops centralized around the throne room and he is inside the room," Calah answered.

"Is it possible retreating is what Lucifer intended for you to do?" Lix asked.

"If it is, then he didn't expect us to move here. Few know of this place, or at least few used to know of it," Morax said and clasped Verin's hand. I realized this had been their private chambers.

Kobal led me over to one of the quartz seats and maneuvered me onto it before taking the seat beside me at the head of the table. Lix sat on my other side and Calah moved to sit beside Kobal. Corson took a seat near the end and Morax helped Verin sit before stepping behind her. All the others spread out to stand behind those seated at the table.

Kobal opened his mouth to start speaking when a solid knock sounded on the boulder blocking the entrance. Morax strode over and pulled the rock out of the way. He stepped aside to allow someone entrance, but I couldn't see who entered over the top of the table. I glanced at Hawk as his eyebrows shot into his hairline. His lips compressed into a flat line and he looked as if he were trying not to laugh or gawk.

I went to rise to see who had entered, but Kobal seized my hand and flattened it on the table, holding me in place. I frowned at him as Verin rose from her seat and strode over to stand beside Bale. A scraping sound filled the air, and I thought the seat Verin vacated was pulled back, but I couldn't be sure.

Straining to try to see what was going on, I nearly toppled out of my seat when a forehead and eyes popped over the table. A pair of deep-set chestnut eyes met mine over the slab separating us and a bulbous nose with a reddened tip rested on the top of the rock. A gnarled hand rose and plopped onto the table beside the eyes, which twinkled with amusement. The demon hoisted himself onto the rock seat before leaping nimbly onto the table.

I understood Hawk's reaction as I tried not to gawk at the three-foot creature striding across the table toward me. His red outfit reminded me of Santa's suit, only the belt was green, as was the top hat he wore slightly askew. A red belt ran around the middle of the top hat.

The man's brown hair hung in ringlets, and with every step he took, they bounced against his shoulders. Due to his knobby knees bowing out to the sides, his gait was awkward and hitching. If he'd been wearing shoes with bells on them, I wouldn't have been able to stop myself from laughing, but his hairy feet were entirely bare and his pink toenails neatly trimmed.

Stopping in front of me, he tilted his head to the side to study me and set down the small, black pot he'd been holding. I blinked at the yellow liquid swirling within the pot as a wave of steam wafted from it.

It can't be! My mind screamed at me. However, when I lifted my head to take in the little man as he crouched before me and rested his hands on his knees, I couldn't deny I was waiting for a rainbow to sprout somewhere behind him.

"River, this is Lopan," Kobal said.

Lopan the leprechaun. I almost laughed, but I had a feeling this little leprechaun would tear my throat out instead of granting me wishes or giving me his pot of steaming yellow stuff.

"It is good to see you, Lopan," Kobal said.

The little man's eyes darted to him. "You also, my king. You have been missed. There are still five leporcháins on your side."

Leporcháins? That must be what type of demon Lopan was, but were they pulling my leg with this? Was this one of Magnus's illusions? I glanced at Magnus, but I knew he wouldn't try something like that right now, and Kobal wouldn't play along with it. Not while they were discussing how to kill Lucifer.

"The other five leporcháins remain on Lucifer's side?" Kobal asked.

"Four. I killed Dragsi," Lopan replied.

When he spoke, he revealed his mouthful of razor teeth. He may not look overly intimidating, but this leporcháin could inflict a lot of damage. He wouldn't be here if he wasn't a formidable opponent.

"I am sorry for the loss of your friend."

"Dragsi stopped being a friend when she chose the false king over our true king," Lopan replied. "Jumping Jehoshaphat! She has angel eyes, my liege."

I somehow managed to keep my shock hidden over this abrupt shift in conversation and his choice of words.

Rising, Lopan extended his tiny hand to me. "Howdy!" he greeted. "What's cracking?"

"Ah, I'm not sure," I replied and glanced at Kobal. He'd propped his chin on his palm and conveniently placed his hand over his mouth to hide a smile. I stretched my hand out to take Lopan's. "Hello."

Lopan lifted his other hand and clasped mine within both of his as he leaned forward to peer more intently at me. "Much power, much strength, a fine queen, for a mortal," he said as he patted my hand.

I was saved from having to think of a response when he released me, turned away, and bent over his pot. He waved a gnarled hand across the top of it before dipping his hand inside and pulling out a perfect, golden rose. My mouth dropped and Hawk's breath exploded from him when Lopan extended the rose to me.

"Unlike Magnus's tricks, you'll find this will remain intact when touched," Lopan said.

"I'll show you a trick," Magnus muttered.

"For you, mah rejant," Lopan said, ignoring Magnus. "Please, take it."

I stretched my hand out and took the stem of the rose. Solid beneath my fingers and cool to the touch, the rose looked so real that I was tempted to sniff it.

"It's beautiful," I murmured. "Thank you."

"A rose for a flower," he replied, and I couldn't figure out if he didn't know the saying, or he didn't know any other flowers. Either way, it didn't matter. Lopan bowed his head and lifted his pot. He tottered back to the other side of the table and set his pot down. Settling himself on top of the slab, he sat crossed legged as he gazed at all those within the room. "Now, where were we?"

I kept the rose in hand as I drew it closer to me. Kobal leaned over to whisper in my ear. "The leporcháin do not often part with their treasures. That is a rare gift from one such as them. I think he has also tried to learn some human sayings for you and might be confusing them."

"It's sweet that he tried," I murmured.

A smile curved Kobal's mouth as he leaned closer to me. "I've never heard another refer to the leporcháin as sweet. Murderous fiends, yes. Bloodthirsty, most definitely, but never sweet. Lopan is a strong ally."

"You sent the demon in the cavern to find him and bring him here," I said.

"Yes. When I learned Lopan still lived and had simply been elsewhere engaged when we arrived, I wanted him here for this."

He'd been with the nymphs most likely, or some other demon, I realized. I turned and pressed my lips to Kobal's ear as I spoke. "Is he really a leprechaun?"

"Yes and no." Kobal clasped my hand within his. "The leporcháin certainly aren't friendly creatures who have a pot of gold and chase rainbows, but they most likely spawned the leprechaun myth amid humans."

I looked from Lopan to the rose and back again. "What's the stuff in the pot?"

"It's not a pot but a caultin. They carry it with them wherever they go, and it is the source of the leporcháin's magic. Their magic keeps the caultin bound to them when they carry it, but it is possible to steal it if they set it down. If it's ever stolen from them, so is their source of power."

"So that's where the myth of a pot of gold came from, and that if you steal one from a leprechaun they have to do what you ask."

"Yes. The leporcháin will do almost anything for their power back; it's their main defense. They can conjure anything from within, as long as it's the size of the caultin or smaller. It's where their clothes come from; for some reason they enjoy wearing those things. I think one of them saw the myth the humans had turned them into and decided to have fun with it, or they are trying to make themselves look even less threatening to demons by wearing the outfit. Though, those who cross a leporcháin know just how lethal they can be."

"Amazing."

I ran my fingers over the rose. A single, midnight blue spark flickered across the tip of my finger to the rose.

"A child of the angels," someone in the room murmured.

I lifted my head to find everyone staring at me. Lowering the rose, I placed it carefully on the table.

"What is the next step, my liege?" Lopan inquired.

Beside me, Lix uncapped his flask and took a swig before turning it over. Not a single drop fell out. I expected him to complain; instead, he recapped his flask and folded his arms over his chest.

"We go after Lucifer," Kobal said.

"No one fighting Lucifer has made it into the throne room since he seized control of Hell," Calah said.

Kobal tapped his fingers against the table. "No one has been able to lure him or his followers out of that room once they hole themselves up in it. We will be able to do so now."

"How?" I inquired.

A muscle in his jaw twitched when he turned his eyes to me. "Bait."

Slowly, he outlined his plan to draw Lucifer into a battle.

CHAPTER FOURTEEN

Kobal

I kept River close by my side when we returned to the main cavern to join with the other demons. They didn't go to one knee again, but they all bowed their heads and stepped aside to create an aisle for us to walk through.

Looking at her, no one would know that her hand briefly trembled against the small of my back as she kept her chin high. She held the gaze of every demon whose eyes she met, and she stopped to speak with those who offered their hands to her.

A tree nymph dashed through the crowd to stand at the front of the gathering. Her blonde hair framed her pretty face and emphasized her green eyes. She practically bounced on her toes while she waved enthusiastically at River. A beautiful smile lit River's face as she stopped before the nymph.

"Lena," she greeted and clasped the nymph's hand in hers. "I'm glad to see you here, and safe."

"You also, my queen. Your highness," Lena said with a bow of her head to me before focusing on River again. "I'm glad you are both well.

My queen, we have a bathing area and some fresh clothes for you. If you would like."

"I would," River breathed.

"I will escort them to the bathing area," Verin said as she stepped forward. "I could use a bath myself."

"So could I," Bale said.

River rose onto her toes to place a chaste kiss against my lips. My arm locked around her waist, holding her in place as I deepened the kiss until she became breathless. Reluctantly, I released her and stepped away. I almost pulled her back to me when she gave me a sultry smile.

"Come, my queen," Lena said and tugged on River's hand. "Our king will still be here when you are done."

"Make sure no one else goes anywhere near her and that they all steer clear of the bathing area," I said to Bale as I watched River walk away with the nymph and Verin. "I will send the hounds with you."

"I'll keep her safe," Bale vowed.

The hounds followed at Bale's heels as she stalked away to catch up with River. A few seconds later, demons filtered out of the side tunnel River entered.

"I will be taking my leave to find some mjéod and some tree nymphs. *Many* tree nymphs," Lix said to me before vanishing into the crowd.

"You should go with him," I said to Hawk as he gazed after Lix with a look of longing on his face. "You need to feed, and we need you at your best for this fight."

"I think I would like some more leisurely activities myself before we go to war." Corson slapped Hawk on his shoulder. "Come, canagh demon, let's make some nymphs happy."

"I bet I make mine far happier than you make yours," Hawk retorted.

"I'm game for a challenge," Corson said, and the two of them broke away to stride through the crowd.

Morax and Magnus stepped closer to me as Lopan and Calah walked with us to the end of the chamber while I greeted everyone within. Before the humans opened the gateway into Hell, Lopan and Calah had been two of my strongest allies and fighters against Lucifer. I'd ordered them to remain behind to continue the fight when I went above with the others.

As we walked, Calah filled me in on the events that occurred since my last trip into Hell. "Things had been quiet since you were last here," Calah said. "There were skirmishes between the two sides, but nothing major, until recently."

I contemplated his words as I left the chamber and started down the tunnel River had entered with the others. "It probably started to change around the same time Lucifer realized we had River."

"From what I've gathered, it does seem that way," Morax said as we walked down the empty tunnel. "He's been preparing for us to enter Hell."

Stopping, I leaned against the wall. I glanced back at the main cavern, but no one had followed us. "And we've brought River to him," I said.

Not only that, but I planned to use her as bait to lure the bastard out. Every instinct I had screamed against following the plan I'd laid out. Everything within me said to get her out of Hell before it was too late, but she'd never know a second of peace, never be completely safe, if we returned to Earth with Lucifer still alive. He would never stop hunting her.

"From what Morax has told us about her, our queen can handle herself," Calah said.

"She can," I agreed. "We received a visit from the fallen angel, Caim, when we traveled through the oracle."

"Truly!" Lopan blurted and set his caultin down to lift his hat and push his hair back. "Did you kill him?"

"Not yet. He stated he would help us against Lucifer and that he believes the angels in Heaven are trying to communicate with River."

"What do you make of that?" Morax inquired, his tail flicking above his head.

"We can't trust him, but I think he's right about the angels trying to speak with River. Whether that means the angels will grow a set of balls and step into this fight or not, I don't know. I do believe they're trying to get some message through to River. However, unlike some of the other children of the angels, she can't receive it."

"Why did you not reveal this to the others?" Lopan asked and lifted his caultin.

"They accept her as their queen; they have no choice. However, it could make some distrustful of her if they learn the angels are trying to get a message to her and that one of the fallen has offered to help her. Some of our fighters have turned to Lucifer's side before; we can't have this information somehow finding its way back to him. *No* one else is to know about this."

"They will not," Calah vowed.

"Whatever is necessary to protect our queen, my liege," Lopan said. "You will also note that none of Magnimus's illusions remain in the cavern."

Magnus's eyes narrowed on Lopan. He shifted his feet as if he were preparing to kick the leporcháin down the tunnel. I placed a hand against Magnus's chest as Lopan grinned at him, revealing all his flesh-rending teeth. The two of them had never gotten along, each believing their capabilities to conjure things superior to the other's.

"I noticed," I said.

Lopan stared at Magnus before shifting his gaze to me. "They did well enough for simple illusions, and were good distractions while they lasted."

"Good," I said briskly. That meant Magnus had upheld his end of things. I already trusted him more than I had upon first encountering him again, but I wouldn't take any chances when it came to River's safety and Lucifer's demise.

"I have a carnival you wouldn't find so simple, and you would make a star attraction in it," Magnus said.

Lopan turned away as if Magnus hadn't spoken. Morax chuckled and all of Calah's eyes rolled. Stepping away from the wall, I started down the side chamber again, stopping when River appeared with Verin and Bale. Behind them, the tiny nymph skipped along with River's clothes in hand. The hounds brought up the rear.

River lifted her head and her amethyst eyes met mine. The black pants and shirt she wore hugged her slender frame. Her wet hair hung loosely against her back and over her shoulders. Watching the sway of her breasts in her shirt caused my cock to swell. Soon, we would be going to war against Lucifer, soon I would be putting her at risk, but before that happened, I would spend as much time with her as possible.

"Leave us," I ordered the others.

Stalking toward her, I swung her into my arms and carried her back the way she'd come from. "Is there a place we can be alone down here?" I asked her.

"There is," she said as she nibbled at my ear.

River

Kneeling in the shadows of the tunnel, I rested my hand on the cool ground. I breathed slowly in and out as I took a minute to rest. We'd been walking for what felt like hours, but we'd finally reached our destination. Finally reached the place where Kobal hoped to draw Lucifer into battle by using me as bait.

It wasn't the most comforting of thoughts, but I'd do whatever it took to end this today.

"I keep waiting for him to declare that they're magically delicious," Hawk said as he knelt beside me.

I did a double take. "What?"

He nodded toward where Lopan stood beside Kobal, looking even smaller as he barely reached Kobal's knee. "Lopan. I keep waiting for him to say that."

"But why would he ever say *that*?"

Hawk rested his palm on the rock floor. "It was from this cereal that existed before the war. It had this… Never mind."

"Oh." I vaguely recalled something like that, but it felt like a lifetime ago now. "I keep waiting for a rainbow to sprout around him," I admitted.

He chuckled. His skin and eyes fairly shone with vitality, and I could feel the swell of his power prickling against my skin. It didn't take a demon to figure out that he'd recently fed.

"You're growing stronger," I commented.

Hawk's indigo eyes slid toward me. "I'm becoming more of a demon every time I feed; I can feel it."

"You have to feed to survive," I said.

"I know. I just wish…"

"What?" I prodded when his voice trailed off.

His lips flattened into a thin line. "That I had a choice. And not a choice about being changed. Nothing could have stopped that, but a choice about what I have to do to survive now."

"I see."

"Do you? Because I don't. At one point in time, I would have been thrilled to have an endless parade of women, but I'm not. Maybe that will change too as I become more and more demon."

"Is that what you want to happen?"

"No."

"You could meet your Chosen."

"And feed from her?"

"I don't know how that would work," I admitted. "I'm sure there are other canagh demons who have met their Chosen before."

"Yeah," he mumbled. "I'm sure there are too."

Kobal stepped away from the end of the tunnel and turned toward us. "We'll do it now," he said as he strode toward me.

Every muscle in my body tensed; a ripple of unease slid down my spine as Hawk and I rose.

"They're never going to forget you," Hawk said to me before walking down to join Lopan, Magnus, and Corson at the end of the tunnel.

Kobal had outlined his plan to everyone in Morax and Verin's room, and I had agreed to it, but I was seriously rethinking my agreement now. If this worked the way he anticipated, he would be going for Lucifer, and I would be remaining here to fight off as many demons as I could.

I'd rather be in on the battle, but Kobal believed my presence below would only be a distraction to his fighters, and I couldn't deny he had a point. Many of them would be more concerned with keeping me safe than killing. I was quite capable of raining down a fair amount of destruction, but if I was below, I could hit Kobal's followers. From above, I'd at least be able to aim better and offer some cover for Kobal and the others.

To join the demons below, Kobal planned to scale down the wall, something I couldn't do with any speed. He might give in and agree to carry me if I insisted on it, but it would only slow him and put us both at greater risk.

Kobal's fingers slid over the back of my hand when he took it within his. He drew me a step closer to him. The flow of his power caressed my skin, causing the hair on my arms to rise. He hadn't bothered to put a shirt on; it would most likely be burned off him as soon as he went into battle and would only be something for an enemy to grab. I'd noticed that most of the demons weren't wearing shirts. The ones who were couldn't fit a slice of paper between their shirt and their skin.

Kobal's gaze burned into mine as he lifted his other hand to brush the hair back from my face. "Are you ready?" he inquired.

"As I'll ever be."

His fingers stilled on my cheek. He kissed the tip of my nose before turning and leading me to the mouth of the tunnel. I swallowed as I stopped at the end. My toes dangled over the edge while I peered out at the massive cavern for the first time.

CHAPTER FIFTEEN

River

A few hundred feet across from me was a wall of jagged black and gray stones. Flickering light drew my eyes a hundred feet below me and to a waterfall of fire tumbling straight from the rocks there. My mind spun as I tried to comprehend what I was seeing. If the waterfall had been lava, I could have grasped it better, but the flames rolling over top of one another as they fell made it more difficult to process.

The waterfall tumbled five hundred feet to the cavern below. There, a river of fire streamed through the center of the cavern, dividing the smooth, rocky floor perfectly in two. Where the floor met the stream, sparks floated into the air, but they didn't make it far before burning out.

A dozen flat rocks started at the floor of the cavern and were spaced throughout the river like stepping stones. Near the bottom of the waterfall, the flames split apart like stage curtains. The stones disappeared beneath those curtains.

"Where do the stones in the river go?" I asked.

"They lead into the throne room," Kobal replied.

"Have you ever seen the throne room?"

"No."

I didn't miss the gruffness in his voice or the slight lengthening of his black fingernails before he retracted his claws. He was so close to claiming the throne taken from his ancestors. For all any of us knew, there might not even be a throne, but something else entirely. Or if there was a throne, it could be something different than what I pictured in my head, which was a chair with skulls and spikes and dead things all over it.

I *really* hoped it was different than what I pictured in my head.

Craning my head back, I tried to see the top of the cavern, but darkness enshrouded it so thickly that I couldn't make out anything over a hundred feet above where we stood. I spotted more tunnel openings above us, but didn't see any more below us.

Movement drew my attention back to the waterfall. I sneered when two bartas stepped out from beneath the flames. I hated the bear-like creatures with their wolverine claws, pig snout, red eyes, jagged fangs, and thick brown coats.

My fire had no effect on the bartas, but my ability to wield life made their hearts explode like overinflated balloons. The hideous creatures had been behind the fifty-fifth seal, but once freed, they became a part of Lucifer's guard. I'd seen some as small as a teddy bear, but the ones below were the fully grown, Winnie the Pooh on steroids variety as they stood almost ten feet tall.

The six-inch-long claws on their feet ticked across the stones as they made their way to the end of the fiery stream before turning back and vanishing beneath the waterfall once more.

I frowned when I realized the waterfall made no sound. There was no pop of the flames like a normal fire, instead there was only an eerie hush.

"How come the waterfall doesn't make any noise?" I whispered.

"The guards inside the throne room couldn't hear anyone approaching if it was loud," Kobal replied.

“How is a silent fire possible?” Hawk asked.

“This is Hell, anything is possible here,” Magnus drawled. “They are not flames as you know them.”

A dull throb started in my temples. I really had to start thinking outside the box more and move beyond everything I’d ever believed possible. Otherwise, I was going to walk around Hell with a permanent migraine.

“Of course they’re not,” I muttered.

“These flames were established to protect the first varcolac. If they made sound, they would also make the varcolac vulnerable within the throne room,” Kobal said.

“I see,” I said, and though my senses were still thrown off by the noiseless fire, I did understand it.

The barta demons emerged again. They walked their same pathway and turned back.

Before coming here, Kobal told me that the last time they tried to attack Lucifer in the throne room, many of the palitons—the demons who fought on his side—were slaughtered and he’d been severely injured. I could see why as they’d been little more than sitting ducks. The tunnels branching off the cavern below had only enough room for two or three to travel side by side, making it difficult to maneuver troops through them. It would be easy to pick off the attackers before they made it into the cavern.

“Have you ever tried to attack Lucifer from up here before?” I asked.

“No,” Kobal replied. “There are numerous tunnels above us in these walls, but this is the lowest one. If we could have somehow lured him out of the throne room before, the jump from this height wouldn’t kill us, but it would break enough bones that we would be picked off below. Those who didn’t jump and remained above, could launch some kind of an attack on Lucifer’s followers, but we still wouldn’t make it into the throne room and Lucifer never would have risked coming out of there before to fight us.”

"But he will now," I murmured.

Kobal's eyes were troubled when they met mine. "I believe he will."

"Is there another entrance into the throne room?"

"Not that I know of, but I'm certain there are hidden ones. The varcolacs and Lucifer wouldn't establish their base in a place with only one way in or out."

"True."

"The next time the bartas appear, you'll blast them."

I glanced between him and the bottom of the cavern again. "I'm not sure I can hit them from this far away."

"Even if you can't kill them, Lucifer will know you're here. You're a prize he wants for himself, Mah Kush-la."

This time Kobal couldn't stop his claws from extending all the way. This was his plan; we'd all agreed it was necessary, but I had no doubt this was an absolute last resort for him.

"I'm going to be fine," I whispered. "I'm way up here."

"The angels can reach here easily enough," he grated from between his teeth.

"I'll be able to see them coming if they do come this way."

"Promise me you'll protect yourself first, that you won't stay for me if things go bad."

"Kobal—"

"Promise me you will not hesitate for me. You *will* leave."

I winced before taking a deep breath. "I'll leave."

He glanced over my shoulder at Corson. "Make sure she does."

"I will," Corson promised.

"We all will," Lopan said.

Kobal held my gaze before releasing my hand and cupping my cheek. "It is time to work your magic."

Glancing at the cavern, I watched as the patrolling bartas reemerged. "It is."

Stepping back, I became hidden from below again. I braced my feet further apart as I closed my eyes to concentrate on the pulse of life flowing through the rocks beneath my boots. It was still more difficult for me to draw on life in Hell than it was on Earth, but I'd gotten better at doing it.

Drawing on the energy in the ground, I pulled on it until it slid through my toes before seeping into my ankles and spreading further up my legs. When I had a solid grip on the life force beneath me, I focused on the far bigger resource standing at my side, Kobal. He'd always been the strongest catalyst for bringing out my ability to wield life. My fingers caressed his as I fed on the flow of seemingly endless power swelling through him.

The hair on my nape rose and my breath came faster as power raced through my veins. Turning my hand over, I opened my eyes as midnight blue sparks lanced across my fingers like mini-lightning bolts. Harnessing those bolts, I focused them into a ball of energy that swelled within my palm until it rose to hover above it.

Moving forward to stand at the edge of the tunnel again, my eyes landed on the bartas as they patrolled across the stepping stones. They stepped onto the main cavern floor before turning to head back toward the waterfall. Flipping my hand over, I aimed the ball at the two of them and released it in a rush of power.

One of them must have sensed something as it looked up at the last second, but the other never saw the ball until it struck its chest. The energy passed straight through the one who had looked up before hitting the other barta. They both stared at where the ball had entered their chests before they lifted their heads and bared their lethal fangs at us.

The first one took a step forward before freezing and glancing at its chest again. It released a low keening sound before its claws grasped its flesh. Behind it, the other did the same thing until they were both tearing at their chests. They succeeded in rending their flesh and ribcages open to expose their still beating hearts.

The second barta roared as the heart of the first one exploded and it collapsed into the flames. Its body was absorbed by the stream seconds before its friend fell into the fire.

The seconds ticked endlessly onward as everyone held their breaths.

Then, all Hell broke loose.

CHAPTER SIXTEEN

Kobal

Echoing shouts reverberated through the cavern as a group of craetons, Lucifer's followers, poured out from beneath the waterfall. Behind the demons, some of the angels swooped in low before rising to soar higher into the cavern. Around forty of the fallen angels who had entered Hell still lived, and over half of them emerged now. One rushed up before us, its body cutting through the air and blowing River's hair back.

I drew her back as more angels flew into the cavern, followed by a horde of manticores. I snarled when I spotted those winged monsters rising higher. I knew the manticores had escaped from the forty-sixth seal, but I hadn't stopped to think about them with everything else that had been set free.

"What are those?" River breathed from beside me as the first wave of manticores winged up the walls.

"Manticores," I replied, pulling her back a step and maneuvering her behind me when the first one passed by where we stood.

The manticore stopped and lowered itself back down. Its translucent green wings beat against the air as it kept its lion body hovering before us. The red of its fur matched the color of the scorpion tail curving beneath its powerful body. Blue eyes gazed at us from a head that was human in form. This manticore was of the horned variety and had three white horns sprouting from the top of its head. It smiled to reveal its three rows of pointed teeth before releasing a trumpet-like call.

"The poison in the tail is paralyzing," I told River as it swung its tail into the entrance, striking at Lopan. "They devour their victims whole after paralyzing them."

"It's hideous," she whispered.

When it struck out again, I seized its tail, careful not to touch the bead of poison at the end. With a yank to the right, I broke the tail in half. The manticore screeched and flapped its wings to escape me. I kept a firm hold on it as fire burst from my palm and spread forward to consume the tail. The manticore jerked in my hold as I dragged it toward me.

Its front paws clawed at the rock wall outside the tunnel, tearing away stones as it sought purchase. Fire blazed from my hand until it fully engulfed the manticore and it screeched loudly. Releasing it, I watched its flaming body spiraling down before crashing onto the floor below. The lower-level demons tilted their heads back to gaze at us as a cry erupted from the tunnels leading into the cavern.

The skelleins were the first ones to burst into the cavern. They released a loud whoop as they swung their swords over their heads. More of the creatures from the seals poured in from the throne room, as more of my followers rushed forward to engage them in battle.

The hounds bounded into the cavern with the demons. Their jaws snapped as they struck down a wave of prey. Bale, Verin, and Morax led the next wave into the main cavern before Lucifer's troops moved to block the entrance.

My fingers flexed as blood rushed through my veins. I was tired of fighting, but I wanted to give River a life of safety and happiness so I looked forward to destroying Lucifer.

River rested her fingers on my back as she stepped beside me to gaze below. "Where is he?"

"He won't come out, not yet. We have to make him think he's beating us first. It's your turn, Magnus," I said.

Magnus's shoulders tensed. "I'm not sure how long I'll be able to keep this up," he stated, not for the first time expressing his doubts. "I'm a creator."

"This is creating, in a way," Corson said.

"Hmm," Magnus grunted. "This is not the type of illusion I weave."

"Can you do it?" Hawk asked.

"Yes, for a bit. It is tiring to me in a way that creating is not. I won't be able to do any other illusions for a while after this."

"That's why you will remain here, out of the battle," I replied.

I understood Magnus's concerns, but for the plan to succeed, there was no other choice.

"I practiced the cloaking illusion over the years, but I was never able to master it. My father was far better than I at it, but my father never created anything solid as I have," Magnus said.

River rested her hand on his arm. "You can do this."

"Oh, I have no doubt I am capable of anything, my queen," Magnus replied with a wink as his normally brazen attitude returned.

River smiled at him and her hand fell away. Bowing his head, Magnus clasped his hands before him as he closed his eyes. Stepping closer to the edge of the tunnel again, I gazed at the battle waging below.

Blood and body parts flew as the two sides clashed with each other. Angels and manticores dove down to snatch unsuspecting victims from the ground. One demon's arms and legs flailed in the air before the angel released him. The fighters below scurried to get out of the way of the free-falling body before it plummeted into the river. Sparks and flames shot up; fire rolled onto the rocks before retreating into the stream once more.

"Now," Magnus murmured.

Clasping my hands around my mouth, I bellowed, “Retreat!”

The word reverberated off the walls until it echoed throughout. None of my followers looked at me; they had all been expecting this command. The palitons divided and a large amount of them battled through the craetons trying to block off their retreat. The rest remained where they were, their number was small enough that the craetons didn’t notice they weren’t a part of the retreating group. Many of the craetons pursued the fleeing palitons.

An angel flew up to hover before us. Her blonde hair swayed to the sides when she craned her head back and forth to examine the tunnel. I studied the soulless black eyes before me, but though I could clearly see her, she couldn’t see me.

“Gone!” she shouted and dove down.

With the angel out of the way, my attention returned to the cavern. Of the nearly hundred palitons who remained below, no one dared to move as some of Lucifer’s followers patrolled the cavern. Cloaked by Magnus’s ability, the craetons didn’t see them.

Morax and Verin crept cautiously backward as a lower-level demon came within inches of where they stood. Bale shifted back when an angel landed beside her. The arm of the angel would have brushed against hers if she hadn’t moved. It would only take one of those creatures bumping into them for the illusion to end.

I glanced at Magnus. Sweat beaded his forehead and his jaw clenched. His pale skin had become nearly translucent. I didn’t know how much longer he could keep this mirage going.

A disturbance in the air brought my gaze back to the cavern. My fangs extended when Lucifer swooped into sight with the handful of angels who had remained in the throne room with him. He flew low across the fire before pulling up and setting down near the stream. He folded his black wings behind him.

The need to destroy him pulsed within me. We’d battled often over the years, but those battles would be coming to an end. One way or another, one of us would sit on that throne and the other would die.

River rested her hand on my arm. Her violet eyes were solemn when they met mine. As much as I despised Lucifer for all he'd done, for the many lives he'd taken over his years in Hell, I wouldn't change any of what had happened.

If Lucifer had never walked the Earth, River wouldn't exist.

She brushed her fingers over my markings when they shifted in anticipation of going after Lucifer. Lifting her hand, I kissed the back of it before drawing her a step closer. Lucifer walked around the chamber, absently kicking at the remains of those who had perished. Spreading his wings, he flapped them to rise into the air.

"I can't keep this up, Kobal," Magnus muttered as sweat dripped off his chin and plopped onto the ground.

Bending, I rested my lips against River's ear. "Remember, yourself first. I will come back for you, Mah Kush-la."

Her mouth turned until her lips touched mine. "I love you."

"And I you, with everything I am."

Releasing her, I held her gaze before taking a few steps back. I had planned to scale down the rocks to the cavern below, but plans had a way of changing. Running forward, I leapt off the edge of the cliff.

Air battered my body and whipped at my clothes as I plummeted downward. My gaze remained locked on Lucifer when he rose higher, directly beneath me. If I missed him, I would break bones on the rocks below. I had no intention of missing him.

I knew the second Magnus lost the illusion as a startled cry erupted from the craetons and they staggered away from the palitons who had been hidden from them.

"Lucifer!" a scream erupted from above me, but I remained focused on his bat-like, black wings. "Above you!"

Lucifer's head tilted back, his onyx eyes widened when he spotted me. He twisted in midair to avoid me, but he wasn't fast enough as my hand snagged his foot. Wildly, he swung one of the silver spikes protruding from the bottoms of his wing at me. It sliced across my cheek, causing blood to spill down my face and onto the floor below.

I dodged the next swing he took at me and seized his foot with both hands. Before he could launch another wing at me, I swung my legs up and wrapped them around his waist. Releasing his foot, I caught the spike as he drove it straight toward me. The tip of it brushed against my eye. The muscles in my arms bulged as I grappled to keep Lucifer from driving it through my skull.

I shouted as I succeeded in yanking his wing to the side. The satisfying crack of bone and the rending of flesh tearing filled the air before his putrid, oily blood spurted into my face. With the wing bent at an unnatural angle, he struggled to stay in the air with the other, but my added weight dragged him toward the palitons and hounds waiting beneath us.

CHAPTER SEVENTEEN

River

My heart lodged in my throat when Kobal leapt off the cliff and plummeted into the cavern. Resting my hand against the rock wall, I leaned forward to watch him crash onto Lucifer. Many of Kobal's followers moved to block the tunnels as they fought the craetons who had remained in the cavern.

Pulling on the flow of life beneath my fingertips, I created another small ball of energy. I aimed it at a manticore diving toward Kobal and released it. The blast tore through the back of the creature. The screech it released made me wince as it spiraled downward. With a loud crack, it hit the ground and its body bounced across the floor. Bale leapt forward to sever its head with her sword.

"Nice blow, my queen," Lopan complimented.

I started drawing from the rocks again as Lucifer battered at the air with his good wing. The bones of the other wing were already knitting back together and his blood didn't flow as freely. He tried to propel himself away from the hounds jumping to nip at his heels.

My breath hissed in when Lucifer swung one of his lethal spikes at Kobal again. The gash in Kobal's cheek had stopped bleeding, but now fresh blood spilled from the flayed open skin and muscle of his back.

"Son of a bitch!" I spat.

Turning my hand over, I released the energy on a blast that discharged in a straight line from my palm. Lucifer's howl echoed throughout when the flow of life tore through his back. I glimpsed his spine before muscle and blood swiftly started to repair itself.

Lucifer's head whipped around. His pitiless black eyes burned into mine as he bared his teeth. No matter what his plans were for me, if he'd been standing beside me right then, he would have torn off my head.

"Shit," Hawk said from beside me.

"Get her!" Lucifer shouted. His flight faltered again when Kobal jerked on him, bringing him toward the ground once more.

"Not good," Magnus stated.

"Time to go," Corson said and snagged my arm.

"Kobal," I breathed. I jerked against Corson's incessant tugging, but he refused to release me.

"You promised him you would go, that you would think of yourself first," Corson said. "Kobal will focus on the fight better if he knows you're safe."

Before I could respond, a manticore flew up to fill the mouth of the tunnel. Corson shoved me against the wall as the tail of the manticore swung in. It slammed into the floor where we'd been standing. Rocks splintered and broke; their shards pelted my legs. The manticore pulled its tail free, lifted it up, and plunged it down again. Lopan yelped and jumped out of the way in time to avoid being pierced by the poisonous stinger.

Setting his caultin down, Lopan dipped his hand in and pulled out a small sword. Gripping it with both hands, he lifted it above his head and swung the sword across the manticore's tail, severing it. The sliced off end flopped on the ground for a few seconds before going still. Green blood gushed out the other end, spraying the walls as the remaining stump of the manticore's tail lashed back and forth. I dodged a wave of blood as the manticore trumpeted a sound that had me slapping my hands over my ears. It reeled away from the entrance.

"Get her out of here, Corson!" Lopan shouted as he kicked the stinger out of the tunnel.

"We'll fend them off," Hawk said and punched the face of the next manticore who rose to float in front of the opening.

I almost tripped over my feet when Corson started propelling me away from the others. Behind me, something crashed against the rocks with enough force to shake the tunnel. As pebbles rained down on us, I blinked against the dust filling the air and wiped it away from my eyes. Corson threw his arm up, trying in vain to protect us when another crash brought down more debris.

"Don't look back," Corson ordered when I twisted to try to see the others.

I turned back to him just as the tunnel and Corson faded away to reveal a woman coming toward me. Her black hair fell to her waist in thick waves. Her stalking steps emphasized the sway of her hips in the low-slung black skirt she wore. The hem of the skirt dusted the floor, but the slits on both sides went to her waist to expose her thighs. Her black, bra-like top pushed her full breasts upward and was cut low enough to reveal the tops of her areolas.

When she lifted her head, her black eyes locked onto mine and a smile curved her full mouth. Behind her, dainty black wings unfurled, and she ruffled them. Unlike the other fallen angels I'd seen, she didn't have foot-long silver spikes sticking out of the tops and bottoms of her wings. Instead, she had shorter, golden spikes. The ones on top stood straight up, but the bottom ones curved to form lethal hooks.

She hovered above the ground for a second before flying at me with deadly speed. Corson had vanished when the vision first started, but he suddenly reappeared before me. Fire light reflected off the steel blade of the angel's sword when it swung out of the shadows; it whistled as it sliced toward Corson. I opened my mouth to shout a warning, but it was already too late.

Corson's warm blood sprayed over my face and clothing. The coppery scent of it flooded my nostrils as his head hit the ground with a dull thud. It rolled over until his sightless eyes stared accusingly up at me. His mouth remained parted in surprise as I gawked at his head.

How had I not seen this sooner? He seemed to be asking, and that was the same question screaming through my mind. Tears burned my eyes as a strangled cry of horror and grief lodged in my throat.

I didn't have time to react before the angel's hand snaked out of the shadows. She grabbed my shirt and yanked me off my feet. Our noses nearly touched as I gazed into her soulless, black eyes. "Hello, niece," she purred.

The drops of Corson's blood dripping from her sword sounded as loud as gunshots when they hit the ground. She twisted her hand in my shirt and wiped her blade on my pants while she grinned at me.

Kobal

My skin thrummed from the energy River had shot into Lucifer. The flow of her power had spread from him and into me, zapping me hard enough that my grip on him loosened. She'd been able to take out bartas with a stream of energy before, but for it to travel through Lucifer and into me was something neither of us realized she could do.

I fumbled to maintain my hold on Lucifer as he jerked awkwardly in the air to stay afloat. Tremors racked his body from the lingering effects of River's blast. Finally, gripping him firmly again, I released my legs from his waist and swung them down. One of the hounds leapt up and snagged my boot, dragging me toward them.

Lucifer grunted as his blood dripped onto my face and spilled downward. I glanced at where I'd left River to find three manticores attached to the wall outside the tunnel. Two had their tails swinging in, while the third was perched to peer inside. My heart thudded with worry for her, but the best way to keep River safe was to make sure Lucifer died. I yanked on his foot, pulling him down until I could wrap my hand around his calf and sink my claws into his flesh.

I never saw the angel swooping toward me until a sword pierced through my ribcage and straight out the other side.

Blood spewed from my lips as every breath I took caused agony to lance through my battered lungs. The angel holding the sword turned it within me, slicing through my heart until blood pumping freely though my chest cavity. Releasing one of my hands from Lucifer's leg, I clutched the sword before the angel could twist it again.

Turning my head, I met the eyes of the angel hovering beside me. The hounds howled as the one holding my foot pulled more insistently on me. When Lucifer jerked in my grasp, I realized that another angel had grabbed his arms and was trying to tear him free.

Flames burst from my palm to set his pants on fire and sear the flesh from his leg. He kicked at me with his free foot, catching me in the jaw and rattling my teeth. The angel with the sword tried to pull it free as the fire spread up Lucifer's front and raced toward his face. His wings may be fire proof, but his flesh was not. His wings swung forward to try to beat the flames out before it engulfed him. The breeze they created only fueled the blaze.

The flap of wings sounded behind me, and I turned my head in time to see a sword swinging at my neck. Releasing my hold on the sword impaling me, I caught the other one before it could sever my head from my shoulders. The blade bit through my hand, slicing all the way to the bone.

The angel released the sword in my hand and flew up to capture Lucifer's wrists as fire engulfed his head. The burnt smell of his hair filled the air as the skin on his face sloughed off in chunks.

I labored to breathe as the angel who still had the sword within me, twisted it again. When the angel started sawing the sword up through my body, my claws were torn free of Lucifer's leg.

Before I plummeted to the ground, I managed to seize the angel with the sword by the wrist and drag him down with me. The second we hit the ground, the hounds pounced on him. His screams reverberated in the cavern as they tore him limb from limb.

Rolling to the side, I staggered to my feet and gritted my teeth as I wrapped my blood-coated hands around the handle of the sword. The blade scoured my ribs as I worked it free of my body and tossed it aside. With the blade free, blood ran down my sides to pool around my feet.

One of the hounds whimpered and rubbed its head against my waist as the angels drew Lucifer upward. The manticores parted so the angels could set Lucifer on the edge of the tunnel where I'd left River and the others.

"River!" my shout came out raw and broken as fresh blood burst from my mouth.

CHAPTER EIGHTEEN

River

I staggered back as the vision abruptly ended and the world crashed around me. I blinked at Corson's back as I struggled to shove aside my vision of the future and ground myself in the present. Still entrenched in the vision, I lifted a hand to wipe Corson's blood off my face before realizing it wasn't there. The image of his head lying at my feet blurred with the image of him standing before me now.

It wasn't real! Not real! My mind screamed at me even as tears burned my eyes and a scream lodged in my throat.

It would become real soon if I didn't do something to stop it. Leaping onto Corson's back, I dragged him down beneath me. I flinched as I waited to hear the whistle of the sword, but the battle waging behind us was the only noise in the tunnel.

"What are you doing?" Corson grunted.

"Onoskelis," I whispered, naming the angel from my vision. "She's ahead of us."

His head turned toward me as I searched the shadows for any hint of the threat I'd witnessed.

"She… she killed you," I stammered. "Your blood, I felt it on my skin. I smelled it. It was *so* real. We have to go back."

"I'm not that easy to kill," he replied in a disgruntled tone.

"You never saw her coming. I didn't either, but she's there. I can feel her in my bones. *We have to go back*," I repeated more urgently.

"There's no way out back there."

"No, but the others are back there. Death is ahead of us, *your* death."

"I will protect you with my life."

"Not when there's no reason to. We're going back or, so help me, I'll fire an energy ball into your ass that will have you skipping back to the others."

"Sometimes I wish we'd never shown you how to use your abilities," he grumbled.

"Too late. Now, let's go."

Peeling myself off him, I tried to remain behind him, but Corson pushed me ahead. "She won't kill me," I reminded him.

"Don't care, go."

The talons that extended from the backs of his hands occasionally scraped against rock as he ran down the tunnel behind me. Rounding a corner, Magnus, Lopan, and Hawk came into view as they worked to fend off the manticores.

"What are you doing back here?" Hawk demanded, and Magnus looked tempted to choke me.

Lopan froze in the middle of chewing off the leg of one of the manticores. The look on his face was that of a kid caught with his hand in the cookie jar. He tore the paw the rest of the way off. The manticore trumpeted and flew out of the tunnel

"My queen—" Lopan started and tossed aside the paw.

"The angel, Onoskelis, is behind us," I said, trying not to look at the blood staining Lopan's mouth. He looked anything but sweet now. "She killed Corson."

"*What*?" Magnus and Hawk blurted. Lopan's gaze went to Corson and a baffled expression came over his face.

"In my vision! She killed Corson in my vision, and she's coming!" I rushed to explain.

"What do we do now?" Hawk inquired.

"Unless you can fly, we make a stand," Magnus replied.

Lopan scurried forward and set his caultin on the ground. Behind him, one of the manticores slid further into the cave. Corson rushed past me before the manticore could move any deeper into the tunnel. He sliced the manticore from its waist all the way to the tip of its tail with his talons. The creature screeched and flung itself backward, only to be replaced by another.

A cold sweat coated my body as an impending sense of doom filled me. I moved closer to the others while they struggled to keep the manticores back. We were pinned in here, but we weren't outnumbered yet.

Settling my fingers against the wall, I ran the tips of them over the rough rock as I worked on drawing life from them. I rested my other hand against the pocket of my pants where I'd placed the rose Lopan gave me and harvested more energy from it. I built a ball within my palm as I searched the shadows for Onoskelis.

I could feel her hunting us, but a sense of calm descended over me while I waited for her. I was so focused on killing Onoskelis that I didn't realize silence had descended behind me.

Turning my head, I watched as Magnus, Lopan, and Corson staggered away from the end of the tunnel. Hawk stepped closer to me and rested his hand on my shoulder, causing a greater influx of life to surge within me. I opened my mouth to ask what was going on just as the manticores parted to reveal two angels at the end. Between them, the angels gripped the sagging form of a creature I couldn't make out.

My jaw dropped when I realized the charred and bloody thing they set down inside the tunnel was *Lucifer*. When they released his arms, Lucifer bent to rest his fist on the ground. Through his charbroiled skin, the glean of some of the bones in his hands, and his collarbone, could be seen. What remained of the burnt skin on his knuckles broke open and blood seeped out to stain the ground.

The wing Kobal had broken remained twisted at an unnatural angle. The fines bones of it stuck through in a few places, but it had healed more since I'd last seen it. His other wing was tucked against his back.

Black bits of clothing adhered to the blistered flesh of his thighs, chest, and neck. The skin on his face resembled a runny, scrambled egg as part of it dripped off to land on the ground beside his fist. Singed remnants of hair stuck in tufts to his pinkened scalp.

Slowly, Lucifer lifted his head and his eyes latched onto me. His eyeballs remained untouched by the fire, but he didn't have eyelids anymore, which made his eyes look as if they were about to pop out of his head. What remained of his lips twisted into a cruel smile.

"Daughter," he rasped.

"Fuck," Hawk breathed.

That sentiment summed this situation up perfectly.

Lucifer raced forward far faster than I would have thought possible for someone who looked as if they'd climbed off a barbeque spit. The other two angels launched at Corson and Magnus while Lopan started slicing at the ankles of one with his sword. Hawk stepped protectively in front of me.

"No!" I shouted, unable to throw the ball of life I still held at Lucifer.

Lucifer didn't even look at him as he backhanded Hawk. The crack of Hawk's jaw reverberated in the cavern, and he was flung away, but not before his feet lashed out and he kicked Lucifer back. Weakened, Lucifer stumbled back before tripping and sprawling onto the ground twenty feet away from me.

I went to throw the ball of energy I held at him, but something swung out of the shadows behind me and bashed my hand. I cried out as the ball was driven straight into the ground. I gawked at my flopping hand as Onoskelis strolled out of the shadows with her sword resting against her shoulder.

"Niece," she greeted with a smile, and I realized she'd used the butt of her sword to break my hand.

Fire burst from my other palm, and I launched it at her, staggering her back. She planted her feet in the ground and bent over backward to avoid the next ball of fire I threw at her. Frustration warred to the forefront of my emotions, but I tamped it down.

If I lost control of my emotions now, I would lose. My toes curled into my boots as I sought out the life flowing through the rocks beneath me. Sparks flared across the tips of my fingers and the bones in my broken hand set back into place with an audible crack. The midnight blue light spreading up to my wrists drew Onoskelis's gaze. Wrath twisted her striking features, and when she lifted her sword, I knew she would chop my hand off.

I released the ball, aiming for her torso. She spun to the side, but not in time to completely avoid it. The ball sliced across her belly, spilling blood down her ivory skin. When she whirled back toward me, I braced myself and waved both my hands in a come-and-get-it gesture before giving her the finger.

She charged at me at the same time that I spotted Lucifer coming at me from the corner of my eye. I turned to avoid his rush, but it was too late. His good wing swung out and hit me in my chest. Before I could fight against him, he swept me backward and smashed me into the wall. The impact caused rocks to break free. They pelted my head and skin as they tumbled down the wall. Warm liquid trickled down my leg, and I realized that Lopan's rose had broken.

I wheezed as I tried to draw air past my bruised and possibly broken ribs, but my brutalized lungs remained uncooperative. Like a fly caught in the spider's web, I was helpless to fight them off as Lucifer and Onoskelis leaned closer to peer at me. I could barely look at the hideous destruction of Lucifer's face. I knew Kobal had inflicted that damage on him.

Where was Kobal? What had happened? He was still alive—I would feel it if he wasn't—but was he badly injured? The sounds of the others fighting the angels at the end of the tunnel drowned out the noise of what was happening in the cavern below.

Behind Lucifer, Hawk moaned and shifted. Onoskelis didn't look at him as she lunged to the side and sank her sword through his heart. "N… n… no!" I managed to get enough air into my lungs to gasp out.

Hawk jerked on the ground and clawed at the sword protruding from his chest. Onoskelis tore it free and lifted it up in preparation to slice his head from his shoulders. I lunged forward, only to be crushed back by Lucifer's wing. My fingers tore at the rock behind me as Hawk rolled to get away, but not in time to avoid taking a blow that cut halfway through his neck.

Blood spilled over Hawk's fingers as he scrambled to cover the wound. Air succeeded in rushing back into my lungs. I screeched in fury and tore at the rocks as sparks of energy flashed over my fingers and swirled toward my arms.

I may not be able to throw anything at Lucifer right now, but I'd launched Kobal across a room when he'd touched me while my body was thriving with energy. At the time, I hadn't meant to hurt Kobal, but I would love nothing more than to step over Lucifer's dead body.

"Bitch," Lucifer snarled.

Before I could draw on life enough to use my ability against him, he punched me in my temple. The world swayed as bells rang in my head. Blinking, I tried to retain consciousness, but as I grasped at it, he hit me again and the world went black.

CHAPTER NINETEEN

Corson

Swinging upward, grim satisfaction filled me as I sliced the angel from groin to ribs. His entrails and blood splashed over the ground as I effectively ensured he wouldn't be fucking anyone for a long time to come. The angel's startled eyes met mine; I grinned at him as I lifted my talons into the air and casually flicked his blood at him.

The black blood sprayed across the angel's face as he staggered back. His heel slipped over the edge, his momentum carrying him out of the tunnel before he could get his wings out.

Lopan and Magnus danced around the remaining angel as he swung his wings back and forth while stalking toward them. The two of them would have to hold him off as only River mattered right now.

My gaze went to her as Lucifer struck her. Her head lolled to the side, and blood streaked down from the broken skin at her temple. She tried to lift her head, but he hit her again and she went limp behind his wing. Rage filled me as I bounded toward them. Not only had he dared to hit my queen, but he'd also hurt my friend. I'd make him pay for that.

Hawk clawed at the floor as he tried to drag himself toward Lucifer. Blood coated his fingers and the floor. His head fell to the side to reveal part of his spine. Onoskelis lifted her sword to deliver the killing blow to Hawk at the same time that I launched onto Lucifer's back, knocking him into Onoskelis.

The tip of her sword hit the rock with a clatter, but I also heard the thick, bloody sound of more flesh rending. I didn't know if I'd thrown her off enough to prevent Hawk's demise, and I didn't have time to check.

I swiped my talons across the wing sticking awkwardly up from Lucifer's back, shredding it. He yelled as the blood spouting from his wing coated my face and the ceiling. Onoskelis spun toward me, her sword whistling as it sliced through the air.

I threw my other hand up to stop her from decapitating me. Sparks flew as my talons, made of a substance harder and thicker than bone, clashed against the blade of her weapon. A screech filled the air as she slid her sword over my talons before lifting it away.

She screamed and gripped the sword with both hands. When she lifted it over her head to slice me straight down the middle, I swung my hand forward. My talons pierced through the flesh and bone of her chest as she swung her sword down. The blade cut into my wrist, nearly slicing my hand off.

Lucifer reeled backward and flung me off him. I had to use my good hand to grip my nearly severed one as my talons were torn free of Onoskelis. Landing on my ass, I bounced across the rock before leaping to my feet. Onoskelis stalked toward me.

"Enough, Onoskelis, forget the pitiful demon. We have to get out of here," Lucifer spat. "We have her, and so we have him."

I knew the *him* Lucifer referred to was not me, but Kobal. As long as Lucifer possessed River, there wasn't anything Kobal wouldn't do to get her back. I lunged at him again, but he spun toward me and thrust River's limp form in front of him. My heart lurched when I nearly sank my talons into her chest before stopping myself in time. The ends of them cut into her shirt and scratched her skin as Lucifer edged her closer to me.

"Tsk, tsk, demon." The hideous remains of Lucifer's face twisted into what I assumed was a smirk. "You nearly killed your queen."

Lucifer had killed my father and, in a way, taken the life of my mother. After my father's death, she had been unable to face living without her Chosen. My entire life, I'd fought relentlessly by Kobal's side, willing to do whatever it took to see Lucifer die, and he now held the one weapon that could turn Kobal against the quest for his throne.

Not only that, but whatever Lucifer planned for River couldn't be good. Over my many years, there were few I'd truly considered a friend; River was one of them. Lucifer would abuse her, he would break her, and in breaking her, he would destroy Kobal. It would almost be best if I killed her now, but I couldn't do that to Kobal, or her.

"Let her go," I grated through my teeth as Lucifer continued to use River's body to push me backward.

Behind me, Magnus released a shout that fell further away as it went on, and I realized he'd been knocked over the edge. Lopan would be little use against the remaining angel, and Hawk had collapsed onto the floor in a growing pool of his blood. I had no idea if he was demon enough yet to survive that amount of damage, or if his head was still attached at all.

"I think I'm going to keep her," Lucifer replied and smirked at me. "She is *my* child after all."

River's head drooped forward. I lowered my hand, afraid something would happen that would cause me to run her through. Glancing behind me, I saw the other angel waiting at the end of the tunnel, grinning at me. Lopan was nowhere to be seen.

I calculated every move the angels made as I tried to plot a way out of this, with River. When Kobal sent me after her during the gargoyle attack, he made it my duty to protect her, and I would not fail in that duty now. Planting my feet, I leapt forward and grabbed for her arms at the same time as her head lifted.

Her eyes had become the pale violet color they turned when a vision took her over, and I realized she didn't see me. Then, color flooded back into her eyes.

"Run!" she breathed when she focused on me. "Corson, *run*!"

Onoskelis hammered the butt of her sword into River's temple, causing her to go limp again. The shadows behind Lucifer shifted and three more angels emerged. Running from danger was not something I did. I attacked it head-on, but I also didn't have a death wish. Six to one odds didn't work in my favor. I couldn't get her away from Lucifer while he continued to use her as a shield, and I couldn't free her from him if I was dead.

I still might have a shot of getting her back, if I could stop myself from plummeting out of here as the others had.

Mind made up, I turned and raced toward the angel blocking the end of the tunnel. Lowering my shoulder, I slammed into him, propelling us both toward the edge. I buried the talons on my good hand into the vulnerable flesh of his stomach. Lifting him, I carried him back three feet as his hands pounded against my bare shoulders. Arriving at the end of the tunnel, I flung him away from me and into the open.

Leaping out behind him, my feet kicked through the air as I spun to the side and threw myself toward the wall. The talons on my good hand sought to get some purchase as I slid down the wall. Stones tore away as the rough surface abraded my chest and my feet scrambled to dig in somewhere on the wall.

Finally, my talons found purchase on a shelf. I dangled over open air for a moment before I lifted my feet and set them on a rocky outcropping. I took a breath and glanced at the tunnel ten feet above my head before focusing on my wounded hand. The bleeding had stopped, muscle was repairing itself, but it remained almost useless. It didn't matter, I could do this without it.

Bracing my feet against the wall, I started climbing by using my legs and one hand. I heard Lucifer and the others approaching the tunnel entrance as I became even with it. Moving faster, I scurried past the opening and rose above it. Settling myself on a ledge, I perched over the opening in preparation of leaping onto Lucifer's back when he exited.

If I could tear River away from him, I could keep her sheltered from most of the impact when we hit the ground. It wasn't the most solid of plans, but it was better than nothing.

A disturbance in the air snapped my head up seconds before a manticore descended on me. I'd been so focused on getting River that I hadn't heard its approach. I leaned to the side, but it was too late. Its stinger pierced through my back and dug in until I felt the tip of it scraping against my spine.

The second I felt the burn of its paralyzing juice enter my body, my limbs went rigid and my heart stuttered a beat. The manticore's tail remained buried in my back as it lifted me off the wall.

CHAPTER TWENTY

Kobal

I was halfway up the wall, my claws around a rock and my feet braced to make the leap to a higher level when an angel flew backward out of the entrance above. He spiraled toward the ground before flipping over and righting himself on the currents of air. Less than a minute before the angel fell out, Lopan and Magnus had toppled out of the tunnel. I'd heard the breaking of their bones when they hit the bottom, but they would survive.

Corson leapt out of the tunnel and swung so that he skidded down the surface before his talons caught on a rock. Scrambling up the wall, Corson settled on a ledge above the tunnel entrance just as a manticore sprang out of an opening, fifteen feet above him.

"Corson!"

My shout of warning came too late as the manticore's stinger pierced through him. Corson jerked before going still. I scaled the wall faster. Bits and pieces of stone gave way beneath me and knocked my grip loose in some places, but I ignored the pain in my still healing body as I climbed.

River. I had to get to her. If the others had fallen out, and Corson leapt out…

Whatever was happening up there was far from good, but I couldn't think on it now. I could only focus on reaching her. Then I would figure out how to get Corson back.

Two more angels appeared at the entrance and spread their wings. It took me a second to realize they held Lucifer's battered body between them as they took flight. They circled over the cavern before rising higher into the air.

Then, another angel appeared. *Onoskelis*, I realized with a sneer as she unfurled her wings. Over the years, she'd swayed numerous male demons to Lucifer's side with her near siren ways. She looked down at me, a smiling curving her mouth.

I was only fifteen feet away from her when part of the wall gave way beneath my hand, causing me to lose my hold. I scrambled to find purchase as I fell, but the rocks I clutched at continued to break away. Pulling my arm back, I rammed my fist through the stone to stop my plunge to the bottom. My healing wounds from the sword broke open, and fresh blood trickled down my sides as I prepared to climb again.

"Don't fret, Kobal. I'll make sure my niece is well taken care of!" Onoskelis called down in her husky voice.

Bending, Onoskelis lifted something off the ground and draped it over her shoulder. I caught a glimpse of River's limp form before Onoskelis spread her wings and soared over the cavern.

"No!" I bellowed as she rose higher to alight on another tunnel entrance further up.

Onoskelis blew me a kiss before slipping away. My markings shifted as they ebbed and flowed with the thundering pulse of my heart. Phenex and Crux begged to be set free, but I kept them leashed.

They have River.

My breath labored in and out of me as my muscles swelled with their need for destruction. I took a minute to steady the rage battering me. If I allowed it to take control of me, there would be no stopping my rampage. Before River, I never would have hesitated before giving into my murderous impulses, but I knew it wouldn't do River any good if I lost control now and tore Hell apart.

No matter what it takes, I will get her back. But first I had to get off this wall, get Corson back, and reorganize everyone. Then, I would hunt Lucifer through every corner of Hell. And if he took her out of here, I would hunt him all over Earth if that was what it took to get her back.

The manticore spread its wings and leapt off the wall with Corson curled over its back. Hawk came into view as he staggered to a stop at the end of the tunnel. Blood coated his clothes, and there was a hole in his shirt over his heart. His hand pressed against the wound oozing blood from the side of his neck. When the manticore flew into view before him, his hand fell away.

Hawk took a few steps back before running forward and flinging himself onto the manticore's back. He wrapped his arm around Corson's waist as he twisted to the side, wrenching the stinger from Corson. A choked cry echoed through the cavern as they rolled across the manticore's back before falling off the side.

Keeping my fist buried in the wall, I shoved the rest of my body off it and snagged Hawk's arm when he plunged past me. I nearly wrenched Corson from his grasp when I jerked him toward the wall. Hawk grunted when he crashed against the rocks and his hold on Corson loosened further. Corson fell a foot before Hawk caught him under the armpit.

"Ahhhh," Corson managed to get out.

The manticore screeched and turned back toward us, determined to reclaim the meal Hawk had stolen from it. Hawk twisted in my hold and managed to get his fingers around a rock. He shifted his grip on Corson and braced his feet on the wall.

"Where's River?" Hawk demanded.

My lips skimmed back to bare my fangs at the reminder of exactly where she was right now, and *who* she was with. Hawk's eyes widened on me and he leaned back. I released my hold on him before I accidentally sliced his arm from his body.

"Climb down with him and I'll hold this thing off," I ordered gruffly.

"I'm not sure I can," Hawk muttered as Corson slid further down and made another squawking sound.

The manticore flattened its wings against its back and dove toward us. Its tail pointed straight at me. "Prick!" I spat.

With my left wrist still in the wall and my left foot perched on a stone, I let go with my other hand and foot and swung out to avoid the poisonous tail. The tail crashed into the rock beside me, creating a crater where there had been none.

Before the manticore could pull its stinger free, I brought my elbow down on its tail, snapping the cartilage and causing the manticore to screech. I sliced my claws across the tail in three hard swipes, severing it. The manticore flew backward, flapping at the air as blood poured from it. Reaching down, I slid my arm under Corson's armpit and pulled him from Hawk's grasp.

"Get down," I hissed at Hawk as the manticore flew into a tunnel.

Heaving Corson onto my shoulder, I descended to the cavern.

Kobal

I felt the awe of those spreading out around me as they gawked at the massive throne room. *None* of us had ever seen it before, and many had probably believed they never would. It had been six thousand years since any follower of the varcolac walked freely through here.

Just months ago, standing in this place had been my entire goal for all my fifteen hundred and sixty-two years of existence. At the end of the room sat my throne, empty and mine for the taking. Lucifer was still alive, but weakened, his numbers drastically lessened, and he'd been removed from this place of power. It was far more than many of my ancestors had achieved.

Only five hundred feet separated me from my throne sitting on a raised dais at the end of the room, but it didn't matter. Without River, it meant nothing.

The multi-colored stones before me created a walkway toward the dais. As I stood at the head of the walkway, the stones gradually changed color. The ones closest to me became pink in hue, while the ones in the middle shifted to a yellow, and further on they became orange, before turning a brilliant red near the throne. Then they rotated so that the red was before me and the other colors moved closer to the throne.

Overhead, the quartz rocks lining the arched ceiling danced with the colors of the pathway. Beside the pathway, the solid black rock of the floor emphasized the shifting color pattern and the way to my seat.

River would love to see this.

My claws bit into my palms until my blood ran freely across the stone. The colors stopped switching and became a solid red all the way to the dais.

Beside me, Morax glanced down at the blood. "We will get our queen back," he murmured.

"Contact Shax and find out if Lucifer has left Hell," I commanded.

Stepping onto the pathway, I stalked toward the end of the room. While I walked, I lifted my hand to free Crux and Phenex from me. Claiming my throne may mean little to me right now, but they deserved to see the place they had also been denied their entire lives.

CHAPTER TWENTY-ONE

Kobal

The two hounds burst from my palm and hit the ground. They stopped before me. Their haunches lifted as their heads lowered and they sniffed at the air before surveying the room. Rising, they released a howl that reverberated off the stones.

They bounded forward to cover the distance between them and the throne in mere seconds. Leaping onto the stage, they prowled around the throne before sitting beside it, one on each side. Their amber eyes and sleek black coats reflected the color of the walkway as they sat proudly on the dais.

The symbols etched onto every inch of the black rock walls shifted with my steps. The vibrant thrum of power beneath my feet made me realize exactly what this room and that throne were… an extension of the Fires of Creation and the oracle. It was a source of power Lucifer had denied my ancestors, and me, when he'd invaded Hell.

Stopping before the dais, I stared at the black throne directly before me. It stood six feet high and was at least three feet wide. At the top of the throne, two howling hellhounds rose out of the sides to frame the arch in the center. Each of the armrests had the intricately wrought head of a hellhound on the ends of them. Ancient symbols covered the surface of the throne, many of them matched the symbols on me.

Everything about it beckoned for me to claim it.

More blood dripped from my palms as I gazed at it, but no matter how much it called to me, I didn't move any closer.

Toward the back of the dais, hidden within the shadows, I spotted a throne nearly identical to mine. The only difference between them was that the one in the shadows was smaller than the one before me. Only two varcolacs before me had found their Chosen, but I knew the smaller throne was for the varcolac's Chosen. It was River's throne.

I would not sit on mine until she sat on hers.

Turning away from the dais, I faced the demons who spread further out in the room. The colors of the pathway started shifting again, the lights from it danced over the faces of those gathered within.

I strode back down the walkway to where Corson, Magnus, and Hawk slumped against the wall near the entry. Calah, Bale, Verin, and Morax stood near them. Hawk was healing slower than the other two, but his neck would be fully repaired by tomorrow. Until then, I would cauterize the wound to stop the bleeding.

Lopan sat on the floor on the other side of the entry with his head bowed. The four other leporcháins gathered protectively around him while he healed his broken bones. Lix and the remaining skelleins stood to each side of the entry, their swords before their faces, and their heads bowed in reverence.

As I approached, Lix lowered his sword and settled the tip of it against the floor. "Mah rhála, we will get the World Walker back," he said with determination.

More blood dripped from my hands as my claws grazed bone. What would Lucifer do to her before then? He wouldn't kill her, that much I knew, but what were his plans for her? Did he truly believe she could somehow get him back into Heaven?

I shook the questions off. I didn't have the answers for them or the time it took to ponder them. "Did you get in contact with Shax?" I demanded of Morax.

"Yes," Morax replied. "He reported that no one has left Hell since the Erinyes broke out."

"Lucifer could have escaped out of the other gateway and entered Earth on the other side of the planet," Bale said.

"He could have," I agreed. I had more troops established around the gateway that had opened in Hungary at the same time the one in Kansas opened. "Can you communicate with someone there?" I asked Morax.

"I need the name of someone at that gateway," Morax replied.

"Bettle is there," Lix said. "You can speak with her."

"Bettle is a skellein?" Morax inquired.

"Yes," Lix answered.

Morax stared at him and didn't blink for a full minute. "She says there have been escapees from the seals, but no angels. I will remain in contact with her in case that changes."

"Lucifer is still in Hell," I said. "Stay in contact with Shax too."

"I will," Morax said.

"Bring me the captives," I ordered.

Morax, Calah, Verin, and Bale turned and walked out of the entry-way. They followed the stones down the three-hundred-foot-long stream of fire leading to the waterfall and the demons I'd left on guard there.

On this end of it, the stream stopped at the entry way and dipped beneath the rocks we stood on. I suspected it flowed down to the Fires of Creation and the Oracle.

Behind me, Phenex and Crux's claws clicked across the floor as they approached. They rubbed my hands when they settled by my sides. Their brethren spread out to stand beside them.

The others returned with two of Lucifer's followers held between them. The lower-level craetons had all been slaughtered, as had most of the upper-levels and escapees from the seals that we'd caught. These two upper-level demons were the only survivors. That would not last.

Both captives hung limply in the hands holding them, their heads bowed as they were dragged forward. One of them finally lifted his head. His eyes went from me to the chamber beyond and his jaw dropped. Strangled sounds escaped him as he tried to get his feet under him to support his weight.

The demon beside him lifted his head, but unlike his fellow traitor, he sagged further as he gawked at the chamber.

"What... I don't understand... *What*?" the one who kept trying to stand, and failing, stammered out.

I seized his chin and jerked his head toward me. He blinked rapidly at me while his tail thudded against the ground in a matching rhythm. His claws extended, but Bale and Calah held him so that he wouldn't be able to swing at anyone.

"Where would Lucifer take her?" My nails bit through his flesh until they scraped against bone and his blood spilled free.

"We... we... were wrong. This..." His eyes spun in his head as he gazed around the room. "We chose the wrong side."

This last sentence was uttered with a sense of doom. His shoulders fell and he went limp in Bale and Calah's hold.

"Yes, you did," I snarled. "Now, where would Lucifer take her?"

"I don't know."

The hounds echoed the ferocious sound I emitted as they crept closer. Releasing him, I swung my arm up to bury my claws under the demon's chin. Bone broke with a crack and the wet sound of sinew tearing filled the room as I tore his head from his shoulders. My shoulders heaved, blood dripped onto the floor as I took a minute to steady myself. I hadn't intended to kill him before learning everything he knew, but I hadn't been able to stop myself. No matter what happened, I could not lose control again.

Stalking over to the other demon, I kept his friend's head in hand as I stopped before him. The demon barely glanced at the head or his cohort's body when Calah and Bale released it. Verin and Morax tightened their hold on the still alive demon's arms. His gaze fell briefly to the head I held before looking to me. His eyes ran over the markings on my body, then the light of the pathway, and finally the symbols on the walls.

"We didn't know," the demon murmured. His red skin deepened in hue when he looked to me again.

"Didn't know what?" I demanded.

"How wrong we were." His white eyes closed. "I've been here, in this room, once before. It was nothing like this. Only darkness resided in here then, only darkness ruled… it all. The symbols couldn't be seen. The stones were all black." Opening his eyes, his resigned gaze met mine once more. "You *are* the rightful ruler."

"Nah ssshhhit." Corson's words came out slurred from the lingering effects of the manticore poison.

"Tell me where he took her, and I will make your death as merciful as your friend's. Otherwise, I will cut you apart piece by *tiny* piece. I will feed each of those pieces to the hounds while you regenerate, and then I'll start all over again," I promised.

"He was not lying, my lord," the craeton replied. "We do not know where Lucifer would have taken her, or what he plans for her."

When I retracted my claws, the head fell from my hand and thudded against the floor. The craeton bowed his head as I leaned closer to him. "Where do you *think* he would take her?"

"I don't know. We weren't exactly part of the inner circle. That is reserved for the angels alone. Sometimes, I think *they* don't even know what he plans."

The craeton spoke the truth, I knew it. No matter how badly I wanted to make him suffer for his betrayal by cutting him into little pieces, I didn't have time for it. If Lucifer hadn't left Hell with River, I could think of only one place he would take her. However, if I was wrong, we would be far from here, and the gateway, should he try to reclaim the throne or decide to flee Hell.

I glanced at the hounds behind me as I came to my decision. "Let the hounds have him."

"Wait…" The demon started to sputter. "I… no… I…" His protests turned into a scream as Verin and Morax released him and the hounds pounced on him. His screams ended when Crux tore his head from his body and tossed it to Phenex who gulped it down.

I turned to face the rest of the demons gathered within the throne room. "Half the troops will remain here to keep watch for Lucifer's return. Morax, you will stay with them to let me know if Lucifer returns. The hounds will search through the tunnels and chambers of Hell for her. The rest of the demons will come with me."

"Where?" Bale asked.

"We'll be returning to the seals."

CHAPTER TWENTY-TWO

River

My head pounded like someone wearing boots jumped up and down on it, but the pounding was nothing compared to the chill permeating my bones. My teeth chattered and goose bumps covered my skin. My eyes were frozen shut. I attempted to huddle deeper into myself for warmth, but that small movement made it feel as if fissures erupted over my bones.

I tried to recall what had happened, where I was, but all I felt was the unending frost and the agony. A single tear slid free and froze almost instantly on my cheek.

"Someone is finally awake," a voice murmured, and a finger brushed the tear away.

My scream caught in my throat as pins and needles fired across my skin where the finger touched. I would have welcomed fifty more stomping boots over this sensation.

"Why won't she open her eyes?" a female voice demanded.

"Because, dear Onoskelis, she is in pain," another voice purred.

"Nothing to be done about that," the first replied. My head stopped pounding long enough for me to realize Lucifer was the first speaker.

Onoskelis had been the angel who tried to kill Hawk, or maybe she had succeeded in killing him. I hurt too badly to fully grasp the memories tumbling through my mind.

I didn't know how it was possible to be this cold in Hell. I wouldn't be surprised to open my eyes and find out we'd left Hell and they'd taken me to Antarctica where they'd placed me naked in the middle of an iceberg.

If I wasn't in Hell anymore, how would I get away from them if they had taken me somewhere so remote that only a winged creature could make it there?

The way I felt now, it was impossible to draw on either fire or life to fight them off. If they'd removed me from Hell, and somehow stripped me of all my abilities, how would Kobal find me if I couldn't reach out to him in a dream?

Breathe. Stay calm and think. Learn your surroundings.

Still unable to open my eyes, I picked up details about my environment from my other senses. The ground was hard and freezing, or was the freezing just me? Either way, it was hard and it was also smooth. On the air, I scented power, but also the coppery tang of blood and the stench of decay.

Would Antarctica smell like death? I had always pictured it smelling like crisp snow, but what did I know? Maybe penguins smelled as bad as they looked cute. I didn't think that was the answer as beneath my fingers I tried to draw life from my surroundings, but no spark came.

Antarctica may be the land of ice, but it still teemed with life. The world felt as dead to me as I felt cold.

Panic crushed my shallow breaths from my lungs. Had Lucifer somehow managed to sever my tie to life? Even as I considered it, I knew I was wrong. I was frozen and miserable, but there would be something worse inside of me if my angelic connection to life had broken. There would be an emptiness so complete that I would be more like him than me.

Then what is going on?

I had to open my eyes to discover the answer to that. Bracing myself, I somehow managed to pull my lids apart enough to see a sliver of my surroundings. The floor before me was silver with maroon streaking across it. Something black twisted around me, blocking most of my view. The black moved too fast to make out what it was.

"Aw, there she is." Lucifer's face appeared before mine. His cheek rested on the floor so that we were eye level with each other when he grinned at me. His flesh no longer fell off him, but puckered scars marred his face, and his skin color resembled a lobster fresh from the pot.

The pinky of his hand nearly touched my nose as he gazed at me and batted the thick lashes of his rejuvenated eyelids. This close, I could see the insanity looming within the onyx eyes only inches from mine.

This fallen angel, the reason for my existence and my powers, was nuttier than squirrel shit.

He was also lethal, malicious, and cunning. And he was more than willing to do anything to me to get what he wanted. But what did he want from me? Back into Heaven? Had he brought me somewhere that would make that possible?

"I love your eyes, daughter," he said, his smile growing. "Mine were once the same shade."

He brushed his fingers over my cheek, causing me to flinch. I tried and failed to get my body to move away from him.

"There's nothing to be done for the pain, for now, but soon it will be eased." His fingers caressing my cheek caused another icy tear to slide free. "My child."

"N-not your ch-child," I managed to get out between my chattering teeth. They'd become so icy that I was certain they would break out of my head.

He grinned at me and pushed one of his fingers into my cheek until I cried out. He scratched his nail across my skin. Tears burned my eyes, but I refused to shed any more of them, not for this monster.

"More like me than you realize," he replied, and grinned at me when he pulled his hand away. He slapped his palm against the floor and rose so fast that I barely saw him move until his toes touched my nose. "Let's get her ready."

His hands seized me under my armpits and lifted me up. I couldn't stop from screaming when my bones shattered into pieces. Their shards slipped into my bloodstream, sliced through my veins, and pounded toward my heart, which beat so fast I was certain it would tear out of my chest. Whether my bones really shattered or not, I couldn't tell, but it felt like it. My screaming stopped when unconsciousness rushed up to drag me into its depths.

River

When I woke again, it was to the same cold, but at least my veins didn't feel as if they were shredding with every heartbeat, and I was certain my bones weren't in pieces. My bond with Kobal made me stronger and caused me to heal faster, but I could never repair every bone in my body, or survive the pieces of them tearing through my veins.

Cracking my eyes open, I watched as my breath plumed out of me. Lucifer stood before me, his face completely healed except for a puckered area on his chin and another running across his forehead.

"Your hair… gr-grew back," I chattered, unsure why that was the first thought that crossed my mind, but at least I grasped my memories now. I recalled what Kobal had done to him as I prayed for Hawk and the others to still be alive.

Lucifer smiled at me as he clasped my wrist. I winced, but I couldn't do anything to stop him from pulling it upward. I fought against the blackness trying to drag me under again. I had to stay awake. I had to know what he planned and where I was.

"Angels are beautiful creatures, my daughter. Imperfections are not allowed. Unlike the filthy demons you've been associating with and rutting with."

"I bet the demons fuck better though," I replied. I should have just kept my mouth shut, but I *despised* this creature before me, and I wanted to piss him off, even if it meant he tortured me more. Maybe he'd kill me before he could do whatever he planned. Better death than being Lucifer's puppet.

"That's no way to speak to your father."

Before I knew what he intended, he hammered something through my palm. I jerked and screamed as my flesh and bones were pierced. Blood seeped out of the wound, briefly warming me before it froze against my skin. I bit my lip to hold back another cry. My screams were probably music to his ears.

When I tried to move my other hand, I realized it also had something driven through it as it hung down by my side. *Am I standing*?

I couldn't tell. I couldn't see behind him as a wall of black swirled there.

Wraiths!

My heart sank as understanding hit me. The cold, the lack of being able to draw on anything, it was because he had surrounded me with wraiths. And not hundreds of them, *thousands* swirled around us.

This had never been a good situation, but I sensed something very, *very* bad looming. Something that would help him, and I was the key to it.

Yes, death was definitely preferable at this point. I couldn't be the cause of this monster becoming stronger. Couldn't be the cause of more deaths if he succeeded in whatever plot churned within his sick head.

I focused on him again. "What are you doing, Lucifer?"

His eyes sparked with malice over my use of his angelic name, but he didn't rise to my bait. "Setting the world free, daughter."

CHAPTER TWENTY-THREE

River

Behind Lucifer, angels walked through the wall of wraiths. Onoskelis moved to Lucifer's right while Caim stepped to his left. Caim's rainbow-kissed eyes held mine, but his face remained blank. Onoskelis rested her sword against her shoulder as she smirked at me.

"She reminds me of you, Satan," Onoskelis said.

Visions of clawing her eyes out danced through my head.

"She does," he agreed as he stepped back to look at me. "So young and naïve, so full of love." He chuckled. "There comes a time when we all learn that love is a farce."

"You might want to rethink this course, brother," Caim said in a low voice. "This could do far more damage than you expect."

Lucifer shrugged. "So be it."

"This could kill her."

"In all the thousands of years of our children walking Earth, none have been as strong as her. She will survive this."

"You cannot be certain."

Lucifer whirled and stalked toward him. Caim took a step back, his head bowing as Lucifer's wings swung out. The silver-tipped points clicked against the ground on either side of Caim. Fury etched Lucifer's features as he leaned toward Caim, who turned his head away.

"Why are you being so difficult about this?" Lucifer spat.

"I am not being difficult, brother." Caim didn't meet Lucifer's eyes as he spoke. "I am simply pointing out the truth. We could take her to Earth now. She may be able to get you back into Heaven, but if you do this, you could destroy her and forever end your chances of such a thing."

Did Caim say that because he had turned against Lucifer and was trying to save me from whatever Lucifer planned? Or did Caim want to return to Heaven too and believed I could help him? Maybe it was both.

"Perhaps, but she's not getting me back into Heaven," Lucifer said.

Caim chanced a glance at Lucifer before bowing his head again. His actions reminded me of a beaten animal, broken down by its master, but I knew this animal might still have some bite, or at least some nibbling left in him.

"I see," Caim murmured.

"Do you?" Lucifer inquired as he leaned closer. Caim didn't say another word. Lucifer pulled his wings back and tucked them away. "At least she's not getting me into Heaven without an army behind me. There are troops on the surface now, waiting for me, but we all know the best ones remain locked away. The ones, I *really* want."

My stomach sank and an awful suspicion grew in the back of my mind as I tried and failed to take in more of my surroundings. I didn't have the strength to turn my head to look behind me, and the wraiths blocked my view of everything else. Lucifer clasped his hands behind his back as he strolled toward me once more with an odd little skip to his step.

"And if she can open a gateway into Heaven…" His head tilted back as his voice trailed off. He looked to me again. "I know how I opened the gateway into Hell; I might be able to use you to get me back into Heaven. Oh, the looks on those bastards' faces when they see me again."

He laughed as he clapped his hands. "That is, of course, before my army and I destroy them all."

"You're insane!" I blurted before I could stop myself.

"Tsk, tsk, that's not very nice. You should show more respect to those who are better than you. To those you should be bowing before, and believe me, when this is all over, child or not, I will have you begging for mercy. I will make you repent for everything you have said or done, or I will cut out your tongue and feed it to you."

I pressed my lips together when he squeezed my cheeks. Two of him swam before my eyes as starbursts erupted across my brain. Lucifer's power washed over me before a wraith brushed against my skin, cutting off the flow. It was then that I realized the malevolent spirits also churned in a thick wave behind me. They stopped me from drawing power from what I feared was a seal behind my back.

"Demons are lower than us, and humans are even *lower*. You may not be entirely either one of them, but you're no better than refuse beneath my feet," he said as his fingers bit into my skin.

"You would know… about refuse," I panted out.

He had to kill me, *he had to*. I couldn't let him use me to open more seals. I didn't know if he could use me for such a thing, but I wasn't willing to take the chance he could. I would not be what my father had been for him: a tool to destroy everything and everyone I loved.

"The angels threw you out of Heaven after all. *The* Morning Star tossed aside like garbage. The supposedly favored son sentenced to death amongst *humans*!"

Caim stared at me as if I'd lost my mind. Perhaps I had; my life hadn't exactly been sanity inducing lately. Onoskelis stepped toward us, her sword lifting off her shoulder as murder burned within her eyes. Lucifer gazed at me like I was a specimen he was about to pick apart.

Get it over with and kill me!

"You turned out to be nothing to them, Lucifer, and you're still nothing." The wraiths crowded closer as my heart jackhammered with every word I spoke. "Kobal is superior to you in every way, and you know it!"

Instead of plucking me apart, Lucifer chuckled. He brushed the backs of his fingers across my cheek as he stepped closer to me. "You are *so* much like me. I see what you're trying to do, but I'm not going to kill you. Despite Caim's concerns, I will not allow you to die during this. You're far too precious to me for that."

He patted my cheek. "Do you know what makes you my most precious acquisition, daughter?"

I tried to keep my mouth shut, to not give in and ask him. As he continued to stroke my face, I found myself unable to resist questioning him, if it would just make him *stop* touching me. "What?"

He slid his hand behind my head. His fingers tangled in my hair and gave it a sharp tug. Pain exploded through my scalp, and a strangled cry escaped before I locked my teeth down on my tongue. Blood flooded my mouth, but I kept my tongue between my teeth so as not to give him the satisfaction of hearing me scream again.

"Because of you, I now have *him*," he replied and pointed at the black mass encompassing us.

The ends of the wraiths flapped in the breeze they created as they parted to form a perfect ball around me and Lucifer. The break in them revealed Kobal standing at the entrance to the last broken seal. The amber of his eyes burned so brightly that I swore I felt the heat of them against my skin.

"No, no, no," I moaned and Lucifer placed his palm on my forehead, pushing me back into the wraiths. I jerked against the icy sensation of them.

Kobal bared his lethal fangs. "Get your hands off her."

"Kobal... please... go back," I managed to stammer through my chattering teeth.

Instead of listening to me, Kobal stalked forward with Phenex and Crux flanking his sides. He paid no attention to the angels, Hell creatures, and lower-level demons gathered within the broken seal. He seemed not to care that he was vastly outnumbered and surrounded by his enemies. Every inch of him exuded murder, and I knew he would make the deaths of those present a gruesome experience. I gulped.

Finally tearing my gaze away from Kobal, I spotted the palitons gathered at the entrance of the broken seal, but they didn't come any closer. Joy shot through me when I saw Corson and Hawk standing at the front of the group. Burn marks marred Hawk's neck and blood seeped from a wound that I now realized had been cauterized.

My joy was short-lived as Lucifer yanked my hair back. Every muscle in Kobal's body tensed to leap forward.

Lucifer lifted his index finger and waved it back and forth in the air. "Uh-ah," he scolded as his other hand wrapped around my throat. "I'd stay where you are if I were you."

"You're not going to kill her," Kobal growled.

"No, I'm not," Lucifer replied. "But a demon cannot stand to see their Chosen tortured, can they, Kobal?"

I shrank back and bit my tongue again when half a dozen wraiths ran their bodies over my skin. *Do not cry!* I kept telling myself this, but when more of them moved over my frosted skin, a tear slid free.

Kobal froze.

"Good boy," Lucifer said.

The sound Kobal released made the angels and demons closest to him step away. Only Lucifer remained unfazed by the power swelling out of Kobal and pulsating the air around him.

"She is more angel than anything," Lucifer murmured. "It's why the wraiths hurt her so badly, and it is *so* agonizing for the poor mortal. If she didn't have *my* DNA in her, the pain of the wraiths would most likely kill her."

Kobal's gaze slid from Lucifer to me. Anguish twisted his features as he took another step forward.

"Don't." Lucifer clamped down on my throat. "Unless you want to hear her scream like the banshees, I'd stay where you are, Kobal."

"This is between the two of us," Kobal said. "Leave her out of it."

"It stopped being between the two of us when you took my daughter as your Chosen," Lucifer replied.

"I'll die before I let you do this to her."

Lucifer laughed and released my hair to slap his hand off his knee. "You're making the mistake of thinking I'll allow you to be killed, but I won't. You see, if you're dead, then a new varcolac will rise. One who may be stronger than you, and that varcolac won't care if she lives or dies. Under normal circumstances, you would sacrifice yourself for her, but you won't do that now, not if it means the one who rises from your ashes will kill her to stop me."

My eyes slid to Lucifer as he turned back to me. "Do you see the *gifts* you have brought me, daughter? Not only are you going to give me an army, but you have also made it so the only creature capable of stopping that army obeys *me*. What lies behind these seals may despise Kobal for what he is, but they won't destroy him if he fights on my side. He will be one of the strongest generals in my army, and you will be his motivation to be a good hound. And maybe one day, I'll allow you two to be together again, if he's a well-behaved general."

"I'll kill myself first," I whispered.

Lucifer giggled, actually *giggled* as he leaned closer to me. "I would never allow *that* to happen either."

"I'd rather we were both dead before allowing you to do this," Kobal said.

"You say that, but…" Lucifer's hand tightened on my neck, and he lifted me as far off the ground as my pinned hands allowed him to. I gasped for breath as my heels kicked against the seal. Kobal lunged forward, Phenex and Crux leaping into movement beside him. "I'll tear her throat out if you don't stop *now*!"

Kobal skidded to a halt when blood trickled down the sides of my neck and my wheezing increased. His chest rose and fell with his rapid inhalations. His eyes reflected the distress twisting within him as he tried to decide what to do. The best option was to kill me, but Kobal would never be able to do it, and he'd never stand by and watch it happen.

"You will do anything for your Chosen," Lucifer said as he set me on the ground and eased his grasp.

I choked in heaping gulps of air as terror unlike anything I'd ever known spread throughout my belly. I wasn't frightened for me, but for Kobal and everyone else here.

"Love bites you in the ass no matter who you are," Lucifer sighed.

Lifting my head, I met Kobal's eyes. "Kill me," I rasped out.

"So brave, this one!" Lucifer clapped me on the chest with enough force to knock whatever air I'd managed to inhale back out of me. "She thinks you have a choice in this, but you're not programmed that way, are you, Kobal? If she wasn't involved in this, you would sacrifice yourself for all those creatures standing behind you now. The pathetic thing is that you don't realize just how far beneath you those creatures are, but that's a conversation for another day."

Lucifer waved his hand in front of his face as if he were brushing his words aside before leaning so close to me that his lips rested against my ear. "Do you want to know a secret, daughter?"

I refused to acknowledge him as I kept my gaze on Kobal and tried to convey every ounce of love I had for him.

"Would you like to know why I never attempted to stop you from trying to close the gateway?" Despite my resolution not to look at Lucifer, my head turned toward him when he asked this and our eyes locked. "I'll tell you, and *only* you, the secret."

CHAPTER TWENTY-FOUR

Kobal

I remained where I was as River's eyes widened on Lucifer. I couldn't hear what he said to her, but whatever it was caused her blue lips to tremble. The small veins beneath the surface of her flesh were visible as her teeth chattered. Pain radiated from her, yet fire had burned in her eyes when she told me to kill her.

She was *my* Chosen. Mine to love and protect, and she was asking to die because I had failed to keep her safe.

Lucifer's mouth twisted into a cruel smile as he kissed her cheek. I lunged forward. I couldn't kill her; I knew that as well as I knew that the Fires of Creation had forged me. However, I would not let him continue to torment her.

I'd already sent a message to Morax, alerting him to where we were and telling him to bring the rest of our troops here. Through our bond, the hounds would feel the bloodlust within me, would feel the battle, and they would come. If I kept Lucifer distracted, I could get River away from him when the others arrived.

Angels burst into motion as they came at me. Behind me, a battle cry erupted and the clash of steel rang against steel as the two sides attacked each other once more. Before I could reach River and Lucifer, Caim turned and planted himself in front of me. His wings unfurled and he swung one at me. The lethal tip sliced across my cheek, spilling blood.

So much for switching sides. For his lies, I'd make him pay almost as much as Lucifer when this was done. Lowering my shoulder, I crashed into his chest. His wings curled around me as his arms embraced me.

"Go for him. I will get her," Caim's words barely pierced through my bloodlust as I dug my claws into his back.

When they did register, they distracted me enough that Caim swung an uppercut into my jaw. The blow staggered me back and knocked my hold on him loose. Caim swept a wing at me, shoving me further away from him.

"Do not kill him!" Lucifer shouted. "I will tame the hound!"

Caim folded his wings behind his back; his chin rose as he held my gaze. The angels smirked as they closed in on us, and some of them took flight to orbit overhead. Phenex and Crux circled my legs, snarling as they kept the angels away, but they wouldn't hold the winged pricks off for long.

Outside the ring of angels, the clash of steel against steel, the cries of the dying, and the snarls of the hounds resonated from the two, battling factions.

"More are coming, my lord!" an angel called from above, and I realized Morax and the others had arrived.

Rushing forward, I shoved angels out of my way as they tried to block me from River. I didn't have the time to engage them in a fight—something Phenex and Crux understood as they leapt forward to drive more angels back, but they didn't go in for the kill.

A wing hit me in the back, nearly knocking me to the floor as River tried to rip herself free. Lucifer placed his hand on her chest and pushed her more forcefully against the seal. Her scream resonated within me until her suffering became my own.

Nothing should have been able to pierce the seal, yet the spikes Lucifer had driven into her hands were buried in it.

Her blood is affecting the seal, I realized as it dripped down her arm. Against the unnatural paleness of her skin, the vibrant red stood out starkly.

"Leave us!" Lucifer barked.

The wraiths stopped circling and rushed upward as one powerful unit. They vanished through the ceiling a hundred feet overhead.

I tore the arm off an angel as I thrust her out of my way and used the bloody stump to bash in the head of another. The spikes on their wings sliced at me, flaying open my back and slicing across my chest, but I barely felt it as I remained focused on one thing: getting to River.

As more blood seeped from her, the ground beneath my feet vibrated before lurching violently and knocking me back a step. Around me, the angels scrambled away from the seal. Their frantic movements opened a pathway between me and River just as a crack spread through the seal behind River.

The crack lanced from her hand down by her knee all the way to the one above her head. One of the jagged lines raced toward the ceiling while the other ran from her palm to the ground. Orange light seeped through the edges of the fissure when it spread behind her.

River screamed as her back arched off the seal. Power crackled over my skin, my markings all shifting to point toward her. The orange light faded to the golden-white color River had emitted before traveling so close to Hell.

The vast power of my ancestors had forged these seals. The symbols etched into the surface of the wall were a power all their own. River had reacted strongly to the seals before, drawing on their energy to help me keep a seal up. When the wraiths were here, they'd kept her from latching onto the power of the seals. It had bottled up inside her, and once the wraiths fled, her ability had unleashed to feed on the seals.

More than that, Lucifer had made her a part of the seal by using her blood to crack it. Her blood seeped deeper into the seal at the same time the power of the seals spread throughout her. Lucifer's hand wrapped around her throat, flooding her with his life force. He bowed his head against the increasing intensity of the light emanating from her.

I blinked as my retinas were seared by the aura burning brighter around her. River's scream grew until the sounds of the battle were drowned out, or perhaps they had all ceased fighting to watch.

An eon seemed to pass as it all unfolded in slow motion, but only seconds elapsed. I ran toward her, my way clear now that the angels continued to stagger away from her.

Lucifer spun toward me, swinging out with a wing. Seizing the wing, I propelled him back and pinned him against the seal, but he didn't release her. River's eyes were the deepest shade of purple I'd ever seen when they met mine. Pain filled their brilliant depths to the point where I didn't know if she saw me before her. I reached to pull her free of the seal.

"No! Don't touch her!" someone shouted as my hand fell on her arm.

The second I touched River, her back bowed further out and a volatile rush of blinding white light exploded from her. It tore through my chest as it lifted me off my feet and flung me backward.

River

I'd never felt anything like the power coursing through me. It crackled over my skin and sounded like a million bees swarming me as it hummed in my ears. It saturated my cells and thawed parts of me that had been frozen solid only seconds before. I was pinned to the seal like some sort of sacrifice, but I didn't feel like a sacrifice when every part of me was alive in a way it never had been before.

At first, I welcomed the warmth, but it swiftly became too much. I struggled to see anything past the golden-white glow as I became certain my heart would tear out of my chest. I tried to shut it down, tried to withdraw from the source of all the power, but I was pinned to that source, and it was consuming me.

Screams resonated in my head. I didn't know if I released those screams or not. I didn't know anything beyond needing it to stop before it destroyed me. I thrashed against the spikes, but whatever they were made of had melted and forged into the seal, making it impossible for me to break free.

Lucifer was knocked aside, but his hand continued to grip my throat. Kobal's face swam before me, and then my body was flooded with more energy. Pushed beyond what I was capable of handling, power exploded from me and nothing existed anymore.

CHAPTER TWENTY-FIVE

River

I'm dead.

That was the only explanation that made any sense. I'd died. And someone had judged me worthy of going to Heaven.

This had to be Heaven as unicorns couldn't possibly exist in Hell.

Unicorns were loving, magical beings that danced over rainbows or some such nonsense. Although there were leg-munching leprechauns, or leporcháins, in Hell, there were no rainbows for them to slide over.

I almost laughed out loud, but death wasn't funny, and I so badly didn't want to be dead. I would give anything to kiss Kobal again and hold my brothers close, but I didn't want to be Lucifer's pincushion either, so death could be preferable. And apparently, unicorns came to visit the dead. Maybe I hadn't made it to Heaven and the unicorns had come to guide me there, or maybe they would decide I didn't deserve Heaven.

I didn't know how it worked, and I hurt too bad to figure it out.

If I was dead, then why did it feel as if every muscle in my body had been stomped on like grapes for wine? Why did I feel as if it would take far more energy than I had to draw my next breath? And why could I feel the warmth of my blood trickling from my palms? I would no longer have a body if I was dead, so I wouldn't be able to experience all those things, or would I?

I glimpsed one of my hands. Whatever Lucifer had used to pin me to the seal was gone, and I could see the floor of the seal through the hole in the center of my palm.

The unicorn stopped before me. Its nostrils flared and it snorted. With a black coat instead of a white one, it wasn't entirely what I'd envisioned a unicorn to be, but it resembled a horse, and the golden horn protruding from its head could only belong to one creature.

A large hare hopped into view and sat beside the unicorn. I could almost believe I was in an enchanted forest or some such thing, but the hare was far from enchanting. Fangs protruded from its upper jaw and jutted over its bottom lip. The four-inch claws attached to its paws could eviscerate a person in a single blow. When the hare turned its head, four sets of red eyes met mine from *both* the heads on its shoulders.

Nope, if I was dead, this definitely was *not* Heaven.

Horror coiled within me, but I was so battered I couldn't move as the two-foot-tall hare hopped closer to me. Its claws clicking against the smooth surface ticked away the last seconds of my life. A sound to the right caused its head to turn in that direction, and it hopped away with a screeching clatter.

The unicorn's head swiveled toward me, and its blue eyes met mine. Exquisite in its beauty, there was still something unnerving about the creature as it snorted again. Its hooves clattered against the seal when it walked over to something else lying on the ground.

Bowing its head, it stabbed its horn into whatever had caught its attention. The striking gold of its horn became red in color. Nausea turned in my stomach when I realized it used its horn to drain the blood from its victim.

Kobal had once told me the wood nymphs most likely spawned the vampire legend. Watching the unicorn drain something's blood, I knew why some humans believed vampires could shape-shift into animals.

More creatures came into view, followed by others who looked more human. I remained incapable of moving, my body too drained to do much more than breathe and blink, as the creatures swarmed over the floor of the freshly broken seal.

A seal that *I* had been the one to break. A lump formed in my throat, but I had no energy for tears. My body and my abilities had been used to bring about the seal's destruction. This had happened because of me, but I was not the cause.

Kobal. Where was he? I recalled his face in front of me before everything exploded. Had he really been there or had I imagined him? Then I recalled the influx of power bursting through me and I knew he'd been there. He was the only one who could have created such an intense deluge of life within me. He must have tried to pull me from the seal.

Had I killed him? Before I would have felt certain I would *know* if he were dead or alive. Now, all I knew was that I'd plunged us deeper into the despairing pits of Hell by unleashing more of its worst occupants.

Kobal

Lifting my head, I scanned the numerous bodies scattered across the floor. River hadn't sent just me flying, but everyone else too. I'd always known she was one of the most powerful beings in existence, but the level of power she'd unleashed stunned even me.

Blood poured from the fist-sized hole River had torn straight through my chest. The blood loss from this wound and the ones I'd sustained earlier left my muscles weak, but they were already repairing themselves, as was the bone beneath.

The click of something had me turning my head toward the newly collapsed seal as the first of the púca emerged from their former prison. One of them paused to feed from a lower-level demon while another hopped over to sink its fangs into an upper-level who groaned but was too weak to fight off the creature feasting on it.

I placed my hands under me and pushed myself up as more angels, demons, and hounds stirred around me. My gaze latched onto River lying on her side near the edge of the seal. I couldn't see her face, as her back was to me, but I saw the subtle rise and fall of her shoulders.

Still alive. I had to get to her before the púca did.

More púca emerged around her, and one stopped to sniff her. The creature had taken on the form of a white unicorn. The color bled from its silver horn in preparation of feeding as it nudged her.

It pawed the ground before nudging her again. I opened my mouth to yell at it to get away when her hand fluttered up and she rubbed the púca's nose. I'd never had any experience with the púcas. They were locked away before I rose from the Fires, but I knew they'd been imprisoned because of their ability to completely desiccate their victims. Their original shape was unknown, and though they could adopt many forms, including demon, they couldn't speak.

The púca hadn't been imprisoned for being gentle, but this one appeared to be trying to take care of River as it nudged her again.

Because she is the one who set them free.

Lucifer had believed they would follow him, but the púca knew River was the one who had brought down the seal. The púcas may follow him once they realized she wasn't on his side but on mine and that he had orchestrated their freedom. It wouldn't take them long to realize she was my Chosen either. However, for now they sought to protect her.

A cracking sound drew my gaze beyond River and the still emerging púcas to the fissure racing up the center of the seal behind the one that had just fallen. I leapt to my feet as the next seal toppled and the rokhs were revealed. Many of the large birds had been perched on the ground, but they took flight when the seal fell.

The rokhs' wings, with their eight-foot span, created a breeze in the air that blew back some of the púcas closest to them. Their red, yellow, and orange feathers reflected the fires of Hell outside of the viewing panes where demons had once looked upon those locked within the seals.

Behind the rising rokhs, the fissure raced across the ground toward the next seal, and I knew nothing would stop the remaining seals from falling.

I raced toward River as a rokh swept overhead. Resembling a ten-foot eagle, the rokhs were beautiful, but lethal. Their talons often eviscerated their prey, and the rokhs feasted on their victims while they were still alive. If food was in short supply, the rokhs had been known to let a demon regenerate before picking away its intestines again.

I ran over the bodies surrounding me, my heart hammering as the púca beside River lifted its head and snorted at me before pawing the ground. None of them would have any problem with tearing me apart.

I was still fifty feet away from her when a breeze stirred the air behind me. Turning, the black eyes of the rokh filled my vision. It extended its talons, and I launched a punch at its golden beak. My knuckles cracked as they broke, but the rokh was knocked aside before regaining its balance.

When it came at me again, Phenex and Crux bounded out of the sprawled bodies to leap onto the massive creature. The rokh reeled back as it attempted to shake the hounds off. There would be no escape as Crux clamped onto a wing and Phenex closed her jaws around its throat.

I spun back toward River as the next seal fell with a loud crash. The floor lurched before settling into place. Across the wave of newly freed creatures and, from the bodies littering the floor, Lucifer rose to his feet. Bloodied and battered, his gaze met mine from where he'd been thrown twenty feet away from River.

A smile curved his lips when he realized he was closer. Ignoring the weakness in my limbs, I ran for River again.

A flapping of wings filled the air, and from the corner of my eye, I saw Lucifer lift off the ground. A blur caught my attention before it plummeted from above to land beside River. Caim kept his wings unfurled protectively over her as he gazed from Lucifer, to me, and back again. Crouching lower, he said something to her before embracing her against his chest and flapping his wings until he hovered in the air.

"Take her to Earth, Caim!" Lucifer shouted and flew toward the ceiling as Caim swept overhead.

"*No*!" my roar reverberated through the seals. I changed direction and sprinted back toward my followers. If Caim left Hell with her, I may never see her again.

CHAPTER TWENTY-SIX

Kobal

Caim swooped low with her as the other angels stirred from where they'd been thrown onto the floor. Having been farther away from the burst of power River emitted, my followers were already regaining their feet. Most of the hounds stalked protectively in front of them.

Onoskelis speared a púca before taking to the air as Caim landed behind my followers. The demons closest to him drew their weapons and advanced on him. Caim held River closer against his chest and stepped away from them. His wings unfurled as he prepared to take flight again.

"No!" Corson shouted and he pushed his way through the demons toward Caim.

"Leave him be!" Calah bellowed. He palmed the demons' heads as he shoved them out of his way.

"Caim!" Lucifer shouted. He switched course to fly back toward the fallen angel.

Caim stared at Lucifer as all around him the demons tilted their heads back. They grinned at Lucifer while they gestured with their hands for him to go at them.

"What are you doing?" Onoskelis demanded of Caim as she hovered above him.

"What must be done, what *should* be done, and you know it," Caim replied. "This insanity must be stopped."

The clattering bang of the next seal falling echoed throughout. The ground rose in a wave that nearly knocked me off my feet. Traveling faster with each new seal it brought down, the crack ran up the front of the eighty-third seal as the ouroboros rose out of the remains of the eighty-second one.

The hood of the ouroboros unfurled from the sides of its diamond-shaped head. Its red, forked tongue flicked out to taste the air. The one-hundred-foot-long and twenty-foot-wide, green serpent hungrily eyed its prey from its black eyes.

Every fifteen feet across the ouroboros's back, another snake tail curved out of its flesh. At the ends of those tails were rattles that went off all at once as the ouroboros struck a púca and swallowed it whole. Two of the tails on its back were in the process of regenerating as the ouroboros consumed its own tails when no other food was available.

Lucifer glanced between the falling seals, River, and me. I could feel his fury as his wings battered the air and a throbbing vein appeared in his forehead. He turned and dove toward Caim, but a wave of swords clashing together over Caim's head blocked Lucifer before he could get close to River.

With a shout of frustration, he pulled up and spun away from them. He soared toward the ceiling before fleeing from the seals. The other angels followed behind him. They left the rest of the craetons behind to be slaughtered by the palitons or the escapees from the seals.

"Go!" I shouted at my followers as Phenex and Crux fell in beside me.

We had to get out of Hell before it completely fell apart.

River

"Give her to me!" Kobal commanded when he caught up to Caim.

The angel could have gotten away a lot faster if he flew, but he'd told me he didn't dare take to the air when he had no idea where Lucifer was. On the ground, we were sheltered by Kobal's followers and the craetons looking to flee the creatures emerging from the seals. In the air, there was nothing to protect us.

"You're badly wounded. I can get her from here faster," Caim replied. I suspected he also feared one of the demons might try to kill him if he no longer held me.

"I'll never be too injured to protect her," Kobal growled. "Give her to me."

Caim was right, but I was too weak to protest, and I really didn't want to. If these were going to be my last moments alive, then I preferred to spend them in Kobal's arms. Caim slid me into Kobal's waiting arms. He cradled me against his chest, his mouth brushing over mine in the briefest of touches, but his love for me radiated through the kiss.

The hole in the center of his chest had closed, but blood coated his flesh. I loved him more than I'd ever believed possible. The idea of anyone hurting him made me want to murder whoever had done it, yet *I* had done this to him.

When he adjusted his hold on me, I briefly saw over his shoulder the destruction I'd wrought on the seals as a wave of bizarre creatures trailed behind us.

"Lo-look at what I did," I stammered out.

"Not you," he stated. "Lucifer created this."

"Maybe Lucifer was the reason behind this, but *I* unleashed it. *My* abilities did this."

Kobal's nostrils flared when he glanced down at me. "It's not your fault."

I knew he was right, but a part of me blamed myself for the destruction that had been unleashed here.

Kobal pressed me closer against his chest, flooding me with his energy as he ran through the seals my father had brought down and into the chamber beyond. The rotting body parts of the creatures that my father freed, and the hounds killed, still littered the floor of the chamber. Amongst those remains were the newer ones of the skelleins, angels, and demons who had died here when we stopped my father from bringing down any more seals.

Now I had triggered a domino effect that would not be stopped.

Overhead, the angels flew into the spiraling cavern above us and toward the open gates on Earth. I sneered while I watched them flee like the cowards they were.

Behind us another seal fell with a resounding bang. One of the giant birds flew overhead and dipped down to snatch a demon from the ground. The demon screamed as he was lifted into the air, but his cry was cut off when the bird gulped him down.

"The Fires of Creation." Kobal's gaze drifted to the tunnel leading toward where he'd been born. "The chamber will strengthen you."

"We don't have time for that. We have to get out of here before all the seals fall," Caim hissed from beside us.

"He's right and you are strengthening me," I told him.

Kobal's lips brushed over mine again before he turned away from the Fires. He raced toward the tunnel that all the other demons were funneling into. The last time we were here, Kobal blocked the tunnel by bringing down the rocks above it, but at some point, those rocks had been cleared away.

"Who cleared it?" I asked as Kobal pushed his way into the tunnel.

"Lucifer's followers," Caim replied. "It was the only way for the craetons to get near the seals again."

The clatter of swords and the cries of the dying rebounded off the walls in a near deafening pitch. The stench of blood permeated the air. Craetons, palitons, and seal creatures fell all around us. The enemies clashed against each other as they ran, but they all kept running for they faced certain death if they stopped.

Caim swung his wing out and sank his spike through the eye of a demon with the face of a dog. He pulled a small sword from his side and sliced the demon's head off. Behind Kobal, Corson, Magnus, and Hawk battled more of the lower-level demons. Before us, Bale, the skelleins, Verin, and Morax carved a pathway through the craetons with the help of the hounds.

Calah's head bobbed above the crowd before he bent down. When he rose into view again, he tossed something onto his shoulders. I didn't realize what it was until Lopan hit him in the head with his caultin. However, Lopan held on when Calah swatted at him. I spotted two more of the leporcháins riding the shoulders of palitons as they ran.

The pounding of numerous feet caused the walls to shake. Dust and rocks rained down on us when the next seal toppled. Kobal held me so carefully in his arms that I didn't feel the impact of his strides as he ran.

"The seals have fallen almost to the demons behind the hundredth seal," Corson grunted from behind us.

The demons behind the hundredth seal had been locked away for breaking the laws of Hell thousands of years ago. Unlike the lower-level demons who fought with Lucifer, these demons were more powerful. They were also probably really pissed at the varcolac and all those who had kept them imprisoned. They would be ferocious enemies.

"We'll be out of here before their seal falls," Kobal replied.

I jumped in Kobal's arms when a jackal-faced demon leapt out of a side tunnel at us. Its claws grasped at my leg as it tried to jerk me free of Kobal. Without missing a step, Kobal shifted his hold on me and sliced his claws across the demon's throat. The demon fell back as black blood spurted from his wound. Crux pounced on him and tore the demon's head away as more of the hounds rushed forward to circle us.

Caim sheathed his sword and swung his wing out to smash a craeton so hard against the wall that he propelled him through the rock. Corson gave him an approving look before slicing the demon's head from his shoulders with his talons.

The growing pandemonium and stench of death battered my senses.

It would only get worse as more of the seals fell, but I feared I wouldn't be strong enough to do what needed to be done to stop this.

CHAPTER TWENTY-SEVEN

Kobal

The walls of the tunnel gave way to reveal the open pathway that we'd traveled into Hell. On the way into Hell, I'd still believed there was a chance we could stop this without all the humans learning the truth. Now, there would be no keeping Hell's existence from them.

Hell was on its way to Earth, and there was no changing that, but I would get River out of here. She would *not* die in this place.

Screams rent the air as both craetons and palitons were shoved over the side of the pathway. Their bodies bounced off the rocky walls as they tumbled into the abyss below. Normally, the fall wouldn't kill them, but I doubted any of them would survive what was escaping below.

River grew stronger with every step I took. The holes in her hands were nearly healed, but it wasn't happening fast enough for my liking. The rocks beneath my feet vibrated before heaving upward. Demons cried out and flung themselves against the wall to my left while others staggered to the side and tumbled over the edge.

Chunks of wall broke off and fell from above, crushing those unfortunate not to get out of the way in time. Rocks battered my back and split open my skin as I hunched over River while I ran.

Caim swung his wing out to block a small avalanche cascading toward us. I didn't know why the angel had switched sides—I knew why he said he'd done it—but even the fact he'd returned River to me couldn't make me trust him. However, I would use him in every way possible to get her out of here.

I leapt over a set of falling rocks as the ground shook again and a wave of creatures rose from the pit below.

"What are those?" River breathed as men and women floated past us toward the surface.

"Jinn," I replied. Like the tree nymphs, the jinn possessed an ethereal beauty. Unlike the tree nymphs, they used their beauty and magic to ensnare and destroy other demons. They were some of the most conniving and savage creatures behind the seals. "You also know them as genies."

"You're shitting me," Hawk said as he gawked at them.

"Like rub the bottle and be granted three wishes, genies?" River asked.

"More like, they'll tell you they'll grant you a wish and make it more of a nightmare. Then they'll tear out your heart, or drain you of your essence, as payment. They also have a way of making others do things they normally wouldn't do for the mere promise of a wish," Magnus said. "When I learned what they could do, and what they had done, I admit to a bit of admiration for their ways."

He shrugged when River and Hawk scowled at him.

"They're… devilish," Magnus said as he shoved a demon over the side of the pathway without breaking his stride. "And they're free."

"What seal were they?" River demanded.

"Ninety," I replied.

"Are they all coming down?" Hawk asked.

"Yes," I replied. The amount of power River had released would not be stopped.

"Put me down," River said.

"You're still weak," I told her.

"I'm strong enough to run."

She squirmed in my arms as she tried to break free of my hold. "River—"

"Put me down, Kobal. I did this. I will face it on my own two feet, and I can't be a burden to you right now."

"You did *not* do this, and you could never be a burden," I snarled, but I paused to set her down.

"I *did* do this. Not on my own, and not willingly, but this is because of me," she said as the last of the jinn drifted out of view. "Once those wraiths pulled away, the flood of life and power from the seals and Lucifer, and then you..." Her voice trailed off as her eyes lifted to mine. "I couldn't control it. I didn't know I was capable of so much destruction."

"Of course you are, dear. You are part human, demon, and angel after all. I'm sure you've realized that we can *all* be highly destructive beings." Caim hooked his arm through hers and tugged her forward. "But if you insist on discussing this now, I suggest running as you do."

I slid my arm around River's waist and shot Caim a lethal look. He released her before moving slightly ahead of us. I used my other arm to shield River's head from more falling debris while we ran.

"If your human father, as a wraith, could bring down the seals, then you most certainly could," Caim said as he plunged a spike through the throat of a craeton and tossed him over the edge.

"When Lucifer blocked you from drawing on life by surrounding you with wraiths, he confined your ability in a way it had never been confined before," I said to her.

"And it sought release as soon as it could get it," Corson said. He didn't miss a step as he cut a demon's legs off at the knees before jumping over him.

"When Lucifer confined your power, it built within you," Caim said to River. "Add Lucifer using your blood to puncture the seal and binding you to it, toss in the varcolac grabbing you while Lucifer *also* held you, and you were a powder keg waiting to explode. And explode you did, child. Lucifer may not be able to connect with life anymore, but he is still the strongest fallen angel in existence. However, I don't even think Lucifer saw *that* coming, but then he never expected Kobal's power to be thrown into the mix too, and I think he may have underestimated your strength. I know I did. There was no way you could have stopped what happened once Lucifer set it into motion. And now that it has been set into motion, there will be no undoing it."

CHAPTER TWENTY-EIGHT

Shax

I tossed aside the cards I'd been playing with and leaned back against the metal tailgate of the truck. Across from me, Erin grinned as she scooped her winnings toward her. While in her cross-legged position, she did a dance that caused her whole body to wiggle back and forth. Her black hair bobbed around her ears while her deep blue eyes shone with amusement. She had every reason to be amused; she was kicking all our asses, again.

Vargas scowled at her as she stacked her newly acquired pieces of beef jerky on top of the bread she'd already taken from him. I may not care about the food she'd claimed, but I *hated* losing, and she now had the last of my mjéod. The skelleins seemed to feel the same way as me as their skeletal teeth clamped together. But then, they were losing what remained of their beer supply to her.

They loved when Erin answered the endless riddles they peppered her with, but they found zero amusement in handing their beer over to her.

My gaze traveled to the burned-out grass marking the area where the skelleins bar had stood around the gateway. The remains of the charred lumber had been removed shortly after the fire so we could see anything exiting the gateway. No one had bothered to construct anything new. If all went well, we wouldn't be staying here much longer, and if it all went to shit, we wouldn't survive this place anyway.

Numerous dirt graves lined the edge of the woods encircling our campsite. Each of them marked a human who already hadn't survived and who hadn't required burning with the lanavour remains. Demons didn't typically bury their dead, but then graves wouldn't have been easy to dig in Hell. They could have been buried on Earth, but I'd still ordered the burning of the demons killed here.

Things had been quiet since the erinyes burst free of the gateway five days ago. Those hideous creatures had flown away from here so fast, that no one had been able to launch an attack against them. They were most certainly wreaking havoc somewhere in the world, but that was a problem for later.

For now, we waited, and we continued to lose to Erin.

I hadn't heard from Morax since yesterday morning, when he'd mentally sent me a message telling me the angels had River, and that they might try to escape Hell. After his message, I tripled the guards around the gateway. If the angels came this way, I would not allow them to flee with her. I'd only slept for an hour since, but nothing had emerged from the gateway, and I hadn't heard from Morax again.

I'd been patrolling when Erin suggested a break for all of us. Deciding it was either try for a distraction, or continue to prowl the camp until I drove myself mad, I'd opted for the distraction.

I kept my gaze on the gateway as I collected the cards Vargas dealt. Sitting out the fight against Lucifer had never been my plan. However, these humans had grown on me, and I'd become okay with staying above to help keep them safe. Though, I'd much prefer to be tearing the head off something right now, instead of staring at a pair of twos.

"I swear you're cheating." Vargas shot Erin a pointed look before grimacing at his cards. His nearly black eyes narrowed as he tossed his cards aside. "Not going to attempt this one."

"I would never cheat you." Erin smiled sweetly at him as she batted her eyelashes. "I warned you the first time we played that I was as lucky at cards as I am good at riddles."

"I like her better when she's answering our riddles," one of the skelleins muttered.

"So you did," Vargas said and leaned over to snatch a piece of jerky from her pile.

"Hey!" she protested.

He grinned at her as he took a bite. "You know you're going to give it back to me when the game is over anyway."

And so she did. Every time we played cards, the game ended with Erin having the largest pile before her. She divided it back to everyone, but it had become a point of pride for someone to eventually beat her.

"Not the point!" Erin retorted. "And just for that, I'm keeping some of your losses."

Vargas ran a hand through his short black hair and tried to put the bitten piece of jerky back. She slapped his hand away.

"Children," Wren admonished and placed a can of peas on the pile.

My gaze slid to the woman sitting beside me. Wren had shown up with some of her human friends the day after Kobal and the others entered Hell. At first, I'd been tempted to toss her into the gateway without so much as a second thought. On our journey here, she and her friends had tried to ambush us and been determined to kill us. I'd assumed I'd never have to see her again, so when she arrived here, I was perfectly fine with killing her.

Unfortunately, not everyone agreed with me. After a lot of discussion, Erin convinced me to let Wren and her friends not only live, but to also stay. Wren and company were fighters and survivors, perhaps more so than any of the other humans here. I had to agree that they could prove to be valuable assets. They had survived this long in the wilds after all. They had even survived Kobal leaving them tied up in the woods.

Not only that, but they had tracked us all the way here. I couldn't turn away such talent with a weapon, or knowledge of this world, while our forces were divided and the battle for Hell waged.

Erin and Vargas hadn't been with us at the time Wren and company attacked. They had been with River and Corson, so they didn't dislike or distrust Wren as much as I did. I watched every move she made and made sure demons were with her and her followers at all times. I'd grown to trust her a little more, but not enough to let my guard down around her.

When I'd asked Wren why she risked their lives by following us, she'd told me that Kobal's words intrigued her. She had gazed at me from her blue eyes with her pale blonde hair dangling over her shoulder in a loose braid as she spoke, "Your boss said to me, *'You have no idea what monsters truly are, but if we fail, you will. If that happens, you will look back on this moment and know I was right.'*"

Wren had revealed that she had to learn what Kobal was trying to succeed at doing. If she discovered he was only blowing smoke up her ass, she brazenly admitted that she'd intended to kill him. That statement had made me laugh, the skelleins pull their swords, and the other demons close in around her, yet she'd shown no alarm. I'd decided to let it all play out until Kobal returned to make the final decision about her.

If she tried anything against one of us again, I'd happily rip off her head and use it as a soccer ball. Maybe the sport would be the one thing Erin *wasn't* good at, but I doubted Erin would be willing to use a human head for fun.

The human race was too damn sensitive about things, I realized with a sigh.

One of the skelleins whooped. Its teeth chattered together as it claimed the pile in the middle. High fives went around the circle. Erin so rarely lost a hand that when she did, everyone celebrated it as a win.

Another skellein gathered the cards and started shuffling them through its bony fingers with a speed the humans had trouble following. Their heads bounced up and down and side to side when the skellein flipped some cards through the air before catching them. The skellein dealt out the next hand as a vibration rattled the Earth.

The vibration was so small that I knew no one else felt it, but with my ability to make the Earth move, and therefore a connection to it in this world and in Hell, I sensed the tremor. Rising, I studied the gateway only ten feet away. Nothing moved there, but another quake rattled through the truck.

The skelleins, demons, and humans patrolling the gateway continued their pathways across the charred ground, unaware something had occurred. The ground rumbled beneath my feet again, growing stronger until I felt it all the way to the tips of my fingers.

"Shax, it's your bet," Erin said.

My gaze searched the gateway as the rumbling continued.

"Shax?" Vargas inquired.

Beneath my feet, the Earth heaved. Though none of the others felt it, I knew something had broken.

"Get away from the gateway!" I shouted as I leapt out of the back of the truck.

The humans and demons there all exchanged startled glances and staggered away from the gateway. I raced over to the entrance to Hell and skidded to a halt at the edge. Gazing into the abyss, I sneered as hatred for the place where I'd been born burned through me. I'd come to enjoy the warmth of the sun, the many numerous scents and sights of this planet, and I found human women were often more eager to please in bed than demon women. Demon women wanted to get off and go; humans wanted to impress. I wanted to be part of the fight, would give anything to help tear Lucifer and his brethren apart, but I despised Hell.

Those foul depths were not my home, not anymore.

"Shax!" Erin shouted from behind me. "What is it?"

The skelleins flanked my sides. "What do you feel?" one of them inquired.

"Hell is broken," I murmured.

"How is that possible?"

"I don't know, but it is. We have to move back. Aim your guns at the hole!" I shouted to everyone holding the weapons. "Listen to my commands! If it's not one of ours, *shred* it!"

The words had no sooner left my mouth then the flap of wings sounded and manticores burst out of the gateway. They soared high into the sky.

"Fire!" I shouted, and gunshots pierced the air.

Two of the manticores released an ear-splitting, trumpeting screech. The humans stumbled back as the hideous monsters swooped toward them. Their scorpion tails sank into the victims closest to them. Bracing my feet apart, I readied myself for an attack, but the rest of the manticores flew over the trees and out of view. The two manticores fled with their victims. Three of them remained on the ground, their bodies too riddled with bullets for them to fly again. Demons closed in to dispatch of them.

"What were those things?" Wren demanded.

"Shax!" The intensity of Morax's voice blazing into my mind nearly caused me to go to my knees. *"The seals are falling and the angels are fleeing. They may be coming your way."*

I worked on replying to him. *"I thought the falling of the seals had been stopped."*

"Not anymore."

"What happened?"

"Later. But know that they are all *coming down and we can't stop it."*

My heart sank as I realized the vibrations I'd felt through the Earth were the result of whatever force had been strong enough to bring down the remaining seals. With the gateway open, the entire world was doomed.

"Are Kobal and River alive?" I asked.

"Yes."

"Are all of you going to make it out?"

A protracted silence stretched out before he replied. *"I'm not sure."*

For Morax to admit that, shit had to be real bad. *"The manticores just fled. No angels."*

"Yet."

"Yet," I agreed. *"But that means they're still with you."*

Morax's voice retreated as swiftly from my mind as it burst into it. He often ended his conversations that abruptly, but after what he'd revealed, I couldn't help but wonder if he'd been killed. My gaze ran over the humans and demons gathered around me.

They'd all been prepared for a battle and warned they may not survive it. They would fight to the death, but none of us had been prepared for all the seals to fall and for the worst of Hell to be unleashed at once.

"The seals are falling, *all* of them!" I shouted to them.

"How is that possible?" a skellein demanded.

"I don't know," I admitted. "But Hell is about to come to Earth."

"Ay dios mio," Vargas muttered. He lifted the cross hanging from his necklace and kissed it before tucking it inside his shirt. With a resolute expression, he lifted his rifle to his shoulder and aimed it at the gateway.

"The angels may also be on their way," I cautioned.

The skelleins stomped their feet and their teeth chattered excitedly. "We always enjoy killing ourselves some angels!" one shouted, and the rest released a whoop of joy.

"Crazy bastards," Erin muttered.

Wren stared at them like they'd lost their minds. Perhaps they had, perhaps we all had, but that didn't change the fact that Earth as everyone knew it was about to change again.

From within the shadows of the gateway, the beat of wings resonated against the rock walls as a rokh took shape. It shrieked in excitement when it spotted the freedom it sought. Its gold talons curved as it flapped its wings faster and burst from the gateway.

Bullets riddled its body as it rose higher, its multi-colored wings reflecting the sun behind it.

CHAPTER TWENTY-NINE

River

Keep going. Get out. Get out! You can try to fix this when you're out of here, but you have to be free to do it!

I kept telling myself this, but though I'd gained strength from Kobal, it wasn't enough. I could barely keep my feet under me, and I couldn't let Kobal carry me again. We all needed our hands free as much as possible to survive the craziness surrounding us.

"The manticores are out! Angels are not!" Morax yelled over his shoulder at us.

"Did you communicate with Shax?" Kobal inquired.

"Yes. I can't get in touch with Bettle again, but Shax and the others have been warned about what is coming."

Please let them survive it, I pleaded as my right leg gave out on me.

Kobal lifted me into his arms before I could hit the ground. "Put me down!" I said.

"No." I knew there would be no changing his mind.

The walls shook around us, and more rocks fell as three more demons toppled into the nothingness below. The numbers on both sides of the fight were dwindling.

"Head for the throne room!" Kobal shouted to Morax. "I can open a gateway there that will take us out!"

Morax gave a wave of his tail in response. After another hundred feet, he veered to the left and into a tunnel. Many of the demons, paliton and craeton alike, followed him. Some kept going along the roadway toward the gate above.

Knowing he wouldn't put me down, I draped my arms around Kobal's neck when he entered the tunnel. His muscles bunched and flexed against me. One of his hands shielded my head as the ground heaved upward again. My eyes darted nervously to the ceiling as more dust and pebbles rained down.

"Can't you open a gate here?" Hawk asked from behind us.

"We would have to stop here," Kobal replied. "And it takes time to open one."

The Earth quaked again and larger chunks of stone clattered around us. The dust became so thick I could barely see Lix in front of me. Phenex yelped when a rock caught her on the shoulder.

"I'd prefer not stopping right now," Magnus said as he wiped dust from his hair.

"Agreed," Hawk panted.

Morax took another turn and entered the cavern with the silent waterfall of fire. I gazed into the flames as Kobal ran beneath them. Their heat warmed my skin, but they didn't burn me.

Kobal leapt effortlessly over the stones winding through the red and orange river and into the enormous room at the end of the stream. With every step he took into the room, more colors blazed to life in the pathway of stones beneath him. The symbols etched into the walls twisted and moved toward him as if they were greeting their king.

The power of those symbols crackled against my skin, strengthening me further as the room came alive in a way I'd never dreamed possible.

This place was as much Kobal as the Fires of Creation were.

Kobal

My gaze went to the far dais, my fangs throbbed with the urge to tear something to shreds. *My* throne was gone, and I knew exactly who had it, but why had Lucifer bothered to come here and take it when the weight of it would only slow him down? I had a feeling I would find out the answer to that soon enough.

Beyond where my throne once sat, I saw that River's was also gone.

When she squirmed in my arms, I set her down. She walked away from me to rest her fingers against the wall. Her head bowed and her black hair fell forward to shield her features.

Pulling her hand away, she flexed it as she stepped back. Pink color tinged her cheeks and the black circles under her eyes had lessened. Realizing this room gave her strength, I seized her hand and placed it on the wall again. She tried to tug it from me, but I refused to release her.

"You saw what happened below! What I did!" She jerked at her hand again.

"Those were extraordinary events. You are weakened, Lucifer is still alive, and Hell is coming apart. Take what you need from this place, while you can," I replied, unwilling to relent.

Her fingers unfurled in my hand to rest against the wall. We stared at each other for a moment before I released her. The ground shuddered again. A jagged crack raced out from beneath my feet and toward the dais. Through the crack, the flames beneath us flickered and jumped. The demons stumbled away from it and the hounds backed slowly away.

"Opening that gateway sometime soon would be lovely," Magnus said to me.

"For once, I must agree with him," Lopan said from his perch on Calah's shoulders.

"Step back," I commanded.

River turned and flattened her back against the wall while the demons crept closer to her. Many of them eyed her warily, and only Corson and Bale were brave enough to stand beside her, but beneath the demons' apprehension of her, I also saw admiration. What she'd done to the seals made them nervous, but they respected power, and she had displayed a *lot* of it.

I rubbed my palms together before closing my eyes and focusing on the flow of the symbols marking me. It had been years since I'd opened a gateway, and I'd never done it as often as my ancestors had in the days before Lucifer entered Hell, but the ability to do so came flooding back to me.

The ground heaved again, and gasps filled the air as the temperature in the throne room ratcheted up. Energy crackled over my skin. I didn't have to open my eyes to know the fissure had grown enough to reveal the oracle below.

Opening my eyes, I turned my hands so the backs of them pressed against each other. My markings shifted and flooded down to my fingertips when I pulled my hands apart. The rending of the air caused my skin to ripple as I opened a hole before me. I may not do it often, but the opening of the gateways was a part of me and it brought forth an overwhelming sensation of rightness with it.

River's eyes met mine over the black hole in front of me. At three feet wide and five feet high, the hole had been opened through the fabric of time itself. The ground heaved upward, knocking most of the demons into the wall as chunks of the ceiling broke free to smash into the ground. The force of them dented the ground, and one larger piece crushed a demon beneath it. I didn't have time to open the gateway as wide as I wanted to, or to have it open on the other end where I wanted it to.

This would have to be enough.

"Hurry!" I commanded and held one of my hands out to River. Until I closed it, the gateway would remain open without me now. Taking my hand, she stepped away from the wall. "It won't take you all the way out of Hell," I told her. "I didn't have enough time for that, but it will get you most of the way there."

"I'm not going without you," she stated.

"I will follow you, *after* the others go through."

She glanced at everyone else. "They'll go first, but I'm staying with you."

"No, you're not." Looking beyond her, I focused on the demons. "Start evacuating, now!"

"Your majesty, you should go first," one of them protested, and the others nodded their agreement.

"The Fires will not kill me, but they will kill you. Go."

I didn't have to order them through again as they rushed into the gateway. Many had to duck to enter it, and some could only go through one at a time. The tree nymphs were small enough to fit two or three at a time. The darkness swirled up like fog to block most of their bodies before they were more than three feet in. Within five feet, they disappeared.

"You have to go," I said to River.

"You are their king, and I am their queen," she said. "I will wait until our followers are safe too."

"*I* will survive if this whole place falls, you will not. You're going."

"Kobal—"

"No more arguments." I shifted my attention to Corson. "Get her out of here and don't stop until she's on the surface."

She opened her mouth to protest before closing it. Resting her palm against my cheek, she rose onto her toes to kiss me. Unable to resist, I drew her closer to deepen the kiss.

When the ground heaved again, I pulled away from her. Demons cried out as the fissure in the floor expanded and fire leapt up from below. Sweat stuck River's hair to her face as she leaned closer to me.

"No matter what happens, know I love you with everything I am," she whispered.

"And I you, Mah Kush-la. Now go."

"Come, child, it's time for you to leave this place," Caim said and nudged her forward with his wing.

"Corson, go," I ordered. "Hawk go with them."

"I would like to go too," Caim said as he stepped forward. "If something happens, I can get her from Hell the fastest."

I hesitated before responding. I didn't want the angel with her, but he had a point. "If he tries anything, kill him," I said to Corson.

Corson grinned as he rubbed his chin with the tip of one of his deadly talons. "Gladly."

They all moved forward to follow behind River as she entered the gateway. Sorrow emanated from her as she stared at me over her shoulder until she vanished. Stepping back, I gestured for the others to go through as fire rose to consume the dais.

Bale, Magnus, Lix, Morax, Verin, Calah, and Lopan spread out around me while Phenex and Crux sat next to me. Resting my hands on the heads of Phenex and Crux, I drew them back into me, locking them away as the rest of the hounds prowled nearby. Low growls emanated from them as the fissure in the floor expanded.

CHAPTER THIRTY

River

Within the gateway, the gloom was so absolute that I couldn't see the demons who had entered before me, or Corson behind me. When we'd entered, only inches had separated me from the ones ahead of me, yet it felt as if they had ceased to exist.

I was completely alone in this place and time, something oddly fitting right now. The idea of Kobal back there, still in danger while I traveled away from him, made my teeth grind together. However, standing next to him, I'd realized it was better if we were separated now.

Lucifer's insidious words whispered through my mind. I tried to deny them, but the more I contemplated them, the more I believed that he'd been telling the truth—a truth Kobal would deny. If he was with me, he would never let me do what was necessary to stop the outflux of creatures escaping Hell.

There was no hot, no cold in the gateway. It was a comfortable, warm temperature like a perfect spring day. No sound penetrated the gateway either, not even when I snapped my fingers to create some noise in the vortex did anything penetrate this *nothing*.

Had I somehow lost my way? No, impossible. Kobal would never risk such a thing. But once the idea took hold, I couldn't shake it. Sweat beaded my brow as I lifted my hands to feel in front of me, but they came up with nothing. They didn't create a breeze as no air flowed through here, but I could still breathe.

A pinpoint of light pierced the night before me. The back of a demon materialized, then his head, followed by his legs. The hair on my arms rose at the disconcerting spectacle of the demon coming together in pieces.

I jumped when a hand encased my elbow, and glanced back at Corson. His citrine eyes were filled with concern as he propelled me forward. Behind him, Hawk appeared and then Caim.

Stepping out of the gateway, my back flattened against the craggy wall when I realized we'd emerged on the road leading out of Hell. However, it was a lot different than the last time I'd traveled it.

Before, shadows had concealed the road. Now, it was illuminated by the fires burning below. Sweat dripped down my forehead and cleaved my clothes to my body. The Hell shadows writhed across the walls as they tried to escape the light. Tilting my head back, I gazed at the gateway leading out of Hell only a hundred feet above us. So close, yet so far.

I had to make it there. I couldn't completely fix this mess, but I might be able to staunch the flow of nightmares pouring out of Hell.

Corson tugged me onward as Lucifer's words replayed in my mind. *"Do you want to know a secret, daughter?"*

I shuddered as I recalled the warmth of his breath against my cheek and the humor with which he'd tormented me. *"Would you like to know why I never attempted to stop you from trying to close the gateway?"*

I'd assumed it was because he'd been too cowardly to come out and face those above, especially Kobal. That instead he'd hidden away while he plotted and grew his army, but his whispered words revealed a different reason to me.

Debris crunched beneath my feet as I ran beside Corson. We traveled higher as more seal creatures flew out of the flames or followed along the roadway behind us. Some of those creatures also ran ahead of us, and I knew more were already on Earth.

Glancing back, I searched for Kobal amid the crush of demons and creatures fleeing the demise of Hell, but I saw no sign of him.

He'll be okay. He can survive fire. He's the only one who can help everyone else escape if the gateway above is closed.

My arms and legs pumped faster. If I died in here, there would be no stopping the outflow of Hell, and if I made it out alive…

"I'll tell you and only you my secret," Lucifer whispered through my memories.

I didn't know why he'd told me his secret. Maybe because he believed there was nothing I could do to close the gateway. Maybe because he believed it would inflict more suffering on me and Kobal *if* I escaped and I revealed Lucifer's secret to him. Or maybe Lucifer had simply believed it impossible that I would get away from him. He was arrogant and crazy enough to believe that anyway. And he'd never seen Caim's betrayal coming.

Either way, he had spilled the beans, but was it all a lie?

Most likely, he was a psychotic lunatic after all.

"Must go faster!" Hawk panted from behind me.

My heart sank when I chanced a look back and saw the fires rising higher and still no sign of Kobal. The flames seemed to be chasing us, determined not to let us get away. A few hundred feet below, more demons and seal creatures fled, but others were consumed by the fire as it continued relentlessly onward.

So focused on the rising flames, I tripped over a gobalinus that went screeching past me. Righting my balance, I tore my attention away from the destruction and back to escaping.

Fifty feet, it was all we had until we made it to the top. It felt like a million miles as my legs trembled, my lungs burned for air, and my throat felt as parched as a desert. The throne room had strengthened me further, but I hadn't completely recovered from the effects of the wraiths or the outburst of power that had destroyed the seals, and I felt myself flagging now.

A flap of wings drew my attention overhead as Caim soared into view. He landed soundlessly beside me. "It's time we get you out of here."

Before I knew what he intended, he locked me against his side. My feet continued to run, kicking through the air when he lifted me off the ground. "Wait! Not without my friends!" I shouted.

"Take her out of here!" Corson commanded.

"No!"

My protests were ignored as Caim rose further away from them. His wings beat against the air while he propelled us upwards. I gazed down at the seething fires and the thousands of creatures seeking to escape them. Though the flames still snapped at the air and made me feel as if I'd sweat off about thirty pounds, the fires had stopped rising.

Caim shot out of the gateway like a torpedo. He rose until he became a backdrop against the sun as he held me aloft for a minute. For all I knew, it could be a hundred degrees on Earth right now, yet I felt as if I'd been plunged into a cool lake.

My eyes closed and my head tilted back to absorb the power of the sun's rays and the flow of life on Earth. I'd forgotten how much stronger the energy was here than in Hell, how effortlessly I pulled it into me, and it became easier for me to do so the further from the gateway we traveled.

The energy of the air and the rays of the sun flooded my cells and strengthened me. Particles of the sky brushed against my cheeks. The sway of the trees below caused me to sway with them. The fresh scent of the nearby stream flooded my nostrils and my pulse beat in rhythm with its flow. My fingers dug deeper into Caim's arm as tears pricked my eyes. It was all so beautiful and wondrous.

"Do you want to know a secret, daughter?"

My eyes flew open when Lucifer's words slid insidiously through my mind again. I met Caim's wide eyes. The look of reverence on his face stole my breath.

"I can feel the connection in you," he murmured before shaking his head. "*So* empty."

I knew he spoke of the emptiness within himself from the severing of his bond to life.

"I'm sorry." Those two words felt completely inadequate for the loss he'd endured. However, he'd made his choice when he followed Lucifer. The choices he made now had saved me from Lucifer, but his connection to life could never be reestablished.

He didn't respond as he lowered us to the ground. The clang of steel against steel, the retort of gunfire, and the screams of the wounded and dying pierced the silence that had enveloped me when we'd first broken free of Hell.

Now, all I could smell was blood, gunpowder, and the acrid stench of burning rubber. Caim's feet touched on the edge of the gateway as all around us more died. I spotted Erin and Vargas through the haze of smoke wafting from the inferno consuming one of the trucks. At least half a dozen skelleins were swinging their swords through the air and cutting down anything that got too close.

"It's an angel!"

The bellow came from my right, and Shax charged at us. He swung a broadsword over his head with lethal intent. "Wait!" I cried.

"Whoa, whoa, whoa!" Corson shouted as he leapt out of the gateway to land in front of me. He held his hands up to keep Shax back. Shax skidded to a halt in front of him. "You can't kill this one… yet."

"Thanks," Caim said from beside me.

Corson glanced at Caim over his shoulder as Hawk emerged from the gateway to stand beside him. "Still not sure about you," Corson said to Caim before focusing on Shax. "He claims to be on our side. He saved River and turned against Lucifer in front of all of us. He stays alive unless he tries something, and then have at him."

Shax scowled at Caim before turning to plunge back into the battle.

Hawk and Corson assumed defensive postures before me as they battled back some of the escapees from Hell. Caim fought against my back as a horde of gobalinus poured toward us.

I could see and hear the others, but I felt an odd sense of detachment from the world around me as Lucifer's words ran on a loop through my head.

A look within the gateway revealed that the fires had receded further. The shadows were creeping back in to reclaim the roadway once more. However, those shadows couldn't hide what continued to pour out of Hell. I didn't know what most of those creatures were, but they caused the hair on my nape to rise as they savagely attacked anything in their way.

Screams filled the air as some of them toppled off the road and into the fires. The stench of blood increased as more humans, demons, and escapees were struck down. A breeze blew strands of my hair forward to tickle my cheeks. It was such a normal sensation in a world that had become anything but normal as time slowed around me.

"Do you want to know a secret, daughter?"

He probably lied, I told myself, but what if he didn't?

"Do you want to know a secret, daughter?"

I gazed around the blood and body-covered field. This is what the future held for Earth and humans.

There would never be undoing the damage already done, but what if I could stop more of it from happening?

Then, through the demons and Hell creatures battling on the field, a shimmer of radiance caught my attention. My breath sucked in and my heart kicked against my ribs when Angela materialized fifty feet away from me. Unaware she stood there, the fighters moved through her, but she was as clear as day to me. She stared at me with an expression of such sadness that tears burned my eyes in response to it.

The human Angela had died at seven, but the knowledge in her kelly green eyes made her appear *far* older. Caim had said the angels were using her to try to communicate with me, and gazing at her now I knew he was right.

Her wheat blonde hair took on a golden hue that burned my eyes as it spread over her. Whatever the angels were trying to tell me, they were going to make sure I understood it this time.

The battle faded away from my view as Angela steadily approached me. When she stopped beside the gateway, she lifted her hand over it. She mimicked the gesture she'd made when I sliced my hand open and held my palm over the gateway before entering Hell. At that time, all my blood had succeeded in doing was chasing back the Hell shadows.

"Do you want to know a secret, daughter?"

Angela was ten feet away from me when Hawk staggered away from the lower-level demon he'd been fighting. "Holy shit!" he shouted. His head turned to follow Angela as she strolled unerringly through the battle. "Where the *fuck* did the kid come from?"

They could see her too? I'd been the only one capable of seeing Angela on Earth, but this Angela was vastly different than the last time I'd seen her. She stopped five feet away from me. Corson lifted his arm and planted it against my chest as he shoved me back a step. His shoulders and chest heaved, blood dripped from his blue-black hair as he sneered at her.

"It's okay, Corson," I whispered to him. "It's Angela, and it's okay."

"I know what she is, and she's not coming anywhere near you," he snarled.

"Oh," Caim breathed from beside me. "*Brother*." Then his eyes turned toward me while Angela kept her hand over the gateway.

All around us, the fighters stopped to watch the ethereal child who was as terrifying in her sudden arrival as she was aweing in her beauty. Her golden aura grew stronger until her eyes burned away and light blazed from them.

CHAPTER THIRTY-ONE

Kobal

I watched as the last of my followers slipped through the gateway before turning to those who remained with me. "After you," I said.

I waved my hand at the gateway as the dais at the far end of the room collapsed into the fires. Sparks and flames shot upward in a deafening roar. The hounds crouched; their hackles lifted. The colorful stones of the pathway fell steadily away as the ground crumpled toward us.

The flames devoured more and more of the throne room until the hounds were flattened against my legs and only five feet separated them from death.

"Gallha," I commanded them when Bale stepped into the gateway behind everyone else.

The hounds slid away from me and bounded into the gateway as they followed my command to go. My gaze ran over what remained of the throne room, a room built specifically for me to rule from.

No longer my world. And it wasn't. My world was Earth now. My life was with River, and I had to get to her.

Turning, I watched as the last of the hounds slipped into the gateway before I followed them. I made my way unerringly through the darkness until I stepped out and into the chaos of those fleeing Hell. Glancing into the fiery pit below, I noted the scorch marks left on the walls by the receding flames. Below me, surviving creatures and demons poked their heads out of the side tunnels they'd taken refuge in.

An echoing roar issued from within the flames. The force of the bellow fanned the fires upward as the ground quaked beneath my feet.

"What is that?" Bale asked.

"The one-hundred-first seal has fallen," I replied. "The drakón are free."

"I think that's our cue to *get out*," Magnus said.

"Yes, it is," Bale agreed.

Turning away from the fires, I ran up the pathway behind the others. The hounds carved a line through the lower-level demons and Hell creatures by tearing them in half or knocking them over the side of the cliff. A lower-level demon lunged at me from behind. Its razor-sharp talons sliced down my back before I turned to seize its throat.

I walked it to the edge and tossed it over as another bellow issued from below and the flames shot higher. Morax, Verin, and Calah stopped beside me to peer into the inferno.

"I think continued fleeing would be best," Lopan said and patted Calah on his head.

Calah scowled, but before he could respond, a manticore tail whipped out of a tunnel the shadows had obscured beneath us. The scorpion stinger struck Morax in the center of his chest.

"No!" Verin shrieked.

Blood spurted from Morax's mouth and his body jerked before he froze. Leaping forward, my hand caught in the waistband of Morax's pants as the manticore pulled away. The tearing of cloth filled the air as his pants ripped away from him and the manticore rose away from me.

"Fuck!" I tossed the ruined fabric away as another manticore soared out of the tunnel and pierced Morax's thigh. The creatures snarled at each other as they dipped toward us while they brawled over their catch.

"Closer," I grated through my teeth.

Bracing my legs apart, my muscles bunched as I prepared to leap off the pathway and grab Morax the second they came within reach. They didn't fly closer, but rose higher with Morax's frozen form between them. My claws dug into my palms as I watched them. Morax was one of my strongest fighters, closest allies, and one of the few I considered a friend. I *would* get him back.

The manticores were almost to the edge of the gateway when they tore Morax in half. *He can still regenerate…*

Each manticore lifted their stingers to their mouths and gulped down their half.

"Nooooo!" Verin's heartbroken wail drowned out the triumphant cries of the manticores and the roar of the drakón. Calah snatched Verin back and clasped her against his side when she almost tumbled over the edge.

The inferno below rolled apart to reveal the first drakón rising toward freedom. The gigantic beast released a wall of blue fire from its mouth, its wings fanned the flames below as it soared upward. Opening its skeletal jaws, the drakón swallowed both the manticores whole.

Calah held Verin up when her legs gave out. Lopan shifted to the side when Calah lifted Verin and tossed her over his shoulder. Her sobs were the only noise punctuating the strange hush that descended after the drakón's emergence. And then another drakón roared from below and the fires surged higher once more.

River

"The angels are using a lot of power for this," Caim murmured as he stared at Angela.

"I know they are," I whispered.

Closing my eyes, I became completely still as the warmth of the sun's rays flooded me. For one second in time, it was just me and this powerful world that had helped to forge me into the person I was.

Opening my eyes, I blinked against the sun before returning my attention to the pit. I searched for Kobal amongst the fleeing horde, but he was still nowhere to be seen. He was alive, but I wanted to see him.

I looked back to Angela now encased in a vibrant white light that caused others to stumble out of her way. Corson lifted his hand to his forehead to shield his eyes as he turned his head away from her.

"What are the angels trying to say?" Corson asked as Angela kept her hand over the gateway.

"I don't know," Caim murmured.

I knew, but I couldn't tell Corson. Like Kobal, he would stop me from doing what needed to be done.

The demons and creatures who had fled Hell turned tail and bolted for the woods when the aura surrounding Angela grew stronger. The ones that weren't struck down by Kobal's followers fled into the trees, but no one pursued them. They remained where they were, waiting to see what would happen, and waiting for their king to arrive.

"Is it an angel?" Vargas breathed.

I realized he and Erin had edged closer to us. A pretty blonde woman I didn't recognize stood beside them with her rifle aimed at Angela. I didn't tell her to put it down; bullets wouldn't do anything to the child. If the woman fired her weapon, she would learn that soon enough.

"No," Caim answered. "It's a guide, and it's trying to direct River."

"To do what?" Corson demanded.

"Do you want to know a secret, daughter?"

Closing my eyes, I took a deep breath as my thoughts turned to my brothers. Everything I'd done since childhood was for them. I'd fought to keep them safe and give them a better life than the one I'd had with our mother. Their lives could never go back to what they'd been before Hell opened, no one's could, but Gage and Bailey could still be safer and have better lives, *if* I succeeded in closing the gateway.

Everyone on Earth would be safer and happier if I succeeded in that.

Sorrow tore at my heart as I recalled the last time I'd seen my brothers. It had been right before I left the wall behind to come here. Gage had grown to become a stoic young man. Bailey cried when I embraced them both.

"They told me I have to let you go, but I don't wanna!" Bailey had sobbed, his tiny face flushed with his distress.

"I know, B, but I have to go. I promise to do everything I can to see you again as soon as possible. I love you," I'd whispered to him.

I loved them so much that there wasn't anything I wouldn't do for them. And then there was Kobal. There was nothing I wouldn't do for him either. He may never rule Hell now that it was collapsing, but he would rule Earth. He would gather the demons and he would work to establish control over the annihilation being leveled against this plane. He would succeed in killing Lucifer.

However, if all the creatures of Hell and from the seals continued to pour onto Earth, not even Kobal, the most powerful being I'd ever encountered, would be able to destroy or control them all.

I opened my eyes to gaze into Hell once more. My breath sucked in when I spotted the monstrosity soaring toward us. *What…?*

"Is that… a fucking… dragon?" Hawk asked.

Yes, yes it was, if dragons were skeletal creatures with a fiery blue glow crackling over all the bones making up their easily hundred-foot-long frame. Holes were interwoven throughout the black, leathery flesh connecting the bones of its wings.

A bright blue flame formed a ball at the end of its tail as it released a bellow. Everyone near the edge of the gateway scrambled away from the creature rising toward them. Its eyes were also made up of blue fire, but I felt it when the creature's gaze settled on me. My heart leapt into my throat as the dragon burst free and soared high into the sky, leaving a trail of blue fire in its wake.

As it rose to be silhouetted against the sun, I couldn't help but think how beautiful it would be if it wasn't so freaking terrifying.

"It's the one-hundred-first seal," Corson murmured.

If the gateway wasn't closed, and if the creatures caged within the seals could survive fire, there were still over a hundred more seals that could crumple and release their prisoners onto Earth. The fires of Hell were receding too. Soon enough it might not matter if the creatures could survive the flames or not when they were set free.

"Fall back!" Corson shouted as the dragon craned its head to look down at all of us and blue fire spiraled out of its nostrils.

"No," I breathed as another loud roar reverberated from Hell.

This could *not* be allowed to continue, not when I might be able to stop it. My gaze fell to Angela as her aura swelled.

"Do you want to know a secret, daughter? Would you like to know why I never attempted to stop you from trying to close the gateway? I'll tell you and only you the secret."

The joy Lucifer took in spinning me within his web of evil brushed over my skin once more.

"I never tried to stop you, because even if you did figure out how to close the gateway, Kobal never would have allowed you to do it," he had murmured with glee. *"Because to close the gateway—"* He'd taken a deep breath, his smile growing as he spoke. *"—you have to die."*

When he uttered those words, I'd been unable to stop myself from looking at him. His onyx eyes burned into the fiber of my being while he continued speaking. *"Life's blood, that is what the gateway requires, the sacrifice it needs. Along with a little extra... life,"* he purred the word *life* like he was a cat getting scratched behind the ears. *"I was mortal when I sacrificed myself to open the gateway. I used the last of my connection to the Earth and my angel blood to open it. I became immortal again upon entering Hell, but you will stay the mortal you are now and simply die."*

He'd giggled when he revealed this and steepled his fingers before his nose to study me over the top of them. *"I never stopped you, because Kobal would have."*

And I knew he was right. No matter how many more seals fell,

Kobal would never allow me to die to close the gateway, even if it was the best for everyone.

But Kobal wasn't here now, which was the reason I'd agreed to leave him behind. If I succeeded in closing this gateway, Kobal would be able to form his own gateway to exit Hell. The remaining seals would still fall, but they wouldn't be able to leave Hell and roam Earth. All those I loved would be safer.

Corson shoved me further back when Angela rested her hand over her heart in a gesture I knew meant to show me love and support.

"Tell Kobal I love him and that I'm so sorry for this. Please take care of my brothers. Make sure they're safe," I said to Corson as I felt the swell of life flowing into my feet and surging up my body toward my hands. Sparks danced across my fingertips as renewed vitality flooded me.

He turned his head to look at me over his shoulder. "What are you talking about?"

I met Corson's gaze head-on. "I'm sorry."

Before he could react, I hit him with a ball of energy. It hadn't been strong enough to maim him or knock him out, but it flung him ten feet away from me. Spinning toward Caim, I ripped the small sword from his side before hitting him with a blast of energy as well. I didn't know if he would try to stop me or not, but I couldn't take the chance he might.

Running forward, dirt skidded out from under me as I fell to my knees at the edge of the gateway. My heart shattered when my gaze landed on Kobal, only fifty feet below and coming fast. Tipping his head back, his gaze latched onto mine.

CHAPTER THIRTY-TWO

Kobal

My mouth parted as I met River's eyes. Tears streaked her face, but a strange sense of peace enshrouded her. Her love for me radiated from her as the golden-blue light crackling around her fingers illuminated her face.

From the other side of her, a blinding light walked toward her. My heart plummeted when I realized the glow came from a child, and exactly *who* that child was.

"What is that?" Magnus breathed.

"Angela," I snarled.

"The angels," Bale stated.

"Yes." I continued running, but I couldn't tear my gaze away from River as her head fell back and Angela's golden aura bathed her.

Over River's head, the drakón circled and roared again. Its cry was echoed from the fires below.

I drew on the power of Phenex and Crux within me as I raced forward. River's head bowed, and the look of resolve on her face propelled me faster when our eyes met again.

I love you, she mouthed to me. She may have spoken the words aloud, but I didn't hear them over the blood rushing through my ears. Lifting her hands, she revealed the small sword she held.

"*River, no*!" I bellowed as she turned the sword and plunged it straight through her heart.

RIVER

The blade tore through my flesh and scraped bone as I drove it into my chest. Spasms racked me. I opened my mouth to scream, but the sound strangled on the blood clogging my throat. My fingers clenched the handle as I sought to pull it free so my blood could flow faster. Blood spilled from my mouth when I succeeded in yanking the blade out.

Kobal's words echoed in my head as I slumped onto the ground. The dirt beneath me stuck to my cheek and clogged one of my nostrils. The scent and sound of the worms churning beneath the charred earth, drifted to me as I labored to draw air into my lungs.

I'm so sorry, the apology became a mantra in my head.

I had condemned Kobal to a life of suffering and loneliness by doing this. That realization hurt far more than the physical pain racking my body. However, if I didn't try to close the gateway, I would condemn millions to death.

I knew Kobal would survive without me. He would be miserable; he may even hate me for the rest of his days for doing this, but he would continue to live because he was a leader and the well-being of his followers came before his own. No matter what, I knew he would find my brothers and keep them safe too.

Tears streaked my face. I'd never dreamed of finding love before, never believed myself capable of falling as hard for someone as I had for Kobal, but I couldn't recall what it had been like not to love him, not to feel him in every part of me.

He was my heart, my soul, but this had always been bigger than the two of us. We had always known one, or both of us, might not survive.

Golden-blue light danced across my fingers, mingling with the blood beneath my hands and turning it pink. More of my blood seeped across the dirt and spilled into the gateway.

I kept waiting for the hole to close, for something to happen, but it remained open and unchanged.

Lucifer lied, I thought frantically. *The angels weren't trying to tell me to do this, or maybe they did want me dead. Maybe they had only intended to end the last of Lucifer's line. Or maybe they had all truly believed I could close the gateway, but they'd all been wrong. I couldn't do it.*

I may have killed myself and devastated Kobal for *nothing*. No one would be saved, none of it would be stopped. I wanted to will the blood back into my body, to turn back time, but there was no changing what I had done.

Confusion filled the air and the thunder of a large creature battered my eardrums. From where I lay on the ground, I watched feet racing toward me. They did an odd stutter step away from Angela who remained by my side. Blue flashed by me and I dimly realized another dragon broke free.

I failed. Failed! And I'd broken my promise to my brothers and torn Kobal's heart out of his chest in the process.

Then, the golden-blue light encircling my hands became the golden-white sparks they'd been before I journeyed this close to Hell. Those sparks swirled over my blood before following the trail of it into the gateway like fire racing over gasoline. There, the sparks became entirely gold in color as they surged into the air.

The feet racing toward me skidded to a halt and staggered back as the sparks rolled across the gateway like a wave breaking on the beach. From within the gateway, a shriek pierced the air.

Kobal

I kept my shoulders down to barrel through the light flowing over the gateway. A sizzling sounded in my ears. I realized my flesh was burning seconds before a blast of energy flung me back. The force of my body bouncing off the rocks tore boulders free of the wall before I came to a stop against it.

Smoke drifted from my charred skin; I took a second to steady myself before leaping to my feet. I prepared to lunge back at the opening and tear my way through it. A púca shrieked when it hit the golden light. Smoke streamed from its scorched body as it was flung back. It made no sound when it spiraled into the pit.

Already dead, I realized.

My eyes narrowed on the swelling power of life above me. There would be no tearing my way through that. I might be able to break through it with a wall of fire though.

"What is that?" Bale demanded as she gazed at the growing light.

"River." Anguish tore at my chest as I recalled her plunging the sword into her chest. No matter how fast she healed now, she couldn't survive that, not while she was still mortal anyway.

I stumbled back as around me the rocks quaked and a grating noise filled the air.

"What has the World Walker done?" Lix breathed.

"What the angels guided her to do," I growled. "I'll tear every *fucking* one of them apart for this!"

Rocks fell and clattered about my feet as the grinding noise became louder. The hounds all snarled when larger boulders broke free around us. The boulders bounced down the path. I jumped out of the way of one that crashed into a demon behind me and rolled him off the side.

Fire burst from my hands and raced up to circle my wrists before slithering over my shoulders. My markings all shifted toward my finger-tips in preparation for trying to break through the wave of power cascading over us.

I was about to unleash my wrath when I realized that the closing of the gateway was the source of the grinding noise. My flames burned hotter as I stared at the shrinking hole over my head.

No matter how badly I wanted to get to River and do whatever it took to save her, I couldn't stop the gateway from closing.

This was what we'd been working for, and River had figured out how to do it. If there was any chance for demons and humans to survive, the gateway had to be closed. I roared in fury, but the fire encompassing me died away.

"I think it would be best for us to get out of here," Lopan said as more rocks fell and shattered around us.

Some lower-level demons raced past us, screeching and grunting as they ran toward the light. What happened with the púca didn't deter them from their course. They never made it to the gateway as the golden glow spilled down the rocks in a cascading waterfall.

It's following River's blood, I realized when the light flared outward from there and across the lower-level demons. Three of them were flung off the pathway. The one that fell against the rocks near my feet still had smoke coiling out of its now empty eye sockets.

"Best to leave *now*," Magnus said.

The grinding sound of the Earth continued as more and more debris tumbled around us and the gateway crept closer together. Screeches filled the air as creatures and demons rushed toward their closing escape.

River

I struggled to keep my eyes open, but my lids grew heavier with every passing second. Then I realized they weren't closing, but blackness was coming and going over my field of vision. In the beginning, the blood rushed out of me with every beat of my heart. Now, only a small trickle ran down my flesh with every slowing thump.

My mouth parted, I tried to draw a breath, but it was too much effort. Coldness seeped through my limbs, but it wasn't the same kind of chill as the wraiths. This coldness felt… inevitable. Terror clutched at my chest. I was dying. This was the end of everything I'd ever known. I'd chosen this course. I *knew* it was the right one, but still I didn't want to die. I wanted the life I would never have.

The golden light spreading in front of me flared higher before abruptly dying away. Gazing across the scorched Earth, I saw nothing but dirt before me.

In the following silence, I realized my heart no longer beat.

Despite the fact these were the last seconds of my life, a smile tugged at my lips as I realized the gateway was closed. My blood, and my connection to all things living, had succeeded in stopping the mass exodus from Hell. Dirt had never looked more beautiful to me, and if I'd been able to, I would be laughing while rolling through it right now.

A golden aura filled my vision as Angela knelt by my side. Her hand didn't touch my cheek when she tried to hold it against me. She now had enough power fueling her to be seen by everyone, but she was still only a figure the angels had conjured to guide me.

And they had succeeded in guiding me on how to protect the others and give them a chance for a better future.

I hadn't dared to let myself dream too far ahead throughout all of this, but I mourned the loss of dreams I hadn't realized I had. A field of green grass rolled out before me. Children's feet ran by me; their laughter floated on the breeze. I didn't know if it was my brother's laughter or that of the children I could have had with Kobal, but never would. Whoever it belonged to, it made me smile more as I thought of the numerous children who would get to laugh and run now.

Then, the children and the field faded away and I was left with only Angela's white light. I would never have my dreams, but millions of others would.

Peace settled over me, my eyes slid closed, and I knew nothing more.

CHAPTER THIRTY-THREE

Corson

Blinking rapidly, it took my burnt retinas a minute to adjust after the blinding radiance River emitted seconds before. When my vision finally cleared, I wished it hadn't. I gazed between River's unmoving body and the smooth patch of Earth where the gateway had been. My mind spun as it tried to process what happened and *how* it happened.

"Ri… ver?" Erin whispered, her voice hitching as she edged toward River.

I didn't tell her that River wasn't going to answer her. She was as aware of it as I was, but it wasn't something I wanted to acknowledge, and neither did Erin. What had River done? *Why*?

Even as I asked myself this question, I knew the answer. Because she had to.

Because closing the gateway was the only way to stem the tide. The only way to right some of the wrongs inflicted over the course of so many years. If there had been another way, River would have chosen it, but there was no other way.

Lucifer had opened a gateway into Hell six thousand years ago; now, the last of his line had closed the one he'd intended to use to destroy humanity. It would be oddly fitting it happened that way, if I wasn't staring at River's bloody, lifeless body. If it hadn't been *River* who had to be sacrificed to close the gateway.

It should have been Lucifer lying there now, but the gateway wouldn't have closed for him. The powerful magics used here had required a connection to life and a sacrifice. River had known that when she rammed the sword into her heart.

"River?" Erin whispered again. I gripped her arm when she inched closer, drawing her tear-filled eyes to me. "She's—"

"Gone," I said.

And she may have taken Kobal with her. I tried not to recall the desolation on my mother's face while she'd watched my father's demise. She'd thrown herself into the Hell fires rather than go on without her Chosen.

What would Kobal do? If he didn't choose death, he may raze the entire planet to extract his revenge.

No, he wouldn't do that. River had sacrificed herself for this planet, for all of us. He wouldn't dishonor her sacrifice by destroying what she died to protect.

It shouldn't have been River. She deserved better than *this*. She deserved to be able to live out whatever life she could with Kobal and her brothers. She deserved happiness and love. She hadn't deserved a sword through the heart and dying in this burnt-out wasteland.

The sorrow twisting inside me was something I hadn't experienced since the death of my parents, at least not with this intensity. My queen, my *friend,* was gone and it made my chest feel like a vise squeezed it. I'd enjoyed living on Earth with the humans. I was aware it had brought about changes in me, but not of how much I'd come to care for others.

Angela kept her hand close to River's face before she pulled it away. Lifting her hands, she dropped her head into them. Her shoulders hunched up as if she were crying. The angels may have led River to this, but they appeared to be grieving her death. Wasn't this their goal for her?

My gaze slid to Caim. "Did you know this is what the angels planned for her?"

"I'm not exactly on speaking terms with my estranged brothers and sisters who reside above," he replied.

"Did you know this is how the gateway had to be closed? Did you know what Lucifer had done to open his gateway?"

"No," he said, his black eyes resigned when they met mine. "I had no idea how Lucifer entered Hell, or that this is what would be required of her."

"Would you have stopped her if you did know?"

Caim opened his mouth before closing it again. "I don't know," he admitted. "The gateway *had* to be closed."

"No," Hawk said as he strode toward River. "I will *not* allow this to happen."

Shax stepped in his way. "We can't change this."

"We can turn her into a demon," Hawk said. "I was turned. She can be turned too."

"Not without her losing her connection to life," Caim said. "I have suffered the severing of my bond. It would destroy her as surely as death."

"You can't know that!" Hawk exploded.

"Yes," Caim said, "*I* can know."

Vargas draped his arm around Erin's shoulders and pulled her close when tears spilled down her cheeks.

"She can't stay like that," I said as I stepped away from Erin.

I started toward River. I would kick, punch, or claw away the thing kneeling at her side if I had to. I didn't care what it took to get the guide away from her, but I wanted it *gone.* A vivid golden glow emanated from the child as I moved closer to them. Like the blood and life flowing from River earlier, the light increased until it was impossible to look at it anymore.

Stepping back, I threw my arm up and turned my head away from the increasing glow.

Out of the corner of my eye, I saw another gateway opening almost fifty feet away from the one River had closed. My throat went dry when Kobal rose from the bowels of Hell. His amber eyes were the same color and nearly as radiant as the light spreading across the ground from Angela. Behind Kobal, the others emerged with the hounds on their heels as the new gateway started to close.

I stumbled back when a bolt of lightening pierced the earth next to River. Thrown up by the impact of the strike, dirt and rocks pelted me. They stung my face and body as they bounced off me. Grunts of pain and cries of surprise filled the air as the lightening continued to pummel the ground.

The sizzling electricity filling the air caused my hair to stand on end. The loud crackle of it became all I could hear as jagged white bolts broke off from the initial blast. Like arms, or some kind of feelers, those smaller white bolts stretched out to connect with the ground.

I peered at the strange phenomena in glimpses from under my arm as it became brighter before exploding. The explosion flung me back a good fifteen feet and I landed with an *umph*. Much like the blow River had delivered to me earlier, this blast left my skin electrified and a little singed. An oddly metallic taste lingered in my mouth.

Shaking my head, I glanced around the clearing to discover we'd all been thrown back, even those who had emerged from the gateway Kobal had created to leave Hell. Only Kobal remained standing.

From the tangled mass of tossed-aside humans and demons, Caim pulled himself free to crouch beside me. He set a fist onto the ground as his black wings spread out behind him. The look of wonder on his face caused my eyebrows to rise.

Turning my head, my jaw dropped when I spotted the large man kneeling at River's side. No, not just a man, I realized as white and gold wings unfurled from his back and he scooped River's body into his arms. Her head fell back as he cradled her against his chest. The angel rested a hand over her heart as Kobal charged across the clearing at him.

I'd been fighting with Kobal for nearly thirteen hundred years, and never had I seen him look as enraged as he did now. All the markings on his arms and chest pulsed as they shifted toward the angel. Fire crackled over his skin, the flames lashing out around him.

The angel's head snapped up when Kobal's steps thundered through the air. Staggering back, the angel threw up his hand.

A wave of white light shot out of the angel's palm at the same time as a wall of fire erupted from Kobal. I'd seen many, *many* things over my life. I'd never seen anything like that fire smashing into the light. White and red sparks shot out to the sides, pushing those closest to them further away as wherever the sparks fell, the already burnt ground blackened further. A wall of white and red formed between Kobal and the angel as their abilities battered against each other.

Kobal's shoulder lowered as he pushed against the angel. The angels' ability to wield life was supposed to be one of the deadliest, if not the deadliest force in existence, yet somehow, Kobal gained ground against it.

Because the angel has Kobal's Chosen.

However, I knew it was more than that. The Chosen bond made demons stronger, but the power emanating from Kobal reminded me of the Fires of Creation, and I knew there was far more to the varcolac than I'd ever realized. Kobal would not stop until he reclaimed River.

I didn't think to help him; this was not a place for me. Right now, the angel or Kobal would destroy me and not even realize what they'd done. I was a demon, and this was the wrath of Gods.

CHAPTER THIRTY-FOUR

Kobal

My head bowed and my toes dug into the ground as I pushed against the energy flowing from the angel. It was the same kind of power River emitted, but on a *far* stronger level as it battered the wall of fire before me.

Every day, River had become better attuned to what she could do and at controlling her abilities, but she never would have been able to emit a flow of energy this deadly.

At first, the flow of our powers felt equal as they battled against each other. Neither of us gained ground, but we didn't lose it either. Then, I felt the smallest give in the angel's abilities and I gained a few inches on him. I wouldn't allow the angel to win, or keep me away from *her*. There was no way I'd let him do something more than the angels had already done to her. She was *dead* because of them.

If I got my hands on her, I could change her, make her demon and immortal, and fuck the consequences. But turning her into a demon could make her exactly like Lucifer if she survived the change. Not only would I hate myself for that, but she would hate me too.

Every part of me screamed to change her though, to keep my Chosen with me, to not let her go. My brain knew I couldn't change her, but my instincts clamored to give her my blood and keep her with me.

First, I had to stop the angel from taking her from me.

The symbols on my arms, chest, and back vibrated as they flowed toward the wall of fire. Never had my power felt this intense, but this was River, and there wasn't anything I wouldn't do for her.

The angel's power gave way a little more, allowing me to gain a few feet.

"Varcolac, I mean no harm," the angel grunted, and I felt a further weakening in the energy holding me back.

Almost there.

I was only three feet away from him when something bashed into my side and staggered me sideways. Arms wrapped around my waist, and I was torn off the ground. Startled cries rang out through the clearing. As I bounced across the dirt, I saw the hounds and demons who had emerged from the gateway with me scrambling to get out of the way as the angel's ability shot across the clearing.

The sound I emitted would have made the hounds tuck tail and run, but arms remained locked securely around me. A black wing flattened against my back, and I realized it was *Caim* who had intervened as he used his wing to protect him from my fires. The stench of the skin burning on his hands and arms filled my nose as his unprotected flesh blistered before blackening.

"Let my brother heal her," Caim grunted in my ear. "What you will do to her will destroy her."

Flipping over, I snatched Caim by the throat and lifted him off the ground when I rose. His hands clawed at mine as he tried to break free. His feet kicked in the air when I spun to face the other angel. That angel had River bent over his arm and leg as he knelt on the ground.

A golden-white glow radiated from his hand to the bloody hole in her chest. My eyes latched onto the wound she'd inflicted on herself. My hand involuntarily compressed on Caim's throat; he gagged and his eyes bulged, but I didn't ease my grip as I stalked toward the other angel.

River remained unmoving, her skin the color of the snow I'd seen a few times on Earth. Against the pallor of her skin, the blood from her wound was a vivid slash of death.

I understood what had driven Verin to her knees when Morax perished as a vast emptiness opened within me to replace the rage clawing at my insides. That emptiness had caused Verin to sob with abandon. It took all I had to draw my next breath as the loss of River spread within me. It was only a matter of time before the emptiness tore me open.

I released Caim, unable to be bothered with him anymore. He fell to the ground, his hand on his throat as he crawled backward away from me. I stalked across the clearing to the angel and River as Caim's words echoed in my mind.

Let my brother heal her.

I knew some angels had the ability to heal, but I saw no shallow inhalations and didn't hear the thump of her heart. The angel's purple eyes slid to me. Their color was so similar to River's that the sight of them hit me like a punch in the gut. I bared my fangs at him in a promise of death if he didn't do exactly what Caim said he could.

The angel revealed no emotion before he focused on River again. I stopped beside them, my gaze on River's face as I searched for any hint that the angel was affecting her. The hounds crept closer to me, their prowling movements making it clear they would latch onto the angel before he took flight.

Everyone else remained where they were, hesitant to come any closer. The seconds stretching into minutes felt more like the passing of an eternity with every breath River didn't take. I would rain death on all of those who had caused this. Starting with this angel, and ending with the unrelenting torture of Lucifer for the rest of my existence.

Stepping closer to the angel, my hands flexed as I prepared to snatch his wing and tear it from his body. What seethed inside me now made

Lucifer look sane, reasonable, and fun-loving. Madness slithered through my mind, beckoning me toward it as a haze of red blurred my vision and I craved having this angel's blood sliding down my throat.

I would protect the humans. I would honor River's sacrifice, but all those who stood against me, or had aided in her demise, would know my fury as I hunted them from one corner of the Earth to the other.

I was about to start raining down my vengeance on this angel when River gasped and her whole body jerked in his arms. I found myself unable to breathe as she went still again.

Had I wanted her to live so badly that I only imagined she'd breathed? My eyes remained riveted on her chest as I searched for any hint of a rise and fall there, but it remained still. The angel's light continued to pour into her as more seconds stretched by.

Then, the flow of the angel's energy abruptly cut off. River's chest rose and fell, her eyes fluttered open, and a small smile curved her lips when she saw the angel leaning over her.

"Raphael," she murmured before closing her eyes and slumping against his chest.

In the following silence, the steady beat of her heart sounded like a drumbeat in my ears until my heart fell into rhythm with it. Raphael lifted his head to look at me again. I stared back at him, the emptiness within me filling, but something new clawed at my insides. I wouldn't relax until I held her.

"Give her to me," I commanded gruffly.

I was certain he would try to claim her and take her to Heaven, or anywhere away from *me*. He may have saved her, but the angels had never been anything other than my enemy, and I didn't trust him.

Raphael kept River clasped against his chest as he rose with fluid grace to stand before me. His blond hair was only slightly darker than his white robe. Over the robe, he wore a chest plate of silver armor. A broadsword hung from his waist; the blue jewel in the silver hilt caught and reflected the sun as he gazed at me.

Only a couple inches shorter than me, he was nearly as broad through the shoulders, but he would be no competition against me, not when it came to River. Those purple eyes ran over me. I didn't sense the same condescension in his gaze that Lucifer exhibited; his perusal was a simple assessment as he held River out to me.

Afraid he might try something, I kept watch of him as I eased River from his arms. My hands clenched on her when her head lolled against my chest and her breath heated my flesh. That breath, and the warmth of her skin against mine, nearly caused me to groan out loud. All I wanted was to look at her, to touch her and assure myself she really was alive, but I didn't take my eyes off Raphael as I backed away from him.

When the hounds moved forward to stand between us, I dared a glance at her.

She remained unconscious, but her skin had regained the color she'd lost in death and her chest continued to rise and fall with her inhalations. Despite all that, I couldn't bring myself to believe she was alive. I'd watched her kill herself, seen her lifeless form, and felt the overwhelming loss of her threatening to devour me.

Adjusting her in my arms, I lifted my finger to trace it over her lips. Her mouth parted on a sigh and her hands curled into my chest, but she didn't wake.

"It will take time for her to fully heal," Raphael said. I lifted my gaze to him once more as Caim edged closer to us. Raphael glanced at Caim before focusing on me again. "There is much to be discussed."

"There is," I agreed.

"I think it best if we do it away from here. The gateway is closed, but there are many creatures still lurking within the woods."

I didn't want the angels with us, but I did want answers. "We will travel somewhere else."

"Will Michael not be joining you so you can return to Heaven?" Caim asked.

A muscle twitched in Raphael's cheek before his head turned toward Caim. "No."

"Have you been thrown out of Heaven too then, brother?" Caim taunted with a smirk.

"I made the choice to leave, to come here, to do what I felt must be done. I was not thrown out, but you know I cannot return," Raphael replied and turned dismissively away from Caim.

"The birds are about to start pecking each other's eyes out," Magnus drawled from behind me.

"No, they're not," I replied. "We have no time for their petty bullshit. It is time for us to leave here."

As soon as I finished speaking, a drakón roared from above and something not of Earth screeched loudly in the woods. Humans and demons fell back when I turned to face them. They all gawked at River before the demons went down to one knee. I knew this gesture was not for me, but for *her*. She'd destroyed the seals and sacrificed herself for all of them. Yes, she still lived, but only because of a miracle.

River hadn't realized an angel would save her when she died, and the demons all knew it. Not only did they admire her vast power, but now they also admired her courage. They would have followed her no matter what because she was my Chosen and, as such, their queen. Now they would follow her because she had earned their respect.

When the humans remained standing, Erin glanced at the demons before looking to River again. Tears still wet her eyelashes when she went down to one knee, followed by Vargas, and gradually the rest of the humans.

Not only would we be the king and queen of Hell, but we would also rule here. I held River closer as I strode through the kneeling crowd toward the handful of remaining vehicles. There were things I had to do before we left, but I wanted to get her away from here as soon as possible.

CHAPTER THIRTY-FIVE

Kobal

The sun had set when I called a halt to the vehicles. Overhead, Raphael flew low through the trees. He stayed out of view of anything that would make him dinner or report him to Lucifer. From the woods, beasts screamed, and not just Hell creatures, but the animals and people who resided on this planet too.

Hell had found its way to Earth, and it was wreaking havoc.

River had woken half an hour ago. She hadn't moved, hadn't spoken, but simply lay in my arms, flinching every time a new sound arose. Hawk's knuckles were white on the wheel as he drove, his shoulders hunched. The bed of the truck dipped from the weight in the back of it. Every square inch of it was packed with humans and demons.

Whoever hadn't been able to fit into the truck, walked behind it. Before leaving the gateway, I ordered the surviving demons and humans, who had journeyed to the gateway to join with us, to return to whatever section of the wall they'd been stationed at before. They would be needed there to guard, and to prepare those still at the wall for what was coming.

There hadn't been enough vehicles for everyone, and some of the groups were entirely on foot. The groups on foot had been given more demons and humans to travel with so they would at least have more numbers on their side until they could find something to use as transportation.

I'd also split the palitons that escaped Hell with us between the groups returning to the wall. Any demon who would prefer to return to Hell would be allowed to in the future, when things stabilized on Earth and in Hell.

I had a feeling few, if any, would seek me out to return to Hell when all of this was settled. Not only was Hell an entirely different, far more treacherous place than before, but I suspected many demons had come to prefer Earth to Hell.

However, Earth was also a far different place than the one we'd left five days ago. From what Shax told me, that was all the time that had passed since we entered Hell. Though it had felt like we'd been in Hell for longer than that, I suspected Earth and Hell ran on the same timeline. It only seemed like more time elapsed because it was impossible to mark its passing in Hell.

River rose from my lap as Hawk put the truck in park. "Are we staying here tonight?" she asked.

"No," I replied. "We will not be stopping for any length of time until we are back at the wall. The humans will eat while we discuss some things with the angels."

Her violet eyes were weary in the moonlight filtering through the passenger-side window. "I have to get to my brothers."

"We will."

I opened the door and kept her hand in mine while she climbed out. She brought my hand up between us and held it against her chest.

"I had to," she whispered. "I never would have chosen to leave you, not if things could have been different. You would have done the same thing."

I drew her flush against me. "I would have, but I am immortal."

"Yes, but even if it destroyed you, you would have done the same thing. I knew you could get free of Hell, knew you would look after my brothers, but the gateway had to be closed before all the seals fell. It might have been the death of everyone, and maybe *everything,* if it remained open."

My teeth ground together as I tried to deny her words, but I knew they were true. I would have done the same and expected River to continue without me. Clasping her cheeks, I drew her closer and kissed her until her knees went weak and she was holding onto me for support. I lost myself in the scent and taste of her as I ran my tongue over her lips before dipping inside her mouth to take possession of it. Blood flowed into my cock, hardening it against her belly. I desired her with a savagery I'd never experienced before, but now was not the time.

Her eyes were dazed, her lips swollen when I broke the kiss to gaze down at her beloved face. It took me a minute to find my voice as I resisted the impulse to pull her away from here and take her into the woods to claim her. We wouldn't leave here tonight though if I did that.

"I understand. I only wish you'd never had to make the choice, that I could have protected you better, or there had been another way," I told her.

"You did protect me, from everything."

"Except from yourself."

"There was no other way," she murmured.

"I know." And I did know. It didn't mean I had to like it. I took her hand and placed it against my cheek.

My attention was torn from her when Raphael landed a few feet away from us. Before he closed his white and gold wings behind his back, I spotted a starburst of gold feathers on the inside of his right wing. Those golden feathers formed a sun symbol. Unlike the fallen angels, he had no spikes coming out of the tops and bottoms of his wings. His wings were rounded and very much what humans had always imagined them to be.

His purple eyes landed on River. When he ruffled his feathers, a small wave of gold dust fell to speckle the road.

"Well slap me silly!" Lopan declared.

"I'll volunteer for that," Magnus said.

"The angels actually have angel dust!" Lopan continued as if Magnus hadn't spoken.

"The *true* angels do," Raphael said with a pointed look at Caim.

"You mean the boring ones do," Caim scoffed. "Or I should say, the ones who blindly obey and follow everything they are told even if it means turning on their own siblings. Yes, *those* ones have angel dust."

The remaining humans and demons gathered closer as the two angels stared at each other with equal disdain. "You chose a poor course," Raphael replied. "That is no one's fault, other than your own."

"*I* chose poorly?" Caim inquired as he pointed at his chest. "I think you forget that *I* was the only one trying to resolve things while the rest of you were all squabbling like spoiled children. The only choice I made was to question certain things."

"Things that should not be questioned."

Caim blinked at him. "I'd rather have the freedom to question than not have it."

"And that freedom to question only got you the rule of Lucifer."

"I don't see Lucifer here, do you?"

"Enough!" I interrupted. "For all I care, the two of you can pluck each other to death after I have my answers, but I will have my answers first. Make sure the humans are given food," I commanded the demon closest to me. "Establish a perimeter and kill any threat that comes close to it. We're leaving in twenty minutes."

I pointed to Corson, Bale, Shax, Magnus, Lopan, Calah, Hawk, Lix, Erin, and Vargas and gestured for them to follow me. Erin and Vargas kept glancing at Lopan and then looking quickly away before their gazes returned to him. Calah waved a hand at Verin, who sat mutely on the ground beside him.

"Stay, I'll fill you in later," I said in response to the question in his eyes.

I kept River pinned against my side as I led the others further away from the humans and demons. Until I knew what the angels would reveal, the humans couldn't hear what we discussed.

"Where is Morax?" River inquired as she gazed over her shoulder at Verin.

"He didn't make it out of Hell," I replied.

"Is he dead?"

"Yes."

"And there is *no* bringing him back," Magnus said.

"You're an asshole," Bale muttered.

"It's true," Magnus replied. "Unless you can catch and cut open that drakón, and then fish out the manticores that ate him, and *then*..."

"We get the point," Hawk interrupted briskly.

"What about Verin?" River asked. "Will she be okay?"

"That's for her and time to decide," Lix replied.

I didn't respond. I knew time never would have eased the vast emptiness I'd experienced when River died.

I stopped when we were out of earshot and turned to the angels. "How long have you been guiding River?" I demanded of Raphael.

"Only since she met Angela," Raphael replied. "My brother and fellow Archangel, Uriel, used his power to guide her the best he could."

"What about when she had that dream, stood up and said 'angels' before passing out?" I asked.

Raphael rested one of his hands on the hilt of his sword as he glanced at Caim. "Uriel was unable to guide Angela into Hell. He didn't have enough power for that. We used the collective power of three of us to try to communicate with her through her dreams, and failed. River must be the one to seek out others to join her in her dreams. We used that same combined power to increase our ability to communicate with her at the gateway earlier."

"That's why Angela became visible to everyone," River murmured. "Uriel tried to show me how to close the gateway before I entered Hell."

"Yes, but at that time, we didn't know it would take life's blood to close it. We had hoped a smaller amount of your blood would suffice."

River's hand went to the hole in the front of her blood-soaked shirt and rested over her healed flesh. "Life's blood," she murmured. Her fingers traced the hole in her shirt and her skin paled further. "When *did* you know?"

"When your blood failed to close the gateway. We knew it would most likely require a great sacrifice."

"So you knew how Lucifer opened the gateway into Hell?" Caim inquired.

"No. When he opened the gateway, he used his ability to distort things to keep us from seeing what he did. We came to suspect blood and life were necessary to close it when everything else she tried failed," Raphael said.

"Why did you save me?" River asked. "I'm Lucifer's last descendent. If I stayed dead, then his line died with me, isn't that what you want?"

"Lucifer still lives. We have no idea how long it will be before he is stopped or how many other offspring he might have in that time. *You* are the one who can counteract or recreate some of the same things he can, and you stand against him. There is no guarantee any of his other children would stand against him too. There is also the chance, that like your human father, Lucifer's children may work *for* him. Without your blood, and it is *incredibly* powerful blood, there may be no stopping him. There is a reason he was known as the Morning Star and favored by the being. His powers have never been matched by any other angel. It took a great effort to cast him out."

"The rest of us were more easily disposed of," Caim stated.

Raphael didn't acknowledge his words as he remained focused on River. "And Lucifer's power resides in his descendant. You had to be saved, no matter what the cost."

"And what was the cost?" I demanded.

"Me," he said simply. "I had hoped, with the combined power of my fellow angels, that I would have the strength to heal her from Heaven, but I didn't. I had to leave Heaven to save her, and I cannot return."

CHAPTER THIRTY-SIX

Kobal

"So, you are a fallen angel now too?" River asked.

Raphael's nostrils flared and his gaze slid to Caim. "No, I could never be one of them. My wings will remain intact, and I will never allow myself to become corrupted as they have."

Caim rolled his eyes and folded his arms over his chest. "Oh, Raphael, so certain of yourself in all things. Remember, pride goeth before the fall. Wait until you feed on your first wraith, because you will have to in order to survive. If their nefarious souls don't start to wear away at your otherworldly perfection, something else will trip you up one day. You are no longer in Heaven, with none of its temptations and all its endless boredom. This is the mortal realm; there is much to enjoy here my arrogant, prick of a brother."

"Enough," I commanded when Raphael's hand tightened on his sword.

"Why can't you go back?" River asked Raphael.

"Each angel has the ability to open a gateway out of Heaven. However, once on Earth, we are unable to open a gateway back into Heaven," Raphael replied. "Michael is the only angel who is capable of opening a gateway from Earth into Heaven. It is against our laws for any angel to come to Earth, and Michael will not come to retrieve me. I knew when I left Heaven that I would never be able to return."

"It's also against the laws for an angel to heal a human," Caim said. "Or at least it was when I was in Heaven."

"Is that true?" River asked. "Was it illegal for you to save me?"

"It was," Raphael confirmed. "Some of the other angels felt it best if we allowed you to die. Others were undecided, and some were adamant it be done. In the end, it was my choice to make. I am the only one with a healing ability strong enough to heal the dead. I've seen countless humans martyr themselves for loved ones and causes before, but with your bloodline and selflessness, I knew I had to make a sacrifice to save you."

"Well lah-dee-fucking-dah for you," Corson said. "*One* of you self-righteous assholes has sacrificed something since you dumped these black-winged dicks on the world six thousand years ago. I'm *really* glad you saved River, but you'll get no sympathy from me."

Hawk snickered and Magnus smiled at Raphael who didn't acknowledge Corson's words.

"Won't you die on Earth like the original fallen angels were supposed to?" River asked Raphael.

"Yes, before I would have perished here," he replied.

"Before what?"

"Before the humans opened the gateway and changed the natural order of things," I answered her. "In the past, the gateways to and from Hell and Earth and Heaven and Earth were opened by creatures who were not of this world. Those gateways were never as large as the one the humans opened, and they never stayed open long."

"What difference does that make?" Erin inquired.

"A big one. Earth has changed, and it will never be the same. The unnatural gateway has forever altered the fabric of all our existences," I explained. "I don't have to return to Hell, or travel to the other side of the world to know the gateway in Hungary closed at the same time as the one on this side of the world. I felt its shutting when it occurred. I can also feel that things didn't return to the way they were on Earth, or in Hell. Demons and other Hell creatures won't have to travel into Hell to maintain their immortality, or to feed. When the gateway closed, there were still wraiths on Earth. Like everything else from Hell, they will now be able to survive here too as Hell and Earth have intertwined with each other."

"Oh shit," Vargas breathed.

River

"Thirteen years was too much time for the gateway to remain open," I murmured.

"Fourteen years," Erin said.

"What?" I asked.

She gave me a wan smile. "It's September. It's been fourteen years since the gateway opened."

I blinked at her, uncertain of what to say or how to respond. *Fourteen years. It's September.* "How long were we in Hell for?" I blurted.

"Five days," Shax replied.

Five days? How was that possible? How could I have missed the anniversary of the gateway opening if we had only been gone for five days? The anniversary had been in July.

"We all missed it," Erin said gently as she seemed to guess at my thoughts. "But then, we've all been pretty damn busy. I didn't realize the anniversary had passed until two days ago when I noticed that fall was settling in."

I gazed over her shoulder at the fading green of the maple leaves. Some of them were already taking on an orange or red hue. There had been a time when the anniversary of the gateway opening would have been as recognized by me as Volunteer Day. However, unlike Volunteer Day, there had been nothing celebratory about the anniversary date.

I realized that Volunteer Day, the anniversary, and all the other things that had once ruled my life felt as if they belonged to a different River now. My life had changed so much in such a short time.

I could never go back to my old life, and I didn't want to. All I wanted from it was my brothers and my friends and I would get them. For the first time, I truly realized how precious time was. Living in the past would only bog me down, and living in the future would make me miss the present.

All any of us had was the now, including the immortals.

My eyes lingered on Verin as she hugged her knees to her chest and rocked back and forth. My heart broke for her sorrow.

"We'd hoped to put things to rights by closing the gateway, but even if the gateway was closed minutes after opening, I don't think the damage would have been fixed," Kobal said.

"So that means all the creatures that broke out of Hell will survive on Earth forever?" I croaked.

"No, it means they will survive until we hunt them down and kill them," Bale replied and pulled her sword free to tap the blade against the palm of her hand. "They don't stand a chance."

I gazed at the humans and demons standing by the truck. "Many people will die before then."

Kobal rested his hand on my shoulder, drawing me closer as he spoke. "Ever since they created this mess, the humans have been trying to hide it. We did the best we could to keep them safe, but it is time for the humans to reap what they have sown. Yes, many will die, but many were killed when the gateway opened, and many have perished since. Death is the way of all the worlds."

"Not for the angels, at least not the ones above," Shax said, his eyes locked on Raphael.

"We experienced our fair share of deaths during the battle with Lucifer. Many of the angels were slaughtered. Even a few archangels, such as myself, lost their lives," Raphael said.

"So it's been six thousand years since you've experienced death?" Vargas asked.

"We watch over the mortal realm. We experience death every single day and in the thousands," Raphael replied.

"The more he speaks, the more I hate him," Corson muttered.

Raphael pinned him with a steely look. "We do not fight amongst ourselves like demons and humans do."

"I think you forgot about Lucifer and his followers," Kobal growled.

"Lucifer wanted too much. He questioned too much and broke our laws," Raphael said. "Angels cannot have the freedom humans and demons enjoy. Because they broke the laws, those who followed Lucifer were denied the glory of Heaven."

"Glory my ass," Caim snorted. "Heaven may be the ultimate goal, but you will experience joys here you would never find in Heaven. *Each* plane has something to offer that the others don't. Without any guidance from the being, it was only a matter of time before some angels started questioning things."

"What do you mean without guidance from the being?" Vargas inquired.

"After the being finished creating all the angels, it established laws for us and retreated from our world. The angels remained to do what they were supposed to do, guide and give bliss to the souls they feed on in Heaven," Caim replied. "And we blindly followed the laws in an unbelievably *boring* fashion. Then, one day, Lucifer asked a simple question."

CHAPTER THIRTY-SEVEN

River

We all stared expectantly at Caim when his gaze focused on something in the distance. It seemed he'd forgotten he'd been speaking. "What was the question?" I finally asked.

Caim's head turned toward me. He blinked before spreading his palms out before him. "The question was why. Why are we doing this? Why do the demons and humans have free will? Why do they do different things, while we are simply here, existing and *bored*? You have no idea how mind-numbingly brutal it is to do the same thing day after day, year after *thousands* of years. It wasn't long after the being retreated that Lucifer started thinking outside the box.

"At one time, the archangels Michael and Ariel walked the Earth. I had assumed that maybe one day we would all be allowed to do so too, but I never asked if we would. I was a follower too then."

"Why were Michael and Ariel allowed to go?" Erin asked.

"Michael was chosen to go because he could return to Heaven and Ariel because of her extremely strong connection to nature and people," Caim replied. "Then, one day, they were forbidden from going to Earth and prohibited from speaking about their time there. The being forbid us to question them about the human realm. *None* of us asked why they weren't allowed to return, or why it was forbidden for angels to walk Earth when we'd all been gifted with the ability to open a gateway to it. After the being left us, Lucifer asked why we couldn't travel to the human realm. With his simple '*why*,' he got many of us thinking, and that was unacceptable to some of our brothers and sisters."

Caim puffed out his chest and thumped his fist against it. "Angels are to follow the laws laid down for us. We are to obey. But here's the real question, *brother*," he spat as he looked to Raphael. "*Why* did we have to obey those laws? *Why* couldn't things be different for us? *Why* could the humans' laws change with the times, and the demons create their own laws, while the angels rigidly followed laws set down by a being no longer there? A being who perhaps expected *us* to evolve *with the times too*?"

Caim practically shouted the last of his words as his wings spread out behind him and fury emanated from every inch of him.

"But no, regal Raphael, the great Gabriel, the admirable Ariel, and *mighty* Michael," Caim said in a singsong voice, "wouldn't hear of such a thing. We were punished for your inabilities to bend. Lucifer went absolutely nuts when you all turned on him and threw him out. *You* made him what he is now when you left us to die. He was once the kindest of us all, the brightest, *the* Morning Star! We were brothers and sisters, and *you* broke those bonds over a fucking question, you asshole."

Stunned silence followed Caim's impassioned words. Despite everything that had happened, I felt a twinge of sympathy for Lucifer and the other fallen angels. I couldn't imagine the kind of betrayal and devastation it had taken to make Lucifer so malicious and insane. That betrayal caused Caim's face to twist in grief as his eyes drifted from Raphael to the humans and demons beyond.

"And now I have turned against him too," he murmured and his wings collapsed at his sides as his head bowed.

Without thinking, I rested my hand on Caim's forearm. Kobal tried to pull my hand away, but I refused to relinquish my hold. Caim's sorrow over what occurred with the angels and his betrayal of Lucifer was palpable. He had chosen me and this world over a brother he clearly loved.

"Okay, so he's still got some deep-seated anger issues." Hawk waved his hand at Caim before turning to Raphael. "But I have to agree, that was a dick move."

"It is our laws," Raphael replied. "For better or worse, they are to be obeyed until we are told differently."

"Didn't you break the laws by throwing the angels out of Heaven?" Shax asked.

"Yes, we did," Raphael said. "Angels were never supposed to walk Earth again. However, the war in Heaven was spiraling out of control. Something had to be done before we were all destroyed, and though most of you probably wouldn't have a problem with that"—a lot of nods followed this statement—"Earth and Hell would have been destroyed too without Heaven functioning as it should.

"We had no choice but to remove the problem before it ended existence as we knew it. With only Michael being able to open a gateway while on Earth, we never expected Lucifer to find a way to open a gateway too. However, we couldn't have done things differently. I also wouldn't change what I did today even though it broke our laws. I may have saved you for you to die tomorrow," he said to me, "or you could live for thousands more years. Even if you are our greatest weapon against Lucifer, I will not intervene again. I cannot continue to rewrite your life in such a way. Fate will designate the rest of your course, not angels."

I snorted. "I like your optimism, but I doubt I have thousands of years left in me."

Raphael shrugged. "Perhaps not, but there is no way to know how long an immortal could live."

"I'm not immortal. In case you forgot, I *just* died." I couldn't stop the shudder running through me at the reminder of Caim's sword plunging into my heart. My hand went to the hole in my shirt again. The pain, the coldness, the *emptiness* of dying flooded me once more. Yet there had still been a sense of peace and a knowing that everyone I loved would be okay.

"You entered Hell. We felt the outburst of your power all the way in Heaven when you toppled the seals—"

Raphael stopped speaking when Erin, Vargas, and Shax inhaled sharply and their eyes swung toward me.

"I didn't do it on purpose," I said defensively. "Lucifer didn't exactly give me a choice on the matter."

"I will fill you in later," Kobal said to them, but their eyes still bored into me.

"You are the Chosen of the varcolac," Raphael continued. "You wield fire and life, have premonitions and are capable of entering other's dreams. You are more angel than demon, but more than that, you are more immortal than you are mortal."

I glanced questioningly at Kobal who stared at Raphael like he was trying to figure out if the angel was screwing with him. When his claws lengthened, I knew he would kill Raphael if he was.

"I don't understand," Erin said. "We *all* saw her plunge a sword through her heart, close the gateway, and *die*. I've seen demons regenerate ears and hands, watched more than a few of them get stabbed, burnt, bleed out to the point where nothing could survive it. Yet somehow, they did survive. River was dead. *You* wouldn't be here if she hadn't died."

"She was dead," Raphael confirmed, "but she is and will be an immortal."

He made my head hurt more than Magnus ever had. Releasing Caim's arm, which I hadn't realized I'd still been clutching, I lifted my fingers to rub my temples. "I don't understand," I muttered.

"I do," Caim said. "You haven't frozen into your immortality, yet. You are too young to have stopped aging. You *are* mortal now, but you won't be once you come into everything you are."

I opened my mouth to reply before closing it. I couldn't form words in my head to get them out.

"We would have sensed that," Corson said. "Demons know when another is still a youth."

"Would you have?" Raphael replied. "She is not a demon such as you know them to be."

My gaze shot to Caim. "Did *you* sense this?"

"I haven't spent much time with you, but no I didn't, and I probably wouldn't. I am more demon than angel now, or at the very least I am something different than all of you."

"*I* should have sensed this," Kobal grated.

"You are too close to her and all of this, and you are also extremely different than her," Raphael replied. "She is far more angel than demon."

"I realized in Hell I felt more angel than anything else," I murmured as I tried to process everything he'd revealed and what it all meant. After everything that happened today, my brain seemed completely incapable of absorbing this knowledge.

"I can sense her youth in her, but I can also sense she is nearing the end and will freeze soon," Raphael said. "Keep in mind, soon for an immortal may still be years."

"So I will stop aging and become an immortal?" I inquired, too afraid to believe what Raphael said.

"If you live to freeze into your immortality, then yes, you will become immortal."

Unexpected tears burned my eyes as I grabbed Kobal's arm. My fingers dug into his flesh, but I couldn't get myself to ease my grip on him. I couldn't look at him; I was petrified I'd see denial in his eyes if I did.

Eternity with *him*, if I survived to make it to immortality.

"So that means the other children of the angels will be immortal now too?" Corson inquired.

"Yes," Raphael replied. "And if there are any surviving children of the demons who once walked Earth, they will also be immortal."

I'd forgotten about the children of the demons, but then the demons had never bothered to track any offspring that may still be walking the Earth.

Kobal wrapped his hand around my head and cradled me against him. "Forever," he breathed.

I released my grip on his arm to hug him close. "Forever."

The others remained silent as we clung to each other.

Finally, Vargas cleared his throat and focused on Caim. "You said the being retreated after laying down the laws for the angels, are you saying there is no God?" Vargas's hand went to the golden cross hanging from his necklace; he rubbed it as he asked his question.

"Did you hear those words come out of my mouth?" Caim retorted.

"No, but—"

"It is believed the being will return," Raphael interrupted Vargas. "It's why the angels have tried to obey the laws. Things will be upheld in Heaven, as much as possible, until the being returns."

I could almost hear Caim's eyes rolling.

"Where did the being go?" Erin asked.

Raphael spread his hands out before him. "That we do not know. Perhaps, the being went to other worlds. Perhaps it simply went to rest, but it will return one day."

"What if you're wrong and it has retreated forever, or ceased to exist?" I asked.

Raphael stiffened. "I am not wrong."

"I guess *that's* a touchy subject," Corson said.

"The being will return," Raphael insisted. "We weren't told when."

"Now would be a good time," Hawk shrugged when Raphael shot him a fierce look. "Just saying, you know with Hell *literally* becoming a part of Earth, we could use some help."

"The being will not interfere with the course we have all walked," Raphael replied.

"So what do we do now?" Erin asked.

"We return to the wall," Kobal replied. "We regroup, and we hunt Lucifer. He has to be destroyed. If he didn't come out the gateway on this side…?" His voice trailed questioningly off as he looked to Shax.

"He didn't," Shax confirmed.

"Then he most likely escaped on the other side, but I would guarantee he escaped before the gateway closed," Kobal said. "When Lucifer is dead, the rest of his followers will scatter. Once scattered, it will be easier to pick them off. It will take time, and many will die, but with Lucifer dead, the rest will fall eventually too."

Kobal focused on Raphael and Caim. "What do the two of you plan to do?"

"I will stay with the offspring," Raphael replied.

My eyes narrowed on him. "The offspring has a name, and it's River."

"I am sorry. It is what you are known as in Heaven. With the many we watch die every day, detachment is easier."

"Lovely," I muttered.

"Don't worry, child, the angels are like that with everyone," Caim said. "I will also be coming with you."

"You turned on the angels and then Lucifer, and you think I'm going to let you stay with her?" Kobal inquired of him.

"I *never* turned on the angels. I sought the answers to Lucifer's questions and I paid for it. I warred with the angels because it was either fight or die. I turned on Lucifer to save us *all.* It was not an easy choice to make, and I would not have made it if Lucifer hadn't forced my hand," Caim replied. "I chose her, and I will stand by that choice no matter what happens from here on out."

"I believe him," I said. "He's coming with us."

"River—" Kobal started.

"He saved my life. He made the choice to do that in front of Lucifer, and Lucifer will kill him for it. He's coming with us."

Caim smiled at me as he ruffled his feathers. "You have chosen a wise queen, Kobal." Before anyone could respond, he shifted into raven form and soared into the trees.

Erin and Vargas staggered away from where he'd stood. "What was that?" Erin breathed.

"Caim is the raven of Heaven," Raphael replied. "I am surprised to see he can still shift into that form. It is a special gift bestowed on him by the being, but his connection to the raven seems to have left him with more of a conscience than the rest of the fallen."

"Or maybe it's because what he says is true, and he never wanted to break from all of you, as I'm sure some of the fallen wanted to do after being tossed aside in such a way," I said. "Maybe because of the raven, he was able to keep more of a connection to his angelic side after he lost his connection to life."

Raphael gazed at me for a long minute. "Perhaps," he murmured.

I had a feeling he'd never considered such a thing before.

In the distance, a thunderous boom shook the night. "It's time to leave," Kobal said.

CHAPTER THIRTY-EIGHT

River

Hawk decided to walk with the others to give Kobal and me some time together, but neither of us had spoken since we'd climbed into the pickup truck. Kobal sat awkwardly behind the wheel, his large body barely fitting into the small space as he kept his gaze focused on the dark road as only the moonlight guided us onward. Kobal didn't want to risk stopping, and neither did I, but we couldn't keep the headlights on either. It would only attract something to us.

In the woods, the darker outline of people, demons, and the hounds walking through the small trees lining the roadway could be seen. The further we got from the closed gateway, the healthier and larger the trees became.

We'd lost many of the humans and some of the demons who originally drove to the gateway with us, but we'd gained skelleins, hellhounds, and some of the palitons who had fled Hell. Every hour, those riding in the bed of the truck would switch out with some of the walkers and new riders would climb aboard. I hoped they were getting some sleep, but I doubted it.

My mind spun as I tried to process everything that had happened in such a short time. I kept opening my mouth to speak and then closing it again. I had no idea where to start or if I could put into words the chaos running through my mind.

"I should walk with the others," I murmured.

"You are my queen; you will stay with me."

"Kobal—"

"The humans must accept that things are different now." His head turned toward me and his eyes flickered amber. "You must accept it too."

"I have, in many ways. My views of the world are far different than what they were before we traveled to the gateway and into Hell. The angels are not all that is good, and Lucifer is not all that is evil. He is evil though, in his own way. The things he did…"

Kobal squeezed my hand when my voice trailed off.

"I was so cold, with those wraiths," I said. "I've *never* felt anything like what he did to me with them. Never felt anything like the influx of power that came from him and you touching me at the same time. I thought it would kill me, or that I would kill everyone near me."

Turning away from him, I rested my forehead against the passenger-side window as I tried to suppress the memory. Squeezing my eyes shut, I winced as an unearthly screech pierced the air.

"Listen to the night," I whispered. "This isn't Earth, not anymore. These things are free because my abilities set them free. My choice or not, they are here because of me."

"This is not your fault, do not blame yourself," he said.

"I'm not blaming myself; I'm stating a fact. If I'd been given the choice, this wouldn't have happened. This is not my fault, I was forced to do something I didn't know I could do, but I'm still the catalyst behind it. I have to live with that knowledge."

His thumb stroking the back of my hand sent shivers down my spine. It felt like it had been forever since I'd been able to lose myself in his embrace. Sparks danced across the tips of my fingers when I turned my hand over to clasp his. The light spread to encompass both our wrists.

"When you hit Lucifer with that blast of energy while I was fighting him in the cavern, it went through him and into me," he said as he gazed at the life swirling around us.

"Really?" I gasped. "I didn't know that could happen."

"Neither did I, but it was like a jolt of electricity that ran through him and into me. You are becoming stronger, and Lucifer knows that."

"He'll come for me again," I whispered.

"Yes."

"But he'll be coming for me to get you too."

His eyes revealed no emotion when they met mine again. "And he will die because of it."

"Yes," I agreed, but unease churned in my belly.

"We will get through all of this together."

"Yes, we will," I vowed. My gaze was drawn to the passenger window when a blue glow shone over the trees. "It's one of the dragons."

"It's a drakón," Kobal replied.

"Drakón," I murmured. "I saw them both exit the gateway. One of them flew by me whilc…"

"While what?" he inquired when a lump lodged in my throat.

"While I was dying." I focused on him again when his hand clenched around mine. "I died."

"I know," he grated from between his teeth. "I watched it happen, until the gate closed over me."

"I knew you would be able to get out. Otherwise, I would have waited until you were free before…" I swallowed the lump. I had been the one to drive the blade through my heart; I had to be able to say it out loud. "Before I stabbed myself."

A vein throbbed to life in Kobal's forehead as he released my hand to grip the wheel. "I realize that."

"But?" I asked when I sensed more behind his words.

"But you killed yourself, River. You took a sword and plunged it through your heart."

"There was no other way."

Fire skimmed the tips of his fingers, the rubbery scent of the wheel melting filled the cab before he doused the flames. He lifted his hands from the perfect imprints he'd left behind and repositioned them on the wheel.

"It wasn't an easy choice," I whispered. "I didn't want to die. I didn't want to leave you behind, or Gage and Bailey. I promised Bailey I would see him again, and I knew my actions would break that promise. But I couldn't stand back and let *everyone* die when there was something I could do to stop what was happening. I tried to be brave, but when I felt it all slipping away, when I knew it was the end…"

I gazed out the window as I recalled those last moments.

"What?" Kobal inquired.

"I've never been more terrified, but even still, I somehow knew it would be okay and I felt peace."

Releasing the wheel, he lifted my hand and drew it to his lips to place a kiss against the back of it.

"And then there was nothing," I murmured. "Until I opened my eyes to see Raphael. How long was I dead?"

"Minutes only, but it felt like years."

My heart twisted at his words and the anguish I knew I'd inflicted on him.

"How long did it feel to you?" he asked.

"Like one second to the next. I was gone, and then I was back. There was no white light to lead me on, no gateway, just a space of time that I can't recall, but I *know* it passed."

"It's best that way," he said. "I understand your reasons for what you did. *I* would have done the same. If I could, I would have taken your place."

I scooted closer to him. "I know you would, but when Lucifer told me how he entered Hell, I knew I was the only one who could close the gateway."

"*Lucifer* told you what to do?" he bit out.

"Yes." I repeated to him what Lucifer had told me. "The whole reason he never tried to stop us from closing the gateway was because he knew you would never allow me to die."

"He could have been lying to you about *all* of that."

"He could have been, but when Angela arrived, I realized he wasn't. I just didn't know if my abilities would be strong enough to close the gateway, or if my sacrifice would be enough."

Kobal released my hand to grip the wheel with both hands again. His claws lengthened and the veins in his arms stood starkly out. "*Fuck,* River!"

"Kobal…" When I reached for him, he captured my hand and held it in the air between us.

"When you were gone, when you were *dead,* there was this emptiness—" His hoarse words broke off.

I'd seen many emotions from Kobal, but never had I expected to see vulnerability. It shimmered in his eyes when they held mine. It radiated through the tremor in his hand before he steadied himself. That vulnerability, and the knowledge I'd been the one to inflict it on him, tore through my heart more effectively than Caim's sword.

"I wish I hadn't hurt you in such a way," I whispered.

"It was necessary, but the chance you took without knowing if it would work…. You scared the shit out of me!" He focused on the pitted road again when we hit a bump that made it sound like the tires would fly off.

"I'm still here."

"Only because of Raphael. If he hadn't intervened, you wouldn't be here."

"Careful, you might say something nice about an angel," I teased, hoping to coax a smile to his lips, but he remained solemn.

"Don't ever kill yourself again," he commanded.

"I have no intentions of making it a habit." Still no smile from him. "Hopefully no one will create anymore unnatural gateways into Hell. If they do, it seems I'm going to be immortal one day and I'll be able to shut gateways without dying for good, so there is that."

"There is that."

I moved closer until I leaned against his side. Resting my head on his chest, I relished the solid beat of his heart beneath my ear as he wrapped his arm around me. I could feel his lingering anger through the rigid set of his body, but he kissed my temple.

"Do you think Raphael is telling the truth about me becoming immortal?" I asked.

"I don't see why he would lie about it."

"Immortal," I breathed. "It sounds too good to be true. Will I have to feed on wraiths like you, like Hawk now that he's changed, and like the angels who left Heaven do?"

"I don't think so. Hawk has become full demon, the angels fed on souls in Heaven, and adapted to feed on wraiths once they entered Hell. You were born like this. If the gateway hadn't opened, you would have lived a normal, mortal life. Hawk's genetic makeup was changed by blood and death, but in your case, the world has changed, not you."

"What did the fallen angels feed on while they were on Earth? There were no wraiths on Earth before the gateway opened. Did they feed on ghosts?"

"I don't know. You would have to ask Caim that."

"Will the spirits of people who die and deserve to go to Hell still do so, or will they be stuck on Earth?"

"Both," he said. "With the veil between Hell and Earth broken, they will be able to pass back and forth. With more free reign, they will most likely not be punished as severely as they once were, but there are seal creatures who will make up for the lack of demons in Hell. They will feed on the wraiths. Only solid things will be remain on one side of the gateway or the other."

"Unless you open a gateway into Hell again?"

“Yes.”

“Could you open a gateway here, and one by my brothers that we could travel through to get to them?”

“It doesn’t work that way. I am here, the gateway will open into Hell here. On Earth or in Hell, I would have to travel to where your brothers are to open a gateway there.”

“Oh.”

“So eager to go back to Hell?”

“Not at all,” I muttered as in the distance a trumpet sounded. “Manticore.”

“Yes.”

“Will there be some kind of memorial for Morax?”

“Demons don’t do such things.”

“Maybe it would help Verin and the others to get some closure or something. I’d like to say goodbye to him. I didn’t know him well, but he was a good man.”

“He was.”

I yawned and closed my eyes as Kobal’s warmth enveloped me. “I’d like to stop at Pearl’s on the way back,” I murmured.

He tensed against me. “Why?”

“To see the ghosts or, hopefully, not see them. We can’t fix what was broken, but maybe the closing of the gateway made it possible for the ghosts to become invisible to humans again. I hope so anyway.”

CHAPTER THIRTY-NINE

River

I woke when the truck came to a stop and lifted my chin off my chest. We'd been traveling with only a few minutes for breaks to eat and use the bathroom for the past six days. We'd managed to scrounge up a couple more vehicles and gas, but more demons and humans still walked than rode.

I hadn't seen Jackie, Sarah, or Captain Tresden at all in the past six days. I assumed they'd been killed or else Tresden would be trying to lead the humans, and I'm sure Jackie would have complained about something by now. I knew Sarah would have launched herself onto Hawk and not left his side. She had to be dead if she wasn't following him closer than his shadow.

I had seen Lena waving at me a few days ago from the back of the crowd. She'd been with a group of other nymphs, both male and female who had also waved at me. Verin had stopped crying on day two and mutely followed along with a broken look on her face. Calah and Lopan remained at her side, nudging her onward when she stopped walking and stood there as if she'd forgotten what she was doing.

Since I closed the gateway, the demons had become my new best friends, as had a fair amount of the humans who had mostly avoided me like I had the plague before I'd entered Hell. They all knew I'd been used to topple the seals, there was no keeping that secret in the bag when a fair amount of the demons had been there to witness it. Apparently, my willingness to die for them outweighed the fact that I'd let loose a lot of the things we heard screaming and hunting through the days and nights. I was sure the vast amount of power I'd displayed both times hadn't hurt either.

Over the course of the journey, I kept waiting for something to jump out of the woods and eat us all. My nerves were stretched as thin as they could get, and I knew everyone else's were too. It was only when exhaustion completely took over that any of us slept.

Most of the humans, and me, had stopped jumping at each new shriek, bellow, or garbled roar. We'd adapted to our new environment faster than I'd expected, but there was no other choice. It was adapt, turn into a neurotic mess, or die in this world.

Along the way, we'd encountered more akalia vine and other creatures that we'd destroyed. We'd been forced to take a different route because of obstacles that hadn't been in our way before, but we'd finally made it here. Soon we would be back at the wall; soon I would have my brothers with me again.

I tried not to think about it too much. So many things could happen to them before I reached them. Now that I was so close to getting them back, I felt a growing dread that something would happen to them first. The wall didn't offer the same protection it once had, not when there were flying monsters all over the place now.

There was nothing I could do though; we couldn't travel any faster. Caim and Raphael had both saved me, but I didn't trust either of them enough to fly me home, and I knew Kobal would never agree to it. I wanted my brothers back, but I couldn't risk falling into Lucifer's hands by rushing out to them.

I also had to know about the fate of the ghosts.

Wincing, I rubbed at my sore neck before blinking at the gas pumps.

My gaze traveled to the plate glass windows of Pearl's Truck Stop. It had been night the last time I was here, and the place had been creepier than a tomb. Now, the sun shining off the windows made it almost inviting.

"I hope I can't see them," I said.

"Perhaps," Kobal said from beside the open passenger-side window. He'd been walking next to the truck, and me, when I'd dozed off.

"I hope we can't see them either," Hawk said from the driver's seat.

"You're a demon now," Kobal said to him as he opened the door for me. "You'll see them no matter what."

About a mile away from us, a burst of fire from the drakón surged into the air before dying down. "They're going to set the world on fire," I murmured.

Kobal's gaze followed mine. "Their fire won't spread unless they fan it. They're only using it to hunt and not to destroy, for now."

My cramped muscles protested movement when I swung my legs out of the pickup. Kobal gripped my arm when my knees nearly gave out on me. After the first night, Kobal and I took turns walking with everyone else. The raw skin on my feet rubbed against my boots, and ooze from a popping blister squeezed between my toes.

I repressed a wince as I looked at the ragtag group gathering closer to the truck stop. The demons stared at the building like it was a puss-filled space monster, but demons weren't overly fond of ghosts. The humans appeared curious while the hounds sniffed at the air as they patrolled the parking lot.

"Let's get this over with," Lix said and rested his sword against his shoulder.

"I don't think that's going to work on the occupants," Erin said.

Lix lowered his sword to rest the tip on the ground. "But we all wish it would."

"They're not that bad," I protested.

"Hmm," was the grunted response from the demons surrounding me.

I tipped my head back when a shadow passed over us. Raphael

swooped down to land effortlessly on the asphalt ten feet away. Stretching his wings, he shook the extra dust off before settling them against his back. A raven landed behind me on the roof of the truck. The large beak and talons shifted away as Caim took on his angel form. He crouched on the truck, his hand gripping the edge of the roof and his wings tucked securely away.

Caim rose and strolled down the windshield, across the hood, and jumped off to land on the ground. "Ghosts!" he declared. "What fun!"

Seeing him here made me recall the question I'd asked Kobal the first night. "When you were on Earth, before entering Hell, did you feed on ghosts since there were no wraiths or Heavenly spirits or souls or whatever to feed on?"

"Angels call the ones who enter Heaven spirits or souls," Caim replied. "And I'm afraid not. Ghosts don't fall into the same realm as wraiths and souls do. Ghosts are already getting what they deserve and have no reason to be rewarded or punished further. They provide no nourishment for any of us."

"Then what did you feed from while you were on Earth?"

The tilt of his head caused the vast array of colors in his hair and eyes to stand out more. "We didn't feed on anything. We starved. We cut off our wings in the hopes that we could become more human and sustain nourishment from food like they did, but it didn't work. Human food made us sick. We were dying when Lucifer opened his gateway into Hell."

"Oh," I breathed. "You didn't cut off your wings so you would be able to fit in better with the humans?"

"No, *never*," Caim replied. "You have no idea the pain we endured during the removal of our wings. No idea what it did to our already battered connection to life. It was a desperate, last resort."

"Why did all of you cut them off? Why not have one do it to see if it would work?" Magnus inquired.

"Because we are brothers and sisters; the suffering and degradation of one would be endured by all," Caim said.

I couldn't help but shoot Raphael an angry look. More than a few of the humans went, "Aww," which caused all the demons and Raphael to either roll their eyes or shake their heads in disgust.

"Are they really having sympathy for the *fallen*?" Magnus muttered to Corson.

Corson gawked at the humans before running a hand through his black hair. "Unbelievable."

Caim smiled at all the humans in a way that made a few of the women smooth back their dirty, tangled hair and flutter their lashes. Kobal looked like he was contemplating killing them all.

Caim focused on me as he continued speaking. "We didn't remain on Earth long afterward, but the fallen believe the severing of our wings is what twisted us enough that some of the offspring we produced afterward were capable of wielding fire. We felt a shift in us when we lost our wings, felt something within us becoming darker. The fallen remain unable to wield fire, but it became something we could pass on, as Lucifer did to you."

"You were able to have sex after you cut off your wings?" Erin asked in disbelief.

"Of course," Caim replied with a smile. "We weren't crazy enough to cut off our cocks."

"Oh, for fucks sake," Corson said.

"Enough, let's get this over with," Kobal commanded.

I fell in beside Lix and Erin as we followed Kobal and Corson toward Pearl's truck stop. Hawk and Vargas flanked our backs. Everyone else remained in the parking lot, keeping watch and passing out the slim pickings of food left.

"This place makes me think of a riddle, my dear," Lix said to Erin. The tip of his sword clicked against the concrete while we walked.

"Let's hear it," Erin said.

"It cannot be seen, cannot be felt, cannot be heard, cannot be smelt. It lies behind stars and under hills and empty holes it fills. It comes first and follows after, ends life, kills laughter. What is it?" Lix asked.

Erin kept her gaze focused on the building. I tried to figure out the riddle as I placed my hand on my forehead and squinted against the sun's glare coming off the windows.

"Whatever it is, it's depressing," Vargas said, and I couldn't help but agree.

"It's darkness," Erin said after a few more seconds of pondering.

"It is!" Lix declared and spun his sword in his hand. "And what are most ghosts afraid of?"

"The dark," Hawk, Erin, Vargas, and I all answered at the same time.

Ghosts being scared of the dark was still one of the strangest things I'd ever heard, and that was saying a lot given everything I'd been through these past five months.

"Have they managed to stump you with a riddle yet?" I asked Erin.

"Not yet," she replied with a smile.

"She's the reigning champion," Vargas said and threw his arm around her shoulders.

"They'll get me one day, I'm sure," Erin said.

"Doubtful," Vargas replied.

Kobal opened the door and entered the truck stop diner with Corson following behind him. I held my breath as I stepped inside with the hope of seeing nothing within.

CHAPTER FORTY

River

Those hopes were dashed as the grayish figures sitting at the diner counter swung toward me. They all stared at me with sulky expressions on their transparent faces. Before the gateway fell, those serving their time in Purgatory remained on Earth as ghosts, but they couldn't be seen by most humans. The opening of the gateway caused them to become visible to all humans, something the ghosts hated.

Maybe I can still see them because I died too, I thought. I knew it was a long shot given the ghost's morose demeanor, but it might be possible.

"Erin? Vargas?" I asked.

"I still see them," Erin murmured.

"So do I," Vargas said.

"But the gateway is closed! We felt it!" Ethel declared. The ghost planted her hands on her hips as she floated closer to us. Last time she'd screamed at us to get out the second we entered. This time it seemed she had more important things to worry about.

"It is closed," I confirmed.

"Are those *angels* out there?" one of the ghosts breathed from behind me. I turned to find Pompadour with his head through the blinds covering the windows. Only half his pompadour showed as his face was on the other side.

"They are," I said.

"They can help us!" many of the ghosts declared.

"Highly unlikely," Corson drawled, "but ask them. They're such kind-hearted fellas."

"Corson," I warned.

He shooed the ghosts away from the stools as he strolled forward. The ghosts gathered at the counter glowered at him and remained where they were. Corson plopped himself straight through one of them to sit on a stool.

"Revolting, filthy demon!" the ghost Corson sat through shouted. He floated away from Corson, and many of the others nodded their agreement.

Corson paid them no attention as he rested his elbow on the counter. He twisted slightly on the stool to gaze back at me while he spoke. "Letting them speak with the angels is the only way they'll let it go. Don't forget, ghosts are one-way assholes."

"Not as much as demons!" a few of the ghosts protested and many of them gave Corson the finger.

"Why don't you go out there yourselves and ask the angels to help you," Corson said. "It is daytime."

"Oh, we couldn't! What if they say no?"

"The World Walker will ask them for us! She is one of them after all!"

"That one, I think he's fallen. He'd never help!"

"Ask the golden one then!"

The ghosts all shouted different things so fast that I couldn't stop my head from bouncing as I tried to keep up with the conversations.

"Enough!" I shouted. Striding to the door, I pulled it open and stuck my head out. "Caim, Raphael, could you please come here?"

Releasing the door, I stepped away from it and looked over the ghosts in search of Daisy. The young woman had helped us when Azote and the lower-level demons were hunting us the last time we were here. From the back of the large group of specters, I spotted Daisy when she gave me a small wave.

I smiled and gestured for her to come forward. She floated toward me as the door opened and Raphael entered. The ghosts all drifted closer to him until Caim entered. Some of the ghosts zipped away from Caim to hover behind the counter. Others were still irresistibly drawn toward Raphael. Kobal shifted closer so that his chest brushed against my shoulder as he rested his hand in the small of my back. The ghosts couldn't hurt us, but he always moved closer to me whenever Raphael and Caim were near.

"The golden one can help us!" the ghosts chattered enthusiastically as more of them closed in on Raphael.

Raphael didn't pay them any attention as he focused on me. "What is it you require?"

"The ghosts believe you can help them get into Heaven," I replied.

"I cannot," Raphael stated.

"Of course you can!" the ghost who had tried to look down mine and Erin's shirts the last time we were here insisted as he floated closer. *Pervy ghost*, I'd called him. "You're an angel! You can do whatever you want!"

"I cannot open a gateway from Earth to Heaven. You will remain here until your time has been served and you are deemed ready to pass on," Raphael replied.

"See, demons aren't the only assholes in existence," Corson said and smirked at the ghosts when they all shot him furious looks. "You've heard it from the source, folks. You're stuck here."

"Corson," I said, hating that he antagonized them even if they were only focused on themselves.

"What about you?" a ghost demanded of Caim. "Can you help us?"

"*Moi*?" Caim said as he rested his hand over his heart. "I'm flattered, but no, you're on your own with this one."

"But the gateway has been closed," Daisy whispered. "We felt the closing, but experienced no difference in ourselves. The humans still see us."

"There is no repairing the damage the humans created when they opened the gateway," Kobal said. "It is only a matter of time before all humans learn everything that has happened, if they haven't already."

Some of the ghosts made sobbing noises. In the back, one of them threw himself down and started kicking and throwing his hands in the air like a toddler having a tantrum.

Daisy's eyes went to the covered windows. "We've been hearing all sorts of things out there lately," she murmured.

"And there will be more," Kobal said.

"We're stuck here, in this place?" Pompadour asked, and the sorrow in his voice tore at my heart. Some of the ghosts, like Daisy, were here because they'd been unwilling to leave their loved ones behind. Others had been too frightened to pass on. However, most of them were here as penance for things they did or didn't do in life. Even knowing that many belonged here, I wanted to be able to do something for them.

"Yup," Corson said.

"*Get out*!" Ethel shrieked.

"There's the Ethel we all know and love!" Corson declared as he spun on his stool to face her.

"Get out! Get out!" Ethel shouted.

She swooped toward Lix when he tapped his sword against the ground. "Pardon me, Madame." He held up a bony finger as he spoke to Ethel. "Before we go, could you tell me if you have any spirits here." Lix glanced at the ghosts hovering nearby. "Of the alcohol variety, I mean? Preferably a malt beverage."

Ethel looked mad enough to spit nails. "*Get out*!"

"I'll take a look for myself," Lix said and sauntered straight through her. Ethel gawked after him. The rest of the ghosts drifted out of his way as he pushed open one of the metal swinging doors separating the diner from the kitchen and warehouse beyond.

"It's time to go," Kobal said.

The ghosts zipped faster and faster around the room until they became a circling, gray ball overhead. Their distress became nearly palpable on the air.

"Can't be stuck. Don't *want* to be seen anymore," many of them lamented.

Erin, Vargas, and Hawk headed for the door. Corson rose from his seat as the light coming from the bulbs overhead intensified to the point I was certain they would burst. Caim and Raphael looked as pleased with the ghosts as the demons did. Daisy floated closer to me while Ethel continued to shout for us to get out. Kobal pressed his hand more firmly into my back and nudged me toward the door.

"Is it true, World Walker, is there nothing you can do for us?" Daisy whispered.

"Wait!" I breathed and dug in my heels to stop Kobal. "There may be something!"

Kobal tensed at my words and the others all froze. The lights flared brighter before dimming as the circle of ghosts eased. Some of them floated down around us again. They pressed so close that they cooled my skin, but nowhere near as badly as the wraiths did.

"What?" many of them asked at the same time.

Tipping my head back, I stared at the lights before focusing on the see-through crowd again.

"We could use help powering the lights at the wall." Enough ghosts together could generate a fair amount of light. "It's true that ghosts will never be able to hide from humans again, but we can work together to make it better for *all* of us!" I said.

"Please don't say what I think you're going to say," Corson muttered.

"They can help us, and we can help them!" I insisted.

Pompadour gave me a suspicious look as he floated closer. "How?"

"You can light things up and we can use that ability to help keep the wall lit, if it's still standing. The humans at the wall already know about the existence of demons and angels, so ghosts won't be much of a stretch for them. You can come to the wall and help us."

"Aw shit, River," Corson griped, and he looked as if I'd just told him he had to kiss an angel.

Kobal didn't argue my words, but the expression on his face mirrored Corson's. No one else said a word.

Lix kicked open one of the swinging doors, breaking the silence. He strolled out with a crate in his hands. "Jackpot!" he announced before setting it on the counter and heading out back again.

"You expect us to work for you?" Pervy asked.

"I expect you to work *with* us," I replied. "If you do, you won't have to hide. Helping others might also increase your chances of passing on from Purgatory faster."

"We would have to go out there, in the *dark*?" Pompadour squeaked the last word.

"If the wall still stands, we should be back at it in a day or two," I said. "You can make it there faster than us. If you leave at daybreak you could arrive at the wall before nightfall. If you give us two or three days before you leave, we're more likely to be there before you, and we can prepare the others for your arrival."

"Do you really think they won't be afraid of us?" Daisy asked hopefully.

"I'm sure it will take some getting used to you, but they will adapt to you as they have everything else."

CHAPTER FORTY-ONE

River

The ghosts all turned to each other and started speaking over the top of one another again.

"Why should we help them?"

"We should go!"

"I'm not doing it."

"Perhaps it will help us to leave this plane faster! I don't want to be in Purgatory anymore, don't want to hide anymore."

"What if we go and the wall is gone and then we are trapped somewhere with nothing to protect us at night?"

"We can be of *help*!"

This time, I didn't bother trying to follow their rapid-fire conversation.

"You have time to decide!" I shouted into the confusion. "If you decide to come, we'll be at the wall. If not, then maybe we'll meet again one day!"

"How will we know which section of the wall you're at?" Daisy asked me.

I opened my mouth to respond, but I didn't know how to answer that. "Go straight until you hit the wall," Kobal answered. "There should be demons and humans at that section defending it; if it's not us, you can ask the demons where to go."

"They'll never tell us," Ethel snorted.

"Then you will at least be able to follow the wall until you find us," he replied. "There was light at the wall the last time we were there."

I gripped his arm and gave it a grateful squeeze.

"What if we decide to come to the wall and not help? The humans will adjust to us anyway," Pervy said.

"That's not right! No, not fair!" some of the ghosts shouted while others stopped to hear the reply.

"I hate ghosts," Corson said.

"Then you'll most likely be stuck in Purgatory forever," I replied. "Thinking like that is what landed you here and why you're still here now."

Pervy shrugged. I bit my tongue to stop myself from calling him a bastard. Kobal stepped closer to me and leveled Pervy with a look that had the ghost floating back.

"I know of a place that destroys spirits. Didn't think it was possible?" Kobal inquired when Pervy gave him a disbelieving look. "It is. And I am the only one who can gain entrance to it. No matter what happened to Hell, the Fires that gave birth to me still exist. I feel it in these."

He lifted his arm and gestured at the markings on it. "We watched those fires destroy a wraith, and I don't mean they drained the wraith until it could no longer function. I mean the wraith ceased to exist completely. No reincarnation, no chances of moving on. Push me and don't think I won't take you there."

Pervy darted away from us. The other ghosts remained focused on Kobal.

"Impossible," one of them murmured.

"Not impossible," I said. "I saw it."

Most of the ghosts zipped as far as possible away from Kobal.

Lix reemerged with another crate and plopped it on the counter. "Could someone ask my fellow skelleins to come in?" he asked.

"We're leaving soon," Kobal said to him.

"And we will be prepared to do so," Lix assured him before disappearing again.

"What if the wall is gone and you're not there?" Daisy asked me.

"I don't know," I admitted, "but it is worth the chance, or you can all come with us now. You won't be able to have any light when we travel at night."

"No dark!" many of them said at once, and Daisy glanced over her fellow ghosts.

"I think it's best if we wait," she said.

"I understand," I assured her. "We have to go."

"I will see you soon, World Walker," she said.

Kobal opened the door and ushered me out. "Ghosts."

I smiled at the disgruntled tone of his voice. "I think you put them in their place, and they could be helpful."

"Most of them are so selfish they probably won't show up," Corson said as he fell into step beside me.

"I think you're wrong about that," I replied.

He quirked an eyebrow at me as he grinned. "Ever the optimist, my queen. We shall see."

"They could be useful," Kobal murmured before stopping next to one of the skelleins. "Lix requested your help inside. You have exactly five minutes or we're leaving without you."

The skellein turned and gestured to the others before running for the diner as fast as their bony legs would carry them. Kobal leaned against the pickup as Raphael took to the sky and Caim shifted into his raven form. Kobal pulled me against his chest and held me there. Erin had given me the only spare shirt she had to replace my ruined, bloody one. Still, even without all the blood, I knew I stunk. Kobal didn't show any sign of caring.

I inhaled the fiery scent of his flesh while I rested my fingers on his chest. His breath warmed my ear when he ran his tongue around it before nipping it.

"I can't wait to get you somewhere we can be alone," he said.

My toes curled in response to the promise behind his gravelly words. "Neither can I."

The door to the diner opened and the skelleins exited, each of them carrying a crate. I smiled when I saw the clothing and accessories they'd uncovered and put on, most likely from one of the many boxes stacked in the warehouse.

Once again, they each wore something to differentiate themselves. Lix sported a pink shirt with flowers and birds on it and a straw hat. Some of the others were wearing T-shirts, necklaces, a yellow sunhat, and two had on baseball caps, though one wore his hat backward.

"We are good to go, my king," Lix said when he stopped next to Kobal. Shax, Magnus, Corson, and Bale moved closer to us.

"What's in the crates?" Bale inquired.

"Beer!" Lix declared and the other skelleins all clattered their teeth excitedly together.

"Of course," Shax muttered.

"Won't it be bad?" I asked.

"Who cares?" Lix replied.

With a finger, Magnus lifted the top of one to peer inside. "Where do you plan to put the crates?"

Lix pushed the lid of the crate back down and smiled at Magnus. "In the trucks of course. People can sit on them." To prove his point, Lix stood on tiptoe to set his crate in the back of the truck. He swung himself over the side and settled on the box. Leaning against the cab, he crossed his legs and shook his foot back and forth in the air.

Before anyone could respond, Raphael landed beside me. "There are some humans following us. I saw them the other day, but thought they'd broken off to go another way. They're back and on the road behind us."

"Just humans?" Kobal asked.

"Yes."

"How far behind?"

"About fifteen miles," Raphael answered.

"Armed?"

"Yes."

Kobal rubbed his jaw as he glanced at the road we'd traveled to get here. "Should we wait for them to catch up?" I asked.

As if in response, something that sounded like it could peck my eyes out and eat them for dessert screamed in the distance. Kobal rested his hand on my waist. "If they wanted to catch up, they would have already. They're most likely trying to flee what escaped Hell, but we can't allow them to keep following us until we know what they're up to."

"It might be Wren and company," Shax said.

"Who?" Kobal inquired.

"Wren's group were the humans who tried to ambush us on our way to the gateway. We left them tied up in the woods," Shax replied.

Kobal's face darkened, and anger grew within me. I'd never met them, but I knew they'd shot Kobal. Immortal or not, no one was going to hurt him while I was around.

"Why would they be following us?" Kobal grated through his teeth.

Shax held his hands up and took a step back. "Wren arrived at the gateway with some of her friends while you were in Hell. They helped us, and they fought with us, but I haven't seen her since River closed the gateway. I assumed she fled when she saw you. They're not a threat."

I recalled the blonde woman I'd seen by the gateway. I hadn't known who she was, or seen her before, but I suspected it may have been Wren, or one of her friends.

"If they're not a threat, then why are they following us instead of making their presence known?" Kobal demanded.

"She probably still wants to help, but is concerned about what you'll do to her," Shax replied.

"With good reason."

"She's a fighter, Kobal, and so is the rest of her group. They lasted in the wilds when most humans died. They may have hated us before, but when we left them alive they realized that not all demons are out to slaughter everything in their paths. With their knowledge of the wilds and survival skills, we could use their help in what is to come."

Kobal looked to the road again. "Shax, Raphael, and Magnus, take a group of demons and a small number of humans with you to investigate the group following us. If it is Wren and company, and you feel you can trust them, bring them to the wall. If it's stragglers, see what they're doing and make a decision about their fate. If you feel they could become a problem, kill them."

"Kobal," I whispered.

"There are far too many threats right now, Mah Kush-la. We must eradicate as many of them as we can, whether they're human, demon, or angel."

"Ghosts and humans who possibly hate us. Plan to add any more fun things living with us at the wall?" Corson inquired.

"Ghosts are coming to the wall?" Bale asked.

"River invited them to join us," Corson said. "She thinks they could be helpful in keeping the wall lit."

"Joy," Bale muttered.

"They *will* be helpful," I insisted as a drakón roared in the distance.

"The three of you should leave now," Kobal said. "If you don't catch up with us again, we'll see you at the wall."

Magnus and Shax broke away, but Raphael remained. "What is it?" Kobal demanded of him.

"I am not one of your followers to order about," Raphael stated.

Kobal set me behind his back and released me before I could blink. He stepped so close to Raphael that their noses nearly touched as he gazed down at the angel. "You will either do as I say, leave, or I'll kill you. Those are your options. I doubt you'll survive long on your own. There aren't many who are fans of the angels here, not even the golden ones."

My breath caught when Raphael's hand fell to the hilt of his sword. Golden-white sparks danced across the tips of my fingers when I rested them on Kobal's back and drew on his life force. I couldn't pack the punch Raphael could, but I would unleash everything I had on him if he attacked Kobal.

Everyone around us stopped what they were doing to watch the unfolding scene. Behind me, I heard the clatter of Lix's foot hitting the truck bed. Corson and Bale had walked away, but they stopped where they were and edged back toward Kobal.

"You won't get that sword out before your head is in my hand," Kobal promised Raphael.

Raphael's jaw clenched, Kobal's muscles tensed, and I could sense Phenex and Crux stirring within him. Kobal could kill Raphael, but it wouldn't be an easy fight, and it *was* an unnecessary one.

"We are all on the same side here," I said, but neither of them looked at me.

Caim landed next to them and shifted into angel form. Stepping forward, he rested a hand against Raphael's chest and another on Kobal's. "Easy, fellas, fighting each other solves nothing. You're both giant dicks, that's been established. No reason to go at each other again. Besides"—Caim looked pointedly at Raphael—"You were losing to the varcolac when I intervened before. You *will* lose now."

Raphael stared at Kobal for another minute before releasing his sword and shoving Caim's hand away. "Don't touch me again," he spat before stalking away.

"Raphael," Caim said, and the angel stopped to look at him over his shoulder. "The varcolac is the rightful king of Hell, and Earth is more Hell now than not. The varcolac rules here, and you know it. You were a follower in Heaven and you will be one here too."

Raphael stared unblinkingly at him before walking away again. I inhaled a ragged breath and lowered my hands from Kobal's back.

"He will come around," Caim said, his gaze still locked on Raphael's rigid back.

"He has no choice," Kobal replied.

Leaning over the side of the truck, Lix plucked a feather from one of

Caim's wings. Caim gawked at the grinning skellein tucking the feather into his hat.

"Fallen or not, your feathers are much prettier and more colorful than that one's," Lix said and pointed his thumb at where Raphael stood with Shax and the group he was organizing.

Caim continued to gawk at Lix as if he didn't know what had happened. Ruffling his wings, he clasped them fully against his back while he glowered at the skellein. "Don't ever do that again," he commanded.

Lix saluted him before leaning against the cab of the truck again. The metal clanged when he slapped his hand against the side of the bed. "Onward, good man!" he commanded, though no one sat behind the wheel yet.

CHAPTER FORTY-TWO

Kobal

Cresting the top of a hill, I gazed down at the wall spreading across the land. River's breath caught and she slumped against my side. The houses in the town and the massive structure of the wall looked little different than the last time I'd seen them. However, there were more humans standing guard on top of the wall and far less of them training in the field than there would have been on a normal day.

I searched the entire structure before spotting a broken section about three miles to my right. From there, I spotted another crumpled section with smoke still rising from it.

"They've had an attack recently and sustained damage," I said.

"My brothers," River whispered.

"We will get them tomorrow," I promised, "but I have to speak with Mac. We must learn what has happened here, what is going on with the humans, and how far Hell has spread. You also need a break."

"I'm fine."

She wasn't fine. She tried to keep her discomfort hidden, but I didn't miss her winces or the way she sometimes lagged and occasionally fell asleep while she walked. She refused to let me carry her on the journey, and wouldn't spend any more time in the vehicles than the others. A few hours of rest would most likely heal most of her aches and blisters. I would make sure she took the time to recuperate, because she wouldn't.

"Daybreak tomorrow, we'll leave," I promised her.

"Daybreak," she murmured and trudged down the hill beside me.

We were halfway down the hill when vehicles emerged from the town and raced over the grassy field toward us. I nudged River a little behind me. We'd left here as allies, and I didn't expect to be greeted with hostility, but things had drastically changed since we'd last been here.

Before the first truck skidded to a stop in front of us, Colonel Ulrich MacIntyre leapt out of the passenger side. He kept his broad shoulders back as he strode across the grass toward us. There were lines around his gray eyes and mouth that hadn't been there before. His graying brown hair was grayer now, and a haggard air surrounded him, but he smiled at us.

"It is good to see you both," he said as he extended his hand to me. I clasped it and returned his firm shake before he released it and took River's hand. "It looks as if you've all had a rough go of it."

"We did. It seems you've endured some attacks here," I said.

"We have," Mac replied. "Many attacks. Some we beat back, others broke through. We've endured a fair amount of casualties too, but from the info we've received from other sections of the wall, we're faring better than most. Some areas of the wall have been completely demolished, and there are reports of some pretty horrific creatures causing it to happen."

I saw the question in Mac's eyes as I replied. "Most of those reports are probably accurate."

His shoulders slumped before he straightened them again. "Was the gateway unable to be closed?"

"River was successful in closing it, but many things escaped before then. Despite our intention to return things to the way they were, there is no undoing what has been done. We have a lot to discuss. It would be best to do so at your place," I said.

Resting my hands on River's waist, I lifted her and settled her into the back of the pickup Mac had arrived in. I climbed over the side to sit next to her. The others all settled in with us or spread out through the rest of the vehicles. I kept my arm around River while Mac's driver returned us to the wall.

The humans and demons we'd left behind came forward as we drove through the streets of the town toward Mac's residence. Many had dark circles under their eyes, but they all lifted a hand in greeting to us.

"They've had a rough time of it here," River murmured.

"They have, but we will work together to make it better," I replied and tucked a strand of her hair behind her ear. She smiled at me and leaned into my touch as a raven landed on the roof of the truck and ruffled its feathers.

"You may be better off staying in that form, for now. There's no way to know how the humans will react to you," River said to Caim, and he cawed in return.

The truck pulled to a stop in front of Mac's house. My gaze went to the hill above the town and the tents the demons resided in. The canvas sides of the tents rippled in the breeze blowing over the land. Mine remained standing at the front of them all.

River stifled a yawn and rubbed at her eyes when the truck came to a stop. Rising, I lifted her and stepped over the side with her in my arms. "You will rest while I speak with Mac," I told her.

"No, I am your queen. They all must see me as strong."

"No one sees you as anything else. Most of the demons and all of the humans will be going to do the same thing as you."

She opened her mouth to protest before closing it again and gazing at her clothes. "I'd *really* like a shower, some clean clothes, and food. I can shower at Mac's."

I glanced at Mac's house before nodding. "I will have Bale gather some clothes and food for you while you shower, but you will rest after."

"Okay," she relented.

I hid my surprise over her agreement, but her capitulation was the true indicator of her exhaustion.

Kobal

It was nearing midnight when I finally left Mac's house with Corson. We walked up the hill toward the tents. The bonfire wasn't lit, but the faint sounds of music and moans of ecstasy drifted down from the area where the fire had once burned as humans and demons screwed with abandon.

"Do you need me for anything else?" Corson asked as he tugged absently on one of his pointed ears.

I ran a hand through my hair, which was still damp from the shower I'd taken at Mac's. "No, go," I said.

He didn't look back as he broke off to lope up the hill toward the gathering. Bale emerged from the shadows outside my tent when I neared it. Caim strolled out from the other side of the tent. I'd asked Bale to watch over River, but I hadn't expected Caim to be here too.

"River's inside," Bale said before I could ask. "She's probably sleeping."

"Hopefully," I replied. "What are you doing here?" I asked Caim.

"Watching over my niece," he replied.

I stared at him until he waved a hand at the tent. "I gave up everything I knew for her and all living creatures. I will make sure she is kept safe."

"We'll see," I murmured, but I wouldn't deny added protection for River, and Caim was powerful. He knew if he tried anything, I'd kill him. I turned my attention to Bale again. "Have Magnus, Raphael, and Shax returned?"

"Not yet."

"We'll be leaving at dawn tomorrow to retrieve River's brothers. I already let Corson know to gather some demons, and you will join us," I said to Bale. "Mac is assigning humans to come with us as well. We can't risk leaving the wall vulnerable, but at least a hundred humans and demons will make the journey. If Magnus and Shax arrive before we leave, and you see them, tell them they will be coming with us too."

"I will," Bale replied. "How did it go with Mac?"

"He will send out messages to the other groups stationed along the wall to let them know the outcome of the closing of the gateway. Many of those groups will have already heard the result from the demons and humans who were with us and are returning, but there may be some who don't know yet. I told Mac everything that happened in Hell with the seals and River, and at the gateway afterward. There were too many witnesses to it all to try to keep it a secret."

"Do you think it will make the humans fear her more?" Bale inquired.

"It hasn't so far," I replied. "But large groups of panicked humans, who might be looking to blame someone for everything about to come, are far more lethal than smaller groups who witnessed her dying for them. I made it *very* clear to Mac to communicate to everyone that she is to be protected at all costs. If anyone tries to harm her, I will imprison *all* humans from the second they are born until they die."

"That should keep them away from her," Caim said.

"It will," Bale stated.

"Mac also informed me that all communication with his government ceased three days ago," I said. "He doesn't know what happened, or if they still have a government, but it doesn't matter."

"Their old ways are over," Bale said.

"Yes. After we retrieve River's brothers, we will all sit down to discuss it further, but the humans will have to accept a new way of doing things, as will the demons. The humans will still have a ruler who will be the voice for them. I've asked Mac to take that position, and I believe he'll accept, but I told him to think about it while we're gone. Where is Verin?"

"Calah took her to my tent," Bale answered. "I didn't think it would be good for her to return to the tent she shared with Morax."

"No, it wouldn't," I agreed.

"I'd like to come with you tomorrow," Caim said.

"Fine." I'd rather have him where I could see him anyway.

"I'm sure Raphael will also want to come, if he returns before we leave," Caim said.

"Why?" Bale asked.

"He may not heal River again, but he will protect her with his own life. If she dies now, it means he left Heaven in vain. It's why he protested leaving her at the truck stop. He wasn't trying to start a fight, but he doesn't believe himself to be your follower. He will follow *her* though."

"Are you the peace negotiator now?" I growled.

Caim spread his hands before him as he spoke. "You may not know this about me, but amongst the angels, I was the one they came to when they had a problem to resolve. I am known as a good disputer."

"I see," I said.

"Or a smooth talker," Bale said.

"That too," he said with a wink at her.

She scowled at him in return. "Why didn't you resolve the problem before the war broke out in Heaven?"

"I tried to settle the fight with Lucifer before it became ugly, but it got out of hand so quickly that I was incapable of stopping it," he replied. "Truth be told, I never saw it coming. It was such a simple, *stupid* question, and it caused an all-out war. Raphael is unforgiving, often callous. You may not like him, I don't, but he would lay down his life for her."

"And why do you care so much about her?" I demanded.

"I chose this side. I will see it through, and I will make sure she is kept safe. She is kin after all."

I didn't know if he was the smooth talker Bale had accused him of, or if he was being completely honest with me. Either way, I believed him about Raphael, and he did seem truthful about his intent with River.

"You will come to trust me," he murmured.

"We'll see about that."

I lifted the flap to my tent and ducked inside before either of them could reply. Kicking off my boots, I surveyed the small flames dancing in the lanterns on the side bar. A layer of dust coated the table, chairs, and other things I'd collected, but the inside of the tent remained otherwise unchanged.

The cot I'd slept on when River and I were fighting was still against the side wall. I didn't know why she'd chosen the cot over our bed in the backroom, but she lay on it now. Her raven hair fanned out around her sun-kissed face, and her mouth parted as she slept. Now that she'd had a chance to shower, the fresh rain scent of her mingled with the lemon soap the humans used. Unable to move, I breathed in her fragrance and listened to the beat of her heart.

She looked so lovely and innocent, and she shouldn't be here.

Her eyes fluttered open, their violet hue vivid in the dancing lantern light. A smile curved her lips when she spotted me. Sitting up, she swung her feet to the floor. "I'd planned to wait up for you," she said. "I guess it didn't work."

I couldn't respond as my gaze ran over her small scar, her freckles, the beautiful hue of her eyes. All things I knew so well, yet I absorbed the details like it was the first time I'd ever seen her. "You died," I finally stated.

Some of the color faded from her face. Her hands gripped the edge of the cot before she released it and rose. "Kobal—"

"And there was nothing I could do to stop it. I could only stand there and watch as you plunged a sword into your heart."

She took a step toward me. "Kobal—"

I strode toward her before I thought of doing so. Grabbing her hand, I pulled her against my chest.

CHAPTER FORTY-THREE

River

I lost my ability to breathe as Kobal claimed my mouth in a searing kiss that rocked me to the center of my soul. The desperation in the kiss, the hunger, the *love* were all things I'd felt with him before, but never on this intense of a level. A wet heat spread between my thighs as his desire fanned my own.

His hands were on my face before they entwined in my hair. He wrapped it around one of his wrists and cinched it in his hand. My mind spun. I couldn't think as his claws sliced down the front of my brown shirt. The thin material fell back and cool air flowed over my skin.

My flesh became electrified by his touch as he grazed his claws around the underside of my breast before brushing one over my nipple. I was still trying to catch my breath when he cupped my breast. Moaning, my hips surged forward to rub against him. The heady evidence of his arousal pressed into my belly as his thumb stroked my nipple until it became taut with anticipation.

His tongue slid over my lips before plunging into my mouth. His fiery scent and the delicious taste of him overwhelmed me. Unable to stop them, my hands pawed at the shirt he'd donned, but I couldn't get it off him fast enough. I tore at the shirt, ripping the fabric down the front of it to finally expose him to me. Sighing into his mouth, I flattened my palms against his chest and distantly heard the crackle of sparks.

He propelled me backward until my ass bumped into the table. Releasing my breast, his hand slid between the two of us to slice off the button holding my pants together. I wriggled against him when he slid his arm under my ass and lifted me onto the table. Breaking the kiss, he stepped back to tug my pants down my legs before tossing them aside.

The hand wrapped around my hair pulled my head back. My back bowed as his other hand slid between my legs and he pushed my thighs apart. His gaze held mine as he glided his hand up my thigh, scraping his claws against my flesh. I tried to squirm toward him, but his hold on my hair kept me in place.

I stopped moving. My breath came in small pants when his eyes trailed away from mine to run hungrily over my body. Everywhere they touched on me, it felt like his hand did too as my skin prickled with sensation. He retracted his claws when his hand traveled between my thighs to stroke me.

His eyes watched every move he made as he spread my wetness over me before giving my clit a leisurely stroke that nearly had me coming undone. If I'd been able to form words, I would have begged him to put me out of my misery as he stoked the fire in me until I could barely take it anymore.

My legs opened wider. His gaze came back to mine when he pulled my hair back until I couldn't do anything but follow his hand down to the table. He pinned my hair there and held me with my body spread before him. His other hand went to his pants, and he tore the button off them before pulling them down over his waist and thighs.

His erection sprang free, thick and hard with precum already beading on the head of it. I couldn't help but lick my lips in anticipation when he gripped his shaft and guided it toward my entrance.

He teasingly rubbed the large head up and down me, but didn't enter. I squirmed on the table as he continued his leisurely torment of me, but he kept me restrained in a position that made it impossible for me to impale myself on him.

"Too long," I whispered. "Too long without you."

One of his claws stroked my nape. He gave a small tug on my hair that caused me to cry out with my need for more.

"What is it you want, River?" he demanded.

"You," I panted. "Inside of me."

"Like this?" He pushed his head against me, parting my folds but going no deeper. "Or do you crave more?"

"More," I breathed, unable to tear my eyes away from the savage beauty of him as he stretched me until his head fit inside me.

I lifted my hips to take him deeper, but he placed his palm in the middle of my belly and restrained me. Sweat beaded his brow and upper lip from the self-control it took for him not to thrust into me, but he continued to hold back. I didn't know how he could stand this when all I wanted was him inside me while he remained unmoving.

"Kobal," I groaned.

He bent his head to run his tongue around my nipple before drawing it into his mouth and sucking on it. My fingers threaded through his hair, drawing him closer as his fangs grazed my breast. Sparks flashed across my fingertips, illuminating his markings and bronzed skin.

"More!" I cried out.

Releasing my nipple, he swirled his tongue over it and lifted his eyes to look at me as he slid his thumb over my clit again. "Tell me what you want more of, River," he commanded.

"I want *you* inside of me."

"I am inside of you." My fingers dug into his back when he moved his hips in a way that caused his head to rub me in all the right ways, but it still wasn't enough. The demon stilled within me again. "What do you want me to do to you?"

"I want you to fuck me!" I gasped.

"Your wish is my command," he growled.

Before I could blink, he released my hair, withdrew from me, and flipped me over on the table. I was still trying to process what had happened when he pushed my thighs apart from behind and buried himself in me in one thrust. I cried out at the exquisite sensation of finally having him filling me and possessing me again.

His hand clasped my hair. He lifted my head up until my back bowed and sank his fangs into my shoulder. Withdrawing until only his head was inside me again, he wrapped his other arm around my chest and clasped my breast as he thrust back into me. He pinched my nipple before rolling it through his fingers.

He took such complete possession of my body that I no longer had any control over it. I was his to do what he wanted with and I relished it.

The slick feel of his skin against mine aroused me further. He'd possessed me before, but now I felt consumed by him. He released his bite on my shoulder and bit down on my neck, marking me as his again. His corded muscles against my back, his bite, the delicious feeling of him stretching me as he plunged deeper and deeper until I was sure he touched the very core of me, became all I knew.

When he thrust into me again, I came apart with a loud cry. Sparks encircled my wrists as my fingers raked the surface of the table. Waves of bliss spiraled through my limbs, and my legs gave out.

Holding me up, Kobal released my hair and lifted me off the table. Remaining buried within me, he carried me back a few steps and sat on one of the chairs. He placed a hand on my upper back and nudged me forward.

Kobal

I ran my hand down River's delicate spine, savoring the curve of her back as I lowered her further before me. Beneath my fingers, her skin was like spun silk. I drank in the sight of her slender curves and the firmness of her ass as I squeezed it while I guided her against me.

The exquisite sensation of her wet sheath clenching my dick as she rode me had me on the verge of coming. The pressure of semen building in my cock became almost too much for me to take. But take it I would, as I wasn't ready for this to be over.

I needed to be in her, owning her, staking my claim on her until nothing separated us. My gaze latched onto the marks I'd already left on her. My fangs tingled with the compulsion to leave more. Leaning forward, I sank my fangs into her side and smiled when her head tipped back and her body bucked against mine.

Placing my hand on the small of her back, I urged her faster against me. I released my bite to run my tongue over the marks before scraping my fangs against her delicate skin. She squirmed in a way that made it clear she craved my bite again.

Reclaiming her hair, I drew her up until her back was flush against my chest. Over her shoulder, I watched the rise and fall of her breasts with their pert nipples jutting out from her body. A bead of sweat slid down her skin in a tantalizing trail between her breasts. Reaching around her, I followed it with one of my fingers. I'd seen the most beautiful of sirens and canagh demons, but none of them held a candle to River as she completely gave herself over to me.

"You are exquisite, Mah Kush-la," I murmured before sinking my fangs into the tender flesh of her shoulder. Her back arched as she orgasmed again. I barely managed to pull out of her in time to spill my seed against her back. I groaned, my hands clenched on her as my semen flowed from me in a hot wave that branded her back and marked her further as mine.

When the thick stream finally ended, I released my bite on her shoulder and lifted her off me. Turning her around, I settled her so she sat facing me in the chair with her legs draped over the arms. Her dazed eyes met mine, and a smile curved her swollen lips as her fingers played with my hair. The sparks she emitted lit her face and eyes.

I clasped her flushed cheeks in my hands. "You're mine."

Her smile slid away as she leaned forward to kiss me. Lifting her body, she slid herself slowly onto my still, mostly hard dick until I was buried within her again. "Always yours. I love you," she whispered against my lips.

"I love you too, Mah Kush-la. With everything I am."

Her tongue caressed my lips as she rose and fell in a sinuous movement that had me becoming fully erect again. I'd taken her too roughly last time, I knew, so I resisted the urge to drive repeatedly into her again and let her lead the way.

Breaking the kiss, she moved her mouth over my cheeks and down to my shoulder. Her lips skimmed back before she bit into me and marked me as hers.

River

Releasing my bite on Kobal, I lifted my head to look at him again. His amber eyes burned like molten gold, his lips were compressed into a flat line. The angles of his cheekbones and face were sharper as I sensed the savagery still within him. He'd just found his release, he'd marked me and possessed me, but it hadn't been enough to ease the tumult I sensed within him.

We had lost each other.

Clasping his cheeks, I lowered my mouth to his and kissed him again. He nipped at my lip before drawing it into his mouth to suck soothingly on it. Releasing my mouth, he rested his hand on my chest to push me gently back.

His eyes ran over me as I rested my palms on his knees. His knuckles brushed over my collarbone before tracing a line down my stomach. He clutched my hips with both his hands as I continued to set the pace. His claws curled into my flesh, but didn't pierce my skin. My head fell further back, and my movements became more demanding as tension built within me once more.

His eyes burned hotter when they latched onto mine. I locked my legs around the back of the chair and released his knees to drape my arms around his neck. When my eyes started to close, he squeezed my sides.

"Look at me," he commanded in a gravelly voice. "I'm going to watch you come."

My eyes flew open to meet his. I couldn't look away as my body came apart once more and waves of bliss swamped me.

CHAPTER FORTY-FOUR

River

I'd never been more exhausted or sated in my life, yet I found myself staring at the flickering lanterns on the sideboard. We'd been too tired to go into the other tent with the bigger bed, but collapsed onto the cot and continued to make love there until I had no idea what time it was. Kobal's leg was locked over mine, his shoulder beneath my ear as his hand lazily circled my breasts.

"What did Mac say?" I asked.

Lifting his head, he propped it on his other hand. "There have been casualties here and all along the wall. They stopped some of the creatures from going over, but they couldn't stop them all. After the first wave from the seals hit, the ones your father released, they still had communication with the government, but that ended three days ago."

Horror curdled within me. "What happened to cause that?"

"He doesn't know. Before he lost touch with them, the government was working on evacuating some of the towns and relocating people to a more secure area."

"Were they bringing the evacuees to the wall?" I asked as I rolled onto my side to gaze up at him.

"No."

"Where were they sending them?"

"They were grouping them together with surrounding towns to increase the amount of people who could fight. They felt it would be better protection for all and was a safer option than having people traveling to the wall. They didn't want a good chunk of the human population located in one place. I agree with their decision."

"Everyone would be sitting ducks with so many living near the wall," I murmured.

"Exactly. There also aren't enough resources to sustain the surviving human population if too many of them live near the wall."

"Were my brothers moved?"

"Mac doesn't know, but he thinks they're most likely still in the same place, or nearby. You came from a remote area, one that can be better guarded than some of the other towns and has a natural food supply in the ocean."

I took a deep breath to steady my nerves, but I couldn't shake the crushing feeling growing in me. "What could have happened to the government?"

"If they weren't killed, they probably fled. Once we have your brothers, we will work to establish a new rule on Earth. I've asked Mac to work with us and to assume a larger leadership role with the humans. He will require other humans to work with him, of course, but I want him in charge of them. We will receive his answer when we return."

"They may have lost contact with our government, but there were still other ruling bodies around the world. What if those governments decide to bomb us all?"

"All they'll succeed in doing is killing the remaining humans and destroying the rest of their planet. They know bombs don't kill demons, not unless it's a direct hit, and they also know we're their only chance of survival."

I rested my hand over his heart, taking solace in the steady beat of it. "It's going to be anarchy."

"We'll find and kill Lucifer, which will chop the head off the snake. We will work to rebuild this world and make it a place where humans and demons coexist, but the humans will have to accept their new fate if they're to live."

"They'll accept it," I said. "The ones who came to the wall already have. People are resilient, and they'll do whatever is necessary to survive. If anyone can pull everyone together and rule over them, you can—"

"*We* can."

I smiled at him. "Yes, *we* can, especially with the amazing group of fighters *we* have."

He chuckled as he caressed my cheek with his thumb, and his gaze fell to my mouth. I so badly wanted to lose myself in him again, but I couldn't. "We have to get to my brothers."

I started to roll off the cot, but he held me back. "You need rest."

"I did rest, and if I stay in this bed with you, I *definitely* won't get any more resting done."

I tried pulling my hand free, but he planted it against his chest. "Mac is organizing things for us with weapons, vehicles, and troops. It will still be some time before we are ready to leave."

"What if Lucifer gets to my brothers first?"

"He exited Hell on the other side of the world. Even if he knows about your brothers and where to find them, we would most likely still beat him there. He can fly, yes, but his demon followers can't."

"But some of the creatures from the seal can," I protested.

"Yes, and though they are lethal, they are not as cunning, pissed off, or deadly as the upper-level demons he freed from the hundredth seal. He won't risk going after your brothers, and possibly running into us, without a large number of fighters behind him."

My blood ran cold at the possibility of Lucifer descending on my brothers with his army of craeton followers and seal creatures. They'd be terrified, and if he didn't kill them outright, the things he would do to them—

No, I wouldn't think of it. I couldn't. "Kobal, I *have* to go."

He hesitated before leaning forward to kiss my forehead. "We will see how things are progressing with the supplies."

Rolling on top of me, he pinned me to the mattress with his thigh between my legs as he planted his hands on either side of my head. I bit my lip as my body instinctively sought out his.

"I will find your brothers, Mah Kush-la," he promised before rolling over and fluidly rising.

I sat up on the cot as Kobal lifted the tattered remains of my shirt and tossed it onto the table. "Does Mac know the ghosts are coming?" I asked as I rose and walked over to the adjoining tent. Lifting the flap, I slipped inside it. I strode past the bed and opened the doors on the armoire to peer inside.

"I told Mac to prepare for their arrival," Kobal said from behind me.

I turned to find him standing at the foot of the bed. "He must have been thrilled."

He smiled at me as he walked over to stand behind me. His body warmed mine as he reached around me to pull out a pair of pants and a shirt for himself. "About as much as I am about it, but we all must adjust to living with each other now, and the ghosts could prove helpful here."

"Yeah," I muttered as I uncovered some of my clothes.

It was still nightfall when Kobal led me out of the tent and to the house I showered in. He didn't like using human showers, but he took a quick one too while I dressed. Lifting the hairbrush I'd brought with me, I worked the tangles from my hair while I watched Kobal exit the bathroom. My gaze lingered on the bites I'd left on his flesh when he dropped a towel from his waist.

My Chosen, for eternity. That was still going to take time to process, but once I had my brothers back and Lucifer was dead, I would take the time to enjoy having an eternity with this demon. I couldn't wait.

I hastily pulled my wet hair into a ponytail as Kobal finished dressing. Taking my hand, he led me out of the house and back to the area where the demons resided. All their tents formed a circle around an open clearing. On the horizon, the sky had lightened from a velvety black to a deep gray.

We passed three tents before Kobal stopped and rapped his knuckles against the outside of one.

"What?" Corson demanded groggily from within. The murmured complaints of more than one female could be heard as something clattered within.

"Time to go," Kobal said brusquely and pulled me away from the tent.

A giggle from the woods alerted me to a nymph loping through the trees. Two completely naked male demons chased behind her. "The demons are already adapting to their new world," I murmured.

"I think many of those who first came to Earth with me would have stayed even if they had to travel back and forth to Hell to keep their immortality," Kobal replied. "The ones who remained in Hell while we were on Earth will acclimate soon enough."

"The nymphs already are."

"The nymphs could adapt to life anywhere as long as they have trees to play in and partners to satisfy them. But they will make it easier for the other demons to adjust too. They'll make them happier."

"That they will," I agreed.

We stopped in front of another tent. Kobal raised his hand to hit the side of it, but the flap pulled back before he could and Bale stepped out with Verin at her side.

"We're ready," Verin said. She lifted her chin and stared at Kobal as if she were gearing up for an argument.

I opened my mouth to tell her to stay so she could grieve, or cry, or whatever demons did when they lost a loved one. Then I realized that demons fought, and if Verin had a chance to help end Lucifer, she wasn't going to miss it. Nothing would have stopped me either.

Kobal stared at her before speaking, "Good."

Turning, we walked down the hill together. Verin kept her shoulders back, but her eyes remained focused on the ground as she walked and she began to fall behind.

“How is she doing?” I whispered to Bale.

Bale brushed back a strand of her fiery hair as a raven landed beside her. With a ripple of wings and feathers, Caim appeared.

“She is still breathing, but she does not live,” Bale said without so much as a glance at the angel who fell into step beside her.

Her words sounded like one of the skellein’s riddles, but unlike their riddles, I understood what Bale meant. My eyes lifted to Kobal. Knowing that I would have left him like Verin, if not for Raphael’s intervention, made me shudder.

We were almost to the wall when a squeaking noise drew my attention to the field where I’d spent many days training with Kobal. On the horizon, a pickup crested the hill. It idled for a minute before descending toward us.

CHAPTER FORTY-FIVE

River

"Shax and Magnus," Kobal said and halted beside me.

A few dozen humans followed the truck. They walked with their shoulders back and their weapons at the ready. A flutter of wings drew my attention to Raphael as he landed beside Caim and shook some of the dust from his wings.

"How did it go?" Caim inquired of him.

Raphael hesitated long enough that I didn't think he would answer Caim. "Well enough. They are strong for humans," Raphael finally said. "They are ready for war. I've seen them use their weapons, and they are very skilled with them. The woman, Wren, says she can bring more humans to the fight, if she believes they'll be treated fairly here."

"Hmm," Kobal grunted and turned his attention to the pickup as it came to a stop before us.

A pretty woman with pale blonde hair slid out from behind the wheel. I recognized her as the woman I'd glimpsed at the gateway. "Is that Wren?" I asked.

"Yes," Kobal said.

Now that I knew she'd been the one to shoot Kobal, I contemplated setting her ass on fire as I eyed her up and down.

Two men also exited the truck as Shax and Magnus broke away from the other people and strolled forward to join us. "I know what Shax thinks of them, but what do you think?" Kobal inquired of Magnus.

"I think they'll kill any one of us just as easily as they'll spit at us. And unfortunately, I've discovered they're a bunch of spitters," Magnus snickered. "However, they are definitely survivors and could prove valuable."

"They also know the wilds better than any of us," Shax said.

"True," Kobal agreed.

"Perhaps you should be asking us what *we* think of *you*," Wren said as she strolled forward with her rifle against her shoulder.

"I know what you think of us," Kobal replied. "And if you think that gun will help you, you're wrong. I didn't want to kill you before, I won't hesitate now."

Wren slid the rifle down to rest the butt end on the ground. "I've no doubt," she replied.

"I told you if I ever saw you again, I'd kill you," Kobal said to her. "Why would you go to the gateway after that?"

"You said to me that I had no idea what monsters truly are and that, if you failed, we would know. You made me curious about what you meant by that and what it was you were trying to succeed at doing. And when I learned what it was, I decided to help. We've been fighting to survive for years. It's what we do, but we would like for the fighting to end one day."

"That day may never come," Kobal stated.

"Maybe not," she replied. "But we can come together against a common enemy instead of fighting each other. There is also the possibility for a better life for us," she said with a wave of her hand at those gathered around her. "We're not stupid or stubborn enough to think we can survive in the wilds without help anymore, not with everything we saw come out of that gateway."

She turned her attention to me. "Speaking of which, I saw what you did at the gateway. What are you?"

I bristled when her curious gaze raked over me, and Kobal released a rumble of warning. "Do you honestly think I would tell you that?" I retorted.

"No, but I figured it was worth a shot," Wren replied with a shrug of one of her shoulders. "What you did at the gateway was impressive." A few people nodded behind her while the others all eyed me as if they were trying to solve a puzzle. "You died to close it though, so you're mortal, but the angel saved you and the demon looks like he's about to tear my head off for speaking to you. I bet it's a fascinating tale, and one day I hope you'll trust me enough to share it."

I blinked at her, unsure of how to respond to her blunt words, but she was already focused on Kobal again.

"Okay, Beastly, here's what I think of you. You're a demon, you're a prick, and from what I've been told you're the king of Hell, but you're on our side, so the rest of it doesn't matter if it keeps this world from going to complete shit. We'll fight for you if we believe it's the right thing to do, but we'll follow her," she said and pointed her finger at me.

My eyebrows shot into my hairline. I was fairly certain her time in the wilds had rattled Wren's brain, but I kind of liked her brazen insanity.

"Fair enough," Kobal replied. "But she is my queen and will be treated as such. If any of you try to harm her, I won't kill you. Instead, I will have you pleading for death every day for the lengthy lifespan I will allow you to have."

Behind her, the others all blanched. Wren remained unfazed as she studied me. "A *fascinating* tale," she murmured to me. "Understood," she said briskly to Kobal. "If all goes well here for us, I can and will bring you more fighters. We'll also help you map out the wilds that we know. Some of us have been to areas others haven't, and there are some areas *none* of us have ever been to."

"What do you expect in return?" Kobal asked her.

"The added protection of demons fighting on our side, honesty, and the respect we deserve."

"You will get all those things if they're earned. One foot out of place and you will be destroyed, as will everyone who came here with you. No questions asked."

"Good thing I'm pretty nimble then," she said and hefted her rifle into her hands.

"Well, well, well, what do we have here?" Corson drawled as he strolled out from behind us and crossed the field to where Wren stood.

She frowned at him as he circled her. From the tip of his right ear dangled a little star earring, a fish hung from the top of his left ear, and a gold stud was in the bottom of his right ear. He'd been extremely busy last night, I realized.

"What's your name, beautiful?" Corson inquired.

Wren tapped the barrel of her gun against her palm. The malice behind the gesture had Corson grinning back at her.

"Her name is Wren," Kobal said.

"Wren," Corson purred the name and stopped circling to plant himself in front of her. "I like it."

"I don't care what you like," she retorted, and his smile widened.

"Tell me, Wren, do you wear earrings?" The look on her face almost made me laugh out loud as Corson flicked back a strand of her hair to reveal her bare ears. "Pity," he murmured. "I'd be willing to go without them though, for you."

She rolled her eyes at him. "Fucking demons."

"Oh yes, we are quite capable of fucking. All. Night. Long," Corson said slowly.

Wren gawked at him like he was an alien life form. The color creeping through her cheeks wasn't something I'd expected from the brazen woman. A demon threatening to kill her was fine, but one flirting with her completely rattled her.

"I'd be more than happy to take you for a spin," Corson continued.

"Enough, Corson," Kobal commanded.

Corson remained where he was, his eyes locked on Wren's before he winked at her and stepped away. Wren's mouth dropped before she clamped it closed and gripped her gun against her chest.

Kobal turned to face Shax. "I intended for you to come with us today, but I think it best if you stay and get them situated here. I'll send Mac to meet with you once I'm done speaking with him. He'll also have to agree to these humans staying here, but I don't see him turning away help."

"I will take care of it," Shax said.

"Let's go," Kobal said to the others and turned on his heel to head back toward the wall.

I glanced over my shoulder at Wren as Corson gave her a sweeping bow. He claimed her hand and planted a kiss on the back of it before she yanked it away from him. He leapt back in time to avoid the punch she launched at his face.

"Until we meet again, my sweet," he said to her and sauntered away to catch up with us.

"She didn't appreciate your pitiful attempt at flirting," I told him when he fell into step beside me.

"She enjoyed it," he replied with an arrogant smile.

"She tried to knock you out."

He did an odd little skip step. "It was meant to be a love tap."

"I think you're mistaken about that."

"Or I'm right and you're going to be eating your words." He pulled the earrings from his ears and tossed them aside. "Now, let's go find your brothers."

CHAPTER FORTY-SIX

Kobal

River squirmed in the seat beside me. From the driver's side, Hawk shifted away from her. "It looks mostly the same," she whispered as she stared out the windshield.

Resting her fingers on the dashboard, she leaned forward before sitting back again. I placed my hand on her knee when she started tapping her foot on the floor.

"It does," Hawk agreed.

I'd never been to this area of Earth as the demons had been kept secret from the humans residing here. Dotting the landscape were crumpled and burnt-out homes. Many of the wrecked houses were being reclaimed by vegetation.

"We'll be there soon," Hawk said.

River started wringing her hands in her lap.

"Easy," I said and clasped her hands.

Her eyes were turbulent when they swung toward me. "It doesn't look all that different, but something's not right. I *feel* it."

I drew her closer against my side as Hawk eased the truck over a series of ruts. In the passenger-side mirror, I watched more pickups and a larger truck traveling behind us. Calah, Lopan, Lix, and some of the skelleins rode in the truck following us. Through the trees lining the roadway, the hounds loped beside the road. A shadow fell over us as Raphael circled above, and to my far right, a drakón plunged into the woods to feed.

"Why are the drakón still out there?" River whispered. "Don't they have somewhere else to go?"

"They'll move on. They're feeding as they go," I assured her as her foot started tapping again.

A thud behind me drew my attention to Erin, Vargas, Bale, Verin, and Corson sitting in the bed of the truck. Caim cawed loudly from where he'd landed beside Corson and shifted into angel form.

"Anything ahead?" I asked through the open window behind River.

"No," Caim replied. "Nothing that I can see, but I only went so far as the collapsed bridge."

"What collapsed bridge?" River's voice took on a hysterical note. The truck slowed further when Hawk's head whipped toward the window.

"Ahead, less than a mile, a bridge has collapsed into the water below," Caim answered. "I'm sure it has happened to many of them over the years."

"The bridge was intact when I left," River whispered, and her foot tapped faster as she started wringing her hands again. Hawk focused on the road and pressed on the accelerator.

"Careful, Hawk," I said.

He eased off the gas when the truck was rocked by a series of holes in the pitted road. Chunks of asphalt clanked off the bottom of the truck when the tires threw them up.

Turning back to the window, I met Caim's gaze. "Stay low enough that nothing can see you in the air, keep to the trees, and stay within a half-mile radius. Tell Raphael to do the same. We can't risk either of you being spotted if something more than a simple bridge collapse awaits us."

Caim shifted to soar up to Raphael.

"Something's not right," River said again.

"The people on the Cape could have collapsed the bridge themselves," Hawk said. "It would help keep things from getting over the canal and stop people from flooding onto the Cape again, like they tried to do after the gateway opened. Destroying the bridge could have been a measure of self-preservation. They may have destroyed the other bridge too."

"Or they could have been evacuated," I reminded River, "and the bridge collapsed on its own from time and water."

She barely glanced at me before focusing ahead again. When we crested over the top of a hill, the broken remains of a bridge came into view. River's breath sucked in; she leaned forward until her nose almost touched the windshield. I rested my hand on her shoulder, drawing her back as I gazed at the twisted pieces of metal sticking into the air. Looking over the embankment, I spotted more of the massive structure jutting out of the water.

Caim landed in the bed of the pickup again when Hawk started down a road running parallel to the rushing current of a canal. The sun lit the dark blue water, and I scented creatures living beneath its surface. The aroma reminded me of River, but this was tangier than her scent, and it left something sticky on my mouth. Curious to the taste, I licked my lips and found it salty but not unpleasant.

"Did you see anything else?" I asked Caim.

"No, it is clear on this side."

"Good."

Caim inhaled a deep breath and closed his eyes. "The ocean," he murmured. "It reminds me of home."

"The ocean reminds you of Hell?" Vargas inquired.

Caim smiled at him as he leaned back to spread his wings over the side of the truck. The tips of them almost touched the asphalt. "No, I still consider Heaven my home. Heaven is not only made up of endless clouds and sky, but of rivers and seas so deep a purple they are nearly blue. The angels rose from those waters as surely as the varcolac rose from the fires."

River's amethyst eyes widened, and her fresh rain scent intensified. A part of River had also been forged from those Heavenly waters.

"I've always felt a special affinity for water and the ocean," she said.

My hand tightened around hers as I gazed from her to the sea. The powerful current of the water reminded me of her strength; it didn't waver.

Rising over the top of another hill, River cried out when more broken metal sticking into the air came into view. Hawk stopped near the crumpled remains of a second bridge as he put the truck in park. He gripped the wheel as he gazed at it with a dejected expression.

"I have to get out," River said.

I opened the truck door and climbed out of the vehicle. Hawk pushed his door open. River scrambled out behind me and ran toward the edge of the hill with Hawk and me at her side. Dirt and rocks kicked up beneath her feet when she skidded to a halt.

Gripping her elbow, I pulled her back a step when she showed no sign of knowing her toes hung over the edge. In the waters below lay another structure with rust creeping over its silver paint. The water surged over the sides of the banks. It poured over rocks, and a pathway, as it sought to find a new way around the bridge blocking its natural course.

"The railroad bridge might still be standing." River jerked her arm away from me. She ran back to the truck and jumped behind the wheel before anyone could stop her. "Get in!"

I didn't climb into the cab of the truck again, but lifted myself into the bed. Bracing my legs apart, I rested my hand on the roof and searched for any hint of danger. If something came at us, I would be prepared for it. Around me, the others all rose in the bed and braced themselves as they drew their weapons.

Hawk slid into the passenger seat and slammed the door as River hit the gas. She didn't stomp on it as I'd expected, but she still drove faster than Hawk had. The jarring impact of the ruts shook the truck and caused it to groan in protest as it bounced over the road.

"This thing's going to fall apart," Bale muttered.

My eyes scanned the buildings lining the broken street with their faded signs hanging on the front or lying on the ground. Broken windows marred almost every building, but nothing moved through the shadows within them.

Bending, I spoke through the open window. "Is it always this quiet here?"

"Yes." Hawk braced his hand against the roof when River hit a bump that nearly sent all of us flying. I planted my heel against the side of the truck to maintain my balance better. "This used to be a tourist area mostly, stores and stuff catering to them. After the war, there was no need for the things sold here and these buildings were too far from residents to be of much use for anything else."

River pulled into a burnt-out parking lot. The truck lurched and made a grinding noise as she shifted it into park before coming to a stop. Shoving off the side of the truck, I leapt over the edge as she flung open her door. Landing beside her, I stayed close to her side, searching for any hint of danger as she raced toward another metal structure rising into the air. Unlike the other bridges, this one created a pathway across the water.

River

I ran down the embankment toward the railroad bridge. The tracks had been lowered to extend across the canal. Against the blue sky, the two turrets of the bridge stood proudly in the air on either side of the canal.

When I was younger, the tracks were usually in the air to allow the passing of boats and ships beneath it, but they would lower when a train came through. After the war, the trains stopped running so the bridge remained raised. I hadn't seen it down in years.

I went to leap onto the tracks when Kobal pulled me back. "What are you doing?"

I tried to jerk my arm free.

"Slow down." He scanned the trees on the other side of the canal before looking to the sky. "We have no idea what might be ahead."

"Kobal—"

"We will not run into a trap," he said.

"It might not be Lucifer. It might be something else entirely." I was unable to keep the desperation from my voice. I had to get to Bailey and Gage, *now*. "How would Lucifer even know to look for me or my brothers here?"

"How do you know things that no other does? You're not the only one who receives visions."

"And he is Lucifer," Caim said as he strolled toward us. "He has his ways and followers with abilities too."

My gaze went back to the bridge. "We have to find my brothers."

"We will," Kobal said before turning to Caim. "You and Raphael stay ahead of us and stay close. *Do not* allow yourselves to be seen."

"I don't have a death wish, varcolac," Caim replied before shifting and taking to the sky.

Kobal turned to the others. "Grab your weapons. We have to leave the vehicles here." They all scurried to do as he commanded before joining us near the bridge. "Stay by me," Kobal said to me.

"I will."

Releasing my arm, Kobal moved in front of me and onto the tracks where he broke into a loping run. I followed behind him, my heart thudding with every step as my feet pounded over the railroad tracks. Hawk ran beside me, while the others followed us.

Through the slats in the tracks, I could see the deep blue water of the canal beneath us. The cool white spray dampening my cheeks reminded me I was *home*. I'd yearned to return, to see the ocean and my friends and family again, but this felt so wrong.

"This was never down before," I panted to Kobal. "The Guard kept the railroad bridge up to prevent people from entering our side when they weren't supposed to."

"Members of the Guard were always posted on both sides of it too," Hawk said.

Now, no one stood watch.

My feet landed on the asphalt of the bike path next to the canal, a place where I'd spent so much time over the years fishing to feed my family. Frowning, I tried to figure out what was wrong as I gazed at all the familiar things that felt so foreign to me now. The large rocks looked the same, small waves still crested in white peaks and the current still swirled throughout.

My stomach sank as I finally figured it out. *No* one was here. No one stood on the rocks. There were no fishing poles, no laughter, no greetings called out to others. No one walked the water line, picking crabs from the rocks. There were no seagulls or heron perched on the light poles or bobbing on the water. No caws pierced the silence, no mussels or clams fell from the sky as the gulls dropped them in attempt to crack their shells. Remains of those shells littered the walkway, but nothing picked at them.

It didn't matter what time of day it was, there was always someone here fishing, collecting crabs, or checking their lobster pots. There were always birds feasting on the bounty the canal offered them.

The absolute silence and stillness of it all made my skin crawl and frightened me more than being pinned to the seal had.

"Something is so wrong," I whispered.

"Where do we go?" Kobal asked as he rested his hand on my shoulder.

Taking a deep breath, I turned away from the canal and focused on the bike path. "This way."

He released my shoulder, and I raced down the canal path before veering off onto a trail that wound through the woods. My feet landed effortlessly between the tree roots breaking through the dirt of the pathway, but the others grunted as they were caught up in, or tripped by, them. I knew this trail as well as the back of my hand. I hadn't traversed it in months, but I still recalled every detail of it and nothing had changed. Well maintained, not even vegetation crept in to reclaim it.

The last time I'd traveled this path, the birds had been singing and the squirrels chasing each other through the trees. Nothing moved now except for the leaves overhead as they swayed in the breeze of the early September day. Where did all the animals go? Something horrific had to have happened to chase them all away or scare them into hiding.

Gage. Bailey.

Their names ran on a loop in my mind, driving me faster. Turning a corner in the path, my fingers brushed against the trunk of a red maple tree. It was a tree I'd touched often while walking through here. Beneath my fingers, I felt the maple's roots digging into the earth and the worms squirming through them. Before, I hadn't known what it meant to experience this feeling, now the flow of life flooded every cell of my body.

I skidded to a halt when the pathway ended at the neighborhood where I'd grown up. I gazed over the sagging, weather-worn houses. Years of focusing on survival had left little time for people to worry about the upkeep of their homes. Many had paint chipping off them, sagging porches, missing shutters, and overgrown yards, but there had always been warmth here and a sense of welcome. There were always people milling about, greeting others, heading out to fish or coming back for the day. They'd be gardening or swapping supplies at the exchange Mrs. Loud ran from her house.

Now it felt like a graveyard, minus the headstones.

I strained to hear anything, but the silence stretched onward until I wanted to scream. Every breath became increasingly difficult to take.

Kobal gestured to those following us. They spread out through the trees with their weapons at the ready. Some knelt in the shadows as they focused their guns on the homes, others remained standing and ready to move into the town.

Raphael landed beside us. “There’s nothing amid these homes,” he said. “I did not go far beyond, but I will if it becomes necessary.”

“Not right now,” I said. “This is my neighborhood. We’ll search through here for an answer to what’s happened first.”

“Where is everyone?” Erin asked from behind me.

I was both desperate and terrified to learn the answer to that question.

CHAPTER FORTY-SEVEN

River

"They could have all gone to the old army base," Hawk suggested. "They wouldn't be as close to the ocean, but if they felt it was better to be grouped closer together for protection, there are a lot of places on the base for them to stay."

"Or they could have been evacuated and Mac didn't know about it," Kobal said.

I wanted them both to be right, but the pit in my stomach and the strangling sensation in my throat said they weren't.

I took Kobal's hand and led him around the back of Mrs. Loud's house and into the empty town.

They were all supposed to be safe here! Please don't let me stumble across the bodies of all those I've known and loved my whole life.

Turning the corner of another house, I released Kobal's hand and bolted up the steps of the home my friends Asante and Lisa shared. I practically ripped the screen door off its hinges when I threw it open. Grabbing the knob, I turned it and shoved open the door.

"Asante! Lisa!" I shouted and then winced as my cry sounded louder than gunfire in the house. I hesitated for a second, but nothing jumped out to eat me and I heard no explosion of noise from outside.

I hurried down the hall, past the pictures in their frames and the scrawled drawings that Bailey's tiny hands had created, hanging on the walls. The faint hint of cooked apples lingered within, but there was no sign of life.

"Gage! Bailey!" I called.

Throwing open a couple of doors, I barely glanced into the empty bedroom and bathroom before continuing. I froze in my tracks when I came across a room with two twin beds. A worn teddy bear lying on the bed against the wall, and a pair of patched pants lying at the foot of the other bed caused the lump in my throat to grow.

Bailey won't sleep without that bear and Gage is always ripping or outgrowing his pants.

The blue curtains fluttering in the breeze coming through the open window caused shadows to sway over the walls. My gaze ran over the furniture, but I didn't see any dust on it or on the comb set out on the nightstand. It hadn't been that long since they'd last been here.

The board behind me creaked; Kobal stepped closer to gaze over my shoulder into the room. "Gage and Bailey lived here?" he asked.

"Asante and Lisa brought them here after I was taken to the wall." But they weren't here now.

Lisa's parents' house! They could be there! I spun back toward Kobal and tried to shove past him.

"River, slow down," he said and rested his hands on my shoulders.

"I can't. They have to be.... I have to find them. One way or another, I *have* to know what has happened to them!"

"You will." Drawing me against his chest, he hugged me close before releasing me. "But you must take it easy. There could be something we miss if you keep running from one place to another."

He was right, but I wanted to tear this entire town apart with my bare hands in search of them. Stepping back, he framed my cheeks with his hands and tilted my face up. He bent to give me the briefest kiss before clasping my hand to lead me back down the hall. I couldn't bring myself to look too closely at Bailey's drawings, I might burst into tears if I did.

Raphael, Hawk, and Caim stood inside the front door, but the hundred or so other humans and demons remained outside and alert for any hint of danger.

Stepping outside, I released Kobal's hand before leading the way back through town at a brisk jog. My feet stumbled on the pavement when I came to an abrupt halt next to the community garden. On a normal day, any number of people would be within it, tending the vegetables and weeding. Lisa had often worked here to help keep everyone fed.

Now, all I saw were the handful of tomatoes that had fallen onto the ground and remained there.

"They would never let food rot in such a way," I murmured to Kobal.

I didn't recall covering the distance between the garden and Lisa's parents' house, but I found my feet barely hitting the ground as I flew up their porch steps. I glanced at my own house and inwardly cringed before throwing open the door of the screened-in porch and hurrying across it to the other door.

I moved so fast that I couldn't get the inner door open before my shoulder bashed into it. Pain shot from my shoulder to my wrist as I fumbled with the knob. Kobal pulled me back and twisted the knob. He didn't bother to tell me to slow down again; it would be useless. I was too out of control, I knew it, but I couldn't reign myself in.

The door swung open and I stepped into the shadowed interior of the house. My breath caught as the ever-present scent of lavender filled my nose. I stopped for a minute to take in the books lining the shelves, the TV pushed into the corner, and the scarred coffee table with its numerous water rings. I'd created a few of those rings myself.

As I forced myself onward, Kobal walked beside me through the living room and into the kitchen.

No one was there, but in my head, I could hear Lisa's mother laughing as her father flipped pancakes for breakfast, and Lisa talking excitedly about whatever new thing she'd discovered in the garden.

It played out so perfectly in my mind that for a second I saw their images before me, and their laughter replaced the sound of my blood pounding in my ears.

Then, they faded away and I was left with only the chipped wood cabinets, faded yellow curtains, and cluttered counters. I'd sat on those counters and talked with Lisa more times than I could recall. It's where she'd told me she had a crush on Asante, where she'd revealed she was in love with him, and where I'd first confessed one of my strange visions to someone else.

I was left with the hollow certainty that this room would never again know the love and happiness that Lisa's family exuded.

How many times had I sat at that table before the gateway opened and eaten pancakes with my hands? How many times had I sat there before and after the war and felt safe in a way I never did in my own house?

"Who lives here?" Kobal asked.

"It's Lisa's parents' home," I whispered. I ran my fingers over the kitchen table as I walked over to the window in the back door. At one time, there had been a fence dividing this yard from the neighboring ones. The fence had been torn down years ago to make room for more farming area.

"I spent so much time here as a kid that it became my second home, my only *real* home. It's where I came the times my mother kicked me out, or was being especially vicious. Lisa's parents took me in every time without question. They loved me. I… I loved them."

My hands fisted at my sides when I realized I was talking about them as if they were already dead. I struggled to maintain control of myself and blinked away the tears burning my eyes. Turning, I walked past Kobal and back through the living room. I spotted the others standing guard outside as I climbed the steps by the front door to the upstairs.

Kobal stayed close behind me as I went through the rooms above. I knew the house was empty, but I still searched for any hint as to where everyone could have gone, seeking some sign that they were still alive.

More memories assailed me when I entered Lisa's bedroom. The purple walls hadn't changed since we were kids. The dolls, bears, and knickknacks lining the shelves were exactly as they'd been before the war. When I was a child, I'd envied Lisa's toys and secretly coveted some for myself. After the war, they'd become dust collectors that we both forgot about.

She'd never taken them down, never changed them, and as far as I knew, she'd never played with them again. I suspected she'd kept them that way to preserve the memories of happier times, when she'd been innocent and the world had been kinder. Instead of being envious of them, I enjoyed coming here and seeing all the toys that reminded her of better times.

From the window beside Lisa's bed, I gazed at the house only a hundred feet away. Its sagging porch, broken siding, and missing shingles from the roof were in far worse repair than the other homes surrounding it. The front windows were missing their ledges, and one was also missing a pane of glass.

I'd lived in that house for most of my life; just the sight of it caused cold dread to settle in the pit of my stomach. I rested my fingers against the window as I tried to bury the memories of all I'd endured in that pitiful structure.

I was no longer the girl who had grown up there, or the woman taken from there months ago. Yet just thinking about my mother was enough to make me feel like a frightened child, an angry teen, and a resentful woman all over again.

I had no choice but to return to that place.

My shoulders slumped as I turned to face Kobal in the doorway. His eyes ran over the assortment of toys lining the shelves before settling on the pictures set out on the nightstand beside me. The pictures were of

Lisa, her parents, and Asante's school picture from the second grade, but she also had two of us.

One of them was taken when we were seven. We had our arms entangled around each other's necks as we grinned at the camera, revealing our missing front teeth. The other was from when we were sixteen. My jeans were torn, and Lisa's shirt was unbuttoned at the collar as we sat on a rock near the canal. We were both leaning against each other and staring at our feet. I clearly recalled that we'd been kicking our feet back and forth while we talked in the hushed whispers of teenagers who had so many secrets they could never share with the world, and all of them were life and death. At the time, we hadn't realized she'd been there, but Lisa's mother had sketched the picture.

Bending down, I stretched my hand under Lisa's bed and grabbed the strap of the duffel bag I knew she kept stowed there. I pulled it out and rose. With one swipe of my arm, I shoved all the pictures into it. I would return to the other house later to gather things for my brothers, but I wasn't leaving here without those pictures.

I hefted the bag over my shoulder and turned back to Kobal.

"I have to go next door," I said. "I have to return to where I lived."

CHAPTER FORTY-EIGHT

River

I didn't run next door, didn't fly up the stairs with the same reckless abandon I had everywhere else. I couldn't. I may not be the same person who had left here, I'd literally been through Hell and back, yet my feet felt weighted down by cement blocks as I trudged up the steps to a house that had never been a home for me.

The faded gray front door sagged on its rusting hinges. The door-knob had busted off since I'd been here, leaving only the broken mechanical bits inside the door behind. Kobal slid his arm around my waist to pull me closer. My body tensed against his when he pushed in the mechanical bits and something clicked.

Resting his hand on the door, Kobal swung it inward. I couldn't stop myself from wincing at the creaking hinges. I'd faced Lucifer, but this small noise still made me shudder at the thought of waking my Mother. I would pay for it if I did.

I shook my head to clear it of the haunting image of my mother coming at me as a clammy sweat coated my skin.

Shadows played over the hallway from the sunlight filtering in behind us. It illuminated the peeling paint and patches of exposed and, in some places, broken plaster. The stale scent of mildew permeated the air. Cobwebs dangled from the ceiling, and a thick layer of dust coated the walls and hall table. The dirt caking the floor made it impossible to tell if it was hardwood or a rug there.

A few leaves skittered down the hall when a breeze blew through the doorway. The other homes had appeared recently abandoned; this one looked as if no one had lived here in months. My mother had never been one for housekeeping; that had fallen to me and Gage. Then, she'd sold me to the government, Gage had gone to live with Lisa, and no one had helped her anymore.

For many years, the drone of the TV greeted me whenever I opened this door. Now there was only more silence. Swallowing heavily, I set the duffel bag on the ground outside the door and stepped inside.

I walked into the doorway of the living room where my mother had spent most of her life. Standing in the threshold, I gazed at the tufts of yellow stuffing poking through the worn brown fabric of my mother's favorite armchair. Because the springs had busted through the seat years ago, she'd sat on two pillows while she endlessly watched the news reports on TV.

I froze when I spotted the blonde head sitting in the chair where I'd often seen it. I couldn't move as my knees locked and my feet planted into the ground. Blinking, I tried to figure out if I was hallucinating or if my mother actually sat there. The more I blinked, the more I realized she wasn't fading away, or moving.

My *dead* mother sat in that chair! She'd died and there had been no one to notice or care. Had her decomposing corpse been there for months?

Kobal stepped forward. My hand shot out and I gripped his forearm, holding him back. If she'd died months ago, the place would smell worse than mildew, wouldn't it? Maybe the stench of decay would have faded by now, but I believed there would at least be a hint of it on the air. All I smelled beneath the mildew was the faint hint of ocean air, body odor, and rotten food.

If she'd died more recently, she wouldn't stink yet.

No movement came from the chair. If she'd been alive, she would have heard us open the door, or the creak of the floorboards as Caim, Raphael, Hawk, and Corson entered the house. She didn't so much as flinch.

Kobal

I glanced between River and the chair as her fingers bit so deep into my flesh that her nails pierced my skin. Yet, she showed no sign of realizing she clung to me like a lifeline. She'd stared down all the creatures and angels of Hell with less terror than what shimmered in her eyes now.

I'd long ago realized the only thing that made River vulnerable, the only thing she'd ever feared, was her mother—the woman who I believed to be sitting in the chair before us.

I went to draw River closer, but her feet remained planted on the ground. Then, she lifted her chin, took a deep breath, and stepped further into the room. My upper lip curled as I took in the room. Unlike the other human homes I'd entered, with their pictures and small signs of family and love within them, this place was bleak.

How anyone like River had managed to come from this place, I didn't know, but I would ensure she was cherished for the rest of her days.

The blank screen across from the woman reflected her pale face and unblinking eyes as River edged closer. Following River around the recliner, I spotted the plates of food on the floor. Most of the moldy food was unrecognizable, though an apple sat on the floor near the woman's right foot.

"Mother?" River whispered.

There was no response, no sign of a reaction. My other hand fell on River's waist as her nails dug deeper into my arm. Blood welled forth, but I didn't try to ease her hold on me. "We should go," I said gruffly, intending to carry her out of this place and away from that woman forever.

"No. I have to… I have to know."

RIVER

Stepping next to the chair, I gazed down at the woman staring at the TV. Her fingers gripped the threadbare arms of the chair. The stringy blonde hair waving around her face emphasized the shadows lining her eyes. Her face was gaunter than I recalled and far paler, but she was otherwise unchanged.

I still couldn't tell if she was dead or alive as I tried to detect the smallest rise and fall of her chest. When I stretched trembling fingers out to touch her unlined cheek, her watery blue eyes darted to me. Unable to suppress a squeak, I jumped as I snatched my hand back. I would have stumbled away if Kobal hadn't been there to prevent me from doing so.

He rested his hand in the small of my back, his body turning protectively sideways. My heart hammered in my chest as my mother's eyes burned into me. If hatred could take form and kill someone, she would have sliced me open from head to toe with that look.

"The devil's progeny has returned," she grated in a voice that sounded as if it hadn't been used in months.

"Mother," I whispered, unsure of what else to say or what to do. I couldn't deny her words. Lucifer's blood ran through me, and somehow she'd known this, or suspected it all along. Maybe her rotten mind had accidentally stumbled onto the belief she'd born the devil's spawn and never let go of it.

"I'd hoped you'd die when they took you to the wall," she said.

I rubbed my hand over my heart before I comprehended what I was doing and dropped it. I'd come to realize that no matter how much I armored myself against this woman, she always found a way past my defenses. I had no weapons against her, but as soon as I found Gage and Bailey, I would leave her here to rot in this place.

Beside me, Kobal growled and stepped toward her. "No." I placed my hand on his chest to hold him back.

My mother's eyes flicked to Kobal and enlarged when she took him in. "Demon! You brought a demon into *my home*!" Her voice took on a hysterical note that I'd never heard before. "Be gone, demon! Get out!"

"Go," I said to Kobal and nudged him toward the doorway.

"I'm not leaving you with her," he stated as she continued to shriek at him to get out.

"I'll be fine." I pushed harder against his chest. "I have to learn if she knows anything about my brothers, and she won't tell me with you here. Go."

He relented, walked into the hall, and out of sight. The front door opened and clicked shut again, but I knew he hadn't left. That had been for her benefit. My mother continued to shriek like a bird for a full minute before abruptly stopping and turning her head to gaze at the blank TV.

"Mother, where is everyone from town?" I asked.

She didn't respond. I almost shook her, but stopped myself before I could. Touching her would only set her off more, and that would do nothing for me.

"Where are Ga-age and Bailey?" I was unable to keep the hitch from my voice as I asked this question.

"*You* had them taken from me!" she spat. "But then, you took them from me years ago. Because of your evil, manipulative ways, they always liked you more than me."

"Yes, I manipulated them by loving them when you couldn't, or wouldn't."

"If you hadn't been born…"

"What?" I asked when she stopped speaking. "What if I hadn't been born?"

“I could have had a life.” She lifted a hand to run it over her soiled hair and studied her reflection in the TV. “I was pretty and popular. I could have been loved. But no man would stay with me after you. Once they realized they were with the woman who had given birth to the devil’s offspring, they left me.”

More like they left when they realized she had bats in the belfry, but I kept that to myself.

“No man would listen when I told them you were the spawn of Satan himself,” she said.

I knew the others listened in the hallway, but I didn’t hear the ruffle of a feather or an inhalation. I felt no embarrassment over what they’d heard. They knew the truth of my lineage and my mother had never tried to hide her intense dislike of me from anyone.

“Gage and Bailey aren’t the spawn of Satan, and you never loved them either,” I said, unable to bite back the words. I’d never stoop so low as to hit her as she had me numerous times over the years, but I wouldn’t be her verbal punching bag anymore either.

When her eyes slid back to me, they burned with hatred once more. “You *ruined* me! It was only supposed to be a fling, yet I paid for it by having to bear *you*! The entire time you grew within me, I knew you were evil.”

“I’m not evil. I’m…” I stopped speaking to take a calming breath.

It was pointless to argue with her. She would never see me as anything other than what she believed me to be. Ever since I’d learned of my heritage, I’d feared she’d always been right and that I was evil, but in that moment, I knew she was wrong; I would never be what she’d always believed me to be.

For me to lose my bond with life, I would have to take a series of steps that I never planned to take. Even if something drastic happened to push me into taking those steps, I could never be like Lucifer. I had my love of Kobal, my friends, and my brothers to keep me tied to who I was now.

“Where are Gage and Bailey?” I asked.

"I should have aborted you like I planned!"

I did a double-take as those words plunged a knife through my chest. Never, over all my years with her, had she ever said anything like *that* to me. From the hallway, Kobal stepped into view. My mother was so focused on me, she didn't notice him stalking across the room with his eyes burning molten gold.

He'd kill her if he got his hands on her, I had no doubt about it.

CHAPTER FORTY-NINE

River

"No!" I shouted and placed my hand against his chest to stop him. Stepping closer to my mother, I glared at her as she continued to glower at me. "Then why didn't you?" I demanded of her. "Why did you keep me when you didn't want me, didn't love me, and believed me to be evil?"

Kobal wrapped his hand around my wrist. I didn't know if he was offering me comfort or preparing to pull me out of his way. His eyes were focused on her; his claws extended. It would take only one swipe for him to sever her head from her shoulders.

The fight went instantly out of her and she slumped against the chair. "Because they told me not to," she whispered.

I frowned at her in confusion. "Who told you not to? Your grandparents?"

Her parents had passed before I was born; she'd lived with her grandparents until they both died. I didn't recall them, but this had been their house.

She scoffed. "They booked the appointment for me."

Every time she opened her mouth, it felt like a new one-two combo to my gut. However, I remained standing beside her, a glutton for punishment. She'd never revealed this much before; I had to hear her out.

"Then who?" I demanded, and Kobal's fingers tightened on my wrist.

"I was sitting in the waiting room, eager to be rid of you," she whispered. "I knew you were wrong. It was still early in my pregnancy, yet I was exhausted all the time and so weak. Gage and Bailey never did that to me, but I felt you *draining* the life from me."

I closed my eyes against her words, knowing they were true. Even then, I'd been seeking out life, and she had been the only supply available to me. It had to have been terrifying and exhausting for her.

For the first time in my life, I put myself in her shoes. Fifteen and pregnant with a baby she didn't want, and who was draining her from the inside out. I couldn't understand her hatred, but I understood her fear.

"What stopped you from going through with it?" I asked.

"The voices," she whispered as her fingers dug into the chair. "I was waiting for my turn when they whispered to me for the first time. They told me I had to keep you alive, that I had to care for you, and that if I got rid of you they would kill me and I would burn in Hell for all eternity. So many times, I contemplated ridding myself of you and your evil over the years, and every time the voices returned to tell me to keep you safe or I would pay for it."

I didn't know what was worse, her hearing voices or the fact that she'd contemplated killing me *often* throughout my life.

Corson, Raphael, Hawk, and Caim stepped into the doorway, drawing my attention to them. Raphael's face remained blank, but Caim's expression was curious as well as confused.

"When I told the voices there was something *wrong* with you, that you were killing me, that you were evil, they told me to keep you safe anyway," my mother continued. "I told them I believed you were the devil's spawn, and they told me it didn't matter; Lucifer's child must live. They told me I could never tell anyone what they revealed, and I was too afraid to go against them. It doesn't matter anymore though, everyone knows the truth now."

"Son of a bitch," I breathed as my gaze remained pinned on Raphael. Kobal's head turned toward the angel and his eyes narrowed.

"Then, one day, they told me to turn you in, to get rid of you, and I was *so happy*. Finally, it was over. I was free of you, but it was too late. You had already wrapped your evil around Gage, Bailey, and the rest of the town. You turned them all against me."

Her words drew my attention back to her as a memory tugged at me. On the day she'd sold me to the soldiers, or the day she'd apparently been *told* to sell me to them, I had stood beside her just like this. I recalled thinking that despite her hair being a stringy, unwashed mess around her face and her near constant frown, she looked untouched by the years with her smooth, wrinkle-free skin.

Now, I looked past her unwashed hair and clothes again. Past the shadows under her eyes, her emaciated frame, and hollowed-out cheeks to her unlined, youthful skin. She'd been sixteen when she gave birth to me and twenty-five when the gateway opened. She was thirty-eight now, but there wasn't so much as a laugh line next to her eyes or a crease in her brow.

My head spun as I tried to process this information. I lifted my hand to my forehead and swayed on my feet. Kobal steadied me as Magnus's words from when we'd still been in Hell drifted through my mind. We'd been getting ready to travel to the seals, and he'd gone through the scrolls before pulling me and Kobal aside with some of the others…

"There is more to her," Magnus said to us.

Thrown off by his words, I hadn't known how to respond or what to expect. "What though?" I asked.

"I believe some of your vast power with life is because you have found each other and claimed the other as your Chosen. The discovery of a Chosen makes a demon stronger, even a mortal demon such as yourself," Magnus told me and Kobal.

"What do you believe the rest of it is?" Kobal inquired.

"I don't know," Magnus replied. "What I do know is that she is unlike any who have walked before her, and I believe she will be the end of Lucifer."

He'd gone on to say he believed me to be the first *true* World Walker. The first angel offspring who could be capable of walking Earth, Hell, and Heaven, but he hadn't known why.

I knew now.

Lowering my hand, I stared at my mother again. "You haven't aged in thirteen years," I breathed. "Not since the gateway opened."

She blinked at me as if she hadn't realized this, and perhaps she hadn't. I didn't think she had a clue as to what she was. Until recently, no one had known there would come a time when I would stop aging too.

"You are descended from the angels. That is who the voices belong to and why they can speak with you," I said.

For a moment, a light bloomed over my mother's face. A smile curved her mouth and her eyes warmed in a way I'd never seen before. "Angels," she murmured. Then, her eyes dimmed and she slumped against the chair. "They want nothing to do with me, only you. Everything has always been about *you*."

I looked to where Raphael and Caim stood in the doorway. Raphael remained apathetic, but Caim looked like someone had socked him in the gut as he gazed from my mother to me and back again.

"She's not descended from an angel. It's impossible," Caim muttered, though he looked as if he didn't quite believe it. "We know our lines; we followed them. Few of us have any descendants left. I mean, I guess there could be a line we believed to be dead, or a child lost along the way, but I don't think so. She must be insane."

"No," I said flatly. "No, she told me I had the devil's eyes. She's always known who I descended from and the voices… *the angels* told her."

Caim stared at my mother before focusing on Raphael. "Why would the angels talk to her?" Caim demanded. "Why would they—*you*—not want Lucifer's line ended? River *is* the last of his descendants. Why not let her mother have the abortion and be done with it?"

Raphael stared at me for a minute before his head tipped back and he gazed at the ceiling. When he looked at me again, he started speaking. "Before River was born, Ariel received a premonition revealing that she must survive. No matter what the cost."

"The cost was her," I said and waved my hand at my mother. "The angels broke her when they suddenly started speaking to her and told her to keep me when I was *feeding* off her."

"Some humans are not strong enough to handle the voice of the angels, but she had to know to keep you alive and to keep you with her. What happened to her was unfortunate but necessary."

"Unfor… *tunate*?" My voice cracked on the question. "Unfortunate!"

Kobal moved my palm off his chest and drew me closer to him. His hand ran soothingly over my arm, but I wasn't in the mood to be calmed. Flames danced across the tips of my fingers before I snuffed them out. My mother would run straight through the wall if she saw me wielding fire.

"You have no idea what she did to me! The things she's said to me, and the hatred she harbors for *me*. You have no idea what it's like to grow up not understanding why the woman who is supposed to love you unconditionally treats you worse than most people treat their dogs!

"And now, I know it's because she was right. I *am* descended from Lucifer. I am part demon and angel. The angels destroyed the fragile mind of a scared *fifteen*-year-old girl and all you can say is it was *unfortunate*? Why didn't you at least allow her to give me to someone else?"

"Ariel said your path was to stay with her," Raphael replied. "And you have walked it."

"And she will continue to walk *many* more paths," Kobal growled.

"Yes, she will, but we have little knowledge of where they will take her from here. Ariel knew to keep her alive and when to turn her into the soldiers. If River hadn't been born, there would have been no one to close the gateway when the humans opened it, but her father still would have been able to topple the seals. She needed to exist to counteract the man who created her. Ariel never foresaw anything else about her, not even that she would become the Chosen of the varcolac. Though, I suppose that makes sense."

"And why is that?" Kobal demanded.

"Power attracts power and…."

Raphael's voice trailed off when Vargas, Erin, and Magnus crept into the doorway. I hadn't heard them enter, but then I'd been a little distracted. When they looked from me to my mother and back again, I realized they'd been in the house for a while.

"What angel line is my mother descended from?" I demanded of Raphael. "Who else am *I* descended from?"

His lips compressed into a flat line as he gazed at me. Fury burst so hotly through me that I understood the term "blood boiling." If it was possible, I would have choked the life out of him right then. Saved my life or not, I was sick of being toyed with by angels.

"Tell me who she is descended from. Which fallen angel is it?" I asked.

"I'd like to know that myself," Caim muttered.

Raphael remained stubbornly mute.

"Tell her or I'll kill you," Kobal said flatly. "I don't care if you can help defeat Lucifer. I won't tolerate you keeping secrets from her. I will end you here and now."

Corson, Hawk, and Magnus crept closer to Raphael in preparation of capturing him should he try to take flight. Caim leaned against the door-frame and folded his arms over his chest to make it clear he wouldn't interfere.

"Tell her!" Kobal commanded. He hadn't raised his voice, but my mother jumped and the tension in the room ratcheted up.

"You cannot beat this varcolac, Raphael," Caim said quietly. "He was born specifically to fight the angels. It is why he has survived so long with Lucifer in Hell. The girl has the right to know why her life has been played with in such a way."

"You only seek answers for yourself," Raphael replied.

"I seek answers for all of us!" Caim retorted.

Raphael returned his attention to the ceiling. When he closed his eyes, I realized he was communicating with the angels. I peered at the ceiling, but all I saw there were water stains.

Raphael's eyes were a deeper purple hue than normal when they met mine again. "There is an angel line that only one angel knew of, until recently," Raphael said.

"Who?" I demanded.

"When Michael and Ariel walked the Earth, they mingled with the humans, healing them, bringing them peace and the love of the being," Raphael replied. "They granted miracles to the favored humans, and the being did have favored humans back then. More than that, Michael and Ariel brought hope to a struggling people. The being granted them permission for this, and planned to allow the rest of the angels to also walk the Earth, once the humans were more accustomed to seeing them. That is the reason why we can all leave Heaven, but only Michael can allow us to return. Like the varcolac, Michael having such control was a way to keep the angels regulated and the worlds separated as they should be."

"So what changed all that?" I asked.

"The angels were created to obey, but we do slip. While on Earth, Michael fell in love with a human and succumbed to temptation."

A pin dropping in China could have been heard over the hush that followed those words.

"They fathered a child together," Raphael continued. "His name was Adam, and yes it was the Adam who was placed in Eden. Adam is also your ancestor," Raphael said to me. "You are the only human to ever exist where a fallen angel line and the *only* untainted angel line came together. Not only that, but you are the product of the two most powerful angels in existence."

CHAPTER FIFTY

River

The breath exploded from me, but my shock was nothing compared to the expression on Caim's face. Dumbstruck was an understatement. Then it faded away to be replaced with a look so thunderous I expected him to start tearing the house down.

"*Are you kidding me*?" The glass in the window frames rattled from the force of his bellow. "That's impossible! *Impossible*!"

"Easy," Magnus said from behind him.

Caim's head whipped toward him. Magnus held his hands up as he stepped away from the infuriated angel. Then, Caim leveled Raphael with a look of pure murder.

"Michael is the one who was so insistent that we not question anything, so adamant that we follow the laws, yet he never said *why*. Did he know the reason we couldn't leave Heaven was because of *him* and keep it from us?"

"Yes, but he had his reasons," Raphael replied.

"Ooooh, I'm sure he did," Caim snarled. "And just what were those reasons?"

"Yes, do tell," I said.

Raphael folded his hands before him as he spoke. "Unlike the demons, who need a Chosen to propagate and therefore have a form of immortal birth control, the angels experience no desire in Heaven which keeps them from having an overabundance of immortal offspring. However, the mortal realm is different. Those desires come to life in angels and, like the humans that the being formed angels in the image of, we can propagate with anyone. Michael, the most steadfast and loyal amongst us faltered while on Earth. When he did, the being realized that it could happen to any of the angels and ordered Michael and Ariel back to Heaven. The being then commanded Michael to never speak about what happened.

"Concerned the angels would start to prefer life on Earth and not return to Heaven as often as they should, the being set forth the law that angels could never again walk the Earth. Since life cannot evolve in Heaven, the being created more of the lesser angels to ensure there would be enough angels to keep Heaven, and all life, running smoothly."

"I remember the increase in the making of the lesser angels," Caim said through his teeth. "But I don't remember anyone slapping Michael on the back and telling him congrats on becoming the proud papa of a mortal. I must have missed that memo."

Raphael blinked at him. I didn't know if he didn't get Caim's sarcasm or if he had no idea how to deal with it.

"Before he was born, the being cloaked what Adam was to keep him hidden from all angels and placed him in the garden with Eve and some other humans. The being had granted certain humans entrance into paradise before, so none of us suspected anything unusual about Adam, and only Michael knew the truth of it for all these years."

"Lucifer started questioning things shortly after Adam's birth," Caim murmured.

"Yes, the war started soon after," Raphael replied.

"Were Adam and Eve really thrown out of the garden?" Vargas asked.

“No,” Raphael said. “They left.”

“Why?”

“No one had ever left paradise before, so the being didn’t expect Adam to do so when he placed him there, but humans never do what is expected of them. They left around the same time that Lucifer and the angels were removed from Heaven. Adam’s true nature remained cloaked from everyone, but his lineage spread.”

“Holy shit,” I breathed, unable to do much more than that. Kobal clasped my neck and kissed my temple as his fingers rubbed my tensed muscles.

“If the line was cloaked, then how did the angels know they could communicate with her?” Corson asked with a wave of his hand at my mother.

“Michael knew. At the time, he did not reveal how or why he knew she could speak with us. We didn’t question it either. We all assumed she was part of a fallen angel line and Michael somehow sensed this. We did lose track of some of their children over the years.”

“I see,” I murmured.

“That’s why Adam lived so long,” Caim said. “Not because he was favored, but because he was also descended from an angel. He was drawing power from the Earth and we didn’t realize it, not in Heaven or Hell, and certainly not while we were dying on this plane.”

“Yes,” Raphael confirmed. “And I did not question it either.”

“And the Lord said, let them have dominion over the fish of the sea, and over the fowl of the air, and over the cattle, and over all the earth. Genesis 1:26,” Vargas murmured, and his gaze came to me. “Adam was believed to have a special affinity for the earth, to be connected to it, and they were right.”

I had zero response for that. “Michael never said a word. He just let the war go on when he could have stopped it, or at least revealed the reason why the angels couldn’t return to Earth,” I whispered. Somehow, out of all the angels, I’d ended up with the two biggest assholes as ancestors.

"Michael disobeyed the being once, he would not do so again by revealing that which he had been forbidden to reveal," Raphael replied.

"Until now," Caim said.

"Michael knows that when the being returns he will be punished, that he will most likely be destroyed, but he realized the rest of the archangels had to know what she truly is."

"Because you would not have come to Earth for just Lucifer's offspring," I murmured.

Raphael gazed at me, torment evident in his eyes. "Yes, I would have," he finally admitted. "It was unfair to expect you to pay with your life for the numerous mistakes we've all made over the years. However, knowing what I did about you made my decision easier."

"You really are the first true World Walker," Magnus murmured. "It all makes so much more sense now."

"You would think the angels would still want me dead," I said. "My children will carry on Lucifer's line."

Kobal released a sound that set my hair on end and caused most within the room to step back. My mother slapped her hands over her ears and started shaking. He cast her a loathing glance before focusing on Raphael again.

"We do not want you dead. You would be the end of Lucifer's line, but Michael's line continues, and so do the lines of some of the other fallen angels," Raphael said. "The children of the angels have become entangled with the fabric of this world. I will not take out a woman who is stronger than *all* the other angel lines and who is willing to sacrifice herself to stop Lucifer. I am here to help save humanity, not kill anyone. Without humans, we *all* perish."

"I…" Words failed me. I had no idea what to say. *Lucifer and Michael.* Adam and his children. I didn't ask about Cain and Abel; I preferred not knowing. It was all too much. Turning back to my mother, I blinked at her as I tried to comprehend everything put into motion millennia before I was born.

"Michael is *the* one who threw Lucifer out of Heaven," Caim said.

"I know," Raphael replied.

"Do you not understand what it meant to those of us who were driven out of Heaven?" Caim demanded, drawing my attention to him. "How hypocritical it is for Saint Michael to be the one to do such a thing?"

"I do, but he was determined to obey the laws set down after his transgression."

"And when Lucifer started questioning things, Michael saw his opportunity to become the favored son by evicting Lucifer."

"No," Raphael said. "Michael knows he can never be the favored one. He will forever be a constant reminder of the first failure of the being. The being always had a soft spot for Lucifer, and no matter what he has become, he will probably remain the Morning Star to the being. When Lucifer started questioning things, Michael had no good intentions or bad ones; he only saw what needed to be done and did it."

"How do you know that?" Caim demanded.

"Because I have discussed this with him. He is not proud of what was done with the fallen angels, and he is not ashamed. He carried out his duty."

"Wonderful," I said, cutting into their discussion. "They all did their duties, but Lucifer is still on Earth." I focused on Raphael. "You said Michael's line continues without me, you meant my brothers?"

"Yes."

"Does this mean my brothers will one day become immortal too?"

"It does," Raphael confirmed.

"Oh." I had a feeling I would be Kobal's age and still not have absorbed all the things heaped onto me these past five months. "My brothers have no abilities," I stated before glancing at my mother. "But then I never knew she did either."

"You have not seen any manifested abilities from them," Raphael replied. "Perhaps they are drawing from the Earth too. Not as strongly as you, but enough that they would have stayed alive until a hundred and something before the gateway opened. Perhaps, they can do something else, or perhaps their abilities are latent. Because Michael's line was cloaked, many of his descendants haven't shown their abilities."

"We have to find them and the rest of this town," I stated.

"Dead," my mother said, and my blood ran cold.

"Who's dead?" I managed to choke out.

"The town." Her fingers digging into the ends of the chair caused bits of stuffing to fall around the filthy ground. "The town is dead. Killed."

CHAPTER FIFTY-ONE

River

"What?" I gasped. "Why?"

Before I could think, I grabbed her arm. She yanked it away from me and slapped me so fast and hard that I never saw it coming before it staggered me back. "Devil spawn!" she spat.

My hand flew to my stinging cheek, but for the first time, instead of feeling anger and humiliation over her actions, all I felt was an odd detachment. Before, I'd always questioned why she hated me, why she couldn't love me, and now I had the answers. Maybe she still should have loved me. No matter what, I was her child, but the voices had broken her to the point that she was incapable of caring for me.

Kobal closed in on her with his fangs and claws extended. "No!" I cried. I regained my balance and stumbled forward to stop him from killing her. "No!"

"She will not be allowed to get away with hitting you!" he snarled.

"It's fine." I wedged my body between his and hers. "She can't hurt me anymore."

Kobal's muscles tensed to spring as he stared at her with a hatred that vibrated through the air around us. My mother drew her knees up against her chest and hugged them as she made a pitiful mewling sound.

"Demon," she moaned.

I tried to nudge Kobal away, but he wouldn't budge.

"I won't allow her to touch you in such a way," he stated.

"She won't hurt me again, physically or emotionally." I was surprised to realize, I believed this. She'd cut me open with her words more times than I could count, hit me more times than I cared to recall, but she *couldn't* hurt me anymore. I'd believed this so many times over the years, believed myself armored against her time and time again, yet she'd still slipped through to pierce me in one way or another. There would be no more slipping through for her.

"She will *never* hurt me again," I said. He didn't go after her, but he didn't back away either. Turning back to her, I kept myself between them as I spoke. "What happened to the people in town?"

"Taken. Dead. Your father came to claim them," she said in the singsong voice of children skipping rope on a playground.

"Lucifer was here?"

"He came for you." She giggled as she glanced at the TV again. Whatever few screws she'd still had in place in her mind were working their way free right before my eyes. "He found only the people and the children."

"Why did he leave you here?" Corson asked her.

"Left a message for his daughter."

"What is it?" She stared at the TV instead of responding to me. I stepped in front of the TV, forcing her attention to me. "What is the message?"

"That he knows the truth and so should *you*," she said and pointed a finger at me before wrapping her arms around her legs again. "If I go to town today, can I get some rabbits?"

In my head, I heard the clatter of the last screw coming free from her brain and hitting the ground. What had Lucifer done to her? What had *all* the angels done to her?

"What truth?" I asked.

"I think I would like some flowers instead," she murmured.

"Mother, what truth?"

"Not your mother, just the vessel."

"She's broken," Hawk muttered.

"She's been broken for a long time," I said as I knelt in front of her. "Where are Gage and Bailey?"

"Well, they're with him," she replied and clapped her hands. "We're all kin after all, and they are his kin too."

My eyes flew to Caim as terror curdled like rotten milk in my belly. "Does Lucifer know I am a mix of two angels?" I demanded.

"No, or at least he didn't," Caim answered. "I would have known if he did. We *all* would have known if Lucifer learned Michael propagated while on Earth. The fit he would have thrown would have been heard throughout all of Hell. However, if she"—he waved a hand at my mother—"spoke to him about voices, and after seeing what you did with the seals, he may have figured it out."

"He couldn't suspect it's Michael's line," Raphael insisted. "You knew nothing of it."

"Lucifer is not stupid, nor does he have any faith in you assholes!" Caim snapped. "Michael and Ariel were the only two angels who walked the Earth before the fallen. If Lucifer thinks on it, he'll figure it out. And since Ariel never waddled around with a full belly, he'll figure out who *real* quick."

"Oh," I breathed. "Mother, did Lucifer tell you where he was taking Gage and Bailey?"

Her eyes cleared and she bared her teeth at me. "Spawn of Satan."

"Yes, that's already been established," I replied with an impatient wave of my hand. "You were right, but where did Satan go with Gage and Bailey?"

"When we go to town, I'd like to ride the pony," she said and turned away from me. "Play some games as we do, eat the food, *all* the food. Hungry. When the trucks come, will they take me too?"

"Mother, please, where are they?" I implored.

She stared at the screen over my shoulder. "I'd like to go to town to play the games and hear the music before going with the trucks."

"Mother—"

"Devil's eyes! Rotten seed."

She lifted her hand to slap me again, but I caught her wrist before she could. I held on when she tried to jerk it away from me. "No!" I hissed. "I no longer fear you, and I won't allow Kobal to kill you, but you will *never* hit me again." I wanted to tell her she could never speak to me like that again, but I didn't think she knew half the things she spewed from her mouth anymore.

When she jerked at her hand again and sulked like a petulant child, I released her and rose. Kobal's eyes remained fixed on her before sliding to me. "I will find your brothers," he vowed.

"But what will Lucifer do to them before then?" I asked. "Because of me, because of *them*"—I thrust a finger at Raphael—"Gage and Bailey might be suffering right now!"

Kobal took my hand and rested it against his chest. "I *will* find them."

I closed my eyes and took a deep breath to steady the riotous sway of my emotions. If anyone could find them, it was Kobal, and I knew he wouldn't rest until he succeeded in freeing my brothers from Lucifer. My mother said the rest of the town was dead, but I held out hope we would be able to find and free them too. I couldn't think about everything that could happen to them before then; I'd go insane if I did. I had to stay focused on what I could do now. It was the only way to get through this.

"We'll find them," I whispered.

"Yes. Now it's time to leave here."

"The voices told me to find the soldiers and give you to them," my mother whispered as we walked toward the doorway. "I went to town and played the games!" She clapped her hands again, and when I glanced back, she was wiggling back and forth in her seat. "Can I play them again when you go to town now?"

I froze when her words sank in. My abrupt stop halted Kobal. "I know where they are," I said.

"Then we will go there," he promised.

I tried not to shove him out of my way in my rush to get to my brothers as I followed him out the door. Running headlong at Lucifer was a surefire way to have everything implode on us though. Lucifer wouldn't kill my brothers, but he would use them against me, and he would be willing to maim them.

When we exited onto the porch, I turned to two of the men standing guard with Bale, Lix, and Verin. Calah and Lopan stood at the foot of the stairs.

"My mother is inside. Take her back to the vehicles and keep her safe until we return," I instructed the men.

Kobal stiffened beside me, but before he could protest, I turned to face him.

"She was unable to handle what the angels did to her and she broke. She will sit in there until the house falls around her, but she will not die, not anymore. It's no existence for anyone to live, and no matter how horrible she was to me, she doesn't deserve that fate. We will find somewhere at the wall, away from us, where she can reside. I don't ever have to see her again, but I won't leave her to this. I would never forgive myself if I did."

"She wouldn't do the same for you," Kobal said.

"I know, but I'm nothing like her."

He bent to kiss my forehead. For a second, I allowed my eyes to close as I savored the warmth of him. "No, you're not," he murmured.

"Lucifer must be ended," Raphael said when the guards slipped inside.

"He will be," Kobal replied.

"Oh, of course he must be," Caim retorted sarcastically. "Do me a favor, Raphael. The next time you talk to Saint Michael, or I mean *Sinner* Michael, tell him he can go fuck himself from me."

Caim spun away from us and went down the steps so fast, his feet didn't touch them. Tilting his head back, he pointed a middle finger to the sky. "Fuck you, Michael!" he bellowed before pointing both his middle fingers at the sky. "*Fuuuuuuck yoooooou*!"

The humans and demons closest to him exchanged confused looks before edging away from the irate angel who stormed toward Lisa's house before spinning back toward us. I was so focused on Caim that I didn't notice the shadows circling across the ground, until Kobal stepped protectively in front of me. The hounds in the clearing all crouched low, their hackles rising as they stared at the sky.

My stomach sank when Onoskelis landed a few feet beyond Caim. Caim spun toward her and planted his legs in a defensive position. Folding her wings behind her, a savage smile curved Onoskelis's lips as she grinned at him.

"You chose wrong, brother," she purred when more angels touched down around us.

The humans and demons fell back, grouping closer to my house. Shadows crept through the trees before higher and lower-level demons emerged from the woods.

"I bet most of those upper-level demons are from the hundredth seal," Corson murmured.

"How did they get here so fast?" Bale asked. "I doubt the angels were giving them rides across the ocean."

"There are still two airports open," Kobal replied.

"The idea of demons on an airplane is absurd," Hawk said.

"More absurd than the idea of demons in the first place?" Erin inquired.

"Yeah, a little."

"The demons behind the hundredth seal wouldn't turn down helping Lucifer and getting what they feel is a justified revenge, no matter what they had to do to get here," Magnus stated. "Some of them may have exited the gateway on our side and regrouped here."

"Lucifer can telecommunicate," Raphael said. "He could draw his followers in and let them know where he is."

"It doesn't matter how they got here, they're here," Kobal said. "And we are surrounded."

"Satan would like to speak with you, dear niece," Onoskelis called to me. "And he'd really like to kill *you*," she said with another smile at Caim, who remained unmoving. "Raphael," she greeted. "I'd like to say it's a pleasure to see you again, but that would be a lie."

"It would be the same if I were to say it to you, Onoskelis," Raphael replied.

"I bet she was a rotten bitch even before her wings turned black," Magnus said.

"She was," Raphael confirmed.

"It seems some of our ex brothers and sisters have been keeping secrets. Our king is eager to learn all of them. If you'll follow me," Onoskelis said and gave a sweeping wave of her hand toward the woods.

"What do we do?" I whispered.

At least two dozen angels were on the ground now and shadows continued to swirl across the grass from those still circling overhead. The craetons grouped closer and circled my house until it became a sea of black wings, demon faces, and other Hell creatures around us.

"We have no choice," Kobal said. "We can't allow them to willingly take us to where Lucifer is. That's playing right into their hands. We have to fight."

Bale pulled her sword free of the scabbard on her back, and Corson's talons extended as the hounds released a howl that echoed over the land.

CHAPTER FIFTY-TWO

Kobal

"Stay by my side," I said to River. "No matter what."

"I will."

Caim edged closer to us, but Onoskelis tracked him while she tossed her sword handle back and forth between her hands.

"They outnumber us," Vargas said.

"I can help with that," Magnus said.

Bowing his head, Magnus spread his hands before him. Seconds later, images of demons and humans flickered to life around us. The figures wouldn't be a huge distraction, but they would keep the angels and demons guessing as to what was real and what wasn't. More images of River surrounded her and spread down the porch steps. Then he added in some of me throughout the crowd.

"Are you going to make yourself look like me again?" River whispered to him, unable to hide her unease over the possibility.

"If it becomes necessary," Magnus replied as he lifted his head.

Realizing that we weren't going to come willingly, the fallen angels and demons released a battle cry and charged across the open land between this house and the next. Some had weapons at the ready, others attacked with brutal swings of their hands or lethal tails. Gunshots erupted through the clearing as the humans opened fire on those trying to carve them down.

The hounds leapt forward, their jaws crunching on bones. Their prey screamed when they shook them, before ripping them apart. The hounds spit out the heads they tore free to take down more of their enemies. Within me, Phenex and Crux shifted, begging to be set free, but I kept them caged until the perfect time came for them to leap into the battle.

An angel landed with a thud on the sagging roof overhead. Wood creaked ominously as it bowed further beneath the weight of the angel walking across it. Hawk, Erin, and Vargas leapt over the banister seconds before the section of roof over their heads gave way with a thunderous crash. Corson, Bale, and Verin dove down the stairs when the rest of the roof creaked and started to crack.

Lifting River, I pinned her against my chest and leapt over the other banister as the rest of the roof gave way. Raphael's wings created a breeze against my face when he soared out behind us. Hitting the ground, I kept myself protectively around River as we rolled across the grass.

My claws extended as I leapt to my feet. I released River to slice my nails across the throat of the lower-level demon running at me. His head flopped back and blood spurted out to spray my face. Grabbing his head, I tore it the rest of the way off and threw it at an upper-level demon charging toward me.

The wave of fire I unleashed on the demon sent him spiraling back, screaming as the flames melted his flesh and consumed his hair. River rested her fingers on my back. Her ability crackled against my flesh before she unleashed a ball of energy that took out the barta stalking her.

From the other side, a wave of white light erupted. Raphael stood with his legs apart and both hands raised as he aimed the wave at the fallen angels creeping closer to him. Most dashed to the side to avoid it, but one of them ran into it. Screeching, the angel was flung backward and hit the ground with a thump. The angel lay unmoving, his chest torn open and the top of his head a bloody, gaping hole from where the energy had coursed through his chest and exploded out his head. His wings flopped to the sides of his dead form.

Raphael released another pure white ball of energy, but the next angel managed to catch it. The glow of the energy filled the angel's palm as awe radiated over her face. Violet color shimmered to life in her eyes. Then, the violet faded and the black returned. Loathing filled her eyes when she lifted her head to glare at Raphael.

With a flick of her wrist, she flung the ball back at him. Raphael flew to the side to avoid it. I yanked River out of its way and folded myself protectively over her. The ball of energy hit a human. The man's scream ended as soon as it started, cut off by the foot-wide hole torn through the center of his chest.

On the other side of the hole in the man, I saw Hawk's stunned face before he ducked to avoid the ball that hit the tree behind him. The man crumpled to the ground. From behind Hawk, an ominous creaking sound filled the air. Hawk's hands clawed at the ground as he scrambled to get out of the way of the large tree tipping toward him. Wood cracked and splintered; Hawk dove and rolled to the side as the tree swung down. The ground shook when the tree bounced off it before settling into the dent it had created.

The flap of wings sounded over me. I released River seconds before the angel crashed onto my back. The weight of its body staggered me forward. Hands smashed into my skull and clawed at my hair. Reaching over my shoulder, I discharged a wall of fire that caused the angel to scream. Its wings flapped as it tried to rise away from me, but I grabbed its hand and pulled it over the top of my back.

I drove my hand through the angel's chest and wrapped it around his heart. The organ pulsed in my hand when I tore it out and tossed it aside. The angel clawed and beat at me as I seized his head next. Twisting it to the side, I wrenched it from his shoulders. Like demons, the angels could regenerate everything except for their heads.

Lifting my head, I watched as River pushed back the lower-level demons stalking her with bursts of fire. The skin on the face of one melted off. She flung a ball of energy at two others, taking them both out. Magnus, Bale, Corson, and Verin fell into a V formation ten feet in front of her. They worked to beat back the encroaching threat as she continued to take out some of the others. I stayed in front of her, my back facing hers, as we were pushed into the forest by the numerous craetons.

At some point in the battle, Caim had taken flight. Flattening his wings against his back, he plunged out of the sky to slam into the side of a manticore swooping in from the trees. The manticore trumpeted a roar as it went spiraling into a tree. The snap of its back could be heard over the continued gunfire.

"Is everything that escaped the seals going to come for us?" Hawk panted from beside me.

"No," I replied. "The jinn, erinyes, wood nymphs, and other more sophisticated demons will most likely stay out of this. They'll prefer to stake out their own place on Earth, secure it, and use it to unleash their particular form of brutality on anyone unfortunate enough to stumble across them."

"Like the canagh demons did." Hawk swung out with a knife to slice the throat of a demon. Leaping on the demon, he sawed its head the rest of the way off in two quick slashes before jumping back to his feet.

"Yes," I replied when he fell in beside me again. "Earth is a new playground for them, and they're going to enjoy it. Most of them won't be following anyone other than whoever *they* deem to be their leader. Some of them may be here with Lucifer, but I doubt it. The hundredth seal demons are a different story. They're seeking vengeance."

I released another wall of fire that torched a handful of lower-level demons. Beyond the smoke of their bodies, I spotted Lix and the skelleins trying to angle Erin and Vargas toward us. Lopan rode Calah's shoulders as he lobbed gold balls from his caultin. The balls exploded when they hit the ground, pushing back the demons stalking them and leaving small indents in the earth.

When the balls hit the demons, they blew off body parts or broke apart to become a liquid that poured up to their face and into their eyes. Once it was inside them, the demons hit their knees and started shredding their faces in an attempt to tear it free of them.

Whenever one was taken out, more emerged from the shadows to take their place. Three manticores swooped down to snatch humans from the ground and lift them into the air. The humans screamed as they were carried away, but those screams were abruptly silenced by the manticore's stingers.

Driven deeper through the trees, it became tougher to fight against those pushing against us. Too much fire would set the entire forest ablaze and possibly trap most of our allies within it. Magnus's figures were rapidly fading away, and we didn't have the time it would take for him to cloak us.

Sweat beaded River's brow as she drew more life from the ground to use against the demons trying to get at her. As I watched, she lifted both her palms out at her sides. A golden-white ball formed in her right hand while a burst of fire flamed out of her left. She gawked at them for a minute before grinning and flipping her hands over and pushing them away from her. She hurled the energy into a barta demon while the fire set a lower-level demon ablaze.

"New talent?" I inquired as I brought a demon down beneath me. Using my claws, I sliced his head off. I threw fire at more demons trying to close in on us, pushing some back and setting others on fire.

"Apparently," she replied. She lifted her hands, but this time only fire emerged from both her palms. "And sporadic."

Raphael's life force toppled trees left and right, scattering some of the demons and angels, but more fell in to fill the holes. Another ball of Raphael's energy was caught by an angel who heaved it at Corson. Corson threw himself to the ground and rolled before rising to his feet as a manticore turned sideways to dive through the trees at Erin.

Planting her feet, Erin fired her handgun at the creature. Blood burst from the holes in its chest and beaded in the center of its forehead, but it kept going with its stinger raised in preparation to strike. River cried out and shot a ball of energy at it. The manticore spun to avoid taking the hit.

Corson leapt forward. His hand landed on Erin's shoulder, and he used it to propel him higher into the air. With a single swipe of his talons, he sliced the manticore's head from its body. The head rolled to the side, but its momentum caused its body to crash into Corson and Erin. They flew five feet through the air before hitting the ground and bouncing across it. The skelleins ignored Corson as they rushed to help Erin to her feet. They clucked worriedly over her while Corson scowled at them.

Beside me, River released a stream of energy into the bartas encroaching on us. They stood for a second before tearing into their chests to reveal their exploding hearts. My fire took down more of the lower-level demons and three of the trees behind them. The hounds circled us, growing closer and closer as more of my followers fell to the craetons.

One of the hounds released a screech of pain. Within me, I felt the severing of my bond to a mated male. Its female's sorrowful howl echoed through the trees. When she howled again, all the hounds took up her cry, but her heartbroken tone remained distinct from the others.

Then, all at once, the fallen took to the sky. Their sudden absence caused a strange hush to fall over the woods as the humans pointed their guns into the trees. The craetons continued to surround us, but many of them fell back to blend into the shadows. My teeth clenched and my lips skimmed back when I saw what the craetons had herded us toward.

I turned toward River to stop her from seeing what lay beyond, but it was too late. Tears flooded her eyes as she gazed at the wide-open, blood-drenched field before us. Her hand flew to her mouth, and her skin paled visibly before her knees buckled. Grabbing her arm, I kept her on her feet.

Caim landed beside her and folded his wings behind his back. His dismay-filled eyes briefly met mine before they returned to the carnage.

Amid the copious amounts of blood were so many human bodies and parts that it was difficult to differentiate one from the other. I'd seen many atrocities in Hell, had rained down my fair share of torture and death, but I had never seen anything like what lay before us.

We'd found the missing people of River's town.

I held her closer as tremors shook her slender frame. Ducking her head, River wiped away her tears as the first one hit the ground. A soft sob escaped her, but I knew I was the only one who heard it as she clamped her lips together and inhaled a shuddery breath.

When Caim looked back to me, he shook his head. One of the fallen or not, Caim's humanity was evident in the slump of his shoulders and the way he drew his wings forward as if to hug himself. Not even he had expected something such as this from Lucifer. Truth be told, as much as I hated the bastard, I hadn't expected it either. I never would have said Lucifer was sane, but he'd always kept a leash on his insanity. That leash had snapped.

"I have lost my brothers and sisters forever," Caim murmured.

"Did you think there was a chance you hadn't?" I asked.

The rainbow colors of his eyes were more vivid due to the sheen of water in them. "I had hoped that, if I could retain some semblance of sanity and humanity, that maybe they could too. They were…" He shook his head and gazed out at the field again. "I am a fool."

Raphael strode forward to stand beside him. A muscle in his clenched jaw ticked as his purple gaze searched the field.

"It's the whole town," River muttered. "These were my loved ones, my friends. I knew them all. We survived together. We survived *because* of each other. *Why* would he do this?"

"Because he knows who the other angel of your line is," Caim answered and glowered at Raphael. "I told you, you would have heard his fit all the way through Hell if he'd known Michael fathered a child. Now it's been heard throughout this town, and possibly the surrounding areas."

The sight of the massacre had already leached color from Hawk's face, but he paled further at Caim's words. "My family is in the next town over," he said.

"Probably not anymore," Caim replied.

River lifted her head to look at Hawk. "I'm sorry," she said.

"Not your fault," Hawk said gruffly and blinked away the tears in his eyes.

My gaze went to the sky as an angel soared low over the treetops to land amid the scattered body parts. In the middle of all that blood, the angel looked like a crow reveling in the glory of all its carrion. Behind me, the lower and upper-level craetons started pushing against us again as they herded us out of the woods and into the slaughter.

CHAPTER FIFTY-THREE

Kobal

"This is where we came for Volunteer Day," River said. "It was a day of celebration. There were games and food, music, dancing, and laughter. It was the one day a year when we could forget all our troubles and simply enjoy life." She pointed to the brick building on the right of me, and her voice hitched. "I went to school there, for a time."

"He will never do this again, Mah Kush-la," I promised. I couldn't take her anguish from her, or fix this, but I could offer her that bit of solace.

Another angel landed on the field to her left. Fury twisted her features. The ball of energy she threw at it had the angel rising again, but more angels swooped down to stand amid the bodies. The angels spread out through the carnage until they became black sentinels watching and waiting for us to be maneuvered where they wanted us.

The stench of blood filled my nose; the faint odor of decay lay beneath it, but these humans had not died that long ago. Some of the bodies looked as if they had been torn limb from limb, while others appeared to have been dropped from great heights as bones protruded from rumpled flesh and dents pockmarked the ground.

Glancing behind me, I gritted my teeth when I saw more shadows emerging from the trees, but the attack did not resume. There was no reason for it to as hundreds of the craetons slid from the woods. Their numbers alone were enough to push us forward.

"Any shot some of your brothers and sisters will come help us?" Hawk inquired of Raphael.

"Not likely," Raphael replied without a second's hesitation. "It will take a cataclysmic event for them to intervene."

"Fantastic," Erin murmured.

"When we reach wherever they're pushing us, and the battle resumes, I want you to work on keeping the demons behind us held back," I said to Raphael. "River, funnel your ability into him. The two of you should be able to create a wall that will keep our backs at least partially protected."

"I will," she said as she carefully picked her way through the remains. She held her eyes in such a way that I knew she could see where she put her feet to avoid stepping on anyone, but she didn't see the faces of those who had died here.

Cresting the top of a small hill, red filled my vision when I spotted Lucifer sitting a hundred feet downhill from us on *my* throne. River's brothers were with him. I knew then that he'd taken the thrones from Hell with the intent of baiting me into a fight I wasn't prepared for. Before River entered my life, he would have succeeded, but she had calmed me and made it so I at least paused to think before reacting. Even if I did want to fly at him in a rage, I would not leave her unprotected.

River lifted her head and released a startled cry before stumbling forward. Pulling her back, I clasped her firmly against my side when she wriggled to break free of my hold.

"Bailey," she whispered. "Gage."

"I will get them back," I promised. "But you are to stay by me."

Her body tensed to spring forward, but she stopped fighting my restraining hold. From closer than ever before, the roar of a drakón sounded through the day. The shadow of one darkened the ground between us and Lucifer when it flew overhead. My teeth clenched when I realized that they hadn't been hunting as they moved across the Earth; they'd been following us.

Blue fire trailed from the bones of the drakón as it soared low over the trees behind Lucifer and disappeared. Between us, green grass rolled down the hill toward Lucifer as no bodies or blood marked the land. I doubted Lucifer felt any regret over what he'd done to the humans and settled here because he couldn't stand the reminder their bodies provided. He'd chosen this place because the breeze carried the stench of the carnage away from here.

"Remember, you must help Raphael when it becomes necessary," I said in a low voice to River.

She nodded, but flames flared across the tips of her fingers instead of sparks, and I could feel the fury rolling off her.

Lucifer smiled and waved his hand at us in a beckoning gesture. "Come! Come!" he called excitedly.

"I *hate* that guy," Hawk stated.

"We all do," Magnus replied. "It's why he's trying to kill us."

We'd lost the first part of this battle, but I would not leave here until this was ended. Either Lucifer or I would die today.

Lucifer's grin widened as we neared. Resting his elbow on the arm of my throne, he set his chin on his fist. He draped one leg over the other arm and swung his foot idly back and forth while he gazed at us.

Behind Lucifer, the rest of the angels descended from the sky to form a line. Beside my throne sat River's; her brother Gage was seated on it. A barta demon stood behind Gage. Its clawed hand curled around Gage's thin shoulder, pinning the child against the back of the throne. Gage's brown eyes followed his sister. His freckles stood out starkly against the pallor of his skin, but like his sister, he remained stoic in the face of fear.

"That's far enough!" Lucifer declared when we were twenty feet away.

I glanced behind me to the wall of demons and Hell creatures lined up to block our retreat. River tensed against me when Lucifer rested his hand on top of Bailey's blond head. The young child sat before Lucifer on the throne, his blue eyes filled with tears and his fist in his mouth as he sucked on his hand.

Pulling his hand from his mouth, Bailey shouted a garbled, "River!"

The child tried to leap down, but Lucifer held him back.

"Don't!" River shouted.

I held her close when she lurched toward her brothers again. Tears slid down Bailey's flushed cheeks as he tipped his head back to gaze at Lucifer before looking to River. He shoved his hand into his mouth once more.

"You're in no position to tell me what to do, daughter, and apparently, *niece*," Lucifer hissed through his bared teeth.

"It's okay, B," River said. "It's all going to be okay. How are you doing, Gage?"

"I've been better, Pittah. Yourself?"

"Seen better days too," she replied.

Gage glanced at Lucifer and a crack in his brave façade showed as his hands trembled. "Did you see… ah… did you see everyone?" he croaked.

"Yes," River said. "Did you?" Her fingers dug into my flesh as she uttered the question and she didn't breathe.

"Only some," Gage whispered. "When they were dro…" Gage cleared his throat. "Dropped."

River's grip on me eased only slightly. "It's going to be okay. We're going to get you both out of here soon."

Lucifer pressed his lips against Bailey's ear. "My siblings lied to me too. Don't believe anything she says," he said, and more tears streamed from Bailey's blue eyes. "She's descended from one of those liars, but which… one… is… it?"

With each of those last four words, he turned Bailey's head back and forth in a jerking motion. Fire flashed over River's fingers and up to her wrists. Gage gawked at the flames and Bailey sobbed harder.

"I'll take Bailey's place," River offered.

Lucifer laughed when my arm tightened around her. "The varcolac will never let you do that, daughter."

"The children have nothing to do with this," I growled when the flames on River's fingers went out and golden-blue sparks came to life.

"They have *far* more to do with this than I ever could have dreamed possible!" Lucifer declared and started turning Bailey's head back and forth again. "Imagine my astonishment when *her* mother started rattling on about voices, and devil spawn, and yada boring fucking yada. I almost killed her just to shut her up. How did you live with that pitiful creature all those years?" Lucifer asked River.

She glowered back at him.

"Not speaking, oh well," Lucifer replied. "So anyway, she was rambling on when something clicked into place. I mean, I *know* certain humans have special abilities, but amid her endless bullshit, I realized she actually *believes* in angels and demons. She *knew* I was your father, and even if a human has special abilities, they cannot speak with the angels, unless they *are* part angel. Maybe I could have passed her off as just being crazy, but then I recalled all the power you unleashed on those seals, and that *really* got me to thinking."

Lucifer tapped one finger against his temple while his other hand constricted on Bailey's head and he leaned forward. Nudging River behind me, I planted myself firmly in front of her.

"Since I know *my* line, and the lines of all the angels who fell with me, and I *know* your mother isn't descended from any of us, I realized it must be someone else. *But who*? I asked myself. And how could that ever be possible?" Now he tapped his finger against his chin as his foot swung faster.

"I asked myself these questions over and over again," Lucifer continued. "I even said to myself, perhaps we lost a line. We angels are not perfect after all. So maybe we could have somehow lost track of a child over the countless years. But I couldn't quite bring myself to buy it, not when I felt that I would have at least sensed the DNA of another *fallen* angel within you. Eventually I realized your mother speaking to the angels could only mean that the fallen were not the only ones with children roaming Earth. Since I never saw Ariel heavy with child, it could only be *one* other angel."

Lucifer's gaze went from River to Raphael when he came forward to stand on the other side of her. Loathing exuded from Lucifer when he snarled at Raphael. Bailey tried to squirm away, but Lucifer held him in place.

"Raphael," Lucifer bit out.

"Lucifer," Raphael replied blandly.

"That is not my name!" Lucifer snapped. "I forsook it when I forsook all of you."

Raphael bristled beside River.

"Do *not* instigate him when he has the children," I commanded.

Raphael glanced at River before bowing his head.

"Still a follower I see," Lucifer sneered at Raphael. "I bet Michael sent you here to clean up his mess. The angel's large, shiny, warrior lapdog."

Dust fell from Raphael's wings when he ruffled them, but he didn't rise to Lucifer's baiting.

"Deny to me that Michael had a child while on Earth!" Lucifer shouted at him.

"I cannot," Raphael replied.

Lucifer blinked as if he'd never expected to hear the blunt admission. Lucifer released his grip on Bailey's head and began to pet the child as he gazed at the horizon. A distraught sound escaped River, but she didn't try to go after them again.

Then Lucifer stilled completely, and his eyes returned to Raphael. "Adam!" Lucifer spat.

The world slanted precariously as Lucifer unleashed his ability to disorient his prey. The vast wave of power he emitted crackled against my skin. Raphael staggered to the side before planting his feet. River's legs wobbled, but I held her steady.

Around me, the others stumbled back and forth as if the ground lurched from side to side, though it never moved. Lucifer could make the world appear as if it were shifting when it hadn't. More accustomed to this ability of Lucifer's, I remained unmoving.

Lucifer leaned over Bailey, locking the child in a cage created by his arms as he tee-peed his fingers before his face and gazed at me. The world behind him blurred and twisted. River clutched her head.

"It's not real," I murmured to her. "None of it is real."

The earth seemed to shift away before settling into place as Lucifer regained control of his temper. River's hand fell back to her side, but her head remained bowed as she struggled to catch her breath.

"Do you know why the varcolac rises from the fires?" Lucifer asked me.

"I don't care," I replied blandly.

"You were forged from the flames of Hell, and the angels were created from the waters of Heaven," he continued as if I hadn't spoken. "Two opposite elements; two completely different creatures. All of them not born of a mother, but from a piece of their worlds. The angels guided the souls in Heaven, and the varcolac guided the demons in Hell.

"The being knew some horrible things could evolve in Hell, and so it forged creatures"—he waved a hand at the hounds prowling before me—"and a leader who would be capable of ruling those creatures. That leader also had to be able to protect the demons from any threats that may arise in that abysmal place. Like the angels, the demons are a necessary part of the flow of life."

Widening my stance, I felt the others creeping closer as Lucifer's words lured them in. I studied the way he held Bailey as I tried to figure out a way to get the child free, without killing him.

"The markings on the varcolac, on this throne, they can all be found in Heaven too," Lucifer said. "Did you know the first varcolac rose from the fires before the first angel rose in Heaven?

"No, you didn't," he continued when no one responded to him. "When Hell broke from Earth first, the being resided there. But then Heaven came into existence and the being knew it would be needed there too. No matter how powerful the being was, it did not have the power to reside and rule over all three planes. Before it left Hell, it left some of its power behind. That power made it possible to forge a single ruler every time the previous one died."

"Holy shit," Vargas said.

I remained silent as I tried to deny what Lucifer said, but I couldn't. I had been the one forged in those fires after all. I *carried* their vast power with me everywhere I went.

"Then the being created the angels and retreated. It left us to find our own way on this great spinning ball the humans dubbed Earth."

CHAPTER FIFTY-FOUR

River

The dizzying effect of Lucifer's power still had my head reeling as I tried to slip these last pieces of the puzzle into place. My hands clenched on Kobal's back when his muscles rippled against me.

"Are you saying the varcolac is an angel?" I croaked out as I finally succeeded in blinking Lucifer and Bailey back into place. My molars ground together at the sight of my brother sitting with that monster. I'd like nothing more than to tear Lucifer's hands off for touching him.

Remain calm.

Lucifer laughed and leaned back to slap his hand on his thigh. The white shirt he wore carried no hint of blood, neither did his black pants. He must have taken the time to change after he massacred my friends. That somehow made it even worse.

"Not an angel, child, but a creation of the being just like the angels are!" Lucifer declared.

"I am nothing like the angels," Kobal replied with steely calm, though I knew this revelation had to have rocked him too.

I thought back to all the markings on the stones, the vast power within the cavern housing the Fires of Creation, and I finally understood where all that power came from. The Fires of Creation were where the being had once weaved an ancient magic so powerful none of us could ever comprehend it. Not Kobal, not Lucifer, no one.

No wonder the Fires had been capable of destroying my wraith of a father.

"However, it makes him more like angels than it does the demons," Lucifer said.

I realized he was revealing all this in an attempt to drive a wedge between Kobal and the demons.

"If you truly think about it, the varcolac was more favored by the being than any of the angels," Lucifer continued. "The varcolac can enjoy the pleasures of the flesh without penance." He shot a look at Raphael. "If they find their Chosen, they can breed even if they aren't capable of passing on their abilities to their offspring. But then, their abilities aren't really their own, and when they die, those abilities return to the fires that created them and a new varcolac rises with new powers."

My breath sucked in as that little puzzle piece clicked into place too. I'd never really questioned why Kobal couldn't pass on his abilities to his offspring; I'd just accepted it as one of those things that could never be explained, but it made sense now. When a new varcolac rose, their powers would be different from the varcolacs who came before them, but some would remain the same.

"The varcolac was also allowed to walk Earth whenever it chose, and all the while, it was never burdened with the knowledge of what created it," Lucifer continued.

"That's why you destroyed the varcolac when you first entered Hell!" I gasped. "Because you were envious of what it had been given and you had been denied."

"Why should a Hell creature be treated better than any of us? Why should a Hell creature, created by the *same* being as us, refuse to open a gateway for us and deny us the right to walk on Earth like the angels had? What right did it have to control us in such a way! Why were those hideous demons allowed to roam the Earth, while we were denied?" Spittle flew from Lucifer's lips as he shouted this question at me.

Because you would have destroyed the world, but I kept that thought to myself as my gaze shifted to Bailey's flushed, wet face.

"It does not matter." Lucifer leaned forward on the throne to peer intently at me. His movement revealed the intricate carvings behind his back, carvings that mirrored many of the markings on Kobal's arms. My gaze ran over the heads of the hounds on the arms, and the two hounds on top of the stone chair, howling at the sky. My attention shifted to the throne Gage sat on and the intricate symbols etched into it. The vast power in those thrones radiated into the marrow of my bones.

"No one should have denied us access to Earth," Lucifer said. "When I explained to the first varcolac what he was and how alike we were, he still refused to let us out of Hell, so I killed him. I didn't bother to explain it to the next one before killing her too. If we angels could not have Earth, we would have Hell.

"In the beginning, it was great fun to take out each new varcolac—they were the only real challenge in that disgusting place—but the Fires kept learning and twisting and forging them stronger until *he* came out," Lucifer said with a pointed glance at Kobal.

Kobal tensed against me, a rumble went through his chest, but he kept himself restrained from going after Lucifer—most likely because he wouldn't chance letting me go right now.

"Like humans, demons are an evolutionary species too," Kobal said. "It is why they were allowed to walk the Earth. However, they *never* did so freely, and those who broke the rules were punished for it. It seems a fair amount of those demons stand behind you now," Kobal replied.

"And the many demons standing behind you are fighting for a leader who isn't truly one of them," Lucifer replied. "You are so similar to an angel, rather than demon, that you have taken the daughter of *two* angels as your Chosen."

I didn't dare look back at the demons to see their reactions to Lucifer's words. Kobal's claws lengthened against my side. His eyes glowed as hot as the fires he rose from while he gazed at Lucifer before turning his head to level Raphael with a look that made those closest to the angel edge away from him.

"Is that what you meant at the house when you said, 'Though, I suppose that makes sense?'" Kobal snarled at him.

"Yes," Raphael replied with zero remorse. "There is a deep intertwining of all our worlds, and with the strength of both your powers and heritage, it makes sense you would have a connection to each other."

The ceasing of Kobal's breathing had me shifting subtly to stand between them. Kobal tensed to strike, and I knew if he'd been confident I wouldn't go for Lucifer, he would have destroyed Raphael.

"But you must realize the angels didn't know the varcolac was unaware of its true origins until we were in Hell," Caim said as he strolled forward to stand beside me and in between Raphael and Kobal. "Which means Raphael is also just learning that you were unaware of your origins."

I heaved a sigh of relief when Kobal relaxed a little against me, but he kept his eyes on Raphael.

"That is true," Raphael said.

"Look at the cousins squabbling!" Lucifer declared and slapped his thigh again as he laughed loudly.

His words drew everyone's attention back to him, as he'd intended. I'd come to realize that Lucifer needed to be the center of attention; he thrived on it. The hostility from Kobal and the demons behind us ratcheted up as all the angels smirked and a few laughed outright.

Lucifer's laughter abruptly stopped when his gaze shifted to Caim. He eyed him as a wolf eyed an elk. "I have special plans for you, Caim."

"I've no doubt," Caim replied flippantly, but his fingers twitched at his sides.

Lucifer focused on Kobal once more. "So, like me you are not a demon, not an angel, but something more. Something superior to all those around you. There is a reason it is *my* daughter you claimed. You are more like me than any of them."

I shook my head in denial and opened my mouth to respond, but Corson was already speaking as he strolled forward to stand on Kobal's other side.

"Kobal is the only one of us who is born *of* Hell. He has ruled over us for over a millennia and been willing to die for us that entire time. I have walked through the chamber where the Fires of Creation are located. I know the power that forged my king, know what he went through to rise to lead us, and it makes him more demon than any of us!" Corson declared loudly.

"And he's happily killed more than a few of you," Bale said with a smile as she raised her sword. Red stained the silver blade as she pointed it at the angels behind Lucifer.

The other demons all nodded their agreement and crept closer to us. Kobal had not evolved like they did, he was not a demon, not really, but he was their king, and they would fight and die for him.

"Why did the varcolac not know any of this?" I asked. Kobal had once told me he was born with the knowledge of what he was and what he was to carry out. However, he had none of the memories of his predecessors.

Lucifer shrugged and swung his leg back and forth as he absently patted Bailey's head. My eyes helplessly followed each of those pats until I thought my heart would explode.

"Because the Lord works in mysterious ways!" Lucifer threw his hands in the air and waved them about his head before lowering one to Bailey's head and patting it again. "And there are some things the being likes to keep secret. Like little angel babies."

His patting became faster before his movement abruptly stopped with his hand on top of Bailey's head. I wanted to scream at him to let go of my brother, but I bit my lip, refusing to give him the reaction he sought from me.

"A little Michael angel baby named Adam," he murmured. "And now they're named Bailey and Gage and River."

I had to get Bailey and Gage away from Lucifer *now*, but I didn't know how to do that without getting them killed.

CHAPTER FIFTY-FIVE

River

"You will not win this," Kobal said to Lucifer. The quiet of his tone was more unnerving than if he had bellowed the words.

"I won't?" Lucifer inquired. "I have the numbers, the children, my throne."

"Not for long. I am the rightful ruler of Hell and that is *my* fucking throne."

"Let's face it, Kobal, no one is the ruler of Hell anymore. Your Chosen ruined that place, not like it wasn't a hideous pit before her redecorating, but she has made it everything it was meant to be if the varcolac hadn't been there to protect it." Lucifer's eyes shifted to me as he gave a slow clap. "I knew you could bring down some of those seals, but I never expected that. Bravo, child, bravo."

Gage's eyes looked about to pop out of his head. Tears streamed down Bailey's face and snot bubbles popped out of his nose. Anger and sorrow battled within me as I gazed at them. They never should have had to endure this.

Lucifer swung his leg off the throne arm and shifted Bailey to the side. If the hair on my arms stood up anymore, it was going to leap off my body and run away as shadows shifted in the forest beyond Lucifer and the angels. The demons and humans with us crowded closer to Kobal as more of Lucifer's followers emerged from the woods.

"Am I still going to lose, Kobal?" Lucifer taunted.

Kobal turned his attention from the newest arrivals to Lucifer. When he smiled at Lucifer, I almost fell over. I'd expected many reactions from Kobal, but not *that* as he actually seemed amused by something.

"Yes," he said simply.

Lucifer didn't look at all amused by this response as his fingers curled around the arms of the throne. The newest craetons came closer until they were mingling with the angels. I recognized some of them as the unicorn and hare-like things I'd first seen when the seals started falling.

Púcas, I recalled Kobal having called them when we had held up the seal housing them against my father.

Gage leaned away from a unicorn stepping close to him. The unicorn's bright red eyes studied him hungrily as its horn nudged his shoulder.

"Get away from him!" I snapped.

The púca's head turned toward me; its nostrils flared as it sniffed the air. It snorted before stomping the ground with a cloven hoof and prancing back. Shock ran through me as the hares beat their paws against the ground and more of the unicorns snorted. Some of them shifted into human form while others transformed into large cat-like creatures that could make a lion cower.

"What are they doing?" I whispered.

Kobal continued to smile while he studied the púca. "They're confused," he said.

"About what?"

"Lucifer organized their release, but technically *you* released them, and they remember that. However, you are standing with me."

I kind of, sort of, understood his smile a little more now.

"And they hate you," Caim stated.

"And they hate me," Kobal agreed.

The distant roar of the drakón drew my attention to the sky as one of the gigantic, skeletal beasts soared over top of the field again. Most of those standing in the open staggered back as they sought to avoid being lunch for the fire-breathing dragons.

"River, I'm going to step away from you," Kobal said. "Do *not* go for your brothers. If Lucifer gets his hands on you, that will be the end."

"I won't go for them," I promised.

"The púca can't speak," he said. "But they understand what you say to them. Talk to them, get them to listen to you."

"No pressure though," I murmured and forced a smile.

He ran his fingers over my cheek. "None."

His hand fell away from me and he stepped to the side. Some of the púcas moved closer as their eyes traveled between me and Kobal. Resentment blazed from their eyes when they gazed at him, but when they looked at me, I saw their confusion. Lucifer lifted Bailey and set him in his lap.

Instinctively, I stepped forward, my hand stretching out as I sought to get my hands on my brother. I stopped myself before I went any closer, and my arm fell back to my side. When more of the púcas crept toward me, Lucifer hugged Bailey to his chest.

"Let him go!" I cried as Kobal tensed beside me.

I glanced over the púcas as they continued to shift while more and more demons emerged from the woods. Most of them were upper-level demons.

"Kobal didn't put you behind those seals. His ancestors did!" I declared unable to tear my gaze from Lucifer as he hugged Bailey closer. The coward was using my brother as a shield. "And *I* am the one who brought down the seals!"

"But Kobal chose to keep them imprisoned, and *I* am the one who compelled you to set them free, *daughter*. You may have been the catalyst, but I am the one who orchestrated their freedom," Lucifer purred.

"You set them free so you could use them," I replied.

"And what do you intend to do with them?" Lucifer retorted. "Lock them away again?"

The pucás stopped shifting, all their heads turned to me as they awaited an answer. The one closest to Gage rested its horn against his shoulder. Terror flooded me. I'd seen what it could do with that horn.

"No," Kobal said. "No species will be locked away again because of the actions of one, or even a hundred of its kind. Those who slip up will be punished individually and accordingly for the crime they commit. The demons who were placed behind the hundredth seal for disobeying the laws while on Earth"—a good number of the crowd behind Lucifer leaned raptly forward—"have free reign of Earth now. There's no reason for them to be punished anymore, unless they do something on this plane that warrants it.

"It will be the same for all demons, Hell creatures, and escapees from the seals. Some things, like akalia vine, will have to be destroyed no matter what. That can't be allowed to spread across the Earth, and neither can the revenirs and lanavours. However, for everyone else, new laws will be established and those who obey them will find a home here, and freedom."

They also need to go, I thought as a manticore flew overhead.

"If you follow Lucifer, he will keep you enslaved," Kobal continued, and his eyes bored into Lucifer's. The hatred between them sizzled across the air. "He believes you beneath him and expects you to do his bidding."

The púca with its horn on Gage moved it off him. It glanced at its fellow creatures, and some of them backed further away. If they couldn't speak, then they must be able to telecommunicate, I realized as more of them slipped toward the woods.

"And what of you, Kobal?" Lucifer inquired as he bounced Bailey on his knee. "I assume you think *you* will rule over them, force them to obey your laws, and the laws of the humans you work with—humans who are far beneath angel and demon in strength, yet they stand behind you."

"They stand *with* me," Kobal corrected. "And I expect all of us to work together. We all need each other to survive. Your way will be the end of existence. You seek to destroy. We seek to build a new world from the ashes of Hell and Earth."

"And you will rule, of course," Lucifer said and bounced Bailey faster.

Gage threw his hands out toward Bailey when he cried out. His movement caused him to jerk against the barta who slammed him against the throne. "Don't!" I yelled at it.

The barta revealed all its hideously sharp teeth and released a chattering laugh.

"Better I rule than you," Kobal said. Resting his hand on my shoulder, he gave it a gentle squeeze. "I am stronger than you, and as you have pointed out, you may have orchestrated the seals coming down, but my queen, *my* Chosen was the catalyst behind it. The power she contains broke those seals, which you *never* could have done. She is the first and only true World Walker to exist. No one else can do what she is capable of doing."

"She is *my* daughter," Lucifer replied.

"I am also Michael's daughter," I stated and lifted my chin. I despised being considered the daughter of either of them, but my birth parents weren't exactly prize winners either, so I didn't see what difference it made anymore. "I am angel, I am demon, and I am human. You have no claim on me."

Gage gawked at me before his eyes ran over all those standing behind us. A drakón swept overhead again as all the demons around Lucifer halted. The fallen angels crept closer to him.

"I am still the reason those trapped behind the seals are free," Lucifer said. "If I hadn't forced her to do it, if I hadn't discovered a way to unleash her abilities in a powerful blast, the seals would still be standing."

Lucifer shifted his hold to tuck Bailey against his side, almost under his wing. My throat went dry as I realized he planned to fly away with my brother. If he fled here with Bailey, he would use my brother against me every day for the rest of our lives. He would twist Bailey to his way, turn him against us, and tear my heart out in the process.

Gage was too far away for Lucifer to grab him too, but Onoskelis approached the barta until she stood beside it.

"I set the demons free, and if they're to keep their freedom, they must fight for it!" Lucifer called to the demons. "The fires that forged the varcolac were destroyed when Hell fell. Which means Kobal is the last one who can create a seal. If he lives, even if he cannot create seals on Earth, he can still open a gateway into Hell and toss you back in there, for good."

Malice radiated from the demons behind Lucifer as they crept closer.

"There is no power strong enough to destroy the Fires of Creation," Kobal stated with a certainty that had many of those gathered around us nodding their agreement. "If I die, a new varcolac *will* rise. Unlike me, it probably won't be inclined to work with any of you."

The demons on Lucifer's side all froze.

"Or you could be lying about everything," Lucifer said. "I say that having a chance to be free for the rest of your existence is worth fighting for. If you bring the girl to me, we will have control of Kobal and you will never have to fear him working against you again. If you kill him, so be it, we will destroy the next varcolac should one arise."

Some of the púcas approached again while others slipped away into the forest. Lower and upper-level demons vanished into the woods, but more remained. Manticores, bartas, gobalinus, an ogre, and numerous other Hell creatures closed in on us.

"Remember to help Raphael," Kobal said to me.

"I will." I glanced to my brothers once more. *I love you,* I mouthed to them as a bloodthirsty cry rent the air and the battle resumed.

CHAPTER FIFTY-SIX

Kobal

I knew Lucifer planned to take flight with the child. If he succeeded in doing so, he would flee as far from here as possible with the biggest piece of leverage he had over River. No matter what happened, I couldn't allow that.

Turning, Raphael emitted a blast of white hot energy that formed a wall behind us and allowed everyone else to focus on the threat before us. River rested her hand on my arm. Golden-blue light crackled over her fingers and my skin before she moved her hand away and placed it on Raphael's arm.

Her breath sucked in, and the hair around her face waved as light washed over her. The wall of energy behind us grew until it swept thirty feet across the hill in both directions. It would not stop our winged enemies from diving down on us, but any who touched it would be destroyed.

Humans, demons, and Hell creatures surged forward to battle with each other. I fought my way through a wave of barta demons, making sure to keep them away from River as I tossed them ruthlessly aside.

River and Raphael edged forward with us as we gained ground toward Lucifer.

I seized one barta and smashed it into the ground before decapitating it. When I lifted my head to take on the next one, I discovered the rest of them had switched course. Instead of coming for me, they were barreling toward a group of humans led by Vargas, Erin, and Lix.

"River!" I shouted. "To the right!"

Spinning, she placed her other hand on Raphael's arm before releasing a wave of energy on the creatures. Raphael's power fanned hers, making it more white in color than gold. Some of the bartas fell to their knees immediately and started shredding their chests open. Others kept going for a few feet before they started screaming.

I grabbed the horn of a púca before it could stab me and snapped it off in one quick twist. I threw the horn aside as the creature reeled back, screaming as it spewed black blood everywhere. Lucifer rose to stand on the seat of my throne, spread his wings, and gave them a solid flap. The grass around the throne bowed down beneath the breeze he created as he rose gracefully into the air.

Shoving aside a lower-level demon, I broke free of the craetons and covered the ten feet separating me from Lucifer in two bounds. Leaping onto the seat of my throne, I launched myself into the air after him. My hand snagged his ankle. Bailey cried out as my weight jerked Lucifer down a foot.

Using Lucifer's leg as leverage, I swung my other hand up and sank my claws into his stomach. I dug deeper into the soft flesh there to get a better grip on him. He grunted and beat his wings faster as his warm blood pooled in my palm. I formed a ball of fire in my hand and kept it trapped against his stomach to keep Bailey protected from the flames.

Lucifer yelped, and his feet kicked out. One of them caught me in the jaw and jarred my fangs together, but I didn't release him. My fire licked straight into his stomach. The cooked meat aroma of his roasting flesh and sinew filled the air as his skin sizzled and popped.

Lucifer grunted, closing his wings protectively in, but the gesture did nothing to help him protect himself as he dropped five feet. Unfurling his wings again, he swung the sharp tips at me. I dodged the first one and released my hold on his calf to lunge for the second. My blood-soaked hand slid down the tip before I got a firm hold on it. I increased the fire against his stomach until its glow could be seen behind his ribcage.

"You want him, varcolac," Lucifer hissed. "Then catch him."

Before I could respond, Lucifer threw Bailey away from me.

"No!" I shouted and released my hold on his wing so I could swing out to catch the child, but Lucifer had thrown him out of my reach.

Bailey shrieked, his arms and legs flailed as he plunged toward the ground, almost thirty feet below. River released Raphael and raced toward Bailey, but she would never make it to him in time.

"No!" she screamed.

Then, a black blur swooped into view, catching Bailey seconds before he hit the ground. To my amazement, the child laughed as Caim landed with Bailey tucked against his chest. River skidded to a halt, her head turned back to Raphael and she glanced between him and Caim.

"Go!" Caim shouted to her. "I'll protect the child."

She hesitated for a second before running back to Raphael. Returning my attention to Lucifer, I grinned at him and released a ball of fire that tore all the way through his stomach. The tops of the trees could be seen through the cauterized bits of flesh flapping over the hole I'd created in him. My fingers dug into the bottom of that hole and the charred skin there.

His wings drooped enough that I once again grabbed the silver tip of one and yanked on it. I didn't care what it took, I would not let him go again. He would pay for everything he'd done, for every hurt he'd inflicted on River. Killing had always been a necessity for my survival; killing him would be a pleasure.

A series of blows rained against my face as Lucifer unleashed his telekinesis on me. The impact of the blows caved my left cheekbone and knocked all my teeth on that side out. Blood filled my mouth, and I spit out my teeth, but I maintained my hold on him. Pulling on the wing, I attempted to drag him down while he continued to try to rise with his one free wing.

A fist of air assaulted my stomach, knocking the breath out of me. Tired of this game we'd played for too long, I lifted my hand from his stomach and aimed it at his face. He swung his wing protectively in front of him to shield himself from my fire.

Instead of trying to torch him again though, I set Phenex and Crux free.

Phenex burst out of me first. Her claws left bone-deep gashes across Lucifer's chest and wing. He screamed as his wing dropped down. He tried to grab her, but her momentum had already carried her over the top of him and toward the ground. She landed on all fours and bounded into the battle below.

Crux followed behind her. Lucifer's fingers tore at his belly, spilling blood as the hound soared past him. Leaping over Lucifer, Crux spun in the air and clamped his jaw down on his wing. Twisting to the side, Crux's weight bent Lucifer backward as he pulled on the wing.

The hellhound weighing more than both of us, Lucifer couldn't resist Crux's pull on him with his one free wing. More telekinetic blows pummeled my body as Lucifer started to flip over, bringing me with him. The sky and trees filled my vision before gravity took over and my body slammed against Lucifer's so that his feet were in my face.

He continued to beat at me with his telekinesis. My right eye swelled until it became only a slit, and my ribs broke with an audible crack. Sensing my pain, Crux gave a ferocious shake of his head. Half of Lucifer's wing tore apart and blood spilled free. The jagged remnants of delicate wing bones protruded into the air.

Crux hit the ground seconds before Lucifer and I did. My numerous broken bones protested the impact of the unforgiving dirt, and pieces of my ribs dug into my lungs as I rolled off Lucifer and staggered to my feet.

River

My heart lodged in my throat as I watched the battle between Kobal and Lucifer unfold. When they hit the ground, Crux kept his hold on Lucifer's wing as he dragged him back and shook it violently. An invisible burst of energy hit the hound, knocking his head to the side with enough force that he lost his hold on Lucifer.

Seconds later, Crux was thrown aside as if he weighed no more than I did. Energy rose from the dirt, into my feet, and pooled forth to join with the immense force that Raphael released. Some of the craetons were still stupid enough to batter themselves against the wall of energy, only to be thrown back with nothing but smoke curling from their remains. Most of them were going around it now, but our forces waited for them there. Some were struck down, while others broke through to attack.

When Kobal rose to his feet, my fingers curled with the need to murder as I took in his battered face and bloody body. His hand went to his ribs before falling away. A snarl curved his mouth as an angel dropped toward Lucifer. The angels would fly Lucifer out of here if they got to him.

No! This will end now! The white-hot rage filling me increased the sparks on my hands as fire rose to encircle my other hand. I'd never experienced wrath with this intensity before, but I welcomed it.

Lucifer had tormented my brothers, and he had *killed* people I cared about in brutal ways. I refused to live with the fear of him coming for me again, or plotting something more. I refused to allow him to *exist* anymore. That bastard would pay for everything he'd done, and I would make sure he didn't escape here alive.

"Raphael," I hissed.

He glanced over his shoulder at Lucifer as he stumbled toward the angels trying to slip in between the hounds and palitons waiting for them. Kobal released a blast of fire that torched across the ground toward Lucifer. Battering the air, Lucifer managed to get his good wing to work well enough to propel him away from the trail of fire.

"Go," Raphael said.

I released his arm and raced through the battle still waging around me. Leaping back, I dodged the pointed tip of a horn aimed at my stomach. I drove my elbow into the back of the demon's head, knocking him to the ground. I didn't have time to kill him as I leapt onto his back and ran over the top of him.

When another demon tried to tackle me, I shot a ball of fire into his face. He howled as he beat at the flames. The angels were almost to Lucifer when Caim dove out of the air and slammed into the side of one. They tumbled through the air before hitting the ground in a tumult of black wings. I spotted Bailey on the ground by Bale before Caim sliced his wing across the other angel's throat and took to the air again. He swooped down and reclaimed Bailey. The barta demon still had hold of Gage, but Onoskelis was now engaged in a fight with a few palitons.

One of the other angels grabbed Lucifer's shoulder as Kobal released another wave of fire. This one smashed into the other angel's face and spiraled him backward. Lucifer roared and released a telekinetic blast of energy so strong that it rippled over my skin as I closed in on his side. The blast knocked Kobal over and threw back the hounds that had been closing in on Lucifer. One of the hounds released a high-pitched yelp and the others all howled. I realized another hound had been lost as the howl became a mournful keening.

Despite their loss, the massive creatures were regaining their feet. Lucifer flapped at the air with his one good wing until he rose slowly into the air. My blood pounded through my veins, and power surged through me as I drew on the energy of the life teeming in the ground beneath my feet while I ran.

"No!" I screamed when Lucifer was seven feet off the ground. The hounds leapt at him, trying to catch him and draw him down again, but he curled his legs up to stay out of their reach.

Planting my feet, I threw my arms up as power and fury coalesced together. From my right hand a stream of golden-white light erupted, while from my left a wave of fire burst free. I buried my shock over being able to use both abilities at the same time again as I drew my hands closer together until they pressed against each other.

Fire and light came together in a powerful surge that snapped and crackled though the air before it slammed into Lucifer. It hit him in the chest, but instead of tearing through him, it enveloped him in the golden-white light at the same time the fire burst over his body. For a few heartbeats, he was trapped in the air, his back bowed and his head thrown back.

As the light cascaded around him, I got a brief glimpse of the golden angel he'd once been with his black hair, violet eyes, and feathered, white wings. I saw a smile that lit a room and felt the warmth he'd once radiated. I understood why he'd been favored, why he'd been *the* Morning Star.

There had never been an angel so bright and beautiful before, there never would be again, and I wanted him dead.

The fire and light burst off him, radiating outward like a bomb blast that threw those closest to him back. The force of it flung back the angel Kobal had burnt and knocked the hounds to the ground again. Like a burnt-out star, Lucifer crumpled to the ground. Smoke curled off his burnt flesh and wings as he lay unmoving with his broken wing poking into the air. Nothing remained of his clothes.

All around me silence descended. I could feel the gazes boring into my back and saw some of the craetons scrambling to flee, but most remained unmoving as they gazed between me and Lucifer.

And then, just when I was certain he was dead, Lucifer lifted his head to reveal the smoke curling out of the sockets where his eyes had been. My stomach lurched as those empty sockets gazed ahead. Clumps of grass and dirt broke away as his burnt fingers dug into the earth and he started clawing his way forward.

The clashing of swords and the retort of guns pierced the air again. The hounds all yowled, and screams of the injured and dying resonated across the field as Lucifer continued forward. Walking toward him, I watched his charred skin begin to pinken. The whites of his eyeballs slid into place and the black irises took form. His head tipped back, and hatred burned from his eyes when I planted myself in front of him.

"Hi, Dad," I greeted, and Kobal pounced.

CHAPTER FIFTY-SEVEN

Kobal

I fell on Lucifer's battered body just as he flipped over and plunged the top spike of his intact wing into my shoulder. It pierced through muscle and bone before jutting out the other side. Gritting my teeth, I wrapped my hands around the end of the spike and tore it out of me. Lucifer shrieked when I twisted his wing to drive the spike into his thigh. His blistered body bowed off the ground as he tore the spike from his leg.

Before he could launch a new telekinetic attack, I seized his throat and drove my claws into his neck. He screamed, his fingers tore into my face, peeling away skin as more fists of air battered my body. I twisted his neck to the right until it cracked. Beneath my hands, flesh and bone gave way until his head remained attached by only his spine.

With a violent yank, I ripped his head the rest of the way from his body. Grim satisfaction filled me as his wings flapped once more before his body went completely still beneath me. My shoulders heaved, the blood falling from my hair and face dripped onto his flesh.

I had expected to feel nothing but triumph when this moment came. Instead, there was only a hollow sense of relief, of a door closing and a new one opening. Lifting my head, I looked at River. Her violet eyes seemed like shards of steel as she stared at Lucifer before her eyes met mine.

The anger in her gaze melted away as love filled them. I'd only known death before her, but now I would only know what it meant to live.

I became aware of the hush enshrouding the field that had been a battleground only seconds before. My fingers clenched in Lucifer's hair, and my lips skimmed back as I bared my fangs at our enemies. Many of them gawked at me and then at River with fear-filled eyes.

I set Lucifer's head down, grabbed his still intact wing and tore it from his body. Rising, I drove the silver point at the bottom of his wing into the ground before retrieving his head and spearing it onto the top.

"Who's next?" I inquired of Lucifer's followers.

For a second, silence continued, and then more of the craetons turned and fled into the woods. Others were unable to flee and resumed the fight. Most of the remaining fallen angels took to the sky and swooped into the trees. River turned away and ran toward her brothers.

Turning from the palitons she'd been fighting, Onoskelis shoved the barta demon out of the way and snatched Gage from the throne. Closest to them both, Caim lurched toward her before realizing he still held Bailey. He glanced around for somewhere to put the child, but the barta demon was already advancing on them. Caim kept hold of Bailey as he flapped his wings to rise out of the barta's reach.

Gage squirmed in Onoskelis hold, trying to break free, but she kept him pinned against her as she lifted off the ground. I ran toward them, my bones grating with every step as I followed River through the tumble of dead bodies. I tried to catch her, but with her head start and my injuries, she remained fifteen feet ahead of me as she darted in and out of those battling around us.

"Gage!" River screamed.

"I don't think so, *bitch*!" Verin shouted as she charged out of the fray at them.

Leaping forward, Verin caught hold of Gage and yanked him from Onoskelis's arms before the angel could make it five feet into the air. Verin drove her sword forward as Gage landed on his back with an audible thud. Verin's sword plunged into Onoskelis's belly, and she sliced it upward. Blood spewed from the angel's mouth, but she managed to unsheathe the sword at her back. Swinging it down, she cleaved into Verin's neck.

I shoved aside the craetons in my way, ignoring the blood spilling over my lips as I ran. Yanking her sword back, Onoskelis lifted it and swung it down again. Verin threw up her hand to try to protect herself. The blade sliced through Verin's hand and cut the rest of the way through Verin's neck. A sense of loss clenched my gut when Verin's severed head hit the ground.

Onoskelis dove for Gage at the same time River threw herself on top of him. Onoskelis's hands twisted into River's shirt as her wings flapped rapidly. "River!" I roared when the angel rose with River in her grasp.

Blood spilled from Onoskelis's belly and onto River as she flew. River tried to right herself, but Onoskelis entangled one hand in her hair to keep her head down while the other remained entwined in the back of River's shirt. River blindly unleashed a ball of energy into the air over her head. Onoskelis ducked back to avoid it.

Chasing after them, I dodged a manticore tail before punching through the chest of a demon who lunged at me. I tore its heart out as Crux leapt up to tear away its head. The hounds ran forward to come together in a V formation that cut a pathway through the craetons in between me and Onoskelis as she flew toward the woods.

Aiming for Onoskelis's back, a wave of fire erupted from my palm and shot across the air toward her. Onoskelis must have heard it coming as she twisted to the side to avoid being hit by it.

It had been enough to distract her though, which allowed River to swing her hand up in front of her. She blasted Onoskelis in the face with a ball of fire before hitting her with an energy ball from her other hand.

Onoskelis shrieked and released River. Spinning through the air,

River somehow managed to right herself so that her feet would hit the ground first. It didn't matter, at her height the impact would still kill her.

I pushed myself faster, ignoring every one of my broken bones and battered muscles as River fell. She didn't scream, but her eyes were squeezed shut as the air whipped her hair straight up behind her.

She was thirty feet from the ground when Onoskelis dove at her with her wings folded against her back. Her fingers caught in River's shirt. River's weight and momentum plunged them down another ten feet before Onoskelis stabilized them both. The angel jerked River up and rose with her once more.

A loud roar filled the air and a drakón plunged out of the sky. Blue fire streaked behind it as it bared down on the two of them with its jaws wide open. "No!" I bellowed, knowing that the drakón could consume them both in one gulp.

Onoskelis tried to dart to the side to avoid it, but the drakón's jaw clamped down with a crunch that echoed over the open land. The closing of the jaws severed Onoskelis so cleanly that the stumps of her arms remained standing in the air as her hands remained locked on River's shirt and hair.

River remained airborne for a millisecond. Then, gravity won out and Onoskelis's remains fell away as River plummeted toward the Earth from a height of at least a hundred and fifty feet. My legs moved faster than they'd ever moved before as I raced across the ground toward her.

The drakón swept back toward the battle. It roared again before unleashing a torrent of fire on the craetons running toward the woods. Their screams were silenced by the drakón swooping down to scoop them up and swallow them whole.

River was only forty feet above when the massive shadow of the other drakón soared over me and toward River. With a grace I'd never expected from the skeletal beast, it dipped below River. The blue fire surrounding it went out before she crashed onto it. Dirt and grass shot out from beneath my feet when I skidded to a halt beneath them. River kept her hands in the air as if afraid that, if she touched it, it would snatch her off its neck and eat her.

The drakón touched down without a whisper of noise. It curled its tail around its side and turned its head so the flickering blue flames of its eyes met mine. I continued toward the creature as River remained unmoving. A puff of smoke coiled out of its nostrils, and blue fire rose to encircle its tail but went no further when I neared.

"What's going on?" River called out to me.

The other drakón landed in front of its partner. Blue fire engulfed it as it prowled across the ground, its tail swishing back and forth in warning for everyone to stay back. Every step it took left the perfect imprint of its bony feet and car-sized claws in the dirt.

"They've been following you," I realized.

"What?" River asked, her hands still raised in the air and her skin three shades paler than it had been.

"They've been following *you* since Hell. Not hunting, not tracking us for Lucifer, but watching *you*. They're protecting you. Slide down, slowly."

She gazed at me for a minute before resting her hands on the neck of the drakón. It snorted two puffs of smoke and shook its body as if her touch pleased it. "Easy. Be a good boy… girl… it," River said as she ran a hand over the vertebrae of its neck.

When the drakón lowered its head and placed it on the ground, River froze before creeping forward. She slid down its neck, across its skull, and down its nostrils to the ground. She stared at the drakón for a minute before resting her hand on its nose to give it a pet. "Thank you."

It rubbed its nose against her hand before nudging her away. When River was five feet away from it, blue fire erupted over its body once more. With a flap of wings, the drakón rose into the sky with its partner. River glanced back before running toward me and throwing her arms around my shoulders, heedless of the fact I was covered in blood, but then she had a fair amount on her too.

I embraced her against me while the drakóns circled above before disappearing over the trees.

"Why did they do that?" she whispered.

"You set them free."

I turned my attention to the waning battle as more of Lucifer's followers ran for the woods. The surviving angels had all fled. Without Lucifer, there was no one to lead them and they would be hunted down and dispatched of without mercy.

Focusing on River, I brushed the hair back from her flushed face and cupped her cheeks in my hands. "Are you injured?" I demanded.

"I'm fine. You though—"

She tried to pull away, but I kept her against me. "Already healing," I assured her. I had more broken bones than I could count, but they were shifting back into place and already new teeth prodded at my gums.

Her fingers brushed over my crumpled cheekbone. "Look at what he did to you."

"Some might say it's an improvement," I murmured, succeeding in coaxing a smile to her lips.

"Not me. We… we did it," she breathed. "I mean, I know there are still some angels and craetons out there, but *Lucifer* is dead."

"Yes, Mah Kush-la, we did it." I smiled at her as I ran my finger over her bottom lip before bending to kiss her. I inhaled her sweet breath as I tasted the salt of the sea on her mouth. My tongue stroked hers as I drew her closer.

"Pittah!"

The shout caused River to pull away from me. She spun to face Gage as he ran toward her with Bailey on his hip. Stepping forward, she opened her arms to her siblings and hugged them close when they barreled into her. Words, questions, and tears flowed so fast that I couldn't follow what they said to each other, but they seemed to catch it all.

Over their shoulders, I watched as the others walked through the bodies on the ground. They dispatched of any enemies who still lived, while pulling free any allies who required help. Some of them ambled around the thrones, examining them.

It was time to take my rightful place on my throne. To finally claim what was mine for the first time in my fifteen hundred sixty-two years of existence, but I wouldn't pull River away from her brothers. I'd waited this long to sit on it; I would wait longer.

River stepped away from her siblings. Her hands ran over their faces as if she couldn't believe they were there. Then, she turned to me and the radiant smile she gave me robbed me of my breath. This woman had endured every single horrific thing thrown at her with more courage than any other being I'd ever known, and she was mine.

She stretched her hand out to me. I clasped it and rested it over my heart. "Gage, Bailey, this is Kobal," she said. "My Chosen."

"I'm not sure what that means, but hi," Gage said with a shy wave at me.

"Hello," I replied.

"A Chosen is like a husband, but he's also *more* than that," River said. "I'll explain it later."

"Yeah you will," Gage replied and grinned at her.

Bailey stuck a saliva-covered hand out to me, and I clasped it in mine.

"You have funny eyes," he said and giggled as he dropped his head into the crook of River's neck.

"That's not polite, B," River admonished and kissed the tip of his nose.

"It's true; to humans, I have funny eyes," I said, and Bailey giggled again while Gage gazed back and forth between the two of us.

"You are going to tell me what is going on with *every*thing, right?" he asked River.

"I'll tell you everything," she vowed as she started walking beside me toward our thrones. "I'm not sure you'll believe it all."

"Bailey was just bounced on the knee of Lucifer, and a skeletal dragon plucked you out of the sky. I'm sure I'll believe anything you tell me," Gage replied and River laughed.

"True," she agreed.

The humans, demons, and angels stepped back when I led River around to the front of the thrones. "It's time to claim what is mine," I said to her.

She kissed Bailey on the cheek and slid him into Gage's arms. Bailey frowned at Raphael when he spotted the angel near the front of the crowd. "You told me I had to let her go, but she's still here," Bailey said to him.

River froze beside me, her eyes narrowed as her gaze went from Bailey to Raphael. "What is he talking about?" she demanded.

"He told me I had to let you go," Bailey said, unaware of his sister's hostility toward Raphael.

"They told me I have to let you go," River whispered as her gaze shifted to me. "When Gage and Bailey came to see me before we left the wall, Bailey said those words to me. I'd assumed it was the soldiers, or Gage, or someone else who had told him he had to let me go." Her eyes latched onto Raphael again. "But it was the *angels* telling him that."

"Yes," Raphael admitted. "Ariel briefly communicated with the child to offer you and him comfort. We knew it would be difficult for all of you to be apart, and if your mother could be spoken with, then we thought one of the children could be reached too."

"The angels can communicate with Bailey," River murmured. "What about Gage?"

"No angels are talking to me!" Gage blurted.

"He does not possess the ability," Raphael confirmed. "Whatever power he possesses hasn't shown itself yet, or it is so latent it will never be known."

"You tell the angels to leave Bailey alone," River commanded. "Look at the damage they did to our mother."

"He is young—"

"Leave him be!" she shouted.

"There is no reason for them to communicate with him now," Raphael murmured.

"Make sure it stays that way," she said.

"I cannot promise that. There is no way to know if it may become necessary for them to speak with him in the future."

I rested my hand on River's shoulder when fire blazed over her hands and up to her wrists. A protective demon mother had nothing on River right now.

"Whoa," Gage murmured and Bailey's eyes widened on her.

"No matter what happens, we will be here to guide Bailey and Gage through it," I promised her. "Your mother had no idea what was happening to her, but they will know it all."

River's fire died away as she looked to her youngest sibling. "Are you okay with that, B?"

He smiled back at her. "Sure."

"Gage?" she asked.

"Uh yeah, sure."

River turned to me, and I took her hand. Leading her to the smaller throne, I helped her settle on it. She gasped and her hands clinched onto the arms. White sparks burst to life on her fingers, but gold marked the tips of the energy flowing up to her wrists. From there, the energy wrapped around the arms of the throne and swirled around to the back of it as if it were binding her to the chair.

I doubted any other Chosen had received this reaction from their throne, but then they would have been entirely demon. River was not, and the being had forged the angels as well as the varcolac and these thrones. The throne was reacting to the knowledge that a more angelic queen now sat on it.

"Amazing," River breathed, her eyes a deeper shade of violet when they met mine. "There is so much power here."

"There is," I agreed.

"Oh, you are definitely telling me *every*thing," Gage said as he watched his sister with fascination.

Walking over to my throne, I turned to face everyone before sitting on it. Power immediately lashed into my body as all the symbols on the chair shifted toward me. The symbols felt like water flowing over me as they slid effortless into my flesh before running into the throne again.

Fire flared to life from my fingers. It encompassed my wrists before becoming the umber light that had poured forth to grant me entrance to the Fires of Creation.

That glow spread to the entire throne. Lucifer had sat on this throne for six thousand years, within the throne room, and never been able to unlock the power either of them possessed. If he had, he would have leveled Hell thousands of years ago, but when he'd severed his bond with life, he'd severed any connection he might have had to the thrones and the being too.

River possessed that connection though. Reaching out, I rested my hand over hers. Her power spread out to my wrist at the same time mine fastened onto hers. The umber and golden-white lights swirled together until it became impossible to separate one from the other.

All around us, the demons, Vargas, and Erin went to one knee and their heads bowed. Caim, Raphael, and the remaining humans remained standing until the humans also went to one knee. Gage looked to River before holding Bailey closer and kneeling before us. River made a move as if to stop them, but I gave a small tug on her hand. We couldn't show any favor to anyone. Raphael and Caim glanced around before the two angels also went to one knee. Their wings unfurled behind their backs and they pressed a fist to their foreheads.

"Rise," I commanded as the initial rush of power between River and I ebbed and the light faded away. However, the vast power was still there, waiting to be tapped into again if it became necessary.

"The king and queen of Hell are now also the king and queen of Earth!" Corson declared, and a cheer ran through the crowd.

CHAPTER FIFTY-EIGHT

River

Three weeks later,

I set Bailey down in the vast hall. He immediately ran for one of the walls, his short, chubby legs carrying him far faster than they looked like they could. He ran his fingers over the markings within his reach. Above him and all around me, more markings had been etched into every inch of the wall.

Each one of those markings had been chiseled by Kobal's hand, then stained with his blood as well as mine. The power within this room could never be as strong as what I'd felt in the chamber housing the Fires of Creation, but every time I stepped in here, it made my breath catch.

Energy sizzled over my skin, creating sparks at the tips of my fingers while Bailey continued to trace the symbols. At the end of the room, the hammering stopped as Corson, Hawk, Bale, Magnus, Caim, Raphael, and Gage lifted their heads to look at us. They were all working on finishing the last of the dais. My throne had already been placed on it. Lopan sat on the edge of the dais, swinging his small legs back and forth as he sang to himself. Kneeling beside him, Calah hammered a final nail into place.

So much had happened in three weeks that it felt like years had slipped by. Before we'd left my town, I'd made sure that *every*one Lucifer slaughtered was given a proper burial. It had taken four days to dig the numerous graves and to create whatever headstones we could to mark the loved ones who lay there. It would have taken longer, but the demons and angels worked far faster than the humans could.

I'd kept Gage and Bailey away from the field until all the bodies were removed, but I knew they had seen far more than they should have. Gage still had a haunted look in his eyes and jumped at things that never would have caused him to jump before, but he liked it here and he liked the demons. Bailey had woken screaming every night since Lucifer had taken him. The only thing that gave him any real comfort was being held by me, Gage, or Kobal, or coming to this room so he could trace the symbols. I couldn't deny his connection to the angels, but I hoped to keep him sheltered as much as possible until he was older.

Unfortunately, while we'd been removing the bodies from the field, we'd also uncovered the bodies of Hawk's family and his town and buried them. Caim and Raphael had taken to the sky to survey the towns further out on the Cape. The town of Sandwich had also been destroyed, their bodies mixed in with those we worked to identify before burial, but the people in the other towns were still alive. Lucifer's wrath hadn't progressed that far.

A set of mated hounds also perished in the battle. Kobal had stood with the other hounds, watching as their bodies burned on a fire he created. The hounds all howled and whimpered while they mourned their loss.

When we'd finally finished burying or burning the dead, I reclaimed Lisa's duffel bag, filled it with more pictures and some things for Gage and Bailey. Then, we'd returned to the wall. When we arrived, Kobal ordered my mother taken to another section.

I didn't argue the order. I couldn't leave her to rot, but that didn't mean I wanted to see her every day of my life either. Our lives would never intertwine again. Gage hadn't protested the decision either, and Bailey had yet to ask about her, though he'd asked after Lisa and Asante more than a few times.

Tears burned in my eyes at the reminder of the loss of my friends. I'd found their bodies amongst the remains of the others, along with Lisa's parents. I made sure they were all buried together and had wept over their graves. Never forgetting them was the best way to honor them, and I would make sure their memories lived on for as long as I did.

Verin had also been laid to rest in the field, in a fire that Kobal created. The demons didn't believe in memorial services, but I'd asked for one for her and Morax. We didn't have his body to burn, but I'd assembled a small grave marker for them both. They'd died to bring an end to Lucifer, and Verin died saving my brother. They needed something to honor them and to mark them as together again in the end.

I knew angels and demons didn't go through the same birth and death cycle as humans, knew there was no afterlife for them, but I still chose to believe Verin and Morax were reunited now.

The door behind me opened and closed. A few seconds later, Vargas and Erin smiled at me as they strolled past with bundles of wood in their arms. Skelleins flanked Erin. They were still determined to get her to fail at answering a riddle, but I believed they'd run out of riddles before they stumped her.

Each of the skelleins wore some article of clothing or accessory that marked them different from the others, though they all had a flask hanging at their side or in their hand. They'd returned to their more jovial nature now that they were back on Earth. So had Corson, but he'd stopped wearing earrings.

The candles flickering in the sconces on the walls cast shadows across the wood floor as I followed Bailey. More ghosts than I'd anticipated arriving at the wall had shown up. More continued to arrive daily from all corners of the world, much to the annoyance of the demons and the dismay of the humans. The humans were still trying to get used to the sometimes abrasive, often selfish apparitions who unfortunately discovered they enjoyed materializing through walls to scare people.

However, in this hall, Kobal didn't want electricity. I thought he wanted a small piece of Hell on Earth, and this place was it, even if it was aboveground. I preferred the much cozier feel of the candles in the hall too.

With his throne in hand, Kobal strolled in from the hallway connecting this building to the house my brothers had moved into. I knew Kobal hated living in human homes, but I couldn't bring myself to be apart from my brothers anymore.

In compromise, Kobal had torn out a wall on the lower floor of the house and connected his tent to it for us to sleep in. We were no longer on the hill with the other demons, but the house was far enough away from the other humans that he assured me he didn't mind it.

Kobal set his throne beside mine and stepped forward as Erin climbed the steps of the dais to him. They spoke briefly before Erin set the wood she'd been carrying down. She dug into her pocket and pulled something out. Kobal took it from her, said something to the others on the dais, and they all rose.

"Come on, Bailey!" Gage called to him.

Bailey tottered forward until Lix scooped him up and climbed the steps of the dais with him. Despite their lingering trauma over what had been done to them and our town, my brothers were both handling everything well. Gage was fascinated to have the king of Hell as a brother-in-law, and Bailey was fascinated by every demon, angel, and Hell creature he encountered. The skelleins were a real favorite of his, much to their joy.

They all disappeared down the hallway, and I heard the click of the door shutting. Kobal descended the stairs and strode toward me, a smile curving his mouth. My toes curled when I recognized the ravenous gleam in his obsidian eyes.

"I have a present for you, Mah Kush-la," he said as he stopped before me.

"Really?" I inquired eagerly.

Lifting his hand, he kept it fisted in the air before opening it. A shell necklace fell to dangle from between his thumb and forefinger. My hand instinctively flew to where my shell necklace had once hung. It had been torn away from me before we'd entered Hell.

"How?" I breathed.

"Before we left, I gathered shells from the beach," he said.

I recalled strolling the beach with him. I'd been unable to leave home without going to the ocean to say goodbye. I'd absently watched Kobal as he picked up and either pocketed shells or tossed them aside like millions of others had done with them while walking the coastline. Maybe one day I'd be able to return to the sea, but it wouldn't be anytime soon. For now, we would remain at the wall, making sure it stayed secure until the threat of the remaining angels and the worst of the seal creatures were eradicated.

"I've been working on drilling holes in them and threading them into a necklace for you. Erin made the clasp," he said.

Tears filled my eyes as I lifted a hand to run my fingers over the polished pink and white shells. Each shell handpicked by him. "It's beautiful!"

"Turn around."

I did as he said and lifted my hair to let him slip it around my neck and clasp it there. He bent to kiss my nape. My nipples puckered in anticipation as a wetness spread between my thighs.

"I love it," I breathed.

"I must admit, I have a selfish reason for it too," he said as he cupped my ass before sliding his hand between my legs from behind.

My head fell against his shoulder as he leisurely stroked me. "And what is that?"

"I missed seeing you wearing only shells."

"Then I will do it as often as I can."

He turned me in his arms and claimed my mouth. Lifting me against him, he carried me across the room to the dais. His feet thudded as he climbed the steps to the wood stage. Walking over, he set me down in front of his throne. He made quick work of stripping my clothes from me before stepping back. His gaze raked me from head to toe while I stood before him in only the shell necklace.

A smile curved his mouth as he removed his clothes and tossed them aside. Drawing me against him again, he turned to sit on his throne and pulled me in between his legs. The heavy length of his shaft pressed against my inner thigh when he drew me into his lap.

The flow of power running through the chair came to life as he took hold of his erection and teasingly rubbed the head of it over my already wet opening. My hands rested on his shoulders, and I brushed a kiss against his lips as he slid into me.

My body jerked when we were joined together. Energy flooded me and my golden-white light rose around us. He clasped the back of my head and sank his tongue into my mouth while he thrust deeper into me. The power we generated seeped out to make the symbols shift on the walls as the orange glow flowing from him mixed with my light.

Breaking the kiss, I leaned back to meet his eyes. They were alive with golden fire as they held mine. His finger slid over my necklace before dipping down to trace my hardened nipple. The coiling tension building in my belly and the tightening of his muscles beneath my hands told me we were both nearing climax.

"Don't pull out," I whispered as I clasped his cheeks in my hands and kissed him again. "Stay with me. I need to feel you claiming me in *every* way again."

His claws lengthened against my flesh but didn't pierce it as he drove relentlessly into me. When his fangs pierced my shoulder, I came apart in a frenzy that had me scratching at his back. I felt the pulsations of his release and the warmth of his seed filling me as I sank my teeth into his shoulder, claiming him as mine.

EPILOGUE

Kobal

One year later

River's laughter drifted to me before I arrived at the hall. I couldn't stop myself from smiling as the radiant sound of it filled the day and caused those walking nearby to also smile. Over the year, not only had the demons come to love and respect their queen, but so had the humans, other Hell creatures, and ghosts who resided along the wall.

After we had been back on the wall for a month, I'd made the decision to travel through Hell to the other side of the world to see how things fared there. It was not a journey I wanted to make. I hated leaving River alone, but she couldn't travel with me through the minefield Hell had become, and Lucifer had destroyed the airport in Canada. I'd only felt secure in leaving her because I knew she would be safe here; she had more defenders than I did.

With Corson, Shax, Calah, Lopan, and half the hounds by my side, we successfully navigated Hell to reach the other side of Earth. I'd met with the human and demon leaders I'd established there years ago.

Some of those leaders had perished and needed to be replaced, but the rest were still carrying out their duties and doing it well. What remained of most of the human governments throughout the land had crumpled completely after the seals fell. Only England, Australia, and Russia retained any semblance of their old government, but those governments all answered to me and River now too. I'd spent nearly two weeks traveling over there before I'd been able to return to her.

It hadn't been an easy journey to make. When things were settled on Earth, I would work on trying to right Hell again, but there may be no need for it by then. If the remaining residents of Hell had their way, they would all slaughter each other before I could return to fix it.

After my return and once we'd been back at the wall for two months, River and I decided it was time to travel the wall with her brothers and Mac. It was necessary for me to see how the wall fared, meet with other human leaders, touch base with the demons I'd put in charge of certain sections, and firmly establish our leadership over them, as well as Mac's role as the ambassador of the humans.

Some sections of the wall had been lost completely, and whole encampments wiped out, but others held firm. Most of the sections that had crumbled had been rebuilt and a leadership reestablished by now. The wall was still occasionally attacked, but most of the escapees from Hell steered clear of it, unless they could fly.

After a few months of traveling, we'd returned here, to the area that River considered her home on the wall. I would still need to travel from time to time, the world was still far more lethal than it had been, but a firm rule had been established over this new world. Most were coming together to fight for a common cause, survival.

There were humans and demons who still didn't want to cooperate and work together, but they would either come around with time and join us, or stay out of the way completely. If they chose to fight against our new rule and laws, they would be hunted down and destroyed. There were no other options for them, and I'd made that perfectly clear to all.

From around the corner of the hall, a drakón's head emerged. River had named the creatures Flint and Blaze because she couldn't tell if they were male or female, but she did know which one was which. I had no intention of ever learning how to tell them apart. I disliked them as much as they continued to dislike me, but we had called an uneasy truce with each other, for her.

The drakón snorted before taking flight to join its partner circling on the horizon. The drakóns landed and stood guard over River whenever I wasn't near her, as did the hounds and the few púcas who arrived at the wall shortly after the final battle with Lucifer.

It was the only reason I'd felt at all secure with leaving her alone to travel through Hell. No one was insane enough to battle through all of that, as well as the demons and humans residing here, to try to attack her.

Somehow, River communicated with the pucás and drakóns, or they at least listened to her. At her command, they refrained from eating humans and demons. They feasted on Hell creatures who ventured too close to the wall, or went into the wilds to hunt.

After we had traveled through Hell and returned, I'd sent Corson, Bale, Magnus, Shax, Hawk, Erin, Lix, Raphael, Caim, Vargas, and some of the other demons and humans out with Wren and her group. They were hunting down what remained of Lucifer's followers.

It was a brutal job, but they regaled us with stories about it every time they returned to check in, or to take a break. They'd returned last month, bloodied and beaten, but grinning with triumph. After the others had all been back for a week, most had set out again, but Erin and Vargas remained. Vargas had broken his leg and needed time to heal. Erin had asked to stay with him and River.

During their time here, I'd been surprised to realize that I missed the company of my friends.

Before River, I didn't miss things. It was an emotion I never would have had, and I wouldn't have understood it if I did have it. I understood it now, as I enjoyed sharing drinks and laughter with them.

I did not miss the fight. Another thing I wouldn't have thought possible before River. I'd been born to fight; it was all I had ever known. Now, I knew happiness, laughter, love, and family. I'd had enough of the fighting.

I'd also been born to lead, and I did that with firm control, but also leniency. River tempered my more ruthless side, and together we took the time to judge and punish those who broke the laws when they were brought before us.

I belonged here, and leading over this world was what I was meant to do.

Pushing the door to the hall open, the substantial flow of power it contained washed over me the second I stepped into the shadowed interior. River sat on the edge of the dais with Bailey on her lap as she read him a story. Gage sat on the other side of her, pointing at the book and making strange noises. They all laughed at his awkward attempt with the demon language. The three of them were working to learn demonish, but they had difficulty sounding out some of the words.

Lopan sat on the other side of them, his feet kicking against the dais as Calah relit one of the candles. Daisy hovered over River's shoulder, floating back and forth as she stared at the book.

River stopped reading when the door closed and looked up at me. Joy lit her face. On the day of her twenty-third birthday, she'd stopped aging and frozen into her immortality. Other than no longer aging, her body remained human in every other way.

We didn't know if she could regenerate lost body parts, neither of us were willing to risk what that would entail to find out, but she was an immortal. *My* immortal.

She went to lift Bailey from her arms to rise, but I waved her down. "I'll come to you. It is easier that way."

She laughed as I closed the hundred feet separating us in a breath of time. Bailey scrambled from her arms and into Gage's when I stopped before her and bent to kiss her.

Resting my hand on her extremely round stomach, I felt the kick of our child within her. River placed her hand over mine and sparks raced across her fingers. Like her, the babe already fed on life, and she drew constantly on it to keep the child and herself healthy.

"Your son is extremely active today," she said.

"So certain it's a boy?" I asked as the babe shifted and kicked at me again.

"Oh yes, and he's as stubborn and cranky as his father already."

"I'm not so cranky anymore, not with you in my life."

She grinned as she kissed my neck. "True, you are much nicer now than when I first met you."

I rubbed my hand over her stomach and the babe kicked again. By the end of the month, our son would be born. "That's because you have given me everything I ever wanted, and things I never dreamed of having," I replied.

"I love you," she whispered.

I lifted my head to gaze into her violet eyes, shining with vitality. "And I you, Mah Kush-la."

Squirming from Gage's arms, Bailey walked over and held his hands out to me. He wrapped his arms around my neck when I lifted him. The child had become more like my own over the year and he often sought me out when he needed comfort. Gage had become my brother, one who was rapidly growing toward manhood as he grew taller and broader.

"Have you felt this today?" I asked Bailey, and he nodded as he placed his hand next to mine on River's stomach. My son kicked again and Bailey squealed in delight.

Gage leaned against River's side as Lopan, Daisy, and Calah slipped out of the hall to leave me alone with River and our growing family.

The End.

Turn the page for a sneak peek of book 1 in the Hell on Earth series.
Each book in the Hell on Earth series will focus on a different character

from The Road to Hell Series. Book 1 is now available and focuses on Corson and Wren: brendakdavies.com/HEppbk.

Stay in touch on updates and other new releases from the author by joining the mailing list.

Mailing list for Brenda K. Davies and Erica Stevens Updates: brendakdavies.com/ESBKDNews

SNEAK PEEK

HELL ON EARTH SERIES, BOOK 1

Wren

"Help!" I screamed and leaped at the dirt wall before me. My fingernails tore away dirt as I tried to gain purchase on the wall. At least five hundred feet over my head, the dim light of day was a small circle that seemed about as achievable as Heaven right now. "He—aggghh," my scream for help cut off when a hand slid over my mouth.

Pulled back against Corson's solid chest, his breath sounded in my ear as he held me firmly. I clawed at his hands as I tried to break free of his hold. "Quiet!" he hissed in my ear.

Releasing me, he stepped away. I strained to see him as he moved in and out of the shadows, disappearing and reemerging in the dim light while he circled the pit. He stopped before another tunnel and rested his hand against the dirt wall. Leaning forward, he inspected the opening.

I reached over my back when I realized that a familiar weight was missing. Glancing around, I spotted my bow half hidden in the shadows. I strode over and grabbed it. My heart sank when I pulled the pieces toward me. There would be no putting together the snapped wood and broken string.

I glanced around for my quiver and arrows. I spotted the edge of my quiver peeking out from under the deer. Walking over, I lifted the deer with one hand and after some maneuvering and silent curses, I managed to tug the quiver out from under the deer. I lifted the crumpled remains of my quiver and turned it over to dump out my arrows. Their broken pieces bounced across the ground as they scattered around my feet.

Dropping my hands to my knees, I took a second to steady myself before looking to Corson again. "Can you climb out of here?" I demanded of him in a whisper.

He tossed a look over his shoulder at me. "By the time we reached the top, it would be too late."

I blinked at him before glancing at the circle above again. I liked the sound of that about as much as I liked the idea of having my fingernails pulled out. "What does *that* mean?" I asked as I focused on him again.

"It means that our fall and your yelling will have woke the beast. It will be looking for its dinner."

"And we're its dinner?"

"Yes."

***Hell on Earth* (Hell on Earth Series, book 1) is now available: brendakdavies.com/HEppbk.**

FIND THE AUTHOR

Erica Stevens/Brenda K. Davies Mailing List:
brendakdavies.com/ESBKDNews

Facebook page: brendakdavies.com/BKDfb
Facebook friend: ericastevensauthor.com/EASfb

Erica Stevens/Brenda K. Davies Book Club:
brendakdavies.com/ESBKDBookClub

Instagram: brendakdavies.com/BKDInsta
Twitter: brendakdavies.com/BKDTweet
Website: www.brendakdavies.com
Blog: ericastevensauthor.com/ESblog

ALSO FROM THE AUTHOR

Books written under the pen name

Brenda K. Davies

<u>The Vampire Awakenings Series</u>

Awakened (Book 1)

Destined (Book 2)

Untamed (Book 3)

Enraptured (Book 4)

Undone (Book 5)

Fractured (Book 6)

Ravaged (Book 7)

Consumed (Book 8)

Unforeseen (Book 9)

Forsaken (Book 10)

Coming 2019/2020

<u>The Alliance Series</u>

Eternally Bound (Book 1)

Bound by Vengeance (Book 2)

Bound by Darkness (Book 3)

Bound by Passion (Book 4)

Coming August 2019

<u>The Road to Hell Series</u>

Good Intentions (Book 1)

Carved (Book 2)

The Road (Book 3)

Into Hell (Book 4)

Hell on Earth Series

Hell on Earth (Book 1)

Into the Abyss (Book 2)

Kiss of Death (Book 3)

Coming Fall 2019

Historical Romance

A Stolen Heart

Books written under the pen name

Erica Stevens

The Coven Series

Nightmares (Book 1)

The Maze (Book 2)

Dream Walker (Book 3)

The Captive Series

Captured (Book 1)

Renegade (Book 2)

Refugee (Book 3)

Salvation (Book 4)

Redemption (Book 5)

Broken (The Captive Series Prequel)

Vengeance (Book 6)

Unbound (Book 7)

The Kindred Series

Kindred (Book 1)

Ashes (Book 2)

Kindled (Book 3)

Inferno (Book 4)

Phoenix Rising (Book 5)

The Fire & Ice Series

Frost Burn (Book 1)

Arctic Fire (Book 2)

Scorched Ice (Book 3)

The Ravening Series

The Ravening (Book 1)

Taken Over (Book 2)

Reclamation (Book 3)

The Survivor Chronicles

The Upheaval (Book 1)

The Divide (Book 2)

The Forsaken (Book 3)

The Risen (Book 4)

ABOUT THE AUTHOR

Brenda K. Davies is the USA Today Bestselling author of the Vampire Awakening Series, Alliance Series, Road to Hell Series, Hell on Earth Series, and historical romantic fiction. She also writes under the pen name, Erica Stevens. When not out with friends and family, she can be found at home with her husband, son, dog, cat, and horse.